I0763391

AFTERGLOW DUST

Novels published by Midnight Fire Media

Your Own Fate
Night on Earth
Dreams Belong to the Night
ShadowWalk
Alarums of Reality

The Janus Clan series:

The Defenseless
The Slaves
Birds Flying in the Dark
At the End of the Rainbow

Poetry:

Amos Keppler: Complete Poems 1989 – 2003
Secrets - Descriptions of what Cannot be Described

(A few of the) novels to be published:

Afterglow Rain
Season of the Witch
Thunder Road: Ice and Fire
Falling
Black Dragon
Red Shadow
Lewis of Modern York

For a «complete» list of current and current future Amos Keppler and Midnight Fire Media projects see the back of the book and the Midnight Fire/Midnight Fire Media web pages.

One story of Nine

Afterglow Dust

By

Amos Keppler

2014

Midnight Fire Media

http://midnight-fire.net/mfm
For more about Afterglow and the Nine:
http://midnight-fire.net/thenine

E-Mail:
Amos13@midnight-fire.net
manofhood@yahoo.com

Cover, text, design, premedia, art and photos Amos Keppler

ISBN 978-82-91693-16-3

CHAPTER ONE

The woman looked at her. The woman between the streetlights looked poised at, had her eyes on Kathryn Caldwell as she turned the corner. One moment there was that look, and then it was gone. It was doubtful that most other people would have noticed anything, people not used to noticing details, essential details. But eyes were not merely eyes. They were knives in the shadows, ready to stab at any moment.

There was an old newsstand shed, deserted and worn down the street.

Caldwell walked through the rain, in her dark coat and the hood covering most of her head. Only glimpses of her face were visible, even in the dirty glow of the streetlights. Details were sketchy in the drizzly air, reality asserting itself only in glimpses on the dull wall of the gray night. The woman in the red dress walked in the opposite direction. Caldwell looked at her without looking at her. There were quite a few people walking up and down the street. They were all coughing and looking around them with pained eyes. The rain was light, caressing Caldwell's lips, and the lower part of her face, light but persistent, never letting up for an instant, lit by the distant fire raging on the nearby mountain. The prevalent presence of ash in the air bothered others, but not her.

– They did it, a man swore. – They set fire to the forest.

– Our beautiful forest, a woman shouted. – Damn the Council!

Several other people repeated the cries and curses and added their own.

The Triple City council had, against the wishes of many citizens given the green light for the burning of the Talaho Forest.

Kathryn stopped by the newsstand, no longer deserted. A man waited for her behind the desk, hardly visible in the bad light. There was only one working bulb in the tiny shed, and it did not work properly, fading in and out constantly. The wind picked up as Caldwell touched the desk. The rest of the street was silent, eerily silent, but here there was a buzz in the ears, rising to a silent roar.

– The Examiner, please, she said, straining to speak, to overcome the constriction in her throat.

The man behind the desk grabbed a paper with one hand and accepted the money with the other.

– Thank you for buying a paper, he said.

– You love it when people buy something from you, she said dryly. – Love them to death.

The moment she stepped close to the counter there was a tingling, one she had not quite experienced before. She experienced it like her surroundings kind of faded, turning even darker and dirtier, as if pieces of miniature soil levitated in the air and blocked the world.

That was nothing new.

She looked at Stane, the man behind the counter.

– The Gauntlet has begun, he stated, he replied to her shadow stare. – I can tell you this much. I can not guarantee anything. It is a random thing, like firing at one indistinct mark among many in the mist, you know that.

– I know that. Thank you.

There was no sound of gratitude in her voice. The two of them were not having a conversation. They were exchanging growls and grunts.

– So, how is business?

– Fair, thank you, he replied.

The rain picked up a little, but she did not feel it, just noticed it as a matter of fact, of limited interest. The woman in the red dress had reached the end of the street. She approached a woman pushing a baby stroller. There was something about the woman in red, how she seemed to be glowing, how the other seemed dark and wasted in comparison.

– You know… Stane spoke as she turned to leave. – You might not be aware of this, but there is still Hunger in your eyes, and that is one prerequisite for the Gauntlet.

She looked at him for a brief moment, could not help herself, could not stop the slight anger from manifesting in her pose. There was silence, uncomfortable and sinister. She nodded and walked off. Stane the barterer, the provider faded behind her, and when she a few seconds later turned her head and looked back, kicking herself mentally for it, there was once more nothing but the derelict, empty shed there. Even the badly working bulb was gone, leaving only the ruins of what had been a shed.

Caldwell found her umbrella inside her coat, taking it from the belt on her hips. There was a swooshing sound as she opened it, and it prevented the drizzle of water and ash from hitting her, at least from reaching the upper part of her body. It still splashed in the street, and managed, somehow, to make her shoes and legs wet and dirty.

– Big Red Moon shines on us all, a man in a long, dirty and worn coat wailed, - cutting us like knives.

Big Moon was not red, but its powerful light made it dimly visible even through the ash and the dark clouds. For a moment Kathryn shivered so hard that she almost lost her grip on the umbrella.

At the end of the street the woman in red rushed to the woman pushing the baby stroller. Hands sought collar, sought warm skin beneath clothes. The woman in red's face lit up like a lighthouse, one sought by sailors coming in from the stormy sea.

The woman in the red dress quite simply let go of the other woman, and left her, left her there. The stroller-pushing woman seemed a bit shaken, but otherwise none too worse for wear. She had never let go of the stroller, and now she started pushing it forward again. Caldwell followed her, not the other disappearing around the corner singing and jumping up and down like a loon.

The tranquility of the street had not really been disturbed. Nothing appeared to have been changed. There was movement somewhere. Caldwell sensed that. She could almost make it out as she briefly closed her eyes, but she was confident very few others could, make out the sharp, violent movement, many silent steps on the sidewalk. Caldwell heard them, heard the knives cutting flesh, saw pieces of flesh and red cloth fly through the air and hit the pavement.

Silence reigned in the rainy street. The sound was not shoes hitting the pavement, but shoes hitting the film of water covering the ground everywhere. The woman ahead pushed the stroller. Caldwell had to speed up to keep up. She passed people like a ghost, as they strolled along, indifferent to the world.

Caldwell saw the world. It invaded her. She did not let up no matter how much she wished it to.

Onset Street continued into another, opening up into the broad, infamous Ivy Avenue. There were visitors, travelers from around the realm and possibly other realms there, pointing and staring at all the weird Gothic art, among it the statues made during the turn of the century by the insane artist Homer Upcott. Caldwell rushed on.

The woman pushing the stroller was almost speeding now. She was heavyset, not very tall. Her agility and speed made people stare. The sound of the wheels against the pavement was quite distinct, now. The woman ran, and the stroller shook from side to side, as she pushed it in front of her.

– Shut up, she screamed. – SHUT UP!

The baby started hollering. It started as a normal baby cry, but soon evolved into a loud, disturbing shriek.

– You do not think I heard you before? She shouted. – But you are wrong. You are dead wrong! I heard you loud and clear, you fucking banshee.

As her voice rose one octave, two octaves she lifted the stroller, and threw it across the road. It hit the wall on the other side. Ivy was a truly broad street, many steps across. The stroller hit the wall hard, with a force approaching the extreme. People gasped as the baby fell out and towards the ground. It hit the sidewalk with a soft thud. No one should have been able to hear it so far away, but yet they did. The mother rushed to the bundle and picked it up. People sighed in relief, thinking that, now, the insanity would stop. The mother grabbed the body by the small feet, and smashed the tiny form against the wall. People froze in their tracks, and could not stop staring. The woman smashed her child at the bricks once more, far harder, possessed by an uncanny strength and resolve terrifying the spectators. The skull of the little head broke like a coconut. The brain flowed on the brick wall. The woman kept striking the now lifeless body at the barrage. Blood mingled with the remains of the brain and flesh and bones, as all of it slowly made its way down the wet and rough surface.

The horrible noise faded, as the body, reduced to a scar of flesh slipped from the mother's hands and dropped to the ground. The woman stood there for a while, frozen, looking at the people keeping their distance with bewildered eyes.

– I thought it would help, she choked. – I thought it would put a stop to it.

She fell to her knees in the street, in the pool of blood and flesh that had been her son or daughter, shaking uncontrollably.

Seconds, minutes passed. The sound of sirens filled the drizzle air, muted, sharp. The populace slowly relaxed. Caldwell sensed it, sensed their approaching calm as things slowly returned to normal. A couple of guys in trench coats grinned uncertain at each other. Several of the onlookers started to turn their head once every ten seconds, eager for the magistrate vehicles to appear. Caldwell steeled herself and stepped forward. Two young girls snickered as they had fun with the woman kneeling in her child's remains. Suddenly, shockingly she raised her head and turned it towards a section of the circle forming around her. There were horrified gasps, turning louder as she got to her feet. Her movements were suddenly swift and confident. Caldwell sensed it. The certainty shot through her, painful as lightning. The woman walked. She did not run. She walked, she rushed towards a section of the circle, her features a study in intensity and extremities. People began to pull back. It happened slowly, clumsily, so very, very inefficiently. Some began the first, initial steps of a run. A teenage girl had backed off a couple of steps when the woman caught up with her. She grabbed the girl around the neck and held on.

– YES!

The woman shouted in joy, an insane howl cutting through everybody, freezing all those who were not already marble statues, crumbling in the acid rain. The young girl's struggles to free herself seemed more than ineffective and weak. Her efforts to move were even less than those failing to come to her aid. A group of men and women stepped forward, but then they just stopped, joining the other spectators of the macabre play. The woman let out another final triumphant snarl, and let go of her prey. The girl fell to the ground. The woman, covered in her child's remains stood still a bit, turning, giving them all her empty stare, before backing off, before running off, through the wide passage they made for her, as she passed by them and vanished into the night.

The girl coughed, began coughing hard, just as everybody had convinced themselves she was dead. She held a hand to her neck as she desperately attempted to breathe through the constricted throat. A boy rushed forward, kneeling by her side.

Caldwell stared into the darkness. She heard feet on the pavement again, fading in, fading out, sharp blades cutting through the night.

– Where were you? The girl cried accusingly at the boy. – She almost killed me, and you did nothing.

– I am sorry, the boy whined. – I was so scared, so very scared. Please forgive me.

The girl's expression softened a bit, a study in conflicting emotions. Caldwell felt something, felt something move inside. She shook her head in irritation, directing her attention at the approaching magistrates and later paramedics. There were lots of loud and angry voices raised at the uniformed men and women, as people's fear turned to rage, unfocused and arbitrary.

– Where were you? A woman, holding two small boys shouted at the magistrates. – Where the fuck were you?

– Will you please step back, ma'am, one of the magistrates begged. – We need room here.

She struck her umbrella at the ground. The magistrate, turning pale took one step back.

Caldwell breathed faster. Chaos still ruled these streets. Any minute now, she expected the tall, ominous statues to come to life before her eyes, to ask what the fuck all the noise was, explaining somewhat patiently that it was hurting their ears.

The magistrates walked in a wide circle around the woman with the two boys. She looked indeed like she was going to attack them, but instead she stood there mumbling, sometimes swearing, a blank expression dominating her features. The boys whimpered, obviously hurting by the hard grip in which she held them, too afraid to speak up.

The girl, supported by her boyfriend was guided into the ambulance. Caldwell began moving in fast, focused bursts of limbs. She walked to the closest car with a running engine and opened the door.

– *Get out!*

The man in the car took one brief look at her, paled to a crisp, and jumped out as fast as humanly possible. It took time. The ambulance was already leaving the scene. Caldwell jumped into the seat. She pushed down the pedal before the door had closed. The car slid to the middle of the road, sliding back and forth several times, before returning to a kind of equilibrium. The ambulance was one block ahead of her, well within sight reach. Caldwell nodded to herself, and settled down, somewhat in the seat.

It was a brief trip, really, not more than a few blocks or ten. But it seemed to last forever. The drizzle kept covering the windshield and blocking her sight, no matter how fast she made the sweepers work. The surroundings looked like an indistinct, foggy landscape to her.

The ambulance stopped before the front entrance to the General Health Station. Caldwell stopped the car by the corner and stepped outside. A bit ahead she saw the boy follow the girl inside. The girl looked beyond distressed. Caldwell heard her with uncanny clarity:

– She almost killed me! Do you understand what I am saying here? Have you in all of this considered *my* feelings?

The boy looked like a whipped dog, as wet as if he had walked for hours in the rain. One of the ambulance riders attempted to calm her down. She struck the arm reaching out to her.

There was a crack of thunder somewhere. There was nothing visual, but Kathryn sensed it, felt it. It was in the air, but also in the ground, deep down.

– The world is shaking, a man in rags cried.

She shook her head, dismissing him.

– The world is always shaking, she stated.

– I can walk by myself, the girl shouted, a voice strangely thundering above the traffic and city noise.

Caldwell heard the reply, too, even if she was still far away, still had not covered more than half the distance to the entrance.

– It is health station policy, Miss, one of the ambulance riders pleaded with the girl.

– FUCK HEALTH STATION POLICY, the girl screamed at the top of her lungs.

The man backed off, astounded. There was a sudden pain in his nostrils. He touched his upper lip, and when he discovered the blood on his finger, there was fear in his eyes.

They vanished inside, received by nurses and orderlies. Caldwell entered through the sliding doors about ten seconds later. She walked calmly, measured, in no apparent hurry. There was hectic activity everywhere, people, both employees and guests and sick and wounded moving back and forth in a seemingly random pattern, in various stages of stress or panic or both.

She walked right to the elevators, passing the desk and the nurse on duty, the three huge and dodgy-looking guards eying all people entering the building. The girl and the boy were nowhere to be seen. Caldwell looked at the ceiling, seeing the imperceptible shaking in the material, seeing how the very air moving close to the ceiling quivered and boiled. She entered the elevator and pushed the button to the above floor. The sliding doors closed silently. The elevator itself, a miracle of modern engineering hardly seemed to be moving at all.

But when the doors opened she no longer saw the hectic activity of the ground floor, but entered what was basically an empty corridor. There was a thud, a beating of a heart as she left the elevator, as it closed behind her like a mouth, like a gap, snapping close, and she walked through the badly lit place. There were rows of doors bulging before her, as if welcoming her, snarling at her. The pervasive presence was everywhere. It had grown steadily during the evening, but now it was everywhere, and impossible to pinpoint. Caldwell looked into every room in her path, opening all doors that were not already open. Opened and closed doors, they all invited her in. There were rooms where several patients rested, and there were single-room occupancies. Everything looked the same to her. She hardly saw anything beyond her direct line of vision…

… except for the burning daggers in the back of her neck.

She stopped after having checked a room, and turned back and looked again, shaking her head in irritation and frustration. The room still looked the same, still was the same. The woman on the bed still slept or was unconscious, several tubes sticking out of her face and her arms.

Caldwell hurried back to the elevator, pushing the button several times, also after the light, the signal for Approach had been lit. The doors finally opened, long after she had pondered taking the stairs. The time she spent in the elevator vanished in a blur. An orderly was on his way into the elevator as she was on her way out. She grabbed him, resolute, holding him in a firm grip.

– There was a girl admitted just a few minutes ago, she said to him. – What room is she in?

– Two twenty-four, he stuttered.

– Such a polite young man, she grinned. – Never even requesting my credentials or asking if I am a relative or anything. There is hope for the world.

She patted his cheek, before moving on, before forgetting him.

There was a sign on the first door she reached, fairly worn, but easily readable:

271

She walked on, distracted for a split second, listening to her own steps on the polished floor. There was a commotion somewhere ahead. She noticed it the moment she turned the nearest corner. Three people ran towards her in an undeniable state of panic. She muttered a curse and turned abruptly, throwing herself back, behind the corner.

And at that moment the world dissolved in a blinding light and a deafening roar, as the powerful explosion rocked the building, as materials and remains of materials and bodies filled the air. From some undetermined location speakers started broadcasting loud Rock'n Roll, blasting the place and everything in it. Everybody present shook as they slowly gathered their wits, and got to their feet.

– Who turned on the music? A man complained. – Who would do such a thing?

Caldwell began swaying, began dancing to the thundering beat. Her hum was loud and easily heard. She brushed her clothes for dust and debris as the others present stared incomprehensibly at her and each other, eyes glazed, their movement uncertain and shaky, as she left them, left them to rot. Even more because she went towards the disaster area, not fleeing from it as they did, as soon they got their wits somewhat in place.

The explosion had taken out several floors. There was a huge, gaping hole going down and up, and through the wall to the street. And the ragged walls were all red. Caldwell sensed it, felt dying life flow down the walls, saw the ethereal figures as they faded away in the shadows and the mist. The elevator shaft was pretty much gone, too, along with the elevator itself. This time she took the stairs.

There was a dump sound every time her feet hit the steps. There was a nice view through the rather large window to the plaza below, where surviving patients, staff and curious bystanders began to gather. There was nothing of interest for Caldwell there. As soon as she reached the ground she hit the streets, removing herself from the ravaged building, the shocked beyond reason citizens. The car had been totaled. A large part of a wall had landed on it, taking out a large chunk of its engine. She saw some potentially useful cars close by, but decided not to bother.

– Cab! She cried, lifting an arm.

And a cab came, stopped right by her, making it only a few extra steps for her to walk. She opened the door and stepped into the backseat.

– Just drive, she said.

He did. He did not ask why. He did not even turn his head before turning three hundred and sixty degrees in the road and driving off the hospital area. A quiet cab driver. She felt an idiotic burst of gratitude, smiling bitterly to herself.

She hummed a melody, not the one she had heard at the health station. It just began by itself, and continued, in spite of her feeble attempts at stopping it.

As the car drove back and forth in central downtown. As she sat there with her elbow resting on her knee and her head resting in the palm of her hand, and she hummed the melody, and a catching in her throat made her choke a bit, impossible to hear for the driver, but that she easily noticed.

– That is an oldie, right?

It took several seconds before she even noticed and acknowledged that he had in fact spoken. She raised her head, her eyes sparks of irritation.

– Excuse me?

– The one you are humming? It is an old song. It is been years since I last heard it played anywhere.

– Yes, it is old, she replied, shrugging. – Very old.

She laughed.

– I do not even know why I was remembering it. And tonight of all nights.

– Memories may leave us in peace most of the time, he said. – But they will never let us be.

She nodded to herself, both solemn and bemused.

A philosophical cab driver. She supposed that was not necessarily a rare occurrence.

– Mostly they leave us in pieces, she mumbled.

He heard her. She sensed that easily.

She was tapping the fingers on the seat, soundlessly, unnoticeably, just not to her, striking a beat only she could hear.

He drove up the long, very broad Main Street. She looked over at the other sidewalk. People there were so far away that they seemed like insects, like from high above. But while from far above they would look like dots, these resembled thin lines, floating, not walking up and down the street, indistinct, like everything was, hardly visible in the dirty rain the city air had become.

They reached the vast, open Onion Square on Ivy Avenue, a plaza with many streetlights and lanterns. They all glowed dull and dry. There was a road circling the place, with the open area in the middle.

– Well, here we are again, the driver commented. – Why they call it Onion *Square* is beyond me, really. An onion is not square, if you ask me.

It was a vast, gothic landscape, where artists had been given more or less free reign. Homer Upcott's twisted figures stretched towards the sky. The statues' outstretched arms reached for the passing pedestrians with hands formed like claws. It was a park, really, one of mystery and imagination, of wonder and awe and horror.

Kathryn Caldwell surmised that the more even the most unaware person studied it, the more... uneasy that given person would become.

– I wonder what those artistic types they have let loose in this city have in for statues, the driver kept talking. – It is not like they are actually depicting anyone or are made in honor of anybody. At least they are not resembling anybody I have ever heard of...

A burst of rain and ashes hit the window Kathryn stared through, and for a moment the figures she saw looked even more indistinct.

– I will tell you straight: I will never understand modern art. The old masters, like Rutherford and Kane and classics like Augustus Preditus, those I could understand. I could see the purpose behind their expression, if you get my drift, but these new guys...

– Stop! Caldwell said softly.

The driver stopped. He pushed the brakes a bit too hard, and was trust slightly forward, enough to ruffle his feathers. Caldwell sat there calmly, waiting for him to turn. She handed him the money, giving him tips. His features softened a bit, but the apprehension, the expression of being wronged did not leave his face.

She stepped outside, unveiling her umbrella. The light rain hit it like tiny rocks, the pieces of ashes caressed her skin. There was a brush of wind, lasting only a moment, sending shivers through her being.

Beatrice stood before her, a shimmering, transparent figure.

– Now, she cried triumphantly in her ghostly voice. – Now, you will *pay!*

Kathryn wanted to move, to shrug, but she could not do it. She was not afraid exactly and not angry either, but all of the above.

– We are making a painting, Beatrice said, filled with malice. – And you are a vital piece of the canvas.

She was nothing but malice, a mirror for others to face.

And then she faded, and the air returned to the drizzle it was.

On any other night Caldwell's attention would have been locked on what had just transpired. It would have kept churning through her thoughts like a curse, like it had done for years, for an eternity, but not tonight.

Caldwell saw something, at the edge of her vision, and when she focused on it, that was all she saw. There was movement. A woman passed by her, crossing the plaza, a completely ordinary woman walking through the rain. There was nothing extraordinary about her, nothing at all. Caldwell took one step forward, hesitatingly, suddenly apprehensive. She sensed the draft again, a pull in the air. She turned, and there was another woman right in front of her, the comatose patient from the hospital, still with wires sticking to her skin. To Caldwell the woman's face was illuminated in a darkly light.

– I thought it was a blessing at first…

Then the woman grabbed her, and Caldwell was caught in her grip, claws against skin. There was a tingle, a weak, oddly pleasant electrical surge.

– One touch, the stranger mumbled. – One touch is all it takes.

The woman let go, taking a few steps back, exaltation visible in her eyes.

– It is gone, she cried. – And I am still here. Do you understand? I am free, now. Free! The Nine have no hold on me anymore.

Caldwell shook then, imperceptible. Her mouth moved, but there was no sound.

– They know you, you know, like I do, intimately.

The woman looked at her, in scorn, in pity, in joy.

– You will understand. I know that.

She turned then and ran away, ran down Onion Square, jumping up and down in joy, clearly released from all woes. Caldwell followed her. Perception changed for every new step she took. The woman ran into a small alley. Caldwell did not follow her there, but ran into the adjacent street to the left, picking up speed the moment she was hidden from the other's viewpoint, running hard. She ran to the end of the street and turned right, ignoring the beginning of fatigue in her legs, her increasingly ragged breath. There was a pressure in her bladder. Suddenly she got an insane need to pee. She wanted to curse, but was too out of breath to speak. She rushed to the corner and stuck her head beyond it, looking back down the alley.

As expected the woman had not even reached halfway through it. The wide smile was still painted on her face as she in her euphoria danced and hummed.

And then she stopped, frowning. Caldwell saw it easily. There was movement in the shadows. One, two, three, four, five, six, seven, eight and more figures appeared, carrying flashing swords in their hands. The woman saw them, too, uttering a cry, a squeal of protest. They surrounded her, hardly giving her a chance to move before moving in on her. The swords flashed in metal, flashed in red, as they, during a few incredible seconds cut her in pieces. They kept attacking what was left of the body on the ground long after she lay still, before finally returning to the shadows from which they had come.

Caldwell pulled back, very conscious of her labored and loud breathing. Sweat protruding from her skin was abruptly that much more potent.

One block, two she walked, occasionally breaking into a run. She saw nothing more of the sword wielders, fully aware that she would probably not see them… before they were there.

Noise returned, slowly. She entered a more populated area again, a street with shops, cafés and entertainment. Downtown seemed strangely alive tonight, not at all the shallow, deadbeat area Caldwell remembered. She had a coffee at Wesley's. As she received the cup she briefly touched the skin of the woman behind the counter. The woman shook, as if receiving an electric charge.

Kathryn sat down by a window table, remote from the crowd gathered deeper inside the café. Her nostrils twitched as she… as she smelled the coffee. A grin, one without a smile touched her face. The fumes from the coffee entered her nostrils, and she was able to discern the various brands used in the brewing. This in spite of her never having any interest in or knowledge of coffee brewing.

The astuteness pushed at her in waves. She saw without opening her eyes. The grin that was not a smile widened. She knew what was happening to her.

A man took a sip of his cup at the other side of the room. She heard it, divided it from the background noise, from all the other sounds in the room. The crowd, the in-crowd laughed like one person, «happy, pretty people» having a night out. She sensed every little move, every minor twitch in muscles and sinews. The noise from the minor traffic outside suddenly seemed painfully urgent. It cried out to her like a person, a thin wail growing louder and louder each time her heart struck a beat. She drank her coffee. It flowed inside her, spread to all corners of her being. She hurried outside, hurried through the noisy streets, hardly conscious of having left the place.

Breathing remained ragged. It was as if the minutes she had spent inside, resting had done her no good at all. Sweat kept flowing from her skin. But…

… she did not really feel tired, not tired at all.

She was sweaty, but the sweat seemed to evaporate between her skin and clothes, not truly manifesting itself. She did not use her umbrella, but the rain and ash did not… touch her. Doubt lingered for a second, then it vanished. A buzz lingered inside her, telling her where to go, in which direction to rush. There was another clearing ahead, a lesser one, a small piece of green… what was it called, yes, Broker Park. There were lots of people there, gathered for some kind of meeting, the very vocal protest against tonight's burning of the forest. She pondered what was happening to her. It felt like low burning acid flowed through her veins. And the hum, the hum inside rose to insane levels. So many people, but she did not see them. One single figure, one single woman pointed itself out to Caldwell, glowing in her wet eyes. The woman stood out among hundreds, the woman that had passed Caldwell on the Square not that many minutes ago.

There was a storm brewing. She listened to it, listened to its roar, what she could hardly hear.

– Everything is happening in three's, a man told another some distance off. – I do not know if you have noticed this, but I have. I have made notes for three times three times three years or so. I know. The old stories are true. True!

The unknown woman moved, covered in a translucent light. Caldwell heard music from somewhere, but could not tell from which direction. It invaded her, pervasive and overwhelming. Her feet followed the unknown woman by themselves, followed her with a passion, a beyond frightening intensity. Images assaulted her. Sounds, smells and tastes. *Touches without touches*. And whispers and insults, and hopes and dreams. And the people around her heard nothing of it. Her eyes focused on the women ahead, and increasingly that was the only thing her eyes saw. Caldwell was aware, kind of, of her surroundings, but they mattered less and less for every step she took forward, walking the unknown woman's path. The buzz in her head rose to roar. And now she heard it, the roar. Now, it was impossible not to. There was pain, sudden and shocking, and she stumbled, and whimpered.

– The Gauntlet, she mumbled. – You did it, Stane, you son of a bitch. Thank you, thank you, thank you. Oh, goddess. GODDESS!

People stared. She did not notice them. The energy of the Gauntlet rose in her, irresistible, cutting into her like black, black blades, and the pain, the pain increased on a scale from bad to intolerable. She knew her facial tattoos, even those hidden beneath the clothes showed, that everybody present saw them and that fear beyond fear struck them, struck their bones. Her entire system, physical and mental was overwhelmed, causing an overload to end all overloads.

She followed the woman, followed her, gaining on her for every step. Her only thought was to catch up with the woman, and get rid of the pain, the incessant shriek in her guts.

With an effort of will she stopped. She held back, *held back,* biting her lip.

A man left a building on the other side of the street. The woman lit up even more, and she started running towards him. Caldwell rushed after her in a whirl of motion, catching up fast. One touch… one touch was all it took.

And in that whirl of motion was the woman, and everything else around her was shrinking, until there was nothing else but that shimmering figure, glowing, glowing, like a flame to a moth.

The woman passed under a balcony. The sight of the balcony faded in Caldwell's eyes and consciousness, even as she desperately attempted to hold onto it.

She turned, towards the balcony, away from the woman, removing herself from her with every single step.

There was a shout screaming in her, totally overwhelming her senses, but she ignored all that, and moved, ignored the steering wheel, and made the wheels turn on their own. Her feet wanted to turn, her brain wanted the feet to turn, but she ignored the call, the horrible voice screaming at her by an act of impossible will. She ran to the wall and jumped, jumped high. Fingers like claws grabbed the wall, the handle on the balcony, and held on.

In one swift like lightning movement she pulled herself up, her muscles screaming, but filled, filled with energy, with power. It was as if she was an agile animal climbing the wall.

She landed on the balcony, high above the sidewalk, four to five times her own height, light as a bird on her feet, strength coursing through her. The door was open, an open invitation, and she accepted. She was torn apart inside, more so for every step she took, but she kept going. The raging energy-buildup made her deaf, mute and blind. She kept going. The woman outside was far away now. It felt like she was just a step away. She called to Kathryn, with her siren song, the irresistible siren song. Kathryn wanted to go to her. There was nothing she wanted more, nothing in the whole world.

She entered a luxury apartment. Lush and soft carpets dominated the floor and the walls. Burning violet eyes caught two candelabras hanging from the ceiling, furniture from the most acknowledged vendors of antiques. Caldwell had acquired bits and pieces of knowledge on such things.

– A honey trap, she chuckled, – a goddamn honey trap, designed to keep intruders from the true goodie.

There was no way she recognized her laughter, her voice. It was just a buzz, drowning in the louder roar in her ears.

She sensed the true goodie, even saw it with her eyes, deeper in the apartment. It registered in her mind as a warmer spot in all the heat, luring better-informed intruders to its jaws. And then she felt it, felt its pull, so strong that what she had recently felt from the woman moving away a second earlier shrunk to nothing.

The apartment was like a set of ship-locks, each new room she entered, she rushed through, walked through smaller than the rest. There were five rooms, perhaps six, she could not quite decide, and she did not care to.

She sensed the trembling in the ground, the disturbance rising for every step she took forward. A ghoul appeared in front of her, horrible and ghastly, one of the most terrifying sight she ever had had the pleasure of seeing. Puss and insects flowed from its hollow eye sockets. That in itself was frightening, but the direct assault on her brain's fear center was the true aim, vibrations of pure fear in the air, designed to drive any intruder from his or her senses, leaving him or her a wreck of a human being. Everything was just a hum in Caldwell's mind, not affecting her more or less than a song or a lullaby nearby. The power of the Gauntlet had long since overwhelmed her and made all other impressions meaningless.

The ground, her surroundings changed around her, changed constantly, a mosaic of different, conflicting realities. No human being could survive this with her or his mind intact. But she had no mind left to lose.

The ground turned soft, the air moist. Trees rose around her. Branches reached for her. Vile grass attempted to snare her feet. The door ahead remained. She walked through a room. There was no room. Kathryn hissed patronizingly at the ghouls swarming her and they pulled back in horror. Branches reached her. Snake-like things from the ground twined her legs and body. She snarled and the branches, the snakes turned to try twigs in her close proximity. She broke their hold on her with a small burst of power, tightening of muscles, hardly without her breaking her stride. She cried out in contempt.

The door appeared before her in its solid form. Her hand quite simply grabbed the handle and opened it. Her feet moved inside. Reality turned itself inside out again.

It was an ordinary room, a cave, a hall, a valley, a moon. Planets and flies and bats and clouds and stars buzzed above her, close and far, all fading to nothing as she took the five steps, the thousand steps of eternity to the center, the glass exhibition case, the thick hollow log, the thick metal case. Her hands turned translucent, turned immaterial as she raised them, as she looked at them, as she charged forward, as she reached for the glowing orb levitating in there. Her entire body sparked with energy and life. The overwhelming, overloading charge she received from the defenses designed to deal with any type of persistent intruder, he or she or it who had survived this far… felt like a cool shower a warm summer morning.

She grabbed the orb with both hands. The room, the cave, the Universe lit up like fireworks, equaling that of a billion bombs. Numbers were meaningless. Scales were meaningless. As the furnace within the orb disintegrated her a thousand times the power of the Gauntlet burned itself out within her in one mighty discharge of energy.

Silence descended on the remote, foreboding place. Kathryn Caldwell shook and swayed. Reality turned itself outside in again. She stood there, clutching the orb inside a well-lit room, only a room. There were ghosts of tentacles reaching for her. She lifted the orb, held it up in joy and triumph, and they pulled back in horror, screeching and screaming. She stood still, crouching just a bit before straightening again. The familiar mysteries and power of the orb coursed within her. She smiled, strained but good. The door out was closed. She concentrated just a little and it opened wide. The door bowed down to her. The universal forces of vast time and space bowed deeply… to her.

There was something… She tilted her head. Blood. Her mouth was filled with sweet, sweet blood. Her tongue rummaged in there, searched for a while, before encountering a small stiff of flesh, a piece of her tongue. She had bit herself. Smiling some more she turned towards the exhibition case and spat out the bit of flesh. Flesh and blood hit the glass and splashed all over it.

She put the orb inside her coat and walked back, returned the same path she had come. There were six rooms in the apartment turning bigger the further out she walked. It was a nice apartment. Quite stylish, actually.

– I have seen better, she grinned.

She looked at the open door to the balcony she had walked through ages ago, shook her head, and headed for the door, the big and bulky door. She pulled it open without the biggest of difficulties. There were people outside, men and women with «tough» written all over their faces and bulky, lithe and dangerous bodies. They pulled back in horror by her presence. Guns raised were lowered. They did not run, knowing enough to know that flight would be useless. She totally ignored them, walked down the stairs without acknowledging their presence the slightest. There was not a move or flash in her eyes indicating that she had noticed them at all.

One of the women raised her gun again, pointing it at her head. Caldwell sensed that, as easily as if the barrel had touched the back of her neck. The woman's hands began to shake, and then shake violently. The gun was lowered once more, and she sat right down there in the dust, sobbing helplessly.

Caldwell reached the street. The heavy door closed behind her. She unfolded her umbrella, laughing a bit, a short, coarse laughter and strolled away to the right.

Passing people cast her glances. They always did. But tonight those glances of worry and uncertainty were even more worried and uncertain.

She passed one corner, sensing easily the shadows in the rain and night to her right. There were dark streets and alleys in the immediate vicinity of this one, where light, at least this gray, dirty version of it seemed to be everywhere. She turned to the right on the next corner. Several of the streetlights in this street had broken bulbs, as was often the case, a fact that had been strenuously pointed out by a leading representative for those opposing the current City Council recently.

One block, two, down the dark and downtrodden alley, and she was there, and they were there as well. She heard the light steps, easier than she used to do, discerning the nuances of shadows faster.

The sword-wielding women and men dressed in black advanced on her, cautious, apprehensive, smelling uncharacteristically of fear, but that did not stop them, not that alone.

– Yes, she told them softly, – your fear is well founded.

She did not need to. They knew.

But she wanted to.

They stopped. Their advances stopped as if someone had stopped a film from running.

– I have been curious about you boys and girls, she said. – I will give you that much. And I have wanted to find out more about you. Now seems as good a time as ever.

One of the swordsmen, the biggest of them seemed to struggle, struggle to free himself from invisible hands clutching him. But if so his effort was hopelessly inadequate. His face, his face beneath the mask contorted violently. He struggled to move his sword, but he did not have more luck with that than with his efforts to move himself.

– This is so funny. I very much doubt you would have been able to take me on even before this milestone evening, and now you surely can not.

Suddenly he was pulled up in the air, pulled towards Caldwell, thrust towards her with ramming speed. Caldwell held up a hand, and just like that the forward movement stopped.

– Now, let us have a look at you…

Clothes were torn off the big, bulky body by something that seemed very much like the very air itself. Skin and blood mingled with the torn clothes. Pale, very pale skin was revealed as the man's second skin of clothes was removed. He hung there, suspended in the air, totally at her mercy.

– Talk to me, she said. – *Talk to me!*

He did not betray a single sound as she began her intrusion, her pervasive intrusion into his very being, but she heard him anyway.

Pe a pe a peo pe y ye fo…

A song, an ancient and terrible chant.

Something twisted, turned within him. She sensed it and pulled back, pulled out and away from him. He erupted in flames, his entire body devoured in a second by a seemingly spontaneous combustion. It ended quickly. He added to the ashy quality of the city air and his remains fell to the ground, hardly more than a pile of dust. Even his sword burned and was reduced to cold dust. She looked quickly at the others, but if there was anything she could have done to stop what was happening it was already too late.

They stood there, like statues, with empty eyes, as they all were consumed in one, single burst of flame. She saw it all, in what she experienced as slow motion. More ash and dust joined what was already covering the ground.

The street was dark again, wet again, the brief light and dry air gone like a whisper.

A silent, howling wind raced through the street and embraced her, before taking its leave, returning to wherever it came from. It actually made her shudder, and it was a long time since that had happened.

The wind screamed at her, in unimaginable fury, all the way from the far away place from where it had come.

The impressions and images brought by the wind mingled by those glimpsed by her look into the dust's mind. The world seemed to blink out around her for a moment, before once more sort of reasserting itself. She turned and retraced her steps back to the street of gray and dirty light.

Dust danced in the wet air, as she walked. Gray dust. Gray light. She shook her head, and put on speed, setting course for a peculiar looking building at the other side of downtown, the Maximus Tower, one of several landmarks in the triple cities belonging to the Maximus clan. It was not far. So she walked. She discovered that she was moving her lips. There was no sound, but she still spoke.

Pe a pe a peo pe y ye fo…

She saw a well somewhere, not one of water, but of fire. Nine people stood around it, their hands raised, chanting. Something looking like the insides of an old castle.

– The Nine, she said aloud.

A car passed her. It passed in a normal pace, but the sound… the sound sounded like it slowed down to a halt, a deep, slow, roaring bass shaking the Earth. Its front changed to a huge mouth with jagged teeth.

– YOU TOOK SOMETHING THAT'S OURS, YOU FUCKING BITCH. RETURN IT THIS INSTANT OR THERE WILL BE HELL TO PAY

She shook her head in dismay and contempt, practically ignoring the useless display, and walked on. The car sagged and lost all its bounce, and was just a car again.

There was a plaza in front of the building, named after the very building. The building was old money. It had not been here as long as the city, but not far from it. It was not really a building, but rather a symbol of wealth and power, one of the foremost of its kind in the city and the land, and the realm.

She crossed the plaza, passed its water fountains and elaborate setup of art and lighting and scenery without truly looking at it. The vestibule was also vast, a mirror of the stage outside, with one small reception desk at the end, by the elevators. The man behind the desk was the only visible guard. She approached him with a slow, indifferent stroll. He looked up, a few seconds after she had stopped in front of him, another deliberate attempt at making the guests feel small.

– I am here to see Turner Maximus, she informed the man. – We are acquainted of old. He is expecting me.

– He is, is he? The voice was just as snotty as the snottiest of old money gentlemen. – And your name is?

She did not reply. If there was a reaction to his words at all, there was one of total disregard. He was being ignored in a far more pronounced way than he ever did with the people passing his way.

– Mr. Maximus is expecting you, he enlightened her, as if revealing a major secret. – You may go right up, Miss Caldwell.

The elevator doors slid open. She did not hurry but walked inside at a rather slow pace. If it had not been remote-controlled the doors would have slid shut long before she reached it. There was a slight pressure as the ascension began. She hardly felt it. The doors opened up to a large entrance room. There was a secretary behind the desk close to the elevator. Caldwell ignored her and went straight to next room. A man wearing dark glasses and a black suit opened the door for her from the other side. There were several other men and women inside equally disposed. Everybody, in fact except the casually dressed man behind the large, large desk.

– Ah, there you are, Cathy, he greeted her, rolling her name off the tongue in a manner making her cringe, his very features causing her pain. – So nice to see you again. In all honesty I was not certain I ever would.

– Call me Afterglow, she said.

A film covered his sticky eyes. The pretence of kindness ended.

– Afterglow it is, he nodded, to her, to himself. – You have the… object, I trust.

– I have indeed, she shrugged.

She produced it from the pocket inside her coat, and held it up for him to admire. He stared at it, could hardly take his eyes away. She walked to the desk and put it there, right in front of him. It stayed put, as if had been put in a socket, did not roll at all. He picked it up. It did not emanate any light that anybody could see, but shadows played in his face.

– The Orb of Eternity, he said, and the hoarseness in his voice could not be concealed. – Have you any idea what this is?

– I have a fairly good idea, Afterglow nodded.

– With this you could… you could possibly rule the world, he informed her.

– With this you can destroy the world, she enlightened him. – And all it takes is a snapping of fingers. I did. I destroyed worlds. I created worlds.

He put the Orb back on the desk. It still did not roll.

– A drink? He offered casually, as he walked to the bar to the left.

– Thank you, she said. – Sweet Martini with a twist, please.

– What twist?

– You decide, she shrugged.

He mixed the drinks like a pro, and he was, of course. A pro. He handed her the glass. She sipped it. Her eyes narrowed slightly. It was poisoned.

She did a bottoms up to end all bottoms up. The spice and everything created a pleasant stir of echoes inside her.

– I have heard you like your drink, he said pleasantly.

– And you heard right, she grinned.

He mixed another to her, and handed it to her. He returned with fast steps to the desk, to the Eternity Orb.

– And the guards?

– The guards? She smiled. – I do not know why they were there at all. They are not very useful guarding the place, not against the kind of people that might pay the place a visit, and they are totally useless afterwards, one way or another.

– What did you…see?

He leaned forward, almost crouching, as he scrutinized her, as if to possible stare at the answer to his question.

– I told you, she replied. – I destroyed worlds. I created worlds. I saw everything. This universe and many others were in the palm of my hand. I can only recall a fraction of it.

– You are remarkable. He shook his head. – I knew you were some piece of work, but I could never imagine how much so you truly were. The reputation you have gained is truly deserved.

He grabbed the Orb. The shadows once more played in his face.

His index finger pushed a button on his desk. A light changed from red to green.

– At this moment your retainer is placed in your bank account, he said. – You deserve everything.

– Thank you.

She shrugged.

– We are done, then?

She half turned to lcavc.

– We are done. You may go, with my eternal gratitude. You have done the Maximus Enterprise a great service today. It will not be forgotten.

– Whatever, she shrugged.

– Maybe we can do business again some time?

– We might, she told him.

There was an underlying sharpness in her voice that did not escape him. He was not stupid, after all. After thousands of boardroom meetings and dodgy deals one could not avoid learning something about human nature.

She walked to the door, touched the handle, the golden handle.

There was a sharp pain in her nostrils. She touched her muzzle. Her fingers turned red and wet. She turned and gauged Maximus immersed in the weird lights of the Orb.

– I just can not let you go, he said with regret. – As a tool you are quite simply too dangerous to be wielded by someone else, by competitors or anyone. That would have been true even if you had not been a… thorn in our side for so long. And I need… a test anyway. Think about it… The Orb of Eternity… it is screaming to be *used.*

He stared into it, drowning in its lure.

A sharp pain in her gut. She fell back, her back leaning on the door.

She straightened, a dark anger burning in her violet flame. Sweat covered her forehead and made hairs stick to the skin. When she spoke it was in slow, deliberate bursts.

– You do not want to *mess* with me, Turner. If there is one thing I take seriously it is betrayal. We swore an oath, one saying that all old grievances were forgotten. The only thing a human being truly possesses in this world or any other is his or her word. You *know* that!

He laughed. They all did, his echoes.

– You took that silly performance at face value? He actually looked inconvenienced behind his smug smile. – I, on the other hand obvious did not, and I am not too worried.

– You *should* be.

The snarl was hardly noticeable. Not more than a whisper late at night. The first signs of worry revealed itself behind the smug smile. His confidence remained high, though.

Suddenly he screamed. His henchmen jumped out of their skin, drawing their guns.

Afterglow held up a hand, a half fisted hand.

– See this here? This is your spleen.

He stared stunned at it, stared at the shimmering form in her hand, a form resembling his face, a twisted demonic version of his face.

The guards pointed their guns at her. She ignored them.

– I have bonded with it, you see. It belonged to me long before anyone else knew its sweet and horrible touch. I do not have to touch it to use it. It does not belong to you, but to me. I would have let go eventually, though. A deal is a deal. Now… I do not have to.

He gasped.

– If you had been smart you would have waited, biding your time, until you had some semblance of control, but I figured you would not do that.

She *moved*. To the guards it seemed like she just slipped through the air, slid across the floor like a ghost and grabbed Turner Maximus by the throat.

– *Besides*… it is just a trinket anyway, practically useless without the right person to wield it, to be fueled by its raging energies. And you do not know what it is, like I do. I know exactly what it is.

Smoke rose from Maximus' skin, and suddenly, two, three, ten seconds later his entire body was on fire. But it was not ordinary fire, but bluish, briefly touching bright red. It consumed him from within, from everywhere at once. His remains, his ashes and burning parts dropped to the floor without a sound, and there was hardly anything left of him, except the singed hairs of the carpet.

Afterglow turned towards the men and women with guns. She picked up the Eternity Orb from the floor. It had rolled to her feet. She held it in her hand.

– Trinkets do not matter, she told them. – Only the fire, dark and deep burning inside each person. You might want to remember that, the next time you point a gun at someone.

One bullet was fired, reflexively, from a man trained at firing guns from an early age. The bullet rushed through the air, headed for Afterglow. It seemed slow, as if she had an eternity to react to it. She held up a hand, exposing her palm. The air seemed to… thicken ahead of the small piece of lead. The bullet lost all momentum. Afterglow caught it in her hand.

– You are scared, are you not? You do not just look scared, but *are,* to the bottom of your heart.

He fell to his knees. There was no strength left in his legs.

Afterglow smiled, and that smile made him gasp in the grip of absolute terror.

– You all want to run, she said softly. – But you can not. Your feet will not carry you.

They stood there, like statues, like ghosts, some of them peeing on themselves, the stench of body fluid quickly turning old and stale. The contempt in her serene mask hurt more than any fire.

She left, casually joggling the sphere.

– I hold the world in my hand…

She left, left them to rot.

The secretary sat there, writing. Afterglow walked to the bathroom. After a second or two of soul-searching she chose the door marked GENTLEMEN. She saw how the secretary lifted her head. There was no need for her to turn to see that.

Afterglow chose a cubicle. She stepped inside and without closing the door she pulled down her pants and panties and sat down on the cold marble seat. Release was virtually instantaneous. It felt sweet, relieving the pressure inside. There was a harsh stench as she peed and shit the poison out of herself, along the other waste.

– It hurts, she mumbled. – Why must it hurt?

She dried herself. Smoke rose from the toilet paper and she discarded it seconds before it dissolved in her hand. Her feature twisted in disgust. Without pulling up her pants she dragged her feet to the line of washing trays at the other wall. She grabbed a lot of paper from the wall and began rubbing herself with water and soap, a lot of it, hot, steaming water, lovely, lovely soap. There was a sweet pain that slowly faded as she dried herself. She pulled her pants back up, set to leave when she spotted herself in the mirror. There was a lot of mist and shadow, there always was, but she could see herself, distinct from the surroundings. She was able to recognize herself, sort of, in the swirling air.

The door was ajar, inviting her to step through. She shook her head, walked back into the cubicle and picked up the orb and headed out. The secretary had not moved. She still sat there, typing.

The elevator did not feel that different. It was still an elevator. The hall, the streets felt the same. Nothing had changed. She left the building as she had found it.

It was still raining. Somehow it always was. Her pace picked up as she light on her feet walked away.

It was late at night. Most people were on their way home, headed for bed, headed for sleep. Afterglow hummed to herself, hummed to a melody, but it was none of the many she heard from various cafés and bars she passed.

She stopped by The Needle in Hudson Park, another small patch of green with a few well-groomed trees and a nice cut lawn. It was just a needle, forged in stone, pointing at the sky. She pulled the Eternity Orb from her coat, joggled it a bit, looking at it, studying it with an undeniable tint of regret in her eyes. She concentrated, pulling it behind her body a little, before throwing it into the air.

At first it seemed to be nothing but an ordinary throw, but then, as it reached a certain altitude, its speed and momentum picked up, and it rose above the building. The woman, down there, in the cluster of tiny houses and buildings watched it as it was propelled into the air, as it faded into the air, and returned to the eternity from which it had come.

Afterglow stood still for a while, there on the sidewalk, by the stone needle. Eventually she turned and began walking. She ignored the calls from boys and men, the allure from the passing cars and taxis. She did not have far to walk, not far at all.

She found a dark alley and disappeared into it. She walked down that alley, and when she had walked that to its end she headed down another, walking an eternity of steps, slowly fading into the darkness from which she had come.

CHAPTER TWO

There was a vast, deep dark ocean she floated through. There were points, pinpricks of bright light, and then there was Shadow.

We are paintings, hanging on a wall, retouched and polished, and we do not see the large holes, the large fields and chunks missing.

She could never quite identify the voice, even though she felt she should have.

Afterglow woke up, all sweaty, her hair tangled and wet. The daystar was just a red line in the horizon. It was night. It was always night.

She dragged herself out of the bed, stumbled out on the floor. Her feet moved across the floor, to the bathroom. There was nothing to see in the mirror, nothing at all.

Water fell on her like needles. The shower was hot, was cold. The water smothered her. It surrounded her, cotton pushing softly at her skin. So peaceful. A quiet river passing by a hot summer afternoon.

The towel danced in the air around her, rubbing almost dry skin, a strangely pleasing act. She threw the towel in the air. It was big. It floated up there, never really falling, but sailing the room's invisible airwaves. Afterglow wrapped herself in it, wrapped her body, wrapped her mind, and she became the whirling cloth, became the dancing airwaves centering on her.

Her dress danced on her body, as she walked through the streets. Many casual and not so casual eyes were filled with lust when they studied that body, but looked away when they reached her face. She caught glimpses of her face, her jigsaw puzzle in the display windows she passed. It made her want to look away, but instead she was helplessly drawn to all of them. They kept haunting her, long after they had faded from her view.

The entertainment district drew her, like it drew everyone. The sound of glasses meeting and parting, the relaxed and hysterical laughter both rattled her. She found herself seeking desirable male and female faces in the crowd.

No conscious mind guided her feet. She deliberately let go of control. They walked of their own volition, as she scouted for suitable taverns.

Her warm, warm laughter brought more attention from many other lost and found birds in the night.

She sat on the barstool, looking casually into the large mirror behind the barkeep. She looked at her hair. It was part white, part red, part blonde, part black, and other strange hues, besides. The eyes burned at her, in a weird violet catch. She sipped her drink. It was Sweet Martini, nothing fancy.

– How is your drink, the tall barkeep inquired.

– It burns in my throat, she replied. – It is not supposed to, but it does anyway.

He pulled back, clearly hurt in his professional pride, not understanding the deeper textures of her words.

She looked around, turning away from the mirror, looking through the fairly bright room.

It was a noisy place, even though it was possible to engage in a conversation without actually screaming. She actually heard people at the neighboring tables, which was damn near unprecedented in places such as these. Her ass and body danced on the stool, reacting to the rhythms assaulting her.

A man stopped by her side. She sensed it easily, without looking, without needing to confirm it in any way, except with the increased pressure she sensed in the air.

– May I join you?

His voice was rough, unpolished, promising. She turned slightly towards him. He looked all right. Too much cologne and unnatural smell, but she was used to that.

– You may, she nodded mercifully.

He was about to go for a chair when she raised her hand. There was a shift, a breath in the damp air and the chair moved, seemingly by itself to her side.

She saw him freeze, did not need to sense his fear to confirm it.

– Nice trick, he shrugged.

– I can not stand weaklings, she snarled.

He was gone.

She balanced easily on the stool, sipping her drink.

– You know how to treat 'em, the barkeep commented dryly, his Scottish accent quite distinctive.

– There are plenty of fish in the sea. She shrugged.

She sat there with her third Sweet Martini, taking her time. Lights were dimmed after nine, and she kind of liked that. She did not look around much. It looked very much like she ignored the room and everybody in it, but she did not really. The quick, unnoticed glances were absolutely necessary for her. She needed to know, beyond doubt and in advance… if something was up.

Another man approached her. She studied him in a frank and open manner in the mirror, also after he had noticed her doing so. He went right to her, no hesitation, no detours.

He stopped in front of her, blinking a bit, but not taking his eyes off her.

– I like the way you dress, he commented.

She did not glance in the mirror, but she did look at herself, looked at the very revealing black silk dress, the high edge on the round, muscular thighs, the large breasts sticking up from the low top edge, the nipples more than visible through the thin fabric.

– It is just a dress, she shrugged.

– I like your dress, he persisted.

His eyes kept dwelling on her.

– Well, thank you very much, she grinned

– My name is Justin. He reached out a hand.

– I am Afterglow, she said, taking his hand.

He sat down on the empty stool beside her.

– Can I get you anything, Afterglow?

– Thanks, she shook her head. – But no thanks.

– A whiskey, he turned to the barkeep. – Straight up, please!

The man behind the desk looked at him with pity, and probably not because of the drink. He was good that man, good at reading people. Afterglow began to feel the first stings of excitement within.

– I have never seen anything remotely like your eyes before, Justin marveled, carefully consuming his drink.

He was nervous, but that did not turn her off. In her experience it was kind of unavoidable.

– They are pretty, he added.

– Thank you. What a sweet thing to say…

She was flirting with him, with her words, on so many levels. She spread her legs slightly, opening herself up to him, posing for him.

– Cheers. He raised his glass. – To pretty eyes.

Glasses met and parted. The sound echoed pleasantly in her ears.

– Your hair is pretty, too, he stated solemnly.

She dried a little saliva from the corner of her mouth. He caught that, and his staring eyes turned large and deep.

– I want to fuck you, he stated.

There was a thrill inside her, of expectation fulfilled.

Her eyes twinkled darkly as she turned towards the barkeep.

– A Glenmorangie, straight up, she ordered.

She did not reply directly to his bold words, leaving him hanging there a bit, but she gave him the sweetest of smiles.

The small glass slipped into her hand. She downed it in one move. The liquor exploded in her belly.

– One more, she cried.

She drank, as she slid down from the chair, as she slipped closer to him. A bit of the small glass' content flowed from her mouth and down her jaw, a

few drops hitting the naked skin above her breasts.
– What do you say? Do you want to blow this joint?
– Sure, he said hoarsely.
There was no sense of temperature change, as their surroundings changed from the hot room to the fairly chilly night outside.
– Mine or… he began.
– Your place, she said.
– We need to take a cab, he pointed out.
– That is okay, she said sweetly. – That is perfectly okay.
They walked impatiently through a narrow alley to Onion Square, where the cabs lined up like an honor guard. He hesitated again. She looked at him.
– May I ask… what happened to your face?
– It got beaten up pretty bad some years ago, she shrugged. – It never got quite right, afterwards.
– It was not a boyfriend who did that, was it, he said, a clear and present rage in his voice.
– No, she replied. – Not a boyfriend.
It was yet early in the evening, not really any queue of people waiting to be picked up by the cabs. They were the third couple, and it did not take them more than thirty seconds, tops.
The taxi moved, but it did not feel like it was moving. They sat in the back. She looked at him with badly hidden expectation.
– It is not far, he assured her hoarsely.
She sent him a *grateful* smile, and he reddened like a schoolboy.
He lived in Talaho, the Roman city, just across the Accenton Bridge. There was fog under the bridge tonight, hiding the river completely. In the thickset air Talaho just slowly came into view, seemingly growing out of the very night. The architecture changed slightly, to the more old Roman setting, though not being so pronounced here, as it was elsewhere in Talaho.
– I like your place, she said.
– You have not even seen it, yet.
He just had to say that.
– I like the west side, she said. – Close to the mountains and the forest.
The taxi stopped by the moody, old building. There was a bell in its tower, chiming the moment they opened the doors.
– You do not live here, do you, Afterglow wondered cheerfully.
– No, he shook his head, just to make sure she got the message. – It is right over there. No access for cars.
He pointed to a rather nice looking neighborhood across a children's playground.

– Relax, she grinned. – I am just teasing you a little.

The bell still chimed. It was a nice sound, not the usual overwhelming noise coming from similar arrangements. The entire setting struck a chord inside Afterglow. It quivered pleasantly in her bones.

It chilled her blood.

The building spoke to her. Its waves hit her and conveyed what others could not fathom. Silent banshee cries played in her ears.

Everything was visible in her face, in her shifting face.

They walked across the children's playground. The waves from the bell hit her flesh and mixed with that of her own. There were no old Roman buildings in this neighborhood. These were recent constructs.

It still gave off a certain murky mood to her. Desire and caution warred within her, briefly, before desire won by a mile.

Birds flew up from the nearest rooftop. Thrills and shakes both rose from her depths, equally pleasant.

She rushed up the stairs, light on her feet. The stairs squeaked. She giggled, giving him a lewd look. They entered the apartment. He lit the sparse lighting. She nodded as she looked around her, as she looked at him.

– This is so nice, she mumbled, – such a nice apartment.

Her mind looked at it, at all the places her eyes could not reach.

She grabbed him by the collar with both hands and pushed him at the wall. Greedy lips sought his and tasted blood. The buzz in her mind rose to a roar. The sweet itch below turned irresistible. She lifted him up and put him on her shoulder, as she rushed to the bed.

A light twist of her arm and she threw him on his back on the bed. She studied him as he laid there, breathing in anticipation and quite evident worry. There was a grin on her face as she joined him on the bed, as she crawled on top of him.

She saw his hardening cock push against the confines of his pants.

– So, the boy does not mind having the tables turned, huh?

He tried to sit up. She pushed him back down and held him there. He tried to free himself, in vain. She was far stronger than him. He began shivering in lust and fear.

Her body fell on him, and she began kissing his sore lips. She grabbed him below. His cock hardened some more, and he released a loud, dark moan. She began undressing him, in swift, furious moves, more tearing his clothes than actually removing them. Her lips burned on his skin, and he cried out. He attempted to speak, but she put a finger on his lips, stopping the attempt in its infancy. She sat up on him, on his thighs, grabbing his rock-hard and throbbing cock, squeezing it hard.

– Harder than steel, she mewed pleased.

It started twitching, and she began moving her hand up and down on it, as his hips moved up and down as well, and his semen flowed from it like water. She let go of him and began removing her dress, in slow and lazy movements. It was easy, really, only a few twists and turns, and she was there.

– Now, when we have gotten that out of the way we can begin in earnest…

She moved forward and sat on his chest, one leg on each side of the body. After a brief hesitation he began moving his hands, began touching her, and a huge smile spread on her face.

– Good boy, she whispered. – Good boy…

There was early moisture, and he had no problems smoothing it further, and his hands turned wet, and she threw her head back and cast her moan at the ceiling. She patted his cheek and moved back again on his thighs facing his half erect used-up thing. It began twitching, began rising. She bent forwards and grabbed it tenderly, teasingly. It rose, rose high. She licked it and smothered it in her mouth.

She moved just a bit forward, and pushed him inside her, and she began the ride, the wild, wild ride. He cried out, as she a little rough grabbed his outstretched arms, placing them on her breasts, her sore, sore breasts, as he squeezed, and she hardly noticed, except for the itch spreading to pain, sweet, sweet pain. And he pushed his hips up, as she pushed hers down.

– Big boy, she mumbled. – Little big boy.

He was quite muscular, quite big, actually, but a mere toy in her strong arms.

There was a vast, deep dark ocean she floated through. There were points, pinpricks of bright light, and then there was Shadow.

A hole appeared before her, a vortex in the dark ocean, and she dived into it, and everything turned to dark fire.

She gasped, and began moving faster, faster, faster, on the soft flesh beneath her. She held her arms on her back. She wanted to bring them forward, to hold him, to hug him, but knew she would probably kill him, and she kept her arms on her back instinctively, as if bound, in her fever. She saw her hands on her skin, saw the fingers twitch and move.

A large moan rose and faded in her throat, and she fell down on him and felt his hot juice being pumped into her, and she rolled off him and onto her back on the bed, breathing, breathing, breathing, and riding through the dark, slowly fading fire, back to the infinite silver ebony Space.

She woke up back in her own apartment, as the sun slowly set in the eastern skyline.

Her mouth was paper dry. There had been way too much to drink for her hungry mouth. The sweet taste there still lingered. She walked to the sink and turned on the tap. Water tumbled out and she bent down and drank, drank hard and long, feeling almost exhausted afterwards.

Her off-balance face came into view in the mirror. She stopped and stared at it, impassionate. It was not so bad. Uneven, perhaps, like a mosaic, a beauty serene like a mask, but not ugly, and she had gotten used to it by now. The old pain was still there, though, never really letting go. There were glimpses there, there in the mirror, of the old her, but distant, a memory lost in the mist.

Visions of the hundred mirrors she had smashed, of the shaken, broken figure on the floor flashed through her mind, briefly, before once again resting in her murky depths.

She showered again and dried herself again. She dressed again, in slow, lazy moves, the same way she consumed the breakfast by the kitchen table. The chewed, juicy sandwiches just slipped down her throat like the richest of fluids. A content smile briefly touched her lips.

A hand, a passing body turned on the music, loud and passionate, a hand moving across the guitar strings, playing a solo long and deep. It filled the apartment. Her body filled the room, as her feet moved swiftly across the carpet, the soft carpet. The sound filled her, filled her to the brim, making her cry out to the spheres, touch their infinite darkness forever.

In the middle of the song she went to the room at the center of the apartment. She opened the heavy door, walked inside and closed it behind her. There was a click. She had locked herself in.

The music was cut off. The room turned absolutely silent. There was another click. A recording turned itself on. A pleasant, official voice filled the room.

– Greetings, citizen, this is Erina Maximus from the Science Advisory Board again. We would just remind you of the next Town Hall meeting on the sixth of August. All of us here would just *love* if you attended and gave us a piece of your…

Afterglow pushed the button on the right side of the machine, pushed it hard.

There was another click. The sound of a nervous, unknown voice reached her ears.

– Miss Caldwell… Uh, hello. My name is Roland Kotterlich. I have been told about you and your special *status* through the… the grapevine. I believe you can be of some assistance to me. The funds have been deposited in the account I was told about. My address is 36 Hammer Lane, Westfield, not far from your usual… haunts. I will be expecting you tomorrow evening if that is all right with you. I trust this message will reach you, and I am looking very much forward to meeting you in person.

That was all. The machine turned itself off. There were no more messages, and the door to the living room reopened. She walked back out and the door closed and locked behind her.

The music faded in and faded out just as the door opened, as it closed. The apartment turned quiet. She ruffled her hair a bit, pacing back and forth a bit before sitting down in the nearest chair. A hand snatched the phone receiver on the table. A finger pushed a button, making the phone dial a stored number. It lasted a while, more than a while before anyone replied. There was a hesitant, hardly audible «hello».

– I never go to The Island, she said icily. – You know that, right?

She heard the sound of a deep breath.

– Why did you call me? The man's voice was clearly shaky. – How did you get this number? You are not supposed to *call* me. You…

– SHUT THE FUCK UP! She shouted.

There was silence at the other end of the line.

– You brought this on yourself, she snarled in a crushing blow. – You sent me to The Island. The fuck up you are actually sent me to The Island, even though I explicitly told you *never to send me to The Island*. And you have the audacity to whine about a little indiscretion on my part.

– I may have been a little hasty, the man at the other end of the line said hastily. – But it is an important… it is an important *gig*. My contact demanded the best, and it seemed prudent. I sent Cochran…

– You sent *Cochran?*

– Yes, and after his… his very poor performance my contact got very, very cross, and demanded that I put my word where my mouth is, *or else*…

Afterglow rubbed her temple.

– What happened to Cochran?

– I do not know exactly. No one does, at least not anyone I can access. But let us say what is left of the poor sod leaves very little to the imagination.

– I want double payment.

– I…

– I want double payment and I want to stake you through the heart, but I will be content with the former… this time.

– The… the bonus will be in place in your account within an hour, he choked. – And I can assure you that this is a one-time emergency and that it will not happen again.

– Good, she whispered and closed and opened her eyes. – Very good.

She broke the connection. That small act alone felt like she was cutting herself on a dagger. There was pain, mute and brief. Her arm fell. The receiver slipped from her weak hand and fell on the carpet. The dump sound of the impact sounded remarkably sharp and loud. The beep-beep kept going for a while. She could not tell exactly when it stopped, as she sat there for a long time and stared at nothing.

The northern wind, not cold at all cut through her as the ferry approached the quay. Afterglow's thick coat and hood did not protect her against the daggers of the wind. It never did. Streetlights brightened the quay area in general ways, but it seemed to highlight the shadows more than truly illuminate anything. It was raining. She could not tell if it was the usual dirty substance falling from the sky lately or actual rain tonight. One streetlight flickered constantly on and off. The flickers seemed to stretch out, creating their own, distinct reality.

The ferry reached the quay. The door slid open and let the crowd of afternoon commuters out. Afterglow noticed the pale man with the horns on his forehead immediately. He sniffed the air, and he noticed her glance, her casual glance when his features from a past never gone registered in her mind. There was a grin, a scowl, in the face of horror tearing into her.

– The door will close, he hissed at her.

He did not seem to have aged a day or a minute since she had first encountered him as a little girl.

She looked closer at the ferry. The door leading inside is indeed closing, closing prematurely. Other people scrambled to get inside in time, but Afterglow froze and stopped there on the spot. She looked around for the man, but he was gone. The quay covers quite an area, and there is no way for him to have reached far enough to be out of her sight, but he's nowhere to be seen.

The door closed. The ferry left, leaving her behind. She tried to move, but was unable to, unable to move a muscle for a long time. The man was nowhere to be seen.

She sat on a bench an unmentionable passage of time later, shaking like a leaf, and the worst part of it all was that it was impossible for her to tell why.

The man seemed, if possible even spookier, more sinister, imposing, threatening than the other times she had faced him. She easily conjured the image of his face behind her eyelids. The horns on his forehead by the temples resembled knives and they flashed in blood.

Other people joined her in the waiting area, a woman wearing a red dress, a man clutching a briefcase. Local whirls of mist moved close by. She did not really see any of it, even if she never closed her eyes.

The sound of an approaching engine slowly shook her from her paralysis.

The ferry returned, having completed its round trip. The door opened, opened wide. Just like an ordinary door (she added in her thoughts). More commuters left the ferry, having completed their daily task on The Island. More commuters rushed inside, having completed their daily task on the mainland. Afterglow headed inside in a daze. She found a seat, not really looking down at the spots of faded blood decorating the floor.

She sat down in the deep, pleasant seat. Her senses, her vaunted power of observation slowly returned, and she began to study the other passengers. It was fairly obvious they could not see what she saw, and even though this was not unusual for her, the ice-cold trickle rushing down her spine was one of the most powerful she had ever experienced.

The door closed, normally this time. Her unusually overactive nerves kept working overtime, even though her calm and analytical abilities slowly, painfully resurfaced.

Virtually all the passengers glanced at her at one time or another, easily spotting the sorcerer.

The trip across the sound took only ten minutes. She did not really notice the passing of time, she never did. The small talk of the other passengers did not really register in her mind, even though her ears certainly picked it up. A young girl said to her mother:

– There is something seriously wrong here.

Her mother quickly hushed her up. The crowd stared at her and not Afterglow when they all departed the ferry.

The pale man stood at the end of the passenger bridge, his sick grin very much in place.

– Welcome home, Kathryn, he cried. – This calls for a celebration. Afterglow finally returns to The Island.

Nobody else heard him or even saw him. He faded as she gauged him, as she attempted to get a feeling of him, of what he was.

The chaos, the shifting surroundings distracted and confused her, weakening her, and she wondered if that was not the purpose of this entire exercise. She was still nauseous, close to throwing up and she had to fight it back with all her strength of will.

– Is everything all right?

The voice came from far away, from the other side of a long, long tunnel. She straightened, in that moment almost incapable of masking her distress. A woman, a young girl stood there, looking both anxiously and eagerly at her.

– You are Afterglow, are you not?

Afterglow nodded.

– I knew it! The girl brightened. – You felt something, did you not; felt something the moment you set foot on The Island?

– And you are?

The girl reddened.

– Sorry, she reached out a hand. – I am Alice, Alice Thornbridge. I was sent to meet you, to… assist you.

Afterglow ignored the hand and started walking. Alice rushed to keep up with her, breathless after just a few steps.

– I have a car…

They moved through the crowd. Afterglow moved and Alice moved in her slipstream.

– I can not believe you are here, the girl cried excitedly. – I have wanted to meet you since practically forever. You do not look the same, like you used to, but I Knew that, knew you would not, but I still recognized you the moment I saw you.

– You were just a child.

– But I still noticed you and the guys. We all did, whether we wanted to or not.

The guys… the hard ball in Kathryn's throat made it momentarily hard to breathe.

People whirled around them. Afterglow attempted to spot a pattern in the random movements, in the whirl of motion surrounding them. Her vision shifted slightly, and she saw, in flashes, in slow, slow flashes, dark energy instead of skin. But there was no pattern she could discern, and she was not sure whether that was good or bad.

– You drive, she said, with a nervous twitch of her mouth.

And Alice picked up on it, and her eyes turned huge and round.

They reached the tiny car parked a bit away from most others in the lot. The car looked perfectly normal. Afterglow knew that intellectually, but still ants kept crawling under her skin. Five seconds, one second, ten seconds later she had stopped without being consciously aware of it.

– What is it? Alice wondered. – What is wrong?

– The car… grinned at me.

Afterglow whispered, Afterglow shrugged.

She grabbed the girl and turned away. Afterglow walked, and Alice followed. The girl kept casting nervous glances back at the car. As they passed an alley of trees the leaves changed from pale, grayish green to deep red, like droplets of blood suspended in the air. In a world of gray they were like Rubies glowing in the light of fire. Wind shook the trees, but it did not touch them. Not a single breath touched them.

It passed quickly, lasting hardly more than a heartbeat.

– Did you see that? Alice gasped. – Did I see that?
– Yes, Afterglow confirmed.
– I have the talent for this, you know, the girl beamed. – Perhaps you should take me as an apprentice?
Her voice and eyes turned needy, turned begging.
– I can be of help to you. I can!
– I will consider it, Afterglow replied dryly, – if you survive the next forty-eight hours.
The girl backed off then, even though she kept walking at Afterglow's side.
They caught a bus after having waited a few minutes. The public transport was filled with people, of afternoon and evening commuters, dog-tired after today's work. Faces passed by Afterglow's eyes, and they were all the same.
– There is a lot of negative energy here, Alice shivered, and then she added: – Is there not?
– Yes, there is, Afterglow nodded, – but there is no mouth.
The girl's shiver grew even more pronounced.
A guy standing close to them frowned.
– But… the *mouth* just was not there before, the girl wheedled. – I would have noticed… would I not?
Afterglow sighed. She had known from the start that this girl would be very… trying.
– The mouths move around a lot, she explained patiently. – They have to, with their exaggerated hunger. And someone might have placed it there, for us, for me, setting the dinner table for it, so to speak.
The girl suddenly giggled.
– You are so funny, she said. – Laughing in the face of danger. I love that.
Afterglow sighed some more, a thrill of sadness passing through her.
The guy standing fairly close to them made a face, looking like he might hurl. Afterglow smiled sweetly to him. He pulled back several steps. Alice looked at Afterglow with even more admiration and worship in her eyes.
The man and also all others on the bus stayed away from the two after that, well away. It was good in a way. They no longer had any trouble breathing.
She waited until they were well outside the bus, before pulling the other to the side and schooling her.
– Listen, okay, listen carefully.
The grip was so strong that it hurt the girl.
– I would have preferred Cochran as a helping hand. He has some experience in this, but he is… unavailable, and I need a helping hand, and therefore I need you, but you must do exactly as I say, and not deviate from my explicit orders for a moment, do you understand me?

The girl nodded, her eyes big and wet.
– Afterglow can trust me. I will follow her orders, follow them unto death.
And there were more shivering because of the ominous words, and they sort of shared that, making them feel a little better.
They walked, through the close to frosty night. There was a chill tonight independently of seasons. It stuck in Afterglow's bones, and it did not usually do that.
There was a shopping street looming nearby. They passed it on the way to the house.
– Do we not need supplies?
– No! Afterglow shook her head. – Not from there. I always demand the best stuff, the ingredients we can not buy at inflated markets like that one. Juvenile delinquency would be useless here. You are not playing games anymore, little girl.
Her condescending words had the desired defect. The girl shrunk in her tracks, turning even more timid and attentive.
The house, resembling a castle stood on a corner by a crossroads. The dark, pervasive drizzle resembling rain kept up, making the streetlights almost invisible.
– The world is… dark, is not it? The girl whimpered.
– Yes, Afterglow confirmed. – Yes, it is.
– Is it raining? The girl crouched. – Did it rain just, now? I do not think it was, you know, just a few minutes ago.
– It is raining all the time.
Afterglow shrugged, as she turned right into the shingle road to the castle, to the dark, dark castle.
The road to the castle seemed almost illuminated, inviting. There was a bench to their right and that was illuminated as well, an echo from the shine of the road.
The doorframe was made of bricks. Afterglow saw it, illuminated in shadow. She rang the doorbell, a modern, electronic one. It sounded hollow, fake, echoing down her spine.
A man dressed in formal, very formal clothing opened the door.
– I am…
– Ah, Miss Caldwell, we have been expecting you. Please, come in.
It was the Butler, the classic English butler.
The butler did it, she thought.
– Call me, Afterglow, she insisted, suppressing a giggle.
The two women stepped inside. Afterglow glanced behind her, at the illuminated path, the moonlight shining on the bench.

The door slammed shut behind them, or so it seemed, the castle shaking in thunder.

– Very well, Miss Afterglow. The owner of this humble abode is awaiting your pleasure in the library. Tea will be served in half an hour.

– Thank you, Jeeves, Alice giggled, holding a hand to her mouth.

The man frowned a bit, but kept up the appearances, the mask. Of course he did.

He led them to the library. The walk there seemed endless. There were fires in every room and hallway. It was necessary, she supposed, in order to heat this entire drafty building. And as if to stress that fact, a powerful draft caressed them, welcoming them…

A group waited for them in the warm, warm nice library. A man, heavily built, projecting confidence, shaking like a leaf, welcoming them to…

– Miss Caldwell, Miss Thornbridge, I am Roland Kotterlich, I wish to extend our warmest welcome. Welcome to Ravenscourt.

He was young, his hair still completely black, his features smooth, the deep furrow on his forehead hardly noticeable. She took his hand, and Alice did, too, blushing slightly.

Names, faces of the small group, the minor gathering, floated before her eyes, drifted through her mind.

- Allow me to present Blanche, my Companion. Kathryn shook a soft, wet hand.

- My son Peter. A hand shaking uncontrollably. - Alysse, my daughter.

The girl curtseyed, like a servant. Afterglow… liked that.

- My brother Robert. My sister in law, Margaret. My friend James Basset, and his fiancée Susan Howard.

Basset looked at her with eyes like slugs.

– Nice to meet you, Kathryn, Susan greeted her. – I have heard *so* much about you.

– Call me Afterglow.

Susan Howard pulled back, clearly distressed. Afterglow ignored her and kept taking in the room. It was shuttered, dank, a dark place filled with dust and ashes.

Kotterlich stepped forward again, retaking the center stage.

– As Alfred no doubt told you, tea will be served soon. I am sure you are anxious to begin…

– No, not really. A firm headshake. – I am not in a hurry, really. As you no doubt were told, these things take time. They have to happen in their own way, in their own time. We will probably have to spend one night here, at the very least. My arrival will undoubtedly speed up things and increase the

danger, though.
– No one is safe in Afterglow's rain, Alysse cried.
Silence greeted her words. Afterglow walked to the fireplace, taking in the glowing heat, tasting it, taking its measure. The flames seemed to reach for and dance around her outstretched hands.
– You will have to forgive my daughter. Kotterlich spoke hastily. – She has not been herself lately.
– None of you have, Afterglow nodded. – Be thankful for that.
And this time the deafening silence was deeper than the ocean.
The tea arrived. A timid woman in a maid's uniform brought it and put it on the table. The gathering sat down and began enjoying their tea. There were two seats waiting for Afterglow and Alice. Kathryn sat down and Alice followed her shortly afterwards.
Kotterlich turned his head half around, towards the maid.
– Dinner will be served in an hour, Tessa. Please inform Alfred immediately.
– Right away, sir, the maid curtseyed. – Will that be all, sir?
– That will be all for now, Tessa, Kotterlich nodded.
The maid pulled out of the room, and left nothing but a sigh in her absence. She had hardly been there in the first place. Afterglow could sense her by closing her eyes, but only just about.
She reached for the fire again. It touched her hand and spread slowly, pleasantly through her body, but more than that it touched what could not be touched, and strengthened her. The people in the room stared at her, but she did not care about them. It had been a long time since she cared about shocking people's sensibilities.
– So, you have malevolent ghosts haunting you, she said lazily, finally, after letting them stew. – Why do you not tell me about them?
– There is one in the attic, Alysse cried.
– And one in the basement, Susan butted in.
– One in the kitchen.
– Several in the hallways.
Heads turned, as if by magick, or mind reading, towards the same point in the room.
– And one here, Susan added caustically.
Everybody looked at Alysse, at her now transparent figure.
– That was when everything started, was it not? Afterglow turned to Kotterlich. – When she died?
– Yes, he nodded. – There had been… incidents before, but not like *this*.
Afterglow turned back towards Alysse, studying the nothingness in those dark eyes.

– And is this Alysse?
– It is, and it is not, he replied, his voice clearly quivering.
– I surmised as much, Afterglow said.
– Kathryn has returned to The Island, what was not Alysse grinned its twisted grin. – But she has not visited her old haunts, I gather.
The ghostly figure faded, its smile turning even more sinister, and there was no longer anything obvious but the living present, all standing frozen with rapidly beating hearts.
Kathryn's heart beat faster as well. She listened astonished to the sound of her own heart.
– It… knows you? Blanche Kotterlich asked her sharply.
– I do not know, Afterglow replied, somewhat calmly. – It knows of me. That is clear.
Then she shrugged, deliberately, consciously, spontaneously.
– But then again, who does not?
– Afterglow is known and feared both on and off this realm, Alice stated proudly.
Kathryn looked at her, frowning, voices of both worry and pride speaking within her.
She sipped the tea. It was excellent, still hot and tasty. And she could tell better than most people. She could taste all its different flavors. It was like they played her tongue, her buds, creating a stir of expectations in her blood.
There was no aftertaste. She nodded to Alice. The girl blinked, and took a quick sip, before putting the cup back on the table.
Afterglow studied the family and half circle before her. It was, like always, a two-way process. They studied her with both curiosity and fear. She studied them, looking for clues, any clues that could help her, help her gain what might be crucial insight.
– So, how long have you been doing… this, Afterglow? Blanche asked lightly.
– My entire adult life, Afterglow shrugged.
– How did it happen?
That was Peter Kotterlich, clearly more aggressive.
She turned towards him, interested.
– What do you mean? The violet gleam in her eyes turned more pronounced.
– Why did you start doing it? He restated his question, clearly having thought it through. – Was it one particular incident or a series of experiences that did it for you?
– I guess it felt quite natural, she replied, without really answering his

question.

She noticed the soreness in her throat immediately, making it hard to swallow, making her voice turn hoarse. There was no way of escaping it. Everything opened up inside her. Everything she had strived so hard to close.

Margaret Kotterlich played on the old Harpsichord. Its chords stung Afterglow further, making her even more attuned to the mood of the house and laying bare her demons. They all sat there, in silence, listening to their own thoughts, suddenly so very loud.

Afterglow could hear them, in ways that the others could not, and the pain accosted her, as unbidden and unwanted as ever.

A dark, cold laughter rose from the deepest parts of the house, or so she imagined. She saw herself rise from her chair, and run away, run from The Island the fastest way possible.

She did not move, no matter how much she wanted to.

Alfred appeared in the doorway, silent as a ghost. Dinner was served.

They sat around the long table, while The Butler served the wine, and the maid served the food. It was choreographed to an amazing degree, making Afterglow dizzy. The conversation continued. They researched her, without learning anything. She learned about them, about their fears and desires. It was easy. It felt as natural as rain.

– This calf is just excellent, Jeeves, she grinned. – You are a man of many talents.

Everybody stared at her. Alice, too.

The girl sipped the wine, and her cheeks turned a deeper color.

The evening passed, quickly and slowly.

– So, you have… *powers,* Afterglow?

That was Susan again, always at it.

– Oh, yes, I have *powers,* Afterglow nodded. – It is a requisite to do what I do, actually.

– So, you are a professional ghost hunter?

– That is a rather crude and quite incomplete and on the verge of being a dangerously simplistic description, but essentially, yes.

– And the girl, she has powers, too, then?

That was Blanche, butting in.

Alice remained quiet, too timid to respond to the rather rude and patronizing remark.

– Of course, Afterglow shrugged. – Or, as I implied, she would not be here.

Blanche wanted to say more, but Afterglow kept going, deliberately.

– They are not uncommon, though. And quite a few people wander around in the dark, not knowing they have them, not knowing about themselves…

and the world. Most people lack the necessary resolve to use them, to grow beyond their own self-imposed limitations.

She said, very patronizing.

Blanche turned tomato red. Alice giggled behind the hand covering her mouth, looking at Afterglow with even more hero worship in her eyes.

– The thing with the fire was a neat trick, James Basset noted. – How did you do it?

She looked closer at him. He reddened, too. This was perhaps the only non-believer in the house. He did not live here, and had not stayed here very long at the time. Perhaps he had not even actually seen Alysse.

– It is no trick, Afterglow replied. – It is not just physical fire, by the way, but far more. I absorb the fire, not only the flames you see, but the remnant fire of creation, and it is strengthening me. There are many such sources a Wise One can pick up and use.

– The world you see is not the world, Alice explained patiently, as if to a child, clearly having built her courage. – It is just a pale reflection of the world, the giant Shadow beyond.

– This island, or most of it, is a nexus, Afterglow said. – A center of wild and potent energies. One portal to the Crossroads of realities. That is probably why you have the problems you have in this house. It will remain a nexus, no matter what I do.

– So, what is it you can do for us?

Blanche stared at her with something resembling hatred. Afterglow knew that look, knew it very well.

– I can spare you the worst of its consequences… if you are lucky.

– And if you can not?

– Then you should get out as soon as possible… if you are still able.

A grin followed Afterglow's ominous words. She enjoyed herself, even as ants constantly crawled down her spine. But they did not see that. They just saw the confident, cocky woman grinning at them.

Tessa followed the two of them up the stairs. It was midnight, and the big hall clock struck twelve times, breaking the heavy silence. The sound of the clock reverberated from the carpets as if the soft fabric was solid wood.

Their room was quite spacey, with one single large bed.

– It is like being in one of those old, classic theater performances, Alice said breathlessly. – Kotterlich must have used a fortune on this place.

She was right. It did look like a theater setting. Every room, and every little piece of it reminded of past glory.

Tessa still remained, awaiting their command.

– That will be all, Tessa, Afterglow dismissed her.

And the door closed, and the two of them were alone in the room, in the vast building. There was a suitcase on the night table. Afterglow opened it, and looked through its content, and having done so, nodded somewhat content.

– It is satisfactory to Afterglow? Alice wondered anxiously.

– Quite so, the older woman nodded mercifully. – I would be surprised if it was not. My guess is that Kotterlich is as thorough in everything he does. He has probably researched us both from the cradle and to the point when we went off the bus tonight…

She walked to the fireplace and placed herself close to it. The heat hardly touched her. It hardly ever did.

– Come here, she called absentmindedly.

Alice rushed to her side, clearly nervous, and still anxious. Afterglow sensed it in her like a cancer. She turned and lifted her hands towards the girl, her palms exposed. Alice hesitated.

– I have heard…

– Heard people spontaneously combust? Afterglow nodded. – Yes, there is that risk, that, and a thousand others, at least if you drink it, drink lots of it. But you need to do this, need to toughen up several notches until tomorrow evening.

– And, she added, – we need to protect ourselves.

– Why?

Alice asked hoarsely.

– Because everybody is more vulnerable when they are sleeping, Afterglow replied. – That includes us. Our training makes us better protected than others, but that fact also makes us more… desirable, desirable as *trophies*.

Alice turned pale.

– What worries me is that Cochran knew this. He was no novice. But they still got to him, and to whoever was with him.

Eyes met eyes.

– Who *was* with him?

– I do not know. Alice's eyes flickered. – No one knows.

– Someone does, Afterglow stated.

She nodded encouragingly to the other. Alice lifted her hands and placed them front-to-front to Afterglow's.

– Close your eyes. See with all your senses.

The young girl obeyed. A shiver passed through her.

– Attune yourself with yourself, Afterglow whispered, Afterglow hissed softly.

Alice's breathing first turned less loud, than low and then seemingly fading altogether.

– Reach out, now, beyond yourself, to your surroundings, to me.

Afterglow felt it, felt the invasion, and it hurt. It always hurt.

– You are hooked into me, now, she spoke softly, – into my bigger boat. Know this, beyond doubt, beyond fear: I will never give you up, never sacrifice you, not to get the job done, not for any reason. We float and sink together. Do you understand, Alice in Wonderland?

– Yes, Alice understands, and she is grateful to Afterglow for showing her such an honor, for believing in her, and she will not disappoint Afterglow. She will serve her beyond dedication, beyond Death, beyond the Crossroads themselves, and she puts her life, her very essence in Afterglow's mighty hands.

– Good, Kathryn whispered. – Very good…

Afterglow pulled back her right hand. She picked up one of the tiny bottles from the night table, and with practiced skill she unscrewed the cork. The bottle was turned half around and one single drop fell on her hand. And that single drop grew to a deluge, and quickly covered her hand, coloring it blue. She raised her hand to her mouth, and began licking it, quickly, before reaching out to Alice's hungry mouth, and she licked, too. Like acid it burned in their mouths. Like a waterfall it flooded them. They swallowed.

Alice moaned. Afterglow held back, not releasing a single sound. But they both crouched, while clinging to each other. Slowly, slowly, with their hands never breaking the skin-to-skin contact, they straightened. They stood there like statues.

And then the flames in the fireplace began to grow, to grow beyond what most people believed was normal comprehension, to reach for the two rigid forms, and as it did so, it slowly turned colder, turned bluish, and then, in one swift motion, as if being alive, sentient, it embraced and surrounded the two women, and they burned, burned without burning.

– Open your eyes.

Alice obeyed instantly, and as she did so, her eyes opened wide, beyond wide, and it was no longer her eyes, but something beyond eyes, beyond sight. The bluish flames washed over them in waves, like ripples in the very air, in reality itself. In the ripples there were flashes, glimpses of alien landscapes. Alice whimpered, unable to keep the small sounds from escaping her lips. She could not really comprehend everything she saw, except that it scared her, scared her badly.

The flames faded, pulling back into their preliminary confines. The women let go of each other, facing each other. Afterglow touched Alice's cheek, tenderly, roughly, indifferent, intensively, holding her eyes with her own.

– *Now,* you are on the Path, and from this moment on, you will never leave it.

The girl released a tiny sound and took one single step back. Afterglow turned and walked to the night table. She grabbed another bottle there, a bigger one. It was filled with a red ocher powder with an assorted mix of other stuff.

– I put almost everything in this, she said. – It will give us some measure of protection, at least from the inside of the house.

She emptied it on the floor, «drawing» a half circle around the bed, all the way to the wall. Alice hurried inside its confines. Afterglow chanted a few arcane phrases, an ancient spell. The hairs rose in Alice's neck. The powder began glowing, raising a shield, a protective sphere around their bed, around them, down a floor, up a floor, and even outside, in the seemingly eternal ashen rain.

They undressed and went to bed, Afterglow casually, Alice shyly, unable to look at the other. The bed was soft and the blankets, too. Everything about the bed was soft. Afterglow stretched, sighing somewhat content. She put out the electrical lights by using her powers, doing so with an ease making the girl look even more admiringly at her.

It never turned completely black. The fireplace kept burning, kept casting its illuminating reddish glow.

Afterglow felt sleep come, felt the tense day fade. It always surprised her how easily it happened.

Alice yawned, loud and deep. Afterglow felt the girl's excitement and fear fade, too, somewhat, as sleep slowly overcame them both.

– Afterglow…

– Yes?

– How many times have you done this?

Afterglow considered the question, truly considered it.

– I… do not know. I can not recall.

Too many to count, she thought.

She rested on her back, staring at the ceiling. Patterns formed there, were drawn there, in her mind, in the smallest pieces of the fabric's texture. Eyes closed. Eyes opened wide, turning into vast pools of violet darkness.

Sleep came, dream came, a vortex sucking her in, pulling her down.

The vast Wasteland beckoned her, with its horrors, its terrors way beyond comprehension.

After a timeless time she found herself in the bathroom, sitting on the toilet bowl, peeing. She rose, drying her arse absentmindedly. Kathryn stood before the sink, looking into the smooth, milky surface above it. She saw an innocent, glowing, almost forgotten face in the mirror.

The face changed, turning demonic, turning into a skull where the flesh was not quite gone.

And it grinned at her. It grinned horribly at her.

And she could not wake up. She tried, tried hard. Her face twisted even more, in pain and puzzlement, as she choked, as she kept choking, in her monumental efforts. But she could not wake up, no matter what she did. And the silent scream never rose from her throat. She fell on the floor, remaining there, unmoving, her face a rigid mask, her eyes staring at nothing, a little girl afraid of the night.

CHAPTER THREE

Air drifted in the wind, in valleys and on vast plains. Invisible dust danced between the rays of the daystar and the moon.

Drops fell from the tap in the kitchen below. It hit the water in the glass, making it overflow, making it run, run like a river. Thunder rolled across the sky and the land. The river flowed faster, pulling with it everything on both shores, until there was nothing but the river.

The blue and silver taint flooded the land, the land of the moon. There was no rain, no moisture, either in the air or on the ground. A thousand times thousand ripples opened in the air and Afterglow could see a million distant shores simultaneously.

The face in the mirror smiled to her, as the little girl slept and dreamed in the night.

The day did not really bring bright light, but unused as she was to daylight, it still blinded her. She quickly made the dark curtains cover the windows. The shadowy daylight twilight still made tears drop from her eyes.

She rose from bed, the crisp air of the room grazing her naked body. Her eyes stayed open, hardly ever blinking. A part of her, a rather large part remained in the Other World, in the vastness only a blink away. It always did, and in the first few moments, in long, painful minutes, it was almost impossible for her to distinguish between the many surroundings of her reality. She saw the courtyard bathed in moonlight, bathed in rain, and the building's many gargoyles greet her morning, leering at her with their red eyes and open mouths.

The girl yawned and stretched in bed, a smile spreading on her face. Afterglow walked to the bathroom. She stepped into the shower and turned on the water, its cotton flakes hitting her softly, massaging her bruised skin. In the steam dancing on the wall horribly distorted faces hissed at her. She applied soap, and it was a balm on her sore hide.

She returned to the bathroom, drying herself with three towels simultaneously. Alice's eyes turned huge and shiny as she returned to the bedroom. Afterglow sighed. She had, in the heat of the moment actually forgotten, forgotten that she was not alone.

Alice had breakfast, or rather pre-breakfast, croissants with butter, looking like quite the young Lady.

– The maid was here with the plates, she said, and sighing happily. – I could get used to this.

– Do not! Afterglow reprimanded her, but without much sting in her voice.
She sat down, taking on the croissants. They were excellent. She began using one and one towel, using her hands, at the still wet spots on her body.
– So, this is how the wealthy few live? Alice queried, stated.
– Yes, Afterglow replied preoccupied.
There was an echo in the room, a sensation making her wrinkle her brow, something she almost but not quite could fathom.
That was unusual and bothered her by default.
– What you did… with the towels. Alice leaned forward, like the eager kid she was. – Was that… telekinesis?
– Not exactly. Afterglow frowned. – Think of it more as a… a weaving of sorts. I weave the air and my surroundings.
– You can do much, right? I bet you can! Many things. Much more than you have showed me.
– Yes, much, Afterglow replied preoccupied. – Many things.
She dressed. Alice took a shower. Afterglow stood before the mirror, studying herself, very deliberately looking at the stranger her eyes rested on. The sound of the shower halted. Alice appeared from the bathroom, rubbing herself with another of the large towels. Her skin turned pink. Afterglow looked at her with her direct stare, and the girl's skin turned a deeper red. Afterglow turned away. Alice dressed, very conscious of the wrinkles in her clothes. She did her best to soften them, as she stood before the mirror.
– Do you think one of the servants can line my clothes? Is that part of the deal?
Afterglow did not reply. She left the room. Alice followed her quickly, suddenly out of breath. They walked down the stairs. It was dark and murky in the hall. No amount of lighting, and there was a lot of it, seemed to counter that.
Alysse waited for them at the base of the stairs with her cute, sickly grin.
– Sweet Kathryn, she grinned. – Innocent Alice. I have missed you so. Let me yet again wish you welcome to our humble castle. Know that you are welcome, and that you will always be. This will always be your home… in the eternity to be.
The girl's adult, chilling laughter shook them. Alice saw that Afterglow shook, and shook even harder herself.
– BEGONE, FOUL SPIRIT, Alice cried, doing her hand movements, fueled by rage and fear.
They walked straight at her, and the apparition dissolved in a haze, until that, too, faded, once again becoming one with the very castle.
Afterglow nodded her approval, but the girl's pale face did not gain much

color.

– That is no spirit, right?

She attempted to speak, somewhat, with her bluish lips.

Afterglow shook her head.

– Yes, and no, she confirmed.

– I thought as much, Alice said lightly, somewhat succeeding in lightening the mood.

The loud grandfather clock at the end of the hall called eight times. Its waves struck Afterglow, but she did not really acknowledge the stirrings it created within her. The bell ended its banshee cries. Cluttered morning space fell silent. Kathryn's teeth loosened from her lip.

They entered the kitchen, where the entire family and circle, except the wayward, very wayward daughter waited for them, and the light kept shifting in a chaotic pattern. It was a sort of winter garden, with walls and ceiling made of glass, except there were not many plants. All the light from the outside was let in, creating a bright, bright room. Afterglow put on her shades, her eyes already starting to water.

– Breakfast is ready. Blanche welcomed them with her stiff, very stiff smile. – Feel free to join us.

– Thank you, Alice replied haughtily. – I think we will, will we not, Afterglow?

– We will indeed, the older woman nodded.

There were four empty seats. Afterglow looked encouragingly at Blanche.

– Roland had to go to town, to a business meeting, Mrs. Kotterlich said nervously.

It did not surprise Afterglow that Roland Kotterlich worked on what was supposed to be his day off.

– The other seat is for… we still keep a seat for her. She does use it occasionally.

James Basset released a loud, shrieking laughter, catching himself a bit too late.

The light of day did not treat Blanche well. The bags under her eyes and the recently added wrinkles were impossible to hide, even under the tons of makeup she applied.

Afterglow and Alice sat down. Breakfast was served.

– You two slept well, I trust? Susan needled them, as always.

– Like babies, Afterglow assured her.

Susan did not look so good herself. The skin around her eyes was at least slightly swollen. Afterglow suspected that she had not slept much.

None of them had. And they did not want to be here. That was easy to sense.

The unease and hardly concealed panic had long since been written on their faces.

– I think you have all turned nuts, James Basset stated out of the air. – You are all nutty as fruit loops.

Except for him. He was too stupid or rather insensitive to be afraid.

– Denial will not save you, she told him. – The forces roaming this place quite enjoy you «non-believers».

He jumped to his feet.

– Besides, she needled him further, – your friend and master believes, so you, as a good dog have no choice but to grit your teeth and accept it, or he will take away your toys.

The fat man looked at her with pure viciousness in his eyes.

– You are open, now, she told him. – Your festering hatred is a beacon for those very forces. So is your ignorance. They will tease you, tempt you, and goad you, and you will give in, and then you will be theirs.

He sat down, shock written in his face.

– You will do exactly as I say from now on, she told him, told them. – You all will, if you want to survive the coming night. *Do you understand?*

He mumbled a yes. So did the other stricken figures around the table. Alice did, too, adulation painted on her young face.

It was all very quiet after that. Afterglow preferred it that way. She could close her eyes, and pretend she sat alone there, in a nice, quiet winter garden.

The garden outside surrounded Afterglow and her young charge. Alice hardly took her eyes off the older woman. Kathryn sighed.

– You should really let go of that hero worship thing, she told the young girl. – Careful, my apprentice. That can be quite dangerous as well.

– I am sorry, Afterglow, Alice said. – But you are so powerful, so *mighty*. You handled that inedible man so well, treated him like the dirty spot on the ground he is.

They sat down on the stone bench. The garden, like the house was bathed in thick fog. Afterglow could not see through it to the main road below, could not tell if it was actually there, or if her memory played tricks on her. She shivered imperceptibly. Alice did not notice. She kept looking in blind admiration at the older woman.

Than she brightened visibly.

– Hey, she grinned. – Did you just call me your *apprentice?*

It was a slip of the tongue. Afterglow thought glumly and sighed.

Kathryn attempted to level with the girl, to put her worry into words.

– You have to be focused, she said. – You can not allow yourself the luxury of levity. None of us can. You are not my servant. You do not bow to me or are servile in my presence. Dependent people are meat for the maws of the Wasteland as well. Understand?

Her voice and demeanor came out a bit harsher than she had intended, and she could not remake it, remake the moment.

– Yes, Afterglow, Alice said in a low voice, casting her eyes to the ground. – Your apprentice is sorry, and will aspire to better herself.

The echo in the wind haunted and hurt Afterglow.

– You are young and bashful, she heard herself say. – You will learn eventually, one way or another.

She rose, looking patronizingly at the younger woman.

– The same goes for you as for the others, she said sternly. – You will follow my instructions, and you will do so to the latter.

They explored the garden, the big garden further. Whatever was inside was also present here, even reaching beyond the premises, to the road and streets outside. They reached a low alley of trees.

- There is a portal here, Afterglow mused, - or an almost-portal. It has probably never been used. That means using it is an incredibly risky venture.

She felt it right ahead, as her hand probed the thin slice of air in front of her. Her hand, its skin painted an image, a texture just as detailed as her eyes would. She stepped aside and let Alice have a go at it as well.

- Alice is so grateful that Afterglow would bestow this honor upon her, the girl breathed.

Afterglow sighed. They kept exploring the boundaries of the estate.

- Relate to me the functions of the brick wall, she commanded.

- Defense, Alice replied eagerly, - clearly defense. There are precious metals and spelled soil in the foundation, in the strange, rectangular carving visible to the trained eye. It would be Alice's guess that previous owners have been less unaware of the true properties of their home. They were equally unaware of the dangers from inside, though, over the fact the hard walls would only protect them from enemies coming at them from outside the gate. Alice would guess that their lives ended badly.

Afterglow shook her head in amusement, even as the carvings kept speaking to her with its strong, vibrant colors.

- Alice is a boon to her house, she mocked deliberately.

She returned to the house, and the girl, with her good mood gone in a whiff trailed her meekly.

The others sat in the living room, not doing much of anything. They were waiting, waiting for Afterglow.

– I want you to show me the hot or rather cold spots, now, she declared.

Susan jumped to her feet.

– I can do that, she responded eagerly. – I am quite familiar with all of it.

She blushed.

– I… dabble, she added. – So I made notes.

– Very good, Afterglow nodded. – Lead on.

And Susan did, hardly able to conceal her excitement.

They returned to the kitchen. Susan walked to *her* chair, and held it.

– As you know she joins us here sometimes, but then again, she may join us anywhere in the house. There is a man, too, here. He appears by the door, never saying anything, just staring at us with his sinister eyes. He is more of a ghost, a traditional spirit, I guess. If anyone is, that is.

Susan, too, was needy. Afterglow had sensed that about her immediately.

The light shifted. It did that often. They could not spot the daystar, but the light shifted as if clouds raced across the sky, and the daystar cast their shadows.

The hallway met them with its darkness and bright, misty spots. Kathryn saw human faces in those spots, and heard their screams.

– You can see them, can you not? Susan whispered. – They do not actually have to appear to you?

Afterglow shook her head.

– I can see them, she confirmed. – They speak nicely to me, and behind their smile they hiss.

She turned away from the shimmering figures, and they did hiss at her. The two girls trailed her up the stairs, first to the next floor, and then to the attic.

The attic with its large windows and bright lights. It seemed like a different world, or a glance into one. The floor was not a floor. The walls and ceiling seemed to fade, to reveal what was behind.

Afterglow pushed her shades closer to her skin. Her eyes flooded, even with them in place.

But then, the visuals changed for her, as they often did, and she saw only Shadow. The room changed, becoming something strange and different. Her two companions looked around with anxiety, fear and fascination in their eyes.

There were carvings on the walls, resembling those surrounding the estate, but these were… swollen, unhealthy, like they were… were dying.

– Is this… is this real? Susan breathed.

– It is real, Afterglow confirmed.

– It is the bigger world, Alice said breathlessly. – The reality behind the curtain of normality.

Kathryn glimpsed figures there, in the mist and shadow. Some she knew,

and other she fortunately had been spared from knowing.
– We see so much more now, Susan said.
– It is because of me, Afterglow said, – because I am here. They are drawn to me. Kotterlich knew that when he hired me.
They faded then, pulling back into the Wasteland that had become their home.
The three of them walked back down. Afterglow sensed a draft from the basement. She did not feel it physically, but it was there.
– Than there is…
Susan stopped, knowing somewhat that it was unnecessary for her to complete to sentence. Afterglow walked ahead down the stairs, into the moist, deep darkness.
She trembled, and the other two noticed, and began trembling as well.
– It was in the basement he did it to you, was it not? Susan said, cruelty evident in her voice and features.
– Yes, Afterglow replied, somewhat calmly, straining to focus at the task ahead.
She sensed Alice's distress and sympathy, and that only made it worse.
The cellar was fairly mundane. She neither saw nor sensed anything out of the ordinary here, not at first glance. Shaking fingers turned on the lights, and gray illumination flooded the dank hall. This was no typical basement, of course. She saw no brick wall or hard floor. Everything had been clothed in wood, in fair wood, in bright colors. But the place still looked bleak to Afterglow.
This was basically one more floor in the house, with another bathroom, kitchen and living room. But to her it looked… different. Her eyes saw a nice, cozy flat, but her deeper senses experienced it in a totally dissimilar way. She had noted such dichotomy before, but rarely this pronounced.
It was like a vortex, pulling at her. She sensed shapes, blades sharp and swift.
But they were indistinct, distant. There was nothing here, nothing she could touch or that could touch her, nothing instantly dangerous, no portal to that other place over the rise.
Alice and Susan looked excited at her.
– There are only ghosts here. Afterglow shook her head. – Nothing worthy of our attention.
The two girls both looked disappointed or something akin to it. Afterglow shook her head in dismay.
It was just a basement. Nothing else. Afterglow spotted a face briefly in the mist, and shuddered. It was gone in a whiff, and she could not be certain it

had ever been there. She could never be sure.

She pulled herself together by an act of will, a supreme effort leaving her in shambles.

Alice embraced her lightly, giving her a comforting kiss on the cheek. Even Susan attempted a show of affection, and Kathryn felt somewhat comforted. She knew the sight of the altar stone by the opposite wall was a mirage.

– Come. Afterglow straightened. – We have a lot of preparations to do before nightfall.

They returned upstairs. Alysse waited for them, for her in the hall.

– I trust Afterglow's scenic tour was very educational?

The grin was that of a corpse rotting for two hundred years, not a girl.

– It was, Afterglow nodded calmly, with a razor sharp edge to her voice. – Thank you.

The apparition faded, and left only the ever-present stench of rot.

– Evil flees for Afterglow's might, Susan said, admiration visible in her eyes.

– Not yet, Kathryn said. – But it will!

It was posturing. Not on her own behalf, but to benefit those around her. Building their confidence tended to be a crucial item on the list of preparations to nightfall's event. She had learned that, that, too the hard way.

They returned to the living room. The totally fucked-up family waited anxiously for them. Kotterlich had returned and Afterglow realized that longer time had passed than she had realized. Time had fled in the mist and shadow, in the Wasteland's shade. She saw Susan walk to Basset, bending down and kissing him on the cheek before sitting down by his side.

– So, how was your tour, Afterglow? Kotterlich said lightly, not giving an inch of his calm exterior.

– Quite educational, Afterglow replied. – I believe I have an inkling on how to proceed.

– Think? Blanche cried.

Kotterlich stared his wife down, snarled at her, and she turned mute and meek, shrinking in her seat.

They all looked at Afterglow, waiting for her further explanation, but none was forthcoming.

She nodded to Alice, and the girl rushed off. They heard her run up the stairs.

– She goes to fetch the supplies.

Susan enlightened them, prompting a rather nasty look from Bassett.

Afterglow kept studying them, professionally masking her contempt. They were a typically spoiled group, and she knew they would crack, crack at the first sign of the upcoming terror.

She sensed it, physically felt its approach, its marching band. It played havoc on her in so many ways, both subtle and overt that she could not count them.

It invaded her, and she had no way of avoiding that, so she steeled herself and allowed it to happen.

Alice returned, eager, slightly out of breath, and innocent, not exactly clueless, but vulnerable, so very vulnerable.

– It met me in the hall upstairs, she reported brightly. – It attempted to impress me with its bad breath again, in vain.

She giggled, catching herself under Afterglow's stern stare, and she solemnly handed over the suitcase.

Afterglow led on into the library. They all fell in line behind her. Everything had been removed in there. The furniture, all the shelves and books were gone, and only a large, open space met them. Not a single loose object remained. Afterglow nodded to herself, somewhat content.

She turned to them. The close to violet gleam in her eyes turned more pronounced. They looked startled at her.

– Listen, she whispered, – and listen carefully. Everything happening from this point on is a part of the dance, of the ritual and therefore important. Every action you take will impart on the result. You were all a fluid, imperfect part of Alysse's life. You will all be a part of her leaving this plane of existence. If you screw up, and something goes gloriously wrong, we will all take our leave, and end up in the Wasteland or worse. Trust me, you will not *like* it there.

They nodded, with blue lips, as if they stood outside in a cold winter night.

It… began. She nodded to herself, as if to gain a final bit of confidence, and the others knew she needed that, and they grew sore afraid, even a notch more so. Her arms rose, stretched out from her sides, her fingers touching the air like claws.

– I am Afterglow, she called in a ghostly voice. – Hear me, spirits, hear me, world. I travel the costly freeways again. I go where very few go. I am you. I am the world and everything in it. I am what is lurking in the shadows… waiting for *release*.

A wind began blowing, a wind not a wind, strangely inconsistent, blowing, not blowing, touching people's hair one moment, not doing so the next. Alice's face darkened in expectation, brightened in fear. A tear appeared in the carpet, a tear growing, forming a line, drawing a half moon, drawing a circle. A perfect circle formed around them all. The drawing continued, forming a pentagram inside the circle, completing the pentacle.

– O'Samhain, Lord of the Underworld, Gatherer of the Condemned, hear me; remove the thin walls between worlds for me so I can roam free.

The carpet caught fire exactly the moment the pentacle completed itself. Alice grabbed Blanche, making her stay put, shaking the shaking body. The fire ran along the tears, but nowhere else.

– This is pure fire, Afterglow told them, in her dark voice, – have no fear. No smoke will choke you, and steal your breath.

The pentacle of torn fabric became one of fire, burning with a steady, silent flame, seemingly not consuming anything, not even the air.

– Stand now, go now, to your designated position.

They saw her command, visually in their mind, and they obeyed, and they were compelled, as if they were mere puppets on Afterglow's strings. One walked to one point in the star, and four more did the same. Five marked the star. Kotterlich and Blanche were placed in front of Afterglow. Afterglow stood at the base of the star. Alice stood at the other side of the twitching wed couple holding hands, shivering hands. There were footprints marking everybody's spot. The moment Alice stepped into hers the fire rose from the fireplace, reached into the room, bathing them all in its heat, and the room darkened, and darkened visibly.

They were nine. Nine stood inside the pentacle, burning in shimmering fire.

Afterglow glimpsed other faces, superimposed on the eight twitching faces, for a moment before the familiar, unfamiliar faces faded from her consciousness.

– Two other people, Gilbert Cochran and one other came here four days ago, Afterglow said. – What happened to them?

– Yes. Kotterlich nodded. – They came… and left, and we never saw them again.

Afterglow looked at him. He began sweating harder.

– We did not actually see them leave, but they were gone, and we assumed they had left… at first, that they could not, could not handle it, could not take the… pressure.

– You are correct. Afterglow nodded. – They could not, and Cochran, at least is indeed gone. I can not sense him anywhere, and I usually can. His body was shredded to pieces, and his Other, his Shadow is nowhere to be found, and that suggests that the malevolent power involved is indeed mighty and far beyond ordinary parlor tricks.

A collective gasp rose from the gathering.

– Who was with him?

– I think it was… a woman. Kotterlich frowned.

He stood, clearly shocked, shaking his head.

– It is *amazing*. I can not actually say how she looked like. I have only a… a slim impression of her.

– She looked familiar, Margaret said, frowning. – But I could not, can not place her.

– They were shown to their room, Blanche added hastily, – like you were, and that was the last we saw of them… except for the pool of blood on the floor that is.

The vast pool of blood. Afterglow closed her eyes, and when she reopened them the room had changed visibly, to an even darker hue.

– The clean up crew from our common… *contact* arrived quickly. Kotterlich kept reciting in an uncommonly dull voice. – The contact called me after the crew had left, had fled, and told me in more or less blunt terms that he could not do anything for me and said the money would be returned to my account. I insisted that he sent another, though, and after a bit of *persuasion* he assured me he would, and he gave me your number.

– Why are you asking these questions, anyway? Basset said angrily. – Why do you not step on it and do what you are being paid to do so we can stop this nonsense and go on with our lives?

– Because I want to know what happened to the others, Afterglow reproached him mildly, – so we can all possibly avoid their grisly fate. And because knowledge is power, and I want to know *everything*.

She had expected Kotterlich to caution Basset again, but he did not for some reason. She nodded to herself, smiling enigmatically, and both Basset and Kotterlich looked at her with flickering eyes.

It... grew, as she went deeper into herself, as she readied herself in earnest, as she once more cried into the ether.

– O' Samhain, accept my sacrifice, come and fill me with your essence, please grant me your freedom to roam.

She produced a small pen knife from a pocket, and immediately proceeded to cut, to mutilate herself, her hands, arms and legs. Blood flowed from the cuts. She shook her arms, splashing the blood all over the room, on and off the people standing in and forming the pentagram. They shook and some of them whimpered.

– It burns, Margaret cried. – *It burns.*

They heard a loud sound, akin to a bell, a bell and a drum combined, and reality shifted around them, and the walls were no more, and they stared at a misty surrounding landscape they hesitated to call alien. It was simply too strange, and terrifying. Afterglow's voice turned deeper, and violet fire erupted from her eyes.

– We are here, now. There is no longer any turning back.

Shapes, shapes appearing from the dark, bluish mist and changing into two-legged, sort of humanoid creatures rushed towards them, charged the circle with snarls filling the void. They hit the barrier surrounding the pentacle, and were repelled, in a violent outburst of energy. They ran off in pain, their muddled minds filled with terror.

– Stand still, Afterglow cautioned her charges again. – Whatever happens, you must not leave the circle. I trust you now see the common sense in this?

They nodded vigorously. She smiled grimly, scaring them even a bit more, and that fact pleased her.

The walls regrew around them, but not exactly, becoming something ethereal and frail.

– We have returned to the house, but not exactly, she intoned, her voice a deep female bass. – This is a kind of representation, a Wasteland *version* of it. We are still here.

– It's horrible, Blanche cried.

Kotterlich slapped her. The brutal whack brought no particular reaction from the gathering, and no one at all from Blanche herself. She merely bowed her head, and fell docile, fell silent.

– Now, Afterglow declared, – we can begin.

Alice found nine small cups from her bag, and put them on the ground before her. She found one big chalice and began mixing a brew in it, demonstrating a skill that told the others, the uninitiated that she had done this before or that she, at least had been taught more than the basics. The girl glanced nervously, excitedly at Afterglow, and the older woman gave her an encouraging smile.

Smoke rose from the brew. There was no fire, none the seven could see, but the brew still burned. She poured the cups half full. It looked like tea, but something moved down in the steaming fluid, something looking very much alive. Alice put the nine cups on a tray and rose, walking the round to the other eight in the circle.

First there was Kotterlich. He grabbed the cup and drank without hesitation. Blanche hesitated a bit, but drank without any visible objection, as did the others. The only one raising a stink about it was Basset, of course.

– Why should we drink this shit?

He stared at the girl, stared her up and down, embarrassing her to no end, clearly deliberately.

– Because it will save a lot of lives, Afterglow told him from far away, close as a smudge.

– Whose lives? He asked suspiciously.

– Ours, she grinned.

He drank, and Alice smiled to him, or so he thought. Everything just floated away, as if he was the shore by a river, and it transformed into the river, became the river and everything turned equal.

Afterglow and Alice drank last. They gave each other a final nod before emptying the cups.

The fire in the fireplace began stretching, no, not the fire, the fireplace itself. Suddenly it burned on two walls, both images of it equally real. Then it was on three and four, and on the ceiling and on the floor below them.

– Calm, Afterglow admonished them, as the fire licked them, caressed them. – Stay calm. There are things to be afraid of, very afraid of, but this is not one of them.

The fire engulfed them, burned their skin and mind without burning it. Afterglow seemed to grow taller, taller than all of them. In one way they were convinced she grew far beyond the confines of the bubble. In another she remained the same size. One second was one truth, the next was another. Reality kept shifting and changing around them, twisting them inside out. Panic lured just below the surface of skin and bone and blood.

Figures with twisted faces ran through the alien landscape, ran without pause. There was no break from the relentless charge. They froze when they spotted the protective bubble and the giant creature inside it.

The music, always close to her rose from the depths, so loud in Afterglow's ears that a moan escaped her lips. Alice cast distressed glances around her, her eyes growing wide and fearful.

– Be at ease, young one. Do not be confused or afraid, but be wary of all the horrible and beautiful voices. Focus on what you know. Go deep within yourself, and then reach out, and cautiously shake every tail you can find.

All the tails with sharp, sharp blades at their tip.

Afterglow shook and sent ripples through the thick air.

Every move, from everybody produced ripples, though not as powerful as those emanating from Afterglow. They were invisible, or practically invisible, but easily seen, seen now, changing their surroundings. Reality shifted further, as one moment, two, three passed, into the familiar sight of the living room, the living room as it had been. Apparitions of the extended Kotterlich clan of the past revealed themselves. Some of them sat, while others were walking around, all clearly agitated, anxious.

– You said we should not move out of the circle, Margaret cried. – What are you *doing?*

– We have not moved, Afterglow shrugged, – not physically anyway. This is a mindscape, an environment taken and created from our memories, from our joint experiences. Thoughts turn *real* in this place.

– I can not say I find that to be very reassuring, Margaret whispered.

And just like that the scene shifted again, into the dark, dank hall at the base of the stairs. Margaret stood there, shaking violently, confronted by what was not Alysse.

The current Margaret, at Afterglow's side began shaking as well.

– Sweet Margaret, Alysse hissed softly, – knowing nothing, suspecting so much.

– What are you *talking* about? Past Margaret cried near hysterically.

– Sweet Margaret, the apparition grinned horribly, – sweet wife, docile, clueless wife.

What was not Alysse faded away, and Margaret stood there alone, before abruptly rushing off, into a bedroom, into Robert's arms.

– I saw her, she gasped.

– You… saw her? Her husband shook his head in disbelief.

– I saw her, she insisted, too shaken to be angry, staring at the man rubbing her back in a comforting gesture. – She even *spoke* to me. It was horrible, horrible.

And above the two hovered the specters of the present, looking at the specters of the past.

– What is the *meaning* of this? Robert Kotterlich, the present ghost shouted.

Afterglow looked at him, looked at them all with her acid stare.

– There is a secret here, she replied sweetly, – is knowledge to be gained, and lives to be saved, and I want to know what it is, because knowledge, if anything is really the best weapon against the forces aligned against us.

– You are a cruel, sadistic bitch, he spat at her.

The spiteful, thin smile was the only reply he got. She basically ignored him, and brought them further on their Journey.

Robert left his wife crouching on the couch, walking into the kitchen, the pale winter garden. He rushed straight to the small cabinet on the wall by the fridge, where medicines were stored. There was nothing there, nothing useful. Every bottle of prescription drugs was empty. Margaret had been there already, swallowing every pill at her disposal.

The wraith appeared before his eyes, his startled eyes.

– I will bet you are relieved right now, over the fact that there were not more pills, or she would have already taken a bundle.

The tiny, piercing eyes blinked slowly, seemingly gaining even more cunning, even worse insight.

– Or perhaps you would have wanted that? It would have saved you from being constantly reminded of all those awful, unpleasant thoughts, would it not?

He struck at her, at what resembled his niece, struck at nothing. Alysse did not move, did not flinch or react in any way while living flesh passed through her. He looked insanely at her, hardly even noticing the cold sweat making his eyes burn.

– And your docile, dull wife would have returned to be the dull, non present doll.

The wraith faded, its grin cutting him like knives.

– Why? Blanche cried at Afterglow. – Why are you doing this?

– I told you, to gain knowledge, knowledge that is power. And I am not doing anything. We are simply following the Path, and the Path must be followed to its end, or we will never leave it.

– Never? Robert gasped incredulous, fear painted on his very body language.

– Never! Afterglow grinned wickedly.

The scene shifted again. The world turned outside in, and Afterglow felt the queasiness like a pain in her stomach.

Roland Kotterlich, the past ghost stood in front of the mirror, combing his hair and fixing his tie, or doing the useless attempt thereof.

Blanche walked to him, fidgeting her hands nervously.

– Let me do it, she said, virtually begging him.

And he let her.

That night there was a party, a gala at the house. People practically filled the rather large living room and also the adjacent rooms and the winter garden. Even the garden outside seemed crowded. Most of the guests looked indistinct, with little or no facial features to Afterglow and Alice. Only the avatars of the seven fellow ghosts by their side and Alysse, the true, alive Alysse appeared clear and distinct in their mind.

Everything… focused on Alysse, as she walked among the loud-talking adults. Afterglow sensed worry, both in the girl and in Afterglow's traveling companions, her fellow living spirits. They, at least some of them wanted this tour the force to stop, but it was like she had told them: The Journey had to continue until the end, until the festering truth had been revealed, had been exposed for what it was. She could not stop it, even if she wanted to.

And she did not.

Alysse seemed small, very small among all the adults, her face a study in wonder and anxiety, constantly shifting between the two. Daddy spoke to the Councilor. They seemed to be best buddies, laughing a lot among themselves. Daddy spoke to Mr. Sanborn, the owner of one of the major chains of stores in the area. All in all, daddy was very busy. The girl registered everything with her curious, never resting eyes.

She got tired of looking up at people all the time and walked up the stairs, where she could look at it all from a more favorable vantage point.

Afterglow shook. She felt the beneath and around the manor, felt the power, the «neutral» power resting there, the power of the spheres surrounding Ravenscourt at all possible angles, screaming for release.

Alysse walked up the stairs, and stopped when she reached the final step, and turned to look back at the festivities. She saw Daddy, of course, shining like a beacon in the sea of mediocrity. Uncle Robert was there and poor Margaret. Everybody was, really, or almost everybody.

She sensed a draft from behind. It swept her dress and her hair. The entire house seemed to be actually *breathing*. Afterglow and the others felt what she felt, and everybody, except Afterglow and Alice squirmed in discomfort.

No, it was more than that. There were fear and shame in their eyes, in their entire posturing and movement. It sang to Afterglow like a violent discord.

– You did not think we would find out, did you? It did not even occur to you that we had to find out in order to do our job, and to save all our lives, even though you have to know the forces in question here? You must be suicidal or something.

She did not get any reply, vocal or otherwise. They seemed numb and oblivious to what was happening. But she knew they were not.

The draft seemed to pull her, the little girl. It seemed like that to the observers. But in truth she walked, walked to and through the door ajar at the end of the hallway. She pushed it open. It was one of the guestrooms. On the large bed were her brother and mother entangled in a passionate embrace. They were nude and breathing very, very hard.

She rushed out of there, gasping and heaving.

– Is that enough for you? Blanche cried at Afterglow. – Have you seen enough?

– No. Afterglow shook her head firmly. – We have yet to see everything we have to see, and everything needs to be played out.

Alysse rushed down the stairs, into the living room, to her father. She nipped in his pants when he did not spot her or overlooked her. He looked at her, acknowledging her presence.

– Daddy, daddy, she whispered, – mother and…

He stopped her with a finger to her lips, and a very strange expression appeared in his face.

– Go to your room, he said, not really unfriendly, but very, very strict.

– But *daddy*

– Go to your room, *now!*

She left in a daze, tears flowing down her red cheeks the moment she was out of the room. Daddy would have been pleased at her dedication, her holding out for so long. She rushed up the stairs, hardly seeing where she was going. Blanche whimpered. Roland grunted, a sound he made every effort to keep inside, but failed to do. Alysse stumbled in the loose carpet sticking out from the wall the moment she reached the top of the stairs. It was such a curious event. Everything froze, except her and the tears flowing from her huge eyes. It looked as if she was downright jumping. She flew over the banister, falling towards the distant floor below. This was an old house, one where the distance between the floors was quite considerable, and one where the major staircase crossed two floors. She hit the floor below hard, with her head first, and her neck snapped like a twig.

(And the house grinned excitedly).

Afterglow felt it, felt the power swell within the house. Blanche screamed, a piercing wail breaking every eardrum in her surroundings. Afterglow felt blood flow down her neck. The demonic presence stood there revealed, exposed by the truth, Alysse no longer. They returned to the pentacle, the safe haven they had never left, just outside Its reach. It bared Its teeth, Its claws scratching at the barrier.

– Do not bother! Afterglow spat at it. – And please refrain from the scare tactics. They are so fucking boring and useless that they make me want to hurl.

It snarled at her. She was sweating, fully aware of the possible bravado in her statement.

Alice shook hard. Kathryn focused on her a bit, as she kept focusing at the horror so far away, so close.

– Let us finish this, brave one, she stressed, – while we are still able.

The girl nodded, nodded again, the praise making her blush, as she slowly, slowly pulled herself together.

Fear choked Afterglow. She knew what the thing out there truly was, and the reality was far more frightening than the terrifying illusion.

– Begone, foul spirit, from this life, this place, revealed as you are, exposed as you are…

Afterglow's voice began as a normal voice, but changed, turning deep and with an echo-like quality, and when Alice joined in it was as if the entire place turned alive with voices, and it cut into the creature like knives.

The already powerful central voice rose further.

– Let the full light of the moon shine on you and tear you apart.

It was not merely the words, far from it, or their subtext, of course, but the power the two chanting them brought to the table. It created a synthesis, a storm of invisible daggers attacking the form and spirit before them.

– I know you, Afterglow cried. – I KNOW YOU, AND I WILL DESTROY YOU

Though stunned Alice kept chanting, as her words turned strange and ancient, as weird forms began dancing in the air. The forms solidified and dissolved in rapid succession, making it hard, very hard to gain even a semblance of impression about their surroundings. Reality shifted and shifted again, until nothing was solid, nothing was real, not even a person's flesh and bone.

The creature grinned. If it did so out of fear or expectation was hard to tell. Afterglow was cast years back in time, and guilt and rage warred within her. She strived to focus, but the very attempt at doing so made everything slippery like mercury. She felt it slip between her fingers. The creature's reality imposed itself on them, on Afterglow, and everything seemed to… unwrap, to be undone. Openings appeared everywhere, jaws, hungry mouths, a giant vortex pulling them all in, as the Wasteland, as the Crossroads itself reached for them.

– NO! Afterglow shouted. – I KNOW YOU, JANETTE RAVENHOOD AND I BID YOU TO LEAVE THIS PLACE.

Memories of two shaking girls exchanging names and comfort on far off, remote and desolate fields exploded in her mind, and she screamed in pain.

But the other, suddenly a woman, suddenly vulnerable screamed much louder, as bits and pieces of her began loosening from her body. The woman smiled, a terrible and frightening grin.

– You do know me… Afterglow, and you would have destroyed me… if I had not come *prepared*. I will see you again, sometime.

A final hiss, and the woman, becoming a creature again jumped backwards, vanishing from their sight.

The air calmed. The howl of the wind faded, as the room slowly turned normal around them.

– Thank God, Basset whispered, and then shouted: – THANK GOD!

He took one step backwards, half turning, on his way out of the pentacle.

– NO! Alice shouted, rushing forward.

She grabbed him, pulling him back, loosing her footing. They all saw it, remarkably clear, Basset waving his arm, the arm seemingly *falling* outside the force-field, blood flowing from cuts in his skin, a million cuts the mere microsecond it was outside, Alice being pulled into the air, as forces beyond comprehension cut into her, her scream of pain and absolute horror rattling beyond rattling them all, Afterglow reaching out with her hand, sending powerful gusts of wind through the air, through the rekindled vortex around them, Alice being pulled back, to safety, returning to the inside, her and Basset's blood hissing like acid as it opened the barrier, briefly, before that beyond crucial barrier repaired itself, as everything once again turned quiet and calm.

They all looked at Afterglow, waiting for her to tell them, to confirm it was all right, that the world made sense. She nodded, sensing how the barrier, the protective ball dissolved itself, as they truly returned to the living room.

Afterglow dropped to her knees, beside Alice's mangled body. The girl looked at her through hazes, layers of pain. Kathryn had to do several attempts at speaking before finally succeeding.

– You will be all right, she assured the girl. – You are all right.

Alice smiled up at her, trying to nod, too weak, too torn up to move.

The living room was only a living room again. There was no blood, except on the many cuts in Alice's clothes and on Basset's arm.

Blanche carefully, fearfully reached an arm out into the ether. Nothing happened, and she jumped outside the now invisible demarcation line with a happy glee. Kotterlich joined her, and he put an arm around his estranged wide. Everybody, the entire Kotterlich clan began moving about, fidgeting nervously, glancing around them with scared, paralyzed eyes.

Afterglow sat with Alice, as the girl attempted to breathe, to keep breathing. Kathryn Caldwell spat at the gathering, at them all:

– You people always make me sick to my stomach, she spat. – How I despise you all!

They looked like whipped and wet dogs. Somehow that fact did not give her much comfort, did not grant her the consolation she desperately craved.

Someone must have called an ambulance. Kathryn heard the sirens after a while, heard them fade in, until they appeared loud and distinct in her sore ears. She sat with Alice, until they came and took the girl away. She followed the stretcher outside, the blue lights hurting her eyes, reminding her of the Wasteland.

The girl raised a hand, attempting to speak. Afterglow stopped the paramedics and looked down at the pale figure.

– I… survived, Alice whispered, repeating it, perhaps stronger, perhaps weaker. – I *survived.*

– Hush, Afterglow said. – You need…

– I survived, Alice grinned. – I…

She started coughing, convulsing. A chill surged through Kathryn, and she could not stop the whimper from manifesting itself. The paramedics pushed her away and began treating Alice. One of them pushed an oxygen mask at her mouth.

Is there anything I can do, she wanted to ask.

The ambulance grinned at her, shaking its head.

She froze.

The ambulance doors slammed shut. Afterglow stood there, still frozen, staring straight ahead with unmoving eyes. With a mighty roar the engine rose, the vehicle wheels spinning, and the ambulance speeded away, and the blue, blue lights slowly faded, until only the blue darkness of the Wasteland remained.

CHAPTER FOUR

Afterglow walked through the streets dressed in a dark red and green hood and robe. Her eyes kept moving back and forth. Her waves picked up impressions from everywhere around her.

Something, an interest, a trifle, a desire drew her to the Agora, the public meeting place, the plaza by the council building. A man, a stranger spoke there tonight. He had drawn quite the curious crowd. His voice reached everybody present and also carried well beyond the open space and into narrow streets and alleys. His hard waves hit Kathryn softly, but still cut deep, and understanding eluded her.

– The Nine is coming, he cried. – They have always been here, and soon they will start making their presence known, known in earnest. They come from the turning wheel of fire, to the ocean of mankind.

Afterglow stopped moving her eyes and focused solely on him. She tried getting a… grip on him, to discern what he was about, but he was obscure, elusive, not truly there at all.

– The nine worlds will align, he practically shouted, – like they did in ages long gone and the turning wheel will begin burning again. From each of the nine worlds one or two or three will come, and the ocean of mankind will boil.

Afterglow made her way through the crowd towards him, narrowing her eyes, like she would when hunting prey, but she never truly managed to speed up, to gain on the man she sought.

– Think big, the stranger admonished them. – Think big and then think even bigger. The Nine are not mere sorcerers. Once, long ago they stepped into the land of the moon, and were transformed. The moonlight shines on them around thousand fires. Their might rivals those of the gods and those returning from the shattered lands that would challenge them.

Her walk remained slow or seemingly slow. When she finally reached the place he had stood he was gone, his voice and image faded away in the noise from the chatter.

Both preyed on her ears and her mind.

She crossed the plaza again, scribing hastily in her notebook what she recalled of the stranger's words, which was close to everything. A man followed her, not that far behind. She did not turn her head, but she saw him well enough. He did not aspire to hide himself, clearly a part of the ongoing circus surrounding her and her activities, reminding her that they were there. She ignored him as she ignored them.

Big Moon shone brightly behind her. It briefly turned red in her mind. The written word, her own writing turned strange on the paper. It danced and twisted at the edge of her vision.

Her antennas stayed up, as she made her way through familiar streets, as she made ever bigger circles with her feet and her mind, unable to get a grasp at what troubled her.

Allan Mortimer operated a tavern at the waterfront, up river on the Howell side. He stood behind the bar and froze visibly when Afterglow entered the establishment. Two members of his extensive guard detail, a man and a woman moved closer to Afterglow, clearly guarded, ready for anything. He signed for them to stay their hand.

She sat down by the bar.

– I assume you agree that there is no longer any value in silly secrecy, she said. – That whatever is happening has long since outlived such needs, whatever their initial reason.

He looked at her with his small eyes, not voicing any comment.

– I am… curious about what happened to Cochran, she said, she offered.

She observed how he relented, how he and his wall of fear and arrogance softened.

– You and I both.

He let out a barf of something resembling laughter.

– Who was with him?

– I have no idea. All my usual operatives were busy. Until I received information to the contrary I was convinced he went alone.

– You sent an untrained rookie on such an obviously risky mission, and then, after he had been reduced to dust you sent your equally inexperienced niece. Boy, business must be tough these nights.

He did not look good, whether she studied his mask or what showed beneath it when it cracked.

She looked around. The number of guests did not look very impressive, and those present did not seem very comfortable at all. On the contrary, her keen power of observation painted them as antsy and apprehensive. She did not need her enhanced senses to read them either. They wore their emotions pretty much on the outside.

But they were poster children for harmony compared to their boss. He looked even more like the nervous wreck and even shittier than the nervous wreck Kathryn had always pictured him.

– I was pretty confident you could handle it, of course, he shrugged. – And sweet Alice needed the experience.

He grinned wickedly and she knew he was both playacting and not.

He was pretty much the same guy she had imagined during her brief phone calls with him.

She retreated to a table in the corner with full view of the room. There were other sorcerers present, also a few of them sharing her chosen «profession». She nodded to them, her colleagues, even as she studied them, as they studied her.

Their uneasiness was apparent to her. The apprehension rattling them made unrest rise just below their surface.

She did not drink anything, even though several of those present made her several offers, with curiosity and bravery boiling their mind.

The draft struck her the moment she stepped back outside. Two figures, a woman and a man that had not been inside stood still at the other side of the street.

– Greetings, Afterglow, the woman cried. – Well met.

Kathryn knew of them. They were, like Afterglow a part of a pool of sorcerers that offered their occult services, among those that could be called upon by Mortimer and other informal managers for the right price.

– Well, met, Askar Walton and Leona Mojsov, she returned the greeting in a customary fashion, though not completely, as she had not used their full denomination, the one pointing at their clan and ancestry.

Neither had they, to her. They had used her taken name, the one she had chosen for herself.

The wind picked up and the chill in the air deepened.

The three met halfway, in the middle of the street.

– We have a rather interesting proposition to Afterglow, Askar said. – We know she seeks… diversions these nights. Is she interested?

– She is, Afterglow confirmed.

The two turned and headed south without further ceremony, and she followed their lead. The three crossed the bridge to the Talaho side.

– It is said that Mortimer the Manager is experiencing grave troubles these days, Leona remarked casually.

– Oh, how so? Afterglow inquired, just as casually.

– Word, and there might be some truth to it states that he owns a considerable debt to a particular pleasure dome, and that he, in order to keep himself from losing his business is considering giving up his niece for training and work there. It is said that she is quite the peach, at least until her recent misfortune.

– It is quite funny, is it not? Askar mused. – That he, in his desperation possibly ruined his chances of salvation.

– Word is that the girl will recover, though, Leona said, nodding to herself.

Afterglow made no comments, pretty much ignoring their pointed prattle, just like they expected her to do.

She sniffed the air. The other two noticed, no matter how much she tried to conceal it.

– What is it? Leona asked her directly.

Afterglow felt a certain kinship with her, with both of them. It was inevitable. They were sorcerers similar to her, both in their chosen profession and in temperament.

– The waves bring a scent, she replied, frowning. – One both in the air and not.

– What kind?

Afterglow's frown grew deeper, and she was unable to reply.

– You do not know! The other woman stated startled.

Kathryn shook her head.

– I have never sensed its like.

There was a giant airship port south of the city. They could see the hovering oblong balloon with its comparatively small passenger part from far away, of course, its lights and steam-like gas. The walk took them close to an hour. They did not mind.

Cars stopped by the gate to let people off. There were quite a few of them.

– Look at people, Askar mused, – using transport to cross small distances. No wonder obesity is on the rise among certain segments of the population.

There was contempt in his voice. Afterglow found herself nodding.

– Like the number of known sorcerers is going down for each new generation, Leona said. – Human beings are forgetting, forgetting who they are.

She could not hide the sore subtext in her voice.

The symbol drawn in black representing the middle triple cities on the outside wall of the administrative building was a strange one: a thick base and a line straight up, a broken circle and an invisible triangle, with strange blobs and eddies all over.

The airship was ready for departure. The three could easily discern that by the increased activity surrounding it. They walked up the gangway and hurried onboard just before the door closed.

The ship had arrived from the triple cities in the south and would soon depart for the triple cities in the north. It was an ongoing route back and forth the airships made along the eastern part of the continent.

The trio entered the lower section of the passenger segment of the ship. They saw Talaho and also farther away Howell through the windows. The salon was half full, fairly relaxed, even if the usual anxiety inevitably picked up when the three sorcerers entered it.

It was the way they were dressed, of course, but not only that. Afterglow knew that at least some of the people present would have made them even if they had worn completely ordinary clothes.

People had not forgotten, not truly, not deep down.

– A man followed us onboard, Leona enlightened her offhand.

– At least one, Afterglow shrugged.

She moved to a window without seconds thoughts. Memory assaulted her. She always preferred the window tables, no matter how much it sent her down memory lane.

Leona kept studying her, kept digging beneath her surface. Kathryn brushed off that as well.

The three of them sat there, by a table with no other seats taken. The other passengers kept a healthy distance from the sorcerers and that sat well with them.

The moorings were loosened with a thug. The cities below turned smaller from their perspective. The airship's engines brought it east, above the sea. Kathryn closed her eyes. She saw it down there, the whirling mass of air and water.

– Jupiter's Cauldron is acting up again, Leona marveled. – Look at it.

There was a place out there, in the ocean that was usually calm, where there were mostly sunny and clear skies.

But not so tonight. Tonight a storm or something equivalent to a storm was raging out there. It brought mist or steam or whatever it was into the surrounding area, all the way to the coastland and the triple cities. It brought sudden rain and abrupt thunderstorms. It brought holes in the very fabric of reality.

– It is so amazing, Leona breathed, – so beyond remarkable.

Afterglow sat there with her eyes closed, her eyes open. It made no difference. Her perception remained pretty much the same.

Big Moon seethed and burned above them, hovering in the air, the still clear skies, the high tides making the tall waves even taller, flooding the harbors and low land of the triple cities. She imagined she could actually reach out and touch it. In a glimpse she imagined it turned red, but when she opened her eyes and looked, she saw that it had not.

The airship turned left and headed north. The disturbance from Jupiter's Cauldron kept shaking it for quite a while, until they finally reached calmer skies. The ride turned pleasant and uneventful from there.

They were served a meal and wine.

– A toast to our successful venture, Askar said.

Three glasses met and parted, creating the familiar sound chiming in Afterglow's ears. She recalled happy occasions of times past, no matter the bitter taste it brought.

The wine in her glass changed color as she was about to drink. It turned muddy and dark.

– Do not drink! Afterglow cautioned the other two. – Do not eat more.

They had already swallowed a few pieces of the meat. The other two stared at her and the wine and the food.

All three glanced around, alert and ready for whatever would come. Suddenly the entire room seemed clothed in shadow. They were on their feet and rushing towards the kitchen in just a few seconds. Air flowed around them. They scouted for the waiter, but did not see him. Kathryn recalled his features clearly. She had never seen him before, but he stood out as very distinct in her mind and memory.

– The man serving us, she shouted. – Where is he?

The crew did not have to consciously respond. Their flickering glances spoke volumes. There was a door ajar at the back of the kitchen. It brought the sorcerers to the fairly large balcony. The waiter stood by the rail.

And then he jumped. They ran to the rail and to the stunning view of the ragged eastern coastland and wilderness of the continent Asbara, and the ever smaller falling body.

It hit the ocean far below with a tiny splash.

They used the left passageway back to the passenger-section. Sweat kept breaking on their forehead skin while they concentrated on keeping the possible poison from being digested in their system. Afterglow noticed how her companions used the same techniques she used through the haze of her iron focus.

– So, do any of you have any idea who is behind this, what the reason might be?

– I regret to inform you that we do not, Askar gritted his teeth. – It could be a number of reasons and people with old grievances.

– There is a long line to pick from, Leona grinned. – It is the same with you, I imagine, or so I've heard.

Faces, expressions of hatred paraded before Afterglow's half closed eyes.

They threw up, forced nausea on themselves, impatient, fearful, unwilling to wait. Non-digested meat flowed down to the vast sea below. They kept it up until there was nothing but slime and stomach acid left.

– Fuck! Askar dried his lips and the surrounding area of the mouth. – When will they realize that poisoning a sorcerer's food and drink is a lost cause and spare us the aggravation?

The two females looked bemused at him, their skin equally pale.
– I saw that!
A woman, one of the other waiters stood in the open door to the kitchen.
– He jumped, jumped long before you guys reached him.
– Thank you, honey, Leona said quite relaxed, but with distinct relief in her voice. – That will save us a lot of further aggravation.
People glanced at them when they returned to the lounge, but not with truly curious eyes. The other passengers had no idea of what had transpired. The trio sat down in the same seat they had left not that long ago. It was, in some ways like they had never left.
– I will assume the man jumped to his death, Askar said. – That takes dedication.
– It narrows the list of suspects a little, Afterglow said. – Just a little.
They laughed out aloud.
And abstained from eating and drinking during the rest of the journey.
People enjoyed their food and drink, and cast the occasional curious glance at the three and a few others not consuming anything.
Afterglow kept studying everyone onboard she or her senses encountered. She even sent out her waves in order to deliberately measure their echoes and impressions.
There was nothing suspicious, nothing giving her any further clues to what was happening or if anything substantial was. She did not spot any of her tails from earlier, from before the trio had boarded the ship. As far as she knew they were nowhere on board.
She wanted to tell her companions to be ready for anything, but she saw without trying that they already were, that they had reached an elevated level of alertness the very moment the action had begun, and that they had stayed there all the way since.
Various scenarios kept playing out in her head. She remained calm, collected. The sweat on her forehead slowly dispersed.
They went to the restroom and sat down on bowls in order to shit, just to play it safe. There was no really ill-smelling waste appearing from their digestive system, not even a trace of poison. They relaxed, as much as they ever allowed themselves to relax.
– So, what encouraged you guys to go north, of all places? Afterglow asked them when they had returned to their chairs. – It is not exactly a preferred place of our kind.
The other two nodded empathically, quite familiar with the reasoning behind her words.
– We needed a change of scenery, Leona replied lightly, seemingly joking. –

The urge grew quite persuasive actually.
Afterglow nodded without nodding. It was an answer any sorcerer, including herself would often give as a reply to a similar query.
They sat there and did not really talk much, not beyond the exchange of pleasantries, their need for a true conversation lessened, not increased by their experiences. Time passed by, like the vast, ragged landscape and unruly ocean below.
The airship arrived at the dock outside the city of Shen'n, one of the triple cities of the north, the two others being Selad'n and Sil'n. The powerful heat hit them the moment the doors opened. They walked down the gangway and set foot on distant soil.
There was no checkpoint, even though there were a couple of magistrates present. There were no papers to be shown. No one in the three times triple cities was required to carry any. There had been brief occasions in the long history of Arcadia when that had been the case, but that was long ago.
The symbol of the northern triple cities on the wall of the square building was simplistic, straightforward, quite different from both further south.
The two magistrates noticed the three sorcerers, that much was obvious to the travelers. Other people did not see that, but Afterglow and her companions did so with accomplished ease.
The three of them, their moving eyes, their wide open senses did not miss much of anything anywhere on the port.
– There is no one, Leona mused.
– The waiter was a «no one» as well, Askar pointed out.
– That is true, the woman acknowledged with just a slight, hardly visible irritation.
Distracted, they are distracted.
Afterglow focused away from them and their squabble and issues. There was still no one and nothing.
Little Moon was up and at its brightest and strangest, casting a golden, eerie glow even in the middle of the day.
– Look at it, Leona spat. – It welcomes us. Some claim it is Big Moon that will turn red and bring the fulfillment of prophecy, but I very much doubt that.
The venom in the woman's voice surprised Afterglow. She pondered it as she studied her fellow sorcerer.
They left the port, heading into the sizzling streets.
– It is all burning, Leona mumbled.
Afterglow heard her, perhaps not the first time, but the third, fifth or ninth. A chill passed through her. It was so powerful that she was convinced it was

seen by everybody in her close proximity.

Leona's hard gaze struck her like glowing pokers.

People moved around her. The meaning of their dance was more than clear to her, to them. A considerable number of those present took what was a potentially very unhealthy interest in them. They kept moving.

– This is just yet another gauntlet, Afterglow said aloud. – Fuck it!

– What is it? Askar chuckled darkly. – Afterglow does not regret joining us in our venture already?

Afterglow ignored him as much as she could possibly ignore anyone with her powerful presence.

She turned heads and knew positively that did not constitute a threat.

A car passed them, cast in glow, cast in Shadow. They nodded to each other. The car faded away somewhere on the crooked, crooked road fading in in front of them.

This city was distinctly different from all the other triple cities further south. It had a unique quality also speaking to the three sorcerers, to what spoke within them and shadowed the bright shine of the daystar.

All the streets and avenues were straight lines. The trio encountered no crooked streets on their path. A city rail passed them in an adjacent alley. It made no sound.

The building at its center pointed to itself, even though there was nothing particular about it, nothing visible making it different from those surrounding it. There was a kind of pattern one could discern if one looked real hard. Afterglow saw it, but only because she was able to view all angles simultaneously up and down and from the sides.

No sentries guarded the place. They walked right inside without being stopped or slowed down. No one met them or hailed them. People walked back and forth inside the chilly hall, but they had other things on their mind.

Leona and Askar walked up the central staircase and Afterglow followed them.

– Nobody seems to care that we are here, she remarked.

– Someone does, Askar stated. – But they are not here.

The frown crossed Afterglow's face.

– Ah, you are curious, are you not, Leona said.

– They have created a triple blind system to avoid dealing directly with us, Askar said. – It is really quite ingenious.

– They do not care much for sorcerers, Leona said. – The fact that they need us does not make them care more at all.

Afterglow sniffed in contempt.

– Do you sense anything? Askar asked.

His question, his casual, but insistent voice did make her probe her surroundings in a more deliberate fashion.

– No. she shook her head. – There is nothing.

But there was something, a taste in the wind, a scratch she could not quite fathom or grasp.

The upper floor was not exactly crowded either. Afterglow noticed the almost invisible paintings or markings on the walls, leading them right. They ended up in a room at the end of the hallway, one with no furniture except a single table. A white envelope awaited them there.

They approached it as cautiously as they would anything, sniffing the air, probing their surroundings. Nothing of significance happened, except that they reached the table and the envelope without incident.

Leona picked up the white piece of paper, pausing, pondering a bit, before opening it, revealing the sheet inside.

There was a drawing on it, a stylized «α» or Alpha.

– I have seen this before, she said, – on a building at the north point of the city.

– We are supposed to go there? Afterglow wondered.

– That is how it works, Askar nodded.

– They are paying us handsomely for the added effort, the jerks, Leona added quickly.

– At the end of the trail our true task awaits, Askar added.

They attempted to sense a trail, reaching out to their surroundings, but there was nothing, no flow, not inside the building and not outside, not on any of the sides, not even in the direction they were headed.

Afterglow probed the ground beneath their feet, but it was calm, dead. There were waves here, like there was everywhere, but they hardly stirred the surface. This sea was still, almost unmoving.

– It is different here, she remarked.

– Afterglow has not visited this great city before? Askar wondered in a mock grin.

– Once, long ago, Afterglow replied. – It was not a memorable visit.

– Different, as in better? Leona prodded her.

– Different, Afterglow repeated.

She glanced at the two, not able to conceal her irritation.

There was a broad, long avenue here, as there was in Howell, but no twisted banshee statues. The statues on Resio Avenue stood straight on their socket and didn't speak aloud.

They did speak, though, by their silence. Afterglow heard them without trying.

– This is such a proud place, is it not? A boy said to a girl. – I mean, look at all these symbols and accounts of our history, displays of our great forefathers.

The two held hands. She nodded eagerly and looked at him with shiny eyes.

Afterglow shook her head in dismay.

– These people… prefer order. Leona indicated her surroundings with her hands. – I guess they see us as chaos-bringers, which is just as silly as the alternative, of course.

She giggled darkly.

– They are technocrats, Afterglow said, – believing only in what they can see and touch. Our very existence must be a source of endless frustration to them.

– Is not that the truth!

A huge smile lingered on Leona's face.

Afterglow reached out with her waves, pushing their impact a little beyond the casual in an attempt to get a grip on the scenery. It was not hard to see the obvious. The city rail, starting at the south point could be traced through all three cities, the triple cities on a straight line she could easily, somewhat follow to its end. But beyond that there was nothing, there just was not.

Her extended senses touched only air and buildings and ground, and the flesh in-between.

They walked, casually, at a slightly elevated speed, strolled like ordinary visitors through Shen'n's straight streets. People studying them would be hard pressed to decide whether or not they had a specific goal in mind. A woman standing on a balcony not far away stared a little too long at the passing trio. So did a clearly nervous young boy on a corner and a man looking out through an open door ahead. To Afterglow's trained eye they all stood out like an added light glow in the afternoon daystar and moon.

– I can hear the Dark River, Leona said with chill in her voice. – I can sense its flow.

There was a darkness in the very air, an invisible trail they followed with an ease of an experienced hound, a trail deliberately put in their way for them to track. Kathryn could not hold back the shudder.

It was there, here what was all other places as well, more obscure in a sense, but *present*.

The big house at the end of the street pointed to itself in many ways, not only to the sorcerers' enhanced senses. Their power of observation served them just as well. It was a perfectly ordinary building, one not standing out at all, but people still moved differently walking in and out of it.

They entered through the open door and everything, their impression of the place turned more pronounced. The Roman or rather Neo-Roman style on the outside became even more evident. People roamed the hall, walked back and forth in a disorganized pattern. The three sorcerers crossed the tiled floor. They entered the inner sanctum of the building through yet another open door.

There was more distinct change. A comparatively smaller room appeared to them. Music reached their ears from deeper within the structure. There was another opening, a double swing door, where much of what awaited inside was visible well before they entered the warm, humid surroundings. Nude and scant-clad male and females smiled to the newcomers. The Alpha pleasure dome and its inhabitants embraced the three travelers without touching their physical frame.

Afterglow felt the powerful emotions pounding her like velvet gloves. Enticing smiles and body language greeted her and her two companions.

– They have been trained to be pleasing, Askar commented, with a taint of contempt in his voice. – The result is truly quite remarkable.

A man, a young boy approached Afterglow. She could tell that he focused on her, even though there was nothing evident revealing that. He offered himself to her. A moment or two later he pulled away from her and she realized that she had rejected him, and that he had realized that before she did. They were well attuned to other people and their emotions and inner life, almost as if they were telepathic.

Askar grabbed a woman and held her in cruel and invasive ways. The smile stayed on her sweet face.

Afterglow shuddered again, unable to help herself. The others noticed.

– I can not stand anything resembling slavery, she said. – This is close enough.

The pleasure domes, their very existence kept bringing fierce debate to the three times three cities.

The centuries-old social system creating and sustaining the houses remained.

Everybody presented themselves to them, some close, some far away. They were all displaying themselves in subtle and evident ways. The pervasive sensuality made nausea and low-level arousal war within Kathryn.

– They learn what make people tick here, Leona said wickedly to her. – Do not underestimate them. They know how to move in order to make themselves irresistible. If a particular brand of sorcerer added this skill to her or his bag of tricks they would be mighty indeed.

There were legends of such beings, sirens seducing men and women as easy as they snapped their fingers. One theory stated that that was the origin of the houses, that they had once trained assassins and other dangerous individuals and not humble and obedient courtesans.

Afterglow appraised a male and a female. Sensing her interest, no matter how casual they stopped before her. She grabbed them and fondled them. The sounds of desire fled easily from them.

She let go of them, turning away, leaving them behind.

A woman caught her eyes, even more skillfully. She acknowledged her with a shrug.

– May I interest you in something special, My Lady?

She had a pleasant voice and a more than pleasant and enticing hide, her delving smile probing the depths of her interest.

Afterglow moved on, not replying, replying, dismissing her with something less than a taint of contempt.

A man, a boy sat on a cushion in a corner. The α - the alpha birthmark was not exactly concealed. Once again she felt the unfamiliar, familiar chill irritating and baffling her.

It was not his face, not his thoughts or his concealed but evident spite, but something deeper, possibly atavistic haunting the deeper regions of her self.

The three visitors walked to him.

– Greetings, Leona told him.

She said no more, clearly expecting it to be sufficient. Afterglow found herself nodding in approval.

Lights blew, shifted and changed in the room. There was no visible source doing that. The young man looked stricken at them. The other dolls halted their dance. Leona's mouth tightened in a cruel and pleased grin.

The dance froze. Afterglow felt it, how the three of them interacted and acted. It made goose bumps form on her exposed skin.

The male handed Leona a note. She accepted it with a scorn.

It was not folded or anything. It showed a Ω - an Omega.

– How utterly predictable! Leona snorted.

The three withdrew from the house of flesh and dolls and symbols and returned to the hot streets. Afterglow felt something akin to pleasure.

– We are a triskele, Leona boasted. – We are a Gift of the Raven. I knew we would be!

Clouds floated across the sky. Air blew in their ears.

It was a well known phenomenon, past sorcerers forming unions of attachment and power.

She approached Afterglow with a smile and a soft touch.

– I could sense the ants crawling through your veins. You got problems in that regard, do you not?

Afterglow hesitated only a moment before relenting, bowing her head in acknowledgment.

– I was engulfed in madness for a while in my youth, but the madness has passed and only lingers during special moments of terror and emotion and memory.

Leona kissed her tenderly on the cheek.

Kathryn touched the wet point of contact afterwards, as if she was a teenage girl receiving her first kiss.

– Omega is a cave outside the town, Askar offered. – I guess we are expected.

– I guess we are, Afterglow said.

A sense of… urgency grabbed them. A fast walk broke into a run. The whispers invaded Afterglow, penetrating her defenses. She kept them at bay easily enough, but they kept hammering her.

– This was a mistake, Askar mumbled under his breath. – I knew it would be, damn me.

That admission did little to further disturb Afterglow. Her anxiety had long since risen past that level.

They ran, and urgency and temptation and menace ran with them. Afterglow could taste it. She did not have to try.

Leona ran in front, excitement brightening further her already flushed face.

– There are those here, there, with us that do know what they are doing, she stated pleased. – I appreciate that, love that rare occurrence.

– The question then, Askar said, – why, then do they need us?

– Why indeed…

There was something in her voice Kathryn did not quite catch, and she redoubled her focus.

The trees and the plants in this place… they were far apart, lonely trees and vines never touching, except perhaps deep underground, ever a part of the Tree of Life. Kathryn Caldwell shook her head again. It did her no good.

One lone raven sat on a branch of a barren tree. It felt like she was asleep. In her dream she was open. In her dream, in her flashes of forever it was a dark and cloudy day and there were many trees, and a raven in each tree, and the number was nine, and a blue flame burned at its center.

The streets faded. The vision of houses dwindled in both mind and reality. Urban landscape shrank to a single narrow trail through the wilderness. The cave opening towered above them. They entered its mouth, its steaming gap. The dark swallowed them. A gesture from Leona brought fire. Nine tall torches in a circle illuminated the large cave. Flickering flames danced on its wall and ceiling and floor. In the soot covering the ceiling the omega was drawn in glowing red.

The three sorcerers stopped, facing each other in the triangle they formed.

– Whoever is setting this up is indeed more than a common dabbler, Askar remarked.

– They make us jumping through hoops, the assholes, Leona snarled.

A twisted face formed in the mist rising from the lower parts of the cave. It was visible only a moment, an apparition hardly even half there, but Kathryn easily recognized or believed she recognized Bea's features, and heard the chillingly familiar wicked laughter.

It was always present in Afterglow's mind, what could not be heard with the ears, sometimes stronger, sometimes weaker, but always there.

– There is nothing here either, she eventually concluded, – nothing they might want us to «fix».

Askar looked strangely at her, and that made her think twice about what she had said, and how she had said it.

The path, the shadow trail in the air that had accompanied them here led back out as well. They left the cave, following the trail of the labyrinth presented to them. It boxed them in somewhat. They felt its pull.

– They are not attempting to attack us with the spell, are they? Askar touched the boundary of the trail making the very air around them close to solid. – They are not that stupid?

– We could easily break out, Afterglow stated. – It is not truly affecting us. It appears to be a guiding spell and nothing more, crude but effective and not dangerous.

Leona dried sweat from her brow. She was clearly affected and Kathryn could not fault her for that.

They walked the gauntlet, a set path far more rigid than the one Afterglow had recently walked, with real or imagined wasps buzzing their surroundings.

A loud banshee-like whine made her frown and sweat even harder.

Invasive images and sensations continued to trouble them. They felt very familiar to Afterglow, even those she could not instantly place.

– It *is* an attack, Leona mumbled.

One so insidious that there was nowhere to direct their countermeasures or to even decide what they should be.

The city welcomed them back with its silence and stillness, its apparent tranquility. The shadow path stayed visible all the time, now, turning more distinct, strengthening itself.

Turning potent and dangerous.

The troika had reached another house with only open doors. They all saw it. The infestation was more than evident, waxing and waning, pulsing like a dark star.

It flooded them like lukewarm water, hitting them like acid.

– Quickly, Leona cried, somewhat controlled and confident, – take my hands.

The other two, slightly uncertain of what action to take confirmed to her command. They formed a triangle. Kathryn felt it instantly, the power when the circuit, the Gift of the Raven closed. They were connected these three, connected in ways she had hardly felt with anyone else, at least not since, since…

There was no time for preparation. The assault, even though it had been gaining momentum for a considerable time was abrupt, brutal. All three choired one single word in the ancient language: *protect.* A shield, a barrier surrounded them, keeping the most vicious part of the barrage from reaching their vulnerable flesh.

The barrage shredded their mind hundreds of times before they could blink. Their lips kept moving. Incomprehensible words, slowly turning comprehensive flowed from their throats and depths.

They were three, three hardened and skilled sorcerers.

Pain cut them, but they did not surrender to the vicious attack. It was an insidious thing, constantly attempting to sneak through their defenses. Their synapses kept bursting into flame, even as they burned to ashes, even as they kept bursting. Afterglow sensed no presence behind the veil of the storm, only a well-orchestrated design.

The barrage faded slowly, reinvigorating itself a few times, but ending for lack of nourishment. They held hands a while longer than needed, just to make sure there would not be more charging them.

The number 3 decorated the large door to the left. A callous chuckle rose from Leona's throat.

– I knew they honored the numbers here, but not that they, too honor their significance. Their belief in their professed reason is just that: just another facade.

Hands let go. Silence prevailed. Afterglow glanced around. There were no people here. It was a quiet place, almost isolated from the world outside. Afterglow drew breath short and sharp.

When she looked at Leona a certain way…

She still felt it.

The waves blew around her, relentless.

She felt the madness.

A sharp pain shot through her, first in her hands, and throughout her being. She touched her nose. There was blood on her hand. She staggered backwards. Leona filled her vision, as she stopped, as she kept swaying. Waves of weakness assaulted her.

Leona chuckled viciously.

– They made you jump through their hoops, enter their snare. You were doomed from the moment you entered the first gate. Care to wager where it was?

More, images, sensations hit Kathryn, the moments they entered the pleasure dome replaying themselves in her mind. She sensed shame and wicked triumph both in the other woman.

– We are what we are, Afterglow mumbled. – We do not apologize for it. Pride courses through every part of our being.

– They wanted you dead, Leona snarled, brimming with rage, – wanted it *bad,* and I was so happy to oblige. It was easy. You were just another weakling after all.

It was as if the attack came from the inside this time, shaking Afterglow apart at the seams. She was unable to move, frozen like a statue. Leona's face grew bigger and dissolved in her sickeningly impaired vision. The taste of blood set her mind on fire.

Leona gasped. A blue flame began dancing at the top of her head. She frowned, and then she released a loud cry of pain, and just like that the tables had turned. Afterglow was able to move again and her violet eyes twinkled.

The blue flame surrounded Leona, her entire body, doing so from one moment to the next.

She crouched. Then she straightened again, as if someone grabbed her feet and head, and her body was being pulled in opposite directions. Then terror struck her, accompanied with a shriek of almost childish disappointment and rage.

– You knew. I heard you, *hear you*. YOU KNOW!

Afterglow heard her, through the roar of the blue flame within and without. The blue flames did not burn Leona's clothes, but consumed her body. The skull was visible. The eyes stayed in their sockets for a prolonged moment in time, until they were consumed as well. She kept speaking, even without lips, without a throat, casting hateful, ineffectual spells at Afterglow until the end.

Eventually, there was only the heap of clothes and the ashes. If one looked closely one might spot a few scorched bones there.

Afterglow turned towards Askar, staring straight through him with her penetrating gaze.

– She carried a grudge against you, I am afraid, he said apologetic, not very sorry or concerned. – I knew that, but did not know to what extent.

There was cruelty, a cruel disinterest in his voice, but not animosity.

They stood there, facing each other, while Afterglow pondered the issue before she eventually relaxed and he could not keep a sigh of relief from expressing itself.

– The assassination attempt on the airship, was that part of it?

Her voice made it clear that she expected a reply, a good one.

– Not to my knowledge. He shook his head. – And I doubt she had anything to do with it either. It is quite amusing, is it not, how more than one force or faction is present at any given intersection?

She read understanding in his eyes and even pity and rejected it the moment she spotted it.

– It is a laugh riot, she remarked.

She turned her back to him, left him unannounced, with no visible or audible sign of goodbye.

The streets had turned deadly quiet. At least a few of the people walking even remotely close to her looked visibly apprehensive, shaken beyond words. She reached out with her power. It was a little harder than it used to be, in this place of less and lesser magic, but then it was as if she broke through a slight barrier and she was able to get a mental image of the entire town.

She remained tense and battle-ready, even though there was no sign of another, imminent attack. Her outside stayed calm, deadly calm. Her inside simulated some sort of calm, at least. Her lips flowed into a thin streak, as she walked and studied the flow of people moving back and forth in all directions on the street.

Patterns shifted and changed. Most people here just moved around with no particular plan, even those actually on their way to some particular place.

But not all.

She spotted those others easily, those keeping an eye on her without keeping an eye on her. They moved around her in an almost predetermined pattern. She prepared, making herself ready to act, when all those slowly surrounding her pulled back, to what was evidently an inactive, non-threatening position.

Everybody except one.

A non-descript man in his early thirties wearing the Maximus family crest stepped forward. She turned and faced him. They faced each other.

He spoke with a hollow, weak voice.

– You are notoriously hard to destroy and have proven that once again, but we will find a way. Sooner or later, one way or another we will get you.

– A suicide, an expandable, she said casually. – How fucking *refreshing!*

He was no more than a pawn, hardly more than a recording, perhaps hardly even truly aware of his precarious position, the fact that she could snuff his life out like she would a candle at any time and doing so without exerting herself. She shook her head in contempt. He turned to walk away with the others.

– One moment, she called after him.

He turned and faced her once again.

– I have a message myself, a reply to your *masters*.

She kept speaking casually, as if they were having an actual, laid-back conversation.

– Tell them I am sick and tired of this shadow game, and that I will not stand for it any longer. I will overlook this last attempt to get at me, treat it like the mishap that it was, but this is the last time. And I will get to them. Contrary to all the others attempting to get to me you guys are easily accessible. Tell them that.

He turned and walked away without a word, without visibly acknowledging her words.

She turned and walked in a different direction.

It was quite obvious to everybody watching her that she wasn't in any hurry. This looked to all like a woman taking a stroll through a city new to her, a woman enjoying the sights.

She sent out a controlled burst of waves. Dust rose from the ground. Several people in the know close by turned visibly nervous. She grinned at them, spat at them, snarled at them, pleased that she so easily was able to make them see her the way she wanted them to see her.

The image of Leona stayed burned in her vision. It did not matter whether or not she blinked. She hardly did. The woman's face twisted itself perhaps a little more than it had been doing the last few moments of her life.

Beatrice spoke to Kathryn, but there was no sound when her lips moved. Afterglow curled her lips, dismissing yet another sore, vibrant memory.

She returned to the airship port. The ship was still being refitted and would not depart for some time. She walked to a nearby bistro. It was a fairly quiet place, but the buzz picked up the moment she entered. At least some of the patrons knew of her. Once again, her reputation preceded her. A young waiter greeted the new guest at the door. He bowed politely and avoided her steady gaze.

– Welcome to the dining place Maraste, he said. – My name is Leo, is there anything I can assist you with, My Lady?

Her ambiguous smile made him turn a distinct red. Hormones and apprehension warred within his raging consciousness.

– There is indeed, she replied, pausing a bit for effect. – I would like a table for one, please.

– This way, My Lady, he said, eager like the kid he was.

The dinner, the spicy duck excited her buds. She sat there, taking her time, making time, enjoying her dinner. The maintenance crew outside slowly made the airship ready for takeoff. She saw no more Maximus ghosts. Even the lukewarm northern beer held a certain modest attraction to her, as she used it to quell the burning in her sore throat.

– Mmm, excellent, she breathed, as she put down the fork and the knife for the last time, and then, as she stopped briefly by the door: – Give the chef my regards, will you? It is highly likely that I will return here at a later date.

The waiter blushed. Several others, more serious-minded people, not really enjoying their food looked far more uneasy.

The airship was just about cleared for takeoff as she made her way across the port and up the landing stairway. She did not look back, but had all her attention directed forward, into the lounge and beyond.

An army was coming for Afterglow. She saw it march, inevitable, like life itself. Death stood by, observing and pondering it all. A chill equal to that created by the Wasteland passed through her. She still walked the Gauntlet.

A callous, contemptuous laughter rose from her sore throat, a slight apprehension she quickly quelled.

The airship rose, rose high in the sky, falling, like the human beings onboard into the deep, deep waters of mankind.

– Do you have a wand or similar? Afterglow asked an attendant. – I am out of practice, I am afraid. It would be great if it was possible for me to hone my skills somewhere on your beautiful ship.

– I think we may be able to accommodate you, My Lady, the woman wearing a kind of non-standard uniform said. – One moment, please.

The storage room was virtually empty. There were only a few crates. Some were placed there by passengers. Others had been placed there by the crew, packages sent by people in the northern cities to friends and relatives and other intended receivers in the middle and southern triple cities.

Afterglow filled the room, filled it with herself. The wand did not have the superior balance and necessary weight of one made by a master, but it sufficed. It moved faster and faster in her hands, coinciding with the sweat pouring harder and harder from her skin. She remembered. It did not take much to recall her skills, to pull them from the abyss of memory. Her clothes turned wet, turned soaked. The violet eyes never stopped flashing. Kathryn Caldwell returned south and the surrounding Dark River returned with her.

CHAPTER FIVE

Afterglow stands on the roof of her building at night, staring above the rooftops at the forest-clad mountains and the ugly scar of burned-out forest up there. The entire urban area and both rural and wild surrounding lands are hers to peruse and absorb.

She looked down. At the corner below there was a greenish, fluorescent lamp. The garage port further up the street was flooded in an eerie light. The iron box, where the construction crew lived clothed itself in darkness. They slept soundly in there, unaware, at least consciously of all the things going bump in the night. She looked across the bridge, at Talaho, and Talaho Mountains, saw its changing seasons, as mist turned to rain and drought, and back to mist.

The twin cities of Talaho and Howell breathed beneath her, around her. She sensed them and felt them, could not avoid feeling them, in her blood, in her bones and in the Shadow moving and crouching and breathing deep within her.

She retreated into her apartment, stepping through the hatch, floating down towards the floor below, closing, slamming the hatch quietly behind her, as she landed in the living room, the silence of the enclosed space. Kitchen and living room were rolled into one, the bed placed beyond the archway, a fairly broad portal leading to the bedroom and bathroom in the far corner. She undressed and went the short passage to bed, turning off the remaining lights one by one.

Turning and tossing on the large bed seemed to last forever, the various sections of her way too active and relentless mind turning itself off slowly and reluctantly.

Sleep finally came to her after what seemed like hours of writhing and restlessness continuing into sleep, into dream. Images and voices haunted her. People smiled to her and hissed at her. It was all the same, a jumble of horrors there was no escape from. She woke up in a fit of sweat, as she always did when she was not working. The sheets were soaked, as if she had just done hard exercise. She sat on the bed for minutes, rubbing her face, bathing in the dark red light from the dying sun.

She passed the mirror on her way to the bathroom, stopping there, deliberately looking at the wild creature, the seasoned sorcerer there. Water fell on her, drops passing her face colored violet by the gleam in her eyes. She hit the wall repeatedly with her left hand. It did not really hurt, except for the loud, loud echo twisting her ears.

The music filled the room, as she restlessly dried herself. The door to the secret room opened and she walked inside. In the total silence of the enclosed space she heard the click from the answering machine, but there was nothing on it breaking the ghostly mood of the room.

There was no food left, not in the fridge, the drawer she used to stack her bread or anywhere in the apartment. She dressed slowly, methodically. The dark coat and hood fit her like a glove. It comforted her to look at the indistinctive image of herself in the mirror.

She still saw it, burned into her mind, as she opened the door downstairs and started her walk, glimpsing herself in the store display windows. Gulls screamed and howled, as she walked along the harbor, as she passed pier seven. The lights were lit in there. She had discovered that it was often thus, even in the middle of the night.

The harbor was crowded. People sat outdoors, on the broad sidewalks, enjoying their beer. They were coughing as they swallowed too much beer. The prevailing dry ashen rain made them even more eager to wet their sore throats.

– Where does the ash come from? A man complained with pain and bewilderment in his voice. – It should have ended *weeks* ago.

No one voiced any reply, either because they deigned he was not worthy of any or because they were deep in their own thoughts and speculations about its origin and ongoing woes.

It bothered them, bothered them terribly, both what they knew and did not know. The big woman passing them moved on up the busy quay area.

The big clock on the wall to her left was late, as usual. It was always late.

A singer with a guitar entertained the guests in one of the taverns lined up along the road. He could not really sing and he certainly could not play. It was his twelfth night, so logic dictated that the people paying him enjoyed both his singing and playing. Afterglow shook her head in dry amusement.

She left the harbor, and started on her walk up the incredibly long Ivy Avenue. It was a slow, languished walk. She deliberately took her time, quite relaxed in the way she moved. The statues, the first of Homer Upcott's exhibitions dominating the free space and people's perception appeared at the high point of the avenue. These statues looked fairly normal, but they were not. They looked like statues of normal people, but one closer inspection by a watchful eye changed that silly notion. She stopped and studied them, like she always did. It made her dizzy, even nauseous, influencing her the way it always influenced her. She kept going west, until Ivy turned into the even wider Onion Square, where Homer's work definitely took a turn for the worse, with the twisted figures stretching in all directions.

They did not sing to her, but *screeched.* They did not chant to her, but squealed. The low sound cut into her eardrums and threatened to shatter them. This was new to her. She had never experienced this place quite like this before. It had always affected her in some way or another, but not like this. Something had happened to her, happened recently, opening her up, making her even more sensitive to her surroundings, to the eerie workings of the world. She hurried on, knowing fully well, by experience that it would be no good for her to cover her ears. Her walk turned into a run, but the sound did not go away, did not even diminish in her sensitive psyche.

She sat on a cafeteria eating her sandwiches, having her breakfast, in what felt like an eternity later. The hand holding the steaming cup of coffee was steady, but the quiver inside stayed with her, like it always did. The place was busy, but yet peaceful. It calmed her down somewhat, serving its purpose.

People looked at her. For some reason they always did, stolen, anxious glances. Most of them were regulars, but not all. There were some new faces today. They looked openly at her, some hostile, some curious, checking her out, taking her measure. She was used to that, and pretty much ignored them. This was her regular place, too, and she did not bother to make herself less of a target by switching venues now and then, and those staring at her with hostility in their eyes knew that, and whatever grievance they might have or not have with her grew to a boiling point.

She noticed it immediately, the shift, the beyond powerful shift in the air. It was not visible, except as indistinct ripples around the center, but to a sensitive like her it easily separated itself from its surroundings.

He appeared out of nowhere, at the corner across the street, at the spot where the wind was always blowing. By then she had already recognized him. He was an imposing figure, at least to her, who was able to see him for what he was. There was nothing overtly threatening about him. He crossed the street on the zebra stripes like most mortals would. People cast him beyond worried glances, because, inside, where it counted, they, too, knew him for what he was. He entered the cafeteria, and almost before he had taken the first step inside all those hostile and curious guests was scurrying towards the other exit door, grateful beyond belief for the fact that there was one. One look from him was all it took, to make them flee like rabbits from the wolf.

– Hello, Kathryn, he greeted her.

– Hello, Jason, she replied, somewhat calm and collected.

And the fear and loathing and awe in the looks those in the know sent her turned even more pronounced.

He always called her Kathryn, even though he had been one of the first to call her, to baptize her Afterglow. She watched him as he sat down in the chair opposite hers.

– Look at them scurry, he sighed. – Chaos is all around us, but still most people spend their entire life attempting to escape it…

– A hopeless task for sure, she replied dryly.

– You, on the other hand embraced it long ago.

She remembered, like splinters in the mind's eye.

– You always will. He nodded, both somber and excited. – Accept it, and embrace your destiny fully and unreservedly.

She sniffed angrily, irritatingly, knowing he would notice, not caring.

He looked amused at her. Hands grabbed the second last sandwich from her plate, and consumed it with great pleasure in his eyes, his two dark bonfires in the night.

– Why have you come, Jason?

– I just wanted to say hello. He shrugged, sending powerful ripples through the ether. – Is that so bad?

She saw the ripples, felt them, and sensed them on a far deeper level. They were enormously more powerful beyond what most people considered normal light.

He made them, without conscious thought and without effort. His cold heat singed her skin.

She finished the last sandwich, cleaning herself on the lips and around the mouth with a tissue and rose from her chair.

– That will do, she replied ironically.

He rose, too, and they walked outside. They moved as one, awkward at first, then together, moving to a beat not even they understood. At least she did not. He looked to the left, and she realized in an instant that his attention was drawn, inevitably to the mad man's art several blocks away.

– You can hear it, can you not? She grinned at him. – Such a small distance means nothing to Jason Gallagher.

– Distance? He looked distracted away from her, at the empty air in front of his eyes.

– It is amazing, is it not, the way his work dominates and covers so much of the inner city? There would be a lot of room for new, expensive condos here, a dream for developers and house sharks alike, but they are not *here*.

– Yes, he said, very enigmatic, true to her expectations.

She knew so little about him. Even if the brief glimpse he once had given her had been like a flash of eternity, and had sent her mind reeling almost to the point of annihilation, it had been just a flash. She knew what he was or at least had a fairly good idea, but she did not know him.

The flash revisited her right now, like it always did when he was close, every time he paid her one of his «visits». It was a jumble of impressions, of screams and horrors and vast, empty spaces, totally alien and unfathomable to her limited senses.

He grabbed her hands and pulled her to him. She attempted to stop him from doing so, but was unable to offer even the slightest resistance. He was far stronger than her, and it seemed to her as if his seemingly limited shell threatened to burst under the onslaught of what rested beneath that calm surface. She let herself be held. He did not really hold her that hard, and she could break free if she truly wanted to. He knew she loathed being forced or coerced, so he did not.

When he kissed her, kissed her fiercely on the lips she stiffened in his arms, a tiny moment, before she sighed and relented and began responding, increasingly eager to his advances. She hardly noticed when he led her across the street, the happy, expectant buzz in her mind making her giggle and hum.

They crossed the threshold to the portal, and the Vortex engulfed them, even him. Many different paths revealed themselves to them, strands of night and fire pointing to the infinity surrounding them. She let him choose the direction, the destination, not in submission, but in deference. They arrived in a place of mist and shadows, of forests and moors, invisible and not, in front of a house resembling a castle. Afterglow's heart jumped several beats by the mere sight of it.

– What *is* that? She cried. – I have never seen or sensed anything like it.

– You know what it is, he said. – There is such a place on every world. I've merely… personalized it a bit.

– A reminder? She inquired. – Of where you came from?

– Yes. He frowned. – It is so hard to remember sometimes, and this helps focusing my memory.

They crossed the threshold of the house, the building, the dark lodge, and the tingling in Afterglow's bones grew to a shiver. Everything seemed quiet, still, but Afterglow sensed more, the invisible swirling mists and shadows, even more inside than outside. There was no visible light in the rooms without windows, but a glow coming from everywhere kept the hall and all subsequent rooms they walked through lit.

She sensed… images here and there, misty, deep and three-dimensional, at least that, knowing instantly they were not images at all, but dangerous deep wells of reality. She stayed away.

– This place is really only for me, he remarked. – Almost anyone else would be pulled apart by the powerful energies raging here.

She observed it all, inevitably proud by his words, his praise, staying away, approaching it with caution and curiosity, practically a wide eyed kid again.

He took her arm and pulled her close. She let it happen, wanted it to happen. He kissed her and it was not really a kiss but an embrace, a beyond powerful hug. They were in the bedroom. She glimpsed the bed. It was big and inviting and pulled her to it like the powerful and hot vortex of the Crossroads would. She responded willingly, eagerly and passionately to his advances, holding on to him like she would an anchor in a storm.

– I hope you have made it strong enough, she giggled.

They Fell on it, hard, without holding back. It cushioned them, received them in its lap like a living thing. She did not have to hold back, not here, not with him. It dawned on her slowly, the knowledge of past events catching up with her. She kissed him, drawing blood, and his blood was acid, was fire. Water flowed somewhere, a waterfall, a powerful torrent pulling them down a frothing river. A moan rose from her, from her wet and hot center, mixing with his darker roar. She shouted, in joy, in the pleasure surrounding her. A hand grabbed, crumbled the sheet beneath them, pulling at it, failing at pulling it apart. Its fibers were strong, designed to withstand the strongest passion.

She pushed at him, he pushed himself into her, and they were naked, and she could not recall them undressing, could not recall anything the second before this. Her fingers, her claws raked his skin and there were no marks. She felt his hands, his claws on her hard skin, and shouted in joy. He touched her all over, not only with his hands, but his equally sensitive and powerful mind and body. She felt that mind, that body, its power radiating in waves, back and forth between the dark material, the immaterial walls.

He moved within her, without her, and she gasped, as her nipples turned rock-hard, as her body softened, as both their bodies hardened, as both of them felt, sensed each other far beyond any walls, as fire and water and strands of flame and shadow and the Universe surged through them, and their totally limp bodies fell on the bed, and the soaked sheets caught them, and cushioned their fall, and everything turned bright and dark, and everything between.

They relaxed on the bed afterwards, in each other's arms, after countless couplings seemingly lasting an eternity. It felt so good, so peaceful. She shook her head in wonder, laughed a bit, and shook her head anew.

– We would have woken up an entire city. She kissed him. – Hell, we would have left it in ruins, like gods passing through on their path to nowhere.

He touched her cheek briefly, a touch speaking volumes.

In that touch was the world.

They showered together. She still felt hungry, felt needy, never got enough of the sensation of touching another human being.

She dried him with a towel and he dried her with another. They started off doing it with their powers, but then both stepped close and used their hands. Shadows and mists surrounded them and it felt so good.

They dined in the main hall afterwards, sitting by the long table at each end of it facing each other. He was good at this, at entertaining, at being a host. She raised her glass when he did, and they had a toast. They sat too far away from each other for the glasses to touch, but she still imagined she heard the special sound of glasses meeting and parting.

– To what should we toast? He wondered.

– To Infinity? She inquired. – To Eternity?

– To both, he confirmed.

The wine burned in her throat and stomach. The food did as well. But no more than the daggers that was his eyes, the slits wide as the Universe. He knew how he appeared to her. She knew that. He had revealed to her once, and never again what was concealed between that pleasant shell of his.

When he spoke again his voice had not changed.

– The clock ticks in the dark for Afterglow.

His words inevitably sent shivers through her, but not of fear. It was far more primal than that.

She wanted to ask him, ask him what he meant, but she already knew. It was not that his cryptic words were not cryptic. It was just that he in those words and intonations conveyed everything she needed to know. She looked at him in despair, unable to speak.

He bent slightly forward, reaching out with a hand, and she imagined that he touched hers.

– If you could would you come with me to the other side?

She looked at him, holding his eyes.

– I have been there, she sniffed. – It is not much to write home about, not that much different from here.

– What you have seen is only a tiny glimpse of the vastness that is Reality.

She pulled back, shrinking in her chair.

– It is enough for me.

The eerie mood in the place got to her. He got to her. She emptied the glass in one gulp, looking at him with flaring distrust. When she rose it happened abruptly, without thinking. She walked out on the balcony, knowing he would follow her.

It was night, sort of, even though the difference between day and night was not very pronounced in this place.

– It is so beautiful, she whispered. – I have always loved the mists and shadows.

– I know, he said softly in her ear, grabbing her shoulders from behind, – and you will always do so, no matter how many inhuman idiots that will do their best to put out the fire you carry inside, the fire that is worth any sacrifice to keep burning.

– You know that? She turned angrily towards him. – You know that for a fact?

– I do. When you live as long as I have you learn a few truths. There is nothing more important than that fire, not in the entire Universe. Oh, there are people, religious zealots and bunch, and all the other pretenders that will say differently, but it is merely the posturing of an empty shell that has left the most important in the human being behind long ago. You know of what I speak. You have seen it many times.

Yes, she wanted to say, but her voice failed her.

– I do want something from you, he said, – You are quite correct in your suspicion, but when the time comes it will be totally voluntarily on your part, and it will not leave you any worse off, but more powerful and confident than ever.

– You have been following me around all my adult life, she stated. – Perhaps even longer.

He did not say anything. Perhaps his voice failed him or perhaps cat got his tongue, or perhaps he quite simply chose not to reply.

– I will leave now, she declared curtly. – I will find my way back myself, thank you.

– Yes, you will, he replied calmly, her anger rubbing off on him like dry, slow-falling hail, and he sounded so confident, so certain.

She jumped off the balcony and landed easily, like a cat on the ground below. There were just a few steps to the gate, to the whirling mist, the storm between worlds. She stepped through it, without looking back, but imagined she still glimpsed him there on the balcony, waving goodbye, waving «until we meet again».

It was easy to get lost on the path, to choose wrongly at the Crossroads, but to her it had become second nature and she prevailed. Her path glowed before her, paling all other paths. She appeared on the corner of Wayward and Ivy, where she had stepped through with Jason such a short while ago, such an eternity ago.

The wind was blowing. It was always blowing here.

Everything seemed new and fresh to her, even the stench of battery acid from the engines. Tired people glowed and the loud noise of the city did not wear her down.

Dusk settled with a hiss around her and the lights of the city grew dominant, somewhat. There were benches not far away. She sat down on one, straight by one of the large and outlandish and imposing statues. Every other bench was taken, but not this one. People stared at her. She ignored them. Twilight deepened everywhere. She sat there relaxing, not even having to try. Jugglers performed, collecting their reward, not even approaching the particular bench. No one else gathered in the park for the afternoon did either, but walked wide circles around it when they passed by. Afterglow stared at them with impunity and increasingly enjoyed herself the more the others did not, and she nodded to herself, realizing something.

She walked casually through the streets, at a slow pace. First she chose the well-lit, wide street, where everybody walked, and then she headed into the darker and narrow alleys by the harbor. There was a bit of hesitation at first, there, inside the dusty and basically abandoned area, but then she picked up the pace and an aura of determination settled in her form. The stench of salt became apparent. She could not see the ocean, but it was there, just a few blocks away.

It was not instantly apparent where the door was, but she found it easily, pushing a brick on the wall. The door opened a bit to the left, slid open and vanished, as if there had never been a door there in the first place. A deep, dark hole revealed itself. She walked inside, walked through a long, ebony hallway where even she had trouble seeing. There were sounds, both the sound of voices and less familiar noises.

The room did not exactly fall silent when she entered it, but she effortlessly recognized the qualitative change in the air, and so, she knew, did everyone else present. Those that did not know her or know of her knew by the change in mood that she pointed to herself.

– Behold, a man she did not recognize snarled, – The Forsaken has returned.

Dear child has many names.

Voices rose again as people nodded and looked at her in awe and pity and contempt. Virtually everybody present recognized the calling name, and knew her history, what had made her feared and infamous, what had made her what she was. The sick feeling washed over her. The thrill surged through her. She walked straight for the bar.

– Glenmorangie, straight up, she said casually, hoarsely, unable to keep the mixed emotion from her voice.

The barkeep served her, expertly pouring her glass full. He served anyone. Everybody knew that.

She drank. It burned within her. She knew it would.

– Yes, the Forsaken has returned, she cried, – and she's here to stay. Cheers!

She raised her glass to them all, before doing a bottoms-up.

The glass hit the bar again, as she put it down hard and decisively. The barkeep serving anyone filled it to the brim. She took the glass and walked, walked straight to the nearest table. A man, a big bear of a man jumped on his feet and attacked her outright. She struck him with her free left hand, casually, giving him a gentle slap without spilling her drink. He was thrown across the room. His collarbone broke with a loud crack when he hit the wall. He whimpered as he attempted to fight off the pain and get up. She quickly lost interest in him. The whimpers echoed in the room throughout the evening, but she did not know whether or not they were real or only in her mind.

She sat down on the now very available chair. Everybody rose and left the table, except the man sitting opposite her. He stared at her with a look dark and deep.

– You have changed, he said. – I hardly recognize you.

– I hardly recognize myself, Harley, she shrugged.

And then, with the special intonation in her voice when she spoke his name, he knew it was her.

She took a sip of the drink, hardly noticing that she did, her attention fixed on the man she recognized across an abyss of time deep and wide. Harley Corcoran had gray hair at the temples. His face looked drawn and withered, like with any man that had seen too much and too little of life. There was a catching in her throat and she could not stop it, no matter how hard she tried.

And just now, this one moment she did not want to.

– You do not need to, do you? He shrugged, just as deliberately. – Afterglow has gone places, right? She has become a force to be reckoned with and does not need to concern herself with trifles and lesser beings.

He was not so bad himself, having learned the art of irony and sophistication, and how to put it to good use, how to sting an opponent where it hurt the most.

The need to kill him grew almost overwhelming, but she stayed her hand.

He was no pushover, but no match for her, and that thought brought good and warm feelings to her mind.

– Why have you come here?

– It is nothing profound or anything, she replied. – I just wanted to revisit my old digs. Is not that what all people do sooner or later?

– I guess they do, he nodded. – No matter where they go or what they may

have become, they always return to their humble beginnings.
And she did, as he spoke, as she had since she had stepped inside the room, and for so long before that. The familiar pain, suddenly so much stronger surprised her.
– I felt guilty for many years, she told him flat out. – I do not anymore.
– Survivor's guilt, he nodded. – A classic.
His expression spoke volumes as well. For a moment there, they shared all the guilt and shame there was, before it faded from both faces, like yesterday laundry.
– Beatrice was crazy like a loon, he cried. – I tried to warn you, warn you all. Why did you not listen?
Afterglow wanted to respond to him, wanted to concede, give him right, but was unable to.
A man, haggard and sporting wild eyes stood up on one of the corner tables. People sighed even before he started speaking, started casting his gospel at the gathering.
– We live in an Age of Signs, he cried dramatically.
– Another would-be Seer, a woman complained. – Some people want so much to believe one that they throw all critical thought overboard.
– There has not been a true Seer in centuries, a man related to his companion.
– Afterglow, in her youth brought the first recent signs of the age, the man precariously balancing on the corner table proclaimed. – The first signs of the coming of The Nine…
That did cause a stir in the room, among more than one set of drinking buddies. Several of them glanced at Afterglow, but did not dare let their attention linger. Kathryn ignored them, like they expected her to do.
– The Red Moon will return, the man bellowed with his cracked voice. – It will bring travelers to our distant shores and even more players to the game, the Great Game.
He lost his footing, completely and finally, fell and hit the table. It broke beneath him. Ale and beer and drinks splattered all over the place. People jumped from their seats in an attempt to avoid being splattered.
The man did not move. Minutes passed and he seemed to be lying still in the wreckage.
Somewhat eager discussions followed the brief interplay.
- Every would-be Seer evokes The Nine and the Red Moon, one woman spat. – It is a safe bet. It impresses just about everyone, even those not easily impressed.
They could not help themselves. They cast long glances at the hapless wreck

on the floor.

He did not move. No one approached him or checked him to see if he was still breathing. The barkeep kept serving drinks to everybody interested in having a taste or ten.

Afterglow and Harley sat there while the evening grew old, nursing their drinks. The initial hostility in the room directed at Afterglow did not go away, but it lessened a bit, as the hours crawled by. The two of them did not really talk, but exchanged pleasantries like an old married couple, speaking about nothing and everything.

The band played on. She had not noticed it had returned after the break. They played a sad, wicked tune. She shook imperceptibly.

– I saw her, Afterglow finally said.

He frowned, looking puzzled at her.

– What do you mean you saw her? What was it, someone using her appearance or pretending to be her in other ways?

He did not get it, not really.

– I saw Beatrice, Afterglow explained patiently. – She has appeared to me several times, with increasing frequency lately, speaking to me, replying to me. We have had several *conservations*. It was *her,* not some revenant or similar, but her, paying me a visit from the beyond. I would recognize her anywhere.

– Yes, he said slowly, slowly getting it. – I imagine you would. So what does she want?

– Vengeance, I suppose, but also more than that. She wants a *reckoning*. Someone or something has been chasing my heels lately, perhaps even chasing them harder than everything and everyone else, and she is clearly a part of that. How big a part remains to be seen.

Afterglow spoke loud, making sure everyone in the room heard her, and everybody knew she did it on purpose.

It rattled them, but she did not see anyone stick their head out.

They all stared at her when she rose, all of those that could be classified «old guard». She returned the stare, did so without using her eyes. They felt it, the calm, savage confidence emanating from her form, as she was leaving, and they pulled back, one step, two steps, three… doing so without moving.

– Hey, Afterglow! Harley called to her, making her stop in the door. – Have you been to the Island lately?

He knew she had. They all did.

– Yes, she replied aloud.

They, the youngsters, the aspiring climbers waited for her in the alley outside, like she had expected. She gave them a cursory glance, shrugging

deliberately. They stared at her, taking her measure with flickering eyes.
– Greetings, Forsaken, one of them, a sullen girl called out, snarled at her.
– Call me Afterglow.
She waited, knowing fully well that she could have stopped this before it began, but she wanted this. The realization that was not a realization hit her softly. So she waited.
They rushed her. One of the boys attempted to confuse her, to snare her in his spectacle of mist and shadow filing from his hands and eyes. She saw right through his pitiful effort at illusion, shook it off without trying. Waves fired from her hands hit him hard and pushed him at the wall, breaking at least two of his ribs. She took out the others with her physical body. They were slow and dull, but she still appreciated the contact between her hands and feet and their jaws and ribs and heads.
It did not last long, the pleasure passing her too briefly, as was so often the case.
She held up the girl, held her in a grip of body and mind, and her catch stopped struggling almost instantaneously.
– You will serve me every time I come here, she commanded curtly. – You will be respectful and humble, or I will not be lenient, but send you straight to the Wasteland. Your Master is no longer your Master. I am! *Do you understand?*
– Yes, Afterglow. The girl nodded, timid and shaken to her core. – Lola understands and she will convey everything to her former Master, give him your message, doing her best to make him understand as well.
She let go of the girl. Hopefully the waif would succeed in completing the message before her «master» made mincemeat of her.
The girl stood there, curtseying with a bowed head, and Afterglow knew she felt pride, pride over the fact that Afterglow had chosen her, no matter how difficult her life would be as a result.
Afterglow left, making an effort at bringing with her everything of herself that had stayed in this place for so long.
She walked through town, very conscious of where she was going, seeing the maze she walked from above. The night air had become dry, with the occasional spell of mist. She walked in circles, in eclipses, heading nowhere.
The joint Lysande/Park estate pointed to itself when her walk brought her to the eastern hillside. She sensed hectic activity inside. It was not hard. She sensed it as the counterpoint it had become to the Rosen/Maximus fortifications at the opposite side of the twin cities.
This place beckoned her, even as the other repelled her. She moved on.
The archipelago sea twinkled in the summer twilight. It stretched out, to

the south, to Auburn, the city of her birth and adolescence, and The Island. The Island's presence smothered her, even from the considerable distance.

– There is no escape, Cathy, Bea told her. – There never will be.

Afterglow turned, but Bea was not there.

A man stopped at the opposite corner, his attention clearly fixated on her. He started… hooting like an owl. The chilling sound jumped from his open mouth in completely even intervals.

People stared distraught at the eerie sight and hurried away.

Afterglow laughed short and sharp and turned her back to the man in utter contempt.

The man scowled at her and charged her. She did not seem to notice, not until the last moment, when he raised the knife he clutched in his right hand, ready to plunge it into her body. She turned like a whirlwind, grabbed his arm and broke it in one swift move. The knife fell from his weak hand. One brutal strike in his abdomen made blood flow from his still open mouth, where the sinister sound had once originated.

– It is easier to kill you than to let you live, she told him.

She dropped him. He fell and hit the ground, his weakened legs unable to carry him.

He remained there, on the sidewalk, unable to more than groan and twist.

– That was so impressive.

A girl rushed forward.

– It was not, Afterglow shrugged.

– Will you teach me?

– I might, Kathryn said. – But I do not teach a novice. You will have to learn the basics first.

– I will, the girl cried after her, as she walked away. – I will!

Kathryn walked alone again.

– Good girl, she mumbled.

None of the people present at the previous scene attempted to follow her, even from a distance. She noted that easily. None of the pedestrians surrounding her had the same peculiar or similar energy-signature as her poor assailant. She remained alert.

And relaxed, even as she stayed alert, as she made her way through the maze of the modern city, as it revealed itself to her.

Somewhere, somewhere in the streets below, Stane bartered his newspapers, drew to him ever more needy souls, growing more powerful with each trade, his trail of victims growing longer and longer, all of them staying with him, sustaining and empowering him, and he grew to a giant in her eyes. He, one of many on a long list lingered at, tickled the back of her mind.

She did sense movement, one specific to her, and stopped and turned.

Joan Reston, still tall and muscular stood five steps away from her. Kathryn recognized her across yet another gulf of years.

– You have become so effective, the magistrate shook her head, - such a lethal creature. No one even approaching ordinary stands a chance against you.

– You did not follow me tonight, did you, Afterglow mused, - after all those years?

– No, the other replied, - it was more of a coincidence. I was on my way to your place, in order to inform you that Caroline is ready for you, ready to fulfill her age-old obligations.

The catching in the woman's throat was not instantly recognizable, not to others, but to Afterglow it was.

– Look at you, Joan choked. – You have become so strong, so confident. You can take on the entire realm, now, if need be.

Kathryn wanted to say something, too, but she did not, holding back what was most of all in her thoughts.

Joan stepped close to her.

– I could not help you, all those years ago. I was charged with protecting you and I failed, but know that there is nothing, nothing I will not do to defend you, now.

– I was just a girl then, Afterglow said. – That girl has grown up long ago.

She briefly touched the other woman's jaw, an attempt at comfort. Then she turned around and walked away. She knew that Joan did not follow her.

Thunder cracked, as she made her way to her apartment, both above and beneath the ground, but there was no lightning. It was more powerful than she had experienced it in a long time.

The big clock on the wall to her right was late, as usual. It was always late.

But she still heard the heavy bells toll below.

They spoke of sorrow and the past and the future and power beyond comprehension, and she shuddered in the pocket of cold air briefly surrounding her.

People sat there, drinking their beer, unconcerned, or at least concerned with nothing but trivial matters. She felt like she was drowning in the choir of their loud voices. It was merely a few steps before she had put them behind her, but it felt much longer, as if she would never pass by them.

The entrance to her building awaited her in a fairly ordinary, nondescript alley, just a short walk from the people drinking beer.

She met Mrs. Galbraith on her way up the stairs, and ignored her, as she always did, like Mrs. Galbraith ignored her. Afterglow did not look back, even as she looked back, with the eyes at the back of the neck. There were the stairs, and when the stairs ended there was the elevator. She pushed the button and the door slid open, and she walked inside. There were no buttons inside, only a model of a handprint engraved in the wall. It lit up as she entered and the door slid close behind her. She pushed her palm at the print and the elevator shook, and moved upwards. It stopped and the doors slid open to her apartment. The magick wards she had put there were still in place. Everything remained exactly as she had left it.

Nothing disturbed the ether in her Place of Power. She would have known instantly if anything had, felt it far away, even beyond this world.

She found the wand where she had stashed it years ago. It felt good in her hand, the way she remembered it. A couple of swings were sufficient to make the old feeling return. A minute or two later it felt like she had never put it away.

There were no stairs to the roof, only the hatch in the ceiling opening at her mental command. She levitated up through it, pulled and pushed by the waves she formed around her body, into the shadows and mist of the early night. Words whispered in her ears as she moved, words she now knew by heart. Various teachers had hammered them into her, burned them into her mind's wall, until they stuck on her skin like a brand. She attacked the imaginary enemy ahead of her, struck at him or her without mercy or consideration. Every time she made a move against it that shadowy figure whispered words like curses in her ears.

The wand was like an extension of her body, her mind. This was the real thing, not the pale imitation, the lousy loan she had been offered on the airship. When she struck with it, it was like its point was her eyes and ears and senses. She felt so much bigger than her fairly small human frame, and her consciousness extended all over the vast roof.

Afterglow sat there, on the cold brick seat, looking at the city below and far away, soaking wet with sweat. The horizon was still filled with a deep red sky, one she had learned to recognize through countless late awakenings. The night had always been her time. One piece of daylight did not change that.

And Jason was like a walking shadow, anyway, more than powerful enough to black out the strongest daylight. She had met him in her more vulnerable youth and he had shown her, brutally what reality was… what he was. He had, for his own perplexing reasons sought her out on several occasions since then, but she had never been able to look at him, or existence in quite the same way after that night.

The hand tightened around the wand and she rose, continuing her exercise, doubling, tripling her efforts, digging deep into herself, cutting herself open, welcoming the acid burn in her eyes, as sweat flowed from her skin and created a pool-like humidity on the roof's rough surface. She kept pushing herself, until she almost turned blind by the strain, until the thing, the eerie and wonderful and horrible glow within her had changed into an all-consuming flame devouring her, surrounding her like the vortex of the Crossroads.

She returned to the apartment, closing the hatch behind her. Her soaking wet clothes fell to the floor as she made her way to the shower. Her thick hair clung to her body, front and back. Breathing was still shallow, still burned in her throat. She caught her reflection in the mirror and stopped, looking startled at herself, at how changed she seemed.

Her skin tingled and burned when she showered. The increased sensitivity felt overwhelming each time yet another drop of water hit her. She gasped as water flooded her mouth and she hardly noticed it. The water stopped falling, as she turned all the four knobs in the large bathroom with her mind. She remained in there for a while, enjoying the initial sensation of the water drying on her body.

She stepped outside, reaching out a hand, making the towel dance in the air towards her. It felt easier, like the most casual act in the world. She stared into the mirror while drying, rubbing herself. Letters formed on the moist surface, forming words, first in an ancient dialect she could make out, could understand with an effort, than in modern words everyone would comprehend:

#¤39RF
dpnING
COMING
COMING FOR YOU
YOU
YOU
YOU
YOU

It slid off the mirror and started scratching on the carpet, reaching for her. She stood still. It reached her right foot, scratching, scratching at her skin. There was pain, as the skin was peeled off. She stood there, raising her left hand, curling it into a fist, and *pushed*. A howl of rage filled her ears, the entire room and made the air curl outside the apartment, and the presence dissolved and returned to whence it had come.

She looked at her foot, at the broken skin. The manifestation had drawn blood for the first time. It was growing stronger, steadily, and she feared, inevitably. Eventually it would be powerful enough to do just about anything.

Her feet paced the floor without the mind actually following. Her attention remained stuck at the now faded message on the mirror, in the mirror. In the mirror, in that Other World she glimpsed herself covered in blood, saw herself lick the blood from her hands while looking at her other self with glee in her eyes.

She focused on the advanced music box. The play-button looked like a pinprick from the opposite side of the room where she stopped and turned. She pushed the button with hard air, by solidifying the wave, collapsing it at precisely the right moment, and hard guitar riffs and drums, dark and moody music flooded the apartment and her sensitive ears and skin and bones and wide open mind.

The door to the secret compartment opened, slid open in more than one ominous way. She walked inside and the door closed behind her. The phone-answering machine turned itself on.

There was no voice at first, but a disquieting sound that Afterglow easily recognized as sobbing, sobbing and heavy breathing caused by a human being gasping in pain and fear. She recognized Allan Mortimer, her «manager» before he started speaking.

– I have been told to deliver a m-message, he said.

He wanted to say more, she knew he did, but before he managed to utter one more word or even a sound something that Afterglow knew was a knife cut into his flesh and gutted him from left to right, from low to high, and the loud screams began, and there was nothing except that, until she heard the sucking sound of the knife being pulled from flesh and the body hitting the floor.

– I hear you, she said aloud to the empty room.

The message had been delivered loud and clear.

There was no conscious decision on her part. She dressed slowly, not making haste in any way. The hissing sound in her head did not make her change her speed one way or another. She found her sword and put it and its sheath at its place on her back, hidden, easily accessible. That, too, fell easily in place there, like it had done in her hand, like the wand had done.

The streets passed her by as she moved through them. The bus stop on Ivy Avenue was empty. She waited for a few minutes before her transport arrived. Only a few seats were taken.

She went to Mortimer's home, a house outside the suburbs, outside the city limits. It took some time with the bus, even in the late evening light traffic, but she did not mind. She was not in a hurry.

Streets and people and cars and buildings on the northern road passed by outside, and it did not faze her, any more than figures in a bad painting would do. Her mind was not blank, it never was, but she sat there and let her thoughts drift, let them whirl through her head like the waves in the air always surrounding her.

Thoughts raced through her head and cut and sliced like razorblades.

The people on the bus seemed, if possible even more like carbon-copies of real people to her, totally oblivious to what was happening, what the world was, what a horror, what a glory it truly was.

And all of it was visible in the ever-shifting, indistinct face she glimpsed in the window mirror.

The house on the hill, at the end of a shingle road, a Victorian, fairly well-kept building had been surrounded by magistrates and yellow ribbons. They swarmed the entire private road up to the house in the hillside. She knew they covered all the four sides. Their positions were known to her by the mere blinking of eyes. She concentrated, focused her waves, her power inwards. It did not take much, and she faded away, turned invisible to those that would look at her. She walked inside. It was filled with more uniformed people and men and women of the sciences. She slipped between them like the ghost she had become.

Two… slaughters decorated the entrance hall, two of the very capable sentries and «ghost hunters» Afterglow had encountered at Mortimer's tavern not that long ago. They had been placed in what was clearly a ritualistic position.

The house had been infused with a perverted, overpowering mood she could not help but notice. She suspected even the most insensitive of those gathered here noticed beneath their calm surface. *Worry* surfaced in everybody's eyes. They knew, deep down that this was not an ordinary homicide.

She followed the scent to the place in the house where everybody's attention focused. To her it pointed to itself like a scar. It was the kitchen, quite the original twist, not the bedroom, as was usually the case with these kinds of ritualistic murders. Allan Mortimer had been served to his wife and children. He was stretched across the table with missing pieces of his flesh pushed into his wife and children's mouths. They, too, were stone cold dead, tied to their chairs, their throats cut, their empty eye-sockets staring straight at the opposite wall.

– This the entire family? The chief investigator asked his second in command.

– No, There is an adopted daughter, the niece of the deceased male. Her parents died years ago. She was recently released from the health station. We have not been able to get hold of her.

This had been done by a human being, and clearly not by something else. A vengeful spirit or anything similar would not have been this… orderly, but would have cut its victims to pieces in a cacophony of rage. This had been a deliberate act designed to evoke a specific effect, and had been done in cold hatred, with a slow burning purpose seething like ashes.

A woman crouched just like a little child and pushed the back of a hand at her lips. It quickly turned wet with small pieces of vomit. She had skipped dinner today, because she knew what the night would bring. Her colleagues hardly noticed her little indiscretion or had at least grown very good at hiding their keen eye.

Afterglow walked among them, but she stood apart, and would have done so even if she had been visible.

There was nothing for her here, not after she had walked through the building several times and studied every piece of information in the house, and committed it to memory. As she walked away, as she looked at the shocked and revolted faces surrounding her, she wondered, briefly, whether or not she was sad, angry or felt anything, anything at all. The other people here, both those in uniform or not, they saw things like this on a regular basis, but they still felt, still reacted, were still rocked to the deepest of their core.

To her it was merely writing on the wall. The message had been delivered loud and clear. That was all that mattered.

CHAPTER SIX

She walked back that night. Buses passed her on her way, and she could have caught any one of them, but she felt like walking.

Any dark alley or shadow between streetlights snarled at her, and she snarled back. She dared them silently to come for her, but they did not come.

She could have run, fast as the wind, but she walked, calm as a turtle, taking her time, biding her time, prolonging the pleasant walk.

There were long clusters of houses she had to pass by and between, in order to reach the central parts of the twin cities. The area was dead at night. A few lamps brightened the apartments, making the windows glow in a pale light, that was all. Aside from that everything was dead and still, like a cemetery. Except for the fact that these tombstones reached a little higher than they did on ordinary cemeteries there was no significant difference. These were suburbs, spots in urban areas where people were stored like sardines in a box, like dead and oiled sardines in a box. She twisted her lips in contempt.

The murmur reached her ears just like the moving shadows in the dark places registered in her mind, more than through her eyes. They were always there, for all people, but most people did not notice them, not like she did.

Somewhere deep in her very veins something was moving, whispering about the secret workings of the world.

Music reached her from an open window somewhere. It sounded distorted, even though she knew it was not supposed to be. She realized that the waves surrounding her, the presence in the air all around her emanated from her, and distorted any input seeking to reach her senses. It was the first time in eons she had been unable to control her powers. She simmered down with an effort, exposing herself, casting a challenging stare in every direction she turned, at whoever or whatever was watching.

An unknown woman, clearly an observer did watch her from a spot further down the road. Afterglow focused her senses yet another notch.

The music and noise of the slowly awakening city reached her with full force. It was loud and painful. She shook her head.

The woman had vanished, completely disappeared during the few moments Kathryn had been distracted.

A greater frequence of cars and buses began passing her on the road outside the sidewalk. There were still not that many of them, but they growled as they passed by, mostly on their way to the inner city, where offices and stores devoured people each and every day. Commuters yawned helplessly, desperately attempting to rouse themselves from their walking slumber, failing at every turn.

Afterglow walked on, astute to the point where she could sense everyone breathing and hear people's dull hearts beat.

The inner city's taller buildings rose slowly around her. She hardly noticed, not really seeing what others were seeing. The world was not unmoving buildings and dull eyes pretending to be moving, but a dance complex beyond imagining. She wanted to show them, show them the rain, the ashes and fire and dust, wanted it so bad.

Finally, after a walk seemingly endless, she passed the statues, the insane art. As always, they affected her in a multitude of ways, most of them impossible to identify or even approach in her mind. They seemed alive to her. They always did.

She did not take the usual route home from there, but chose a slight variation, a detour through smaller streets and narrow alleys. The… tension in the air had suddenly increased even further, and she found it prudent to at least attempt unpredictability. A man at the opposite side of the street waved his hand by his head, as if a fly was buzzing in his ear. That small act alone made her sense of anxiety grow further.

Alice sat on the stairs, clearly anxious, clearly determined. She brought with her a large bag, most certainly filled with all her perceived important belongings.

– Thank the fates, she said brightly. – I feared I would have to wait for you for days.

That told Afterglow more than the girl probably wanted to convey, and more. She had waited all night.

Alice looked remarkably good, a little pale perhaps, but evidently pretty much healed from her injuries and from what had surely been an ordeal. Afterglow did not say anything, but looked at her with a steady stare. Alice reddened.

– I survived, she said. – I have faced Death twice and come to claim my prize, my dark devours. I have no other place to go and I want this. I want it!

She was clearly nervous beyond the possible uneasiness confronting the older woman would bring and the stark horror last night had brought her. But the stubbornness beyond determination kept burning in her haunted eyes, her shaken self.

– Very well, then, Afterglow nodded. – I will teach you, will educate you in all tings mystical and transcendent, far more than you ever imagined, and you will no longer be the person you were, but a sorcerer fluent in all the horrors and pathways of existence.

Alice in Wonderland rose, shaking a bit, staring defiantly at the older woman.

Afterglow walked right past her and did not look back. Alice followed her quickly, like a bird fluttering her wings.

The room with the elevator looked besieged by shadows. Alice kept close to Afterglow.

Afterglow turned and stopped.

– You should not shy from the shadows, apprentice, but embrace them.

– Yes, Afterglow, the apprentice conceded eagerly and willingly.

She stepped away from her mentor's shadow, into the bigger pale shadow.

– You feel it, do you not, Kathryn hissed in her ears from far away, – feel the pain and glory and danger and joy?

– I do. Alice nodded. – I have always felt it. It used to frighten me, but it does not anymore.

– Of course it does.

Afterglow snarled and smiled condescending and cruel. Alice bowed her head.

– You trust me, do you not, cub? You will follow me through the Wastelands and beyond without question, without conscious thought?

– YES! Alice shouted.

– Stupid COW!

Afterglow slapped her, slapped her hard on the cheek, enough to make her fall. The girl looked at her with wide and wet eyes.

– You are still so innocent, Kathryn Caldwell said softly. – So trusting. Anyone can take advantage of you. They can do so *easily*.

– Like they did with Afterglow? Alice said equally softly. – Like she allowed herself to be used, to be crushed like a dry leaf in the storm?

The tall, imposing figure froze, for just an instant, before looking at the younger woman with her calm, acid stare.

– You will do exactly as I say. You will obey me to the latter, or I will punish you. You will wish you were dead, wish you were exiled to the wasteland.

Alice rose, her lips cold, her entire body numb.

– Yes, Afterglow. It will be as Afterglow says. Alice will strive, beyond striving to become worthy of the honor Afterglow has bestowed upon her.

Kathryn smiled, or attempted to. It felt more like another snarl. Alice followed in Afterglow's steps, in her cold slipstream. Afterglow sensed her fear. She sensed, in spite of it all her eagerness, her doglike gratitude for being accepted, acknowledged by a superior being.

They walked the stairs. The elevator rose into the air. Energy enshrouded Alice the moment she stepped into the living room. She gasped and crouched, before slowly straightening herself, looking at Afterglow through hazes of red and blue.

– A shield, a protective ward?

She spoke through tears slowly dissipating.

– If you had been of the Wasteland, or been corrupted by anything off this world you would have been incinerated on the spot.

Afterglow touched the other's cheek, not unkindly.

Alice looked around her, the wonder once again, in incredibly ways conquering her fear.

– But this, your Place of Power is not fully of this world either.

– No, apprentice, Afterglow acknowledged, – like me, it has one foot on each side of the veil.

Alice looked around her with excitement glowing in her eyes.

– Afterglow's Place of Power, she breathed, breathed hard, – I can not believe I am actually here.

She was an eager kid, looking for pretty baubles on the ground. A sting of pain hurt in Kathryn's chest.

– This is your Fortress of Solitude, Alice nodded, a catching in her throat, – where you retreat and plan your defense.

The girl understood… to a point. Afterglow found her wand, and another she threw to the apprentice. Alice caught it, a little clumsy.

– This is an extension of you, the only one that will ever matter. There will be no further teaching of dark arts before you master the witch's wand, master yourself.

The hatch opened, and she made the wave pull them both to the roof. Alice released a tiny cry of surprise and delight.

The city surrounding them grew around them, engulfed them. Afterglow circled the girl swinging the wand. Alice trembled, holding on to the wand to the point where her knuckles turned white.

– We will find your center, Afterglow said, – the place where your power rests. Do as I do. Follow my lead.

She moved, slowly in her eyes, a whirlwind to Alice. The girl's attempts at keeping up quickly proved themselves futile. Afterglow slowed down to a crawl, and the shadow followed.

– I had the advantage of extreme incentive when I learned this. You will have to go deep, far beyond mere innocent motivation to succeed. You will not leave this place otherwise, because without it you will surely perish out there. You have touched Afterglow's Shadow, and every single adept will recognize her mark on you.

– When they come I will be ready for them, Alice swore.

– Yes, you will!

She struck the girl's fair mouth. Blood flowed and Alice released a yelp of pain.

– Taste the blood. The hiss struck the girl like a thousand needles. – Know its flavor, its deepest secrets, and you will know yourself, know the world, and the world beyond.

They moved side by side, Afterglow with a burning confidence, Alice with blazing uncertainty smoldering in her gut.

– Do not move your wand. Move *with* it. As you move yourself, you move the wand. You and the wand are one.

– *One!* Alice breathed.

– Most people today attempt to move beyond their reach. The wand is your reach, the only manner in which you can extend your arms and feet.

– Wand, Alice mumbled. – Reach. One!

Afterglow did not sweat. Alice did. It poured from her brow and blinded her, its acid burning her eyes. Her arms felt like lead, and the breath stayed labored, even during the few and brief breaks. Afterglow struck her down. She fell and did not rise.

– On your feet! Afterglow commanded.

She dragged herself on her feet, and kept going. It felt like it went on forever. Finally, when the sky reddened in the horizon on a darkening sky Afterglow pulled back and returned them to the apartment. Alice felt like a child in her hands, in her mighty lap. Afterglow knew she did.

– Undress.

Afterglow studied her when she instantly obeyed, and feared that the girl would obey her no matter what her orders were, no matter how unreasonable they were.

Alice stood before the other woman, reddening again under Afterglow's relentless stare.

– Good, now hit the shower.

The girl ran to the shower and not long afterwards Afterglow heard the sound of the water, the relentless rain. She closed her eyes, and let them stay closed for a while, taking in the room, the space around her, sensing the fangs and claws scratching at the walls.

Alice returned, drying herself, not attempting to hide herself, stubbornly revealing her strong, muscular body. She had a few scars after her recent injuries and subsequent hospitalization, but they had already faded, and what remained would fade more or less completely in time.

Afterglow handed her a small flask with a greenish content.

– Rub this on your skin. It will make your muscles less fatigued tomorrow and will help us speed up your physical training.

Alice took the flask and began rubbing herself with the fluid. It was cold at first, but then it turned hot, very hot. Alice moaned a bit.

– You are not in bad shape, Afterglow told the girl. – You will not feel too bad tomorrow. Wait a few minutes after the oil has dried and you may dress, and start on the dinner.

Afterglow undressed, too, and walked to the shower. She felt Alice's eyes on her, felt them long after she had excited the room and the water rinsed her heated skin.

She did her usual routine when drying herself, but wished she had not when she once again saw how admiration and awe lit up Alice's eyes.

Alice had already started on the dinner. She worked fast and efficient, and it was not long before scents of spices and aromas filled the room and Afterglow's nostrils.

It turned dark outside. Alice, very much in tune with Afterglow's mood did not turn on the electrical lights, but lit the many candles in the room. She had removed the wet clothes and found new ones for Afterglow to wear. The clothes, too, fit the sorcerer's mood well.

They sat by the table, at an informal setting. Alice hardly took her eyes off Afterglow, even when she put the fork in her mouth.

– Does Afterglow find the food to her liking? The girl said humbly. – Is she pleased with her servant?

– You are not my servant, Afterglow replied and shrugged. – You are my apprentice, and apprentices do menial work.

The grin forced itself on her against her will.

– But Alice can cook, yes?

She could. Each bite Afterglow chewed brought sensation, brought memories. Afterglow was not certain she wanted more.

– Alice can do far more than cook, Afterglow said dryly. – She can do far more than cook food. It just needs to be pulled from her. She will open like a flower, and be tempered like steel.

The girl shuddered momentarily again, before her good natured mood once more reasserted herself, an incredible feat, especially considering what she had lived through last night.

– This is so exciting, she cried, missing a beat or six from her role as a humble apprentice, – I have wanted to seek you out earlier, to beg for your favors, but I never could work up the c-courage to do it, and now it is like a dark, dark fate brought me into Afterglow's grasp.

Her lips started shaking as she completed the sentence.

– It is true. You might never have sought out destiny if it had not sought out you, but no matter the reason, you were not ready then. You had not experienced death and blood and darkness, like you have now twice over.

Stark fear revisited Alice's face.

– I saw them, she whispered, – but I could not stay, I just could not.

Kathryn re-experienced, like she did the images of her aunt and uncle and siblings, their glaring eyes and butchered flesh.

– Soon you will be able to stare Death in the eye without blinking, apprentice.

The girl bowed her head in humble deference and acknowledgement, in shame and both prevailing horror and numbness.

The seconds passed in silence, while Afterglow waited, dreading what was to come.

– But you had not either. But you still learned.

– It was practically beaten into me, the sorcerer said icily. – I learned blow by blow, stab by stab. You do not want to learn the way I did, apprentice.

Alice pulled back, visibly.

– I am sorry, she whimpered. – Alice is *sorry!*

– It is all right, Afterglow breathed. – It is all right.

Alice crawled close to Afterglow, half onto her lap, so needy and vulnerable and Afterglow comforted her, rubbed her, like she would a pet, and Alice's close proximity was strangely comforting to her, as well.

– Allan Mortimer was my uncle, Alice stated suddenly, as if revealing a secret. – But he hardly behaved like kin. He was my legal guardian, and wanted to keep me away from Magick, keeping me away from my birthright. Only thanks to my grandmother I managed to learn much of anything. She taught me the basics, though far too little to be of any real use, before she died. He did not want to have anything to do with anything even resembling magick, but he lost his day job and was forced to take over the job as broker from my grandmother. There is a long tradition of what grandmother called «our heritage» in the family, but he ruined it with his insane skepticism and ignorance and fear, and it returned and bit him in the ass.

There was passion, both guilt and anger in her voice and tear-wet eyes.

– He sent Cochran, his most inexperienced operative on a dangerous mission, Afterglow mused, – and when Cochran failed miserably and catastrophically, as expected he still sent his dear, untrained niece. He was some piece of work all right.

– You scared him shitless, the girl shrugged. – I wanted to go and told him so, practically begged him. His fear, or/and his greed eventually conquered his intolerance. Some epitaph, I guess.

– Did you sense anything before it happened? Afterglow asked her lightly,

and fooled no one.
– No. Alice shook her head. – But I was not there until after it had happened. The magistrates showed me all of them, so fucking kind and considerate, and after they had taken my statement I came right here. I am the last in my line, just like you are the last in yours, and we are even the lucky ones. Many families, like my uncle are even more successful in keeping the youngest in their line from reaching their potential. Sorcerers, the doers and makers of Magick are a dying breed in this modern age.
Alice was bright, enigmatic and enduringly passionate. Her words created a string of emotions in Afterglow's mind.
– Come, Afterglow suggested, – let us stretch a little, or you will be an unmoving statue tomorrow.
– Kind Afterglow, Alice stated solemnly, rising eagerly, readily.
Afterglow ignored her statement and began her ballet-like exercise. The student did her best to follow her moves. Afterglow turned on music, and it became easier. Everything seemed to flow, from one moment to the next. They danced, and stiff muscles loosened up again.
– I love how you push the button, Alice breathed. – It happens so effortlessly, as if you had used your finger.
– We will find your button, too, the other said, – find out what makes you tick, what is lurking deep beneath that pleasant shell of yours.
– We will! The girl declared excitedly.
Outside, birds were shrieking, were singing their horrible and beautiful song. She listened to it, distracted and attracted and
Afterglow slapped her, not hard, but hard enough to make her stagger backwards and almost fall. Alice froze and looked at the sorcerer with a wounded, stubborn look in her wet eyes.
– You warned me, she whined, – and I still did not get it. I am so foolish, such a silly girl.
She dried a tear from her eye.
– When I did not do it right my master beat me, Afterglow nodded. – Consider yourself fortunate you will not need to repeat my lessons, at least not in my care.
– I can fight, Alice glared at her. – Uncle made me take lessons in Sardone, and I have the broadest belt.
Sardone was the world's best known self defense system. It had originated in the East thousands of years ago.
She attacked and did so savagely. A silent snarl accompanied every thrust and kick and strike. Afterglow avoided it easily, before finally, after several minutes giving her another slap on the cheek. This time it was hard, hard

enough to send the apprentice sprawling across the floor.

Afterglow towered above her.

– Get up!

Alice shook her head in an attempt to clear it.

– Do you taste it? Afterglow asked her.

– What?

Can you taste the blood in your mouth?

She could. Of course she could. It was salty and tasty and…

– Yes, she whispered.

The slap had broken something in there, and caused blood to fill the cavity. The dizziness almost overwhelmed her. Afterglow felt it, felt her.

– You are *inside* me, Alice whispered.

– My senses are fine-tuned through years of practice and desperate need, and work both ways, the teacher taught her. – So will yours. But that is not it, is not what you are, and that is what we will truly be seeking and exploring, and when we find your center we will also find your power, your birthright.

They circled each other, Alice choking focused and angry, Afterglow loose and relaxed. The dance began. Now, the dance began. Kathryn purposely held herself back, held herself in check. As Alice increased her efforts it was as if Afterglow saw her movements in slow motion, increasingly so as she noticed how the blood flowed faster through her veins, and her Hunger grew, the vast and terrible thing inside her. It was still there, after all these years.

– You will not always have time to prepare a spell, apprentice, she stated, attempting to be gentle, but it still sounded like a snarl to her. – You need an edge, more than one actually. You need to be able to be at your *best* at any given time.

She struck the other's jaw, with her fist this time. Alice fell, looking up through a red haze, once more the sweet taste of blood filling her mouth. Afterglow towered even taller above her.

– To be able to hurt, maim and kill without hesitation and mercy.

Alice was up again in a whiff.

– We are bound you and I, having shared the blue flame, the fire of souls. Our destinies will always be linked, linked for all time.

Kathryn heard it, her own words in the girl's nebulous mind, heard it echo in there, as it was hammered into the fragile psyche, strengthening it like a wound. She sensed the first signs of resentment in the other's boiling mind, and nodded content to herself.

– For what it is worth Alice is clearly a tough kid. She has lived through more horrors lately than most others do during a lifetime.

– Afterglow is kind to Alice, the girl said. – She does not need to be.

– Alice may even be too tough for her own good…

Afterglow grumbled.

And Alice bowed her head in acknowledgment and acquiescence.

The bell in the harbor struck midnight, late as ever. The grown woman heard it without hearing it. With the soundless sound came the impressions of the city at night, and beyond. The apprentice noticed it as well, because Afterglow the Sorcerer did. She dared a glance at the older woman, but there was not really anything to see there, except the stoic, expressionless face.

Birds kept screeching outside, sounding like they were inside. They flapped their wings, and feathers dropped from the roof and fell to the far street below. Black eyes fixed their stare at the sorcerer and would-be sorcerer as they moved and fought.

Down on the street a man stood still and watched the building. Afterglow saw him, and therefore Alice did as well.

- … Jason? Alice spoke slowly, dreamily. – Al'rahan Am…

Her eyes turned wide and deep. She renewed her efforts.

The exercise continued, on and on and on, beyond pain, beyond exhaustion, beyond anything, except the need to fight off the hurting of the punishment dished out.

The man had vanished from the spot below, but they still sensed him in the wind, in the birds' screech and flapping of wings.

It finally ended, somewhat, hours later, temporarily, as it had begun, in the red haze of pain and boiling blood. Alice kept exercising, virtually automatically, without thought, kept moving her body, bending her limbs. Afterglow handed her a glass of lemonade, and she drank it empty in a whiff, a flash of time. She undressed and began drying herself with the towel.

– You will not shower this time. You will sleep with the scent of your own body juices in your nostrils, and you will learn to appreciate them and yourself for what they are, what you are. What are you, tiny speck?

The girl struggled with the answer, attempting to speak, but no words came to her, no glimmer of understanding appeared in her muddled mind, and she bowed her head in deference to the teacher.

– You will sleep on the floor.

– What about the couch? Alice tried, a typical response from a bored teenager.

– You will sleep on the floor by my bed. And if anyone or anything comes for me they will take you first. You are my watchdog. It is your sacred duty to protect your Master.

The icy stare froze the girl completely. She stood still, unmoving for a long time. Afterglow had disappeared into the bedroom when she finally mustered the will to follow.

The shadows in there welcomed Afterglow. There were no candles here. She did not really need them, did not need them to see.

She undressed and went to bed, stretching out, slowly smiling, and thoroughly enjoying herself under the blanket. The dog lay down on the carpet. She knew that, even though she did not actually see it with her closed eyes. But she sensed the young one's life force, pulsing, waxing and waning, waxing and waning in the dark.

– Alice is in awe of her master, the girl's childish voice reached her from the floor.

– I know, but you will get over it. You better!

The wind whined outside and also made itself known in the relative silence inside. It never turned completely quiet.

Sleep came to them both. She sensed it, how the young one's distress grew with the catching in her throat, how exhaustion slowly overcame her and she just fell into dreams and a restless but deep sleep.

The sorcerer's dreams spilled over into the other, making her moan in the grip of the night terrors striking her, engulfing her. The lessons continued and kept hammering her. There was no rest, only what might be called a brief respite from the whip hitting both her sore skin and equally wounded and vulnerable mind.

It was dark outside when Afterglow opened her eyes, when they slid open without blinking. Except for the light from the city itself only the narrow red line was visible in the horizon. It was always dark.

She kicked the body on the floor, not hard, but enough to startle and wake up abruptly the sweet, young thing. Alice jumped on her feet, moaning as her sore muscles strained to work, looking disoriented around her, before finally locking her eyes on Afterglow.

– Make breakfast, the sharp voice thundered in her ears.

– At once, Master!

The girl hurried to the kitchen without looking back, stumbling more than she ran or even walked. Afterglow took her time dressing, skipping the shower. She entered the kitchen. The servant was making breakfast quickly and efficiently, making sandwiches and scrambling eggs.

– You did not dress? Afterglow mused. – Very good. I did not tell you to.

Alice did not reply, but kept doing her chores in silence. She set the table with great skill. Afterglow hardly noticed the tiniest little shaking of her hands.

– Breakfast is ready, Master, the pleasant girl stated solemnly and subservient.

– Very good! By all means, let us begin.

Afterglow sat down, and waiting until she had settled on her chair, Alice joined her. Afterglow began feeding, and so, a little later did her servant.

Then, after a while the girl looked up with a sullen, hateful look.

– You are cruel, Alice whimpered and spat, her right hand shaking so hard, holding so hard around the fork that its skin turned swollen and red. – I did not think you would be cruel.

– Of course I am cruel, the older woman shrugged. – Why should I not be? You are beneath me, so far beneath me that you can not even behold my face without trembling.

– What *happened* tonight? I felt your dreams. What did you do to me?

– I did not do anything, little feather, except allowing nature to run its course. My superior might simply overpowered your mind, imprinting my thoughts on your feeble consciousness. The longer you spend in my company the more suited to me and my needs you will be.

– You are lying through your teeth, *master!* Alice spat enraged, eerily calm.

– Why do you not leave, Afterglow suggested calmly, strangely ambivalent. – There is nothing for you here.

– No! A hand struck the table in a controlled, very controlled manner, her face like twisted in a vice. – Damn you, there is everything for me here, and I am gonna have it even if I have to pull it out of me with a knife.

– So you will! Afterglow stated simply.

And Alice was thunderstruck again, frozen again, turned to stone by the gorgon eyes of the sorcerer.

The wands flew through the air, back and forth, meeting and parting, hitting flesh, drawing blood, turning the girl's vision deep red, blurring reality. It was raining, up there on the roof. Afterglow did not feel it. She was attuned to the girl, and the whirling waves of her own power in ways she had not been for a while. Afterglow felt things she had hardly felt.

Alice fed. Her Hunger almost devoured her. Every single cell in her body screamed for sustenance, for nourishment to possibly still the Hunger.

In vain.

– You will be a warrior witch, Afterglow told her. – You will be able to use your powers, physically and mentally at a moment's notice, and protect yourself from harm, from almost anything the world throws at you.

She advanced again, stepping up the speed of the attack, and Alice was struck to the ground.

The girl lay on the table, blue and black and hurting all over. Afterglow was giving her massage, and pulling no punches.

– Almost..? She gasped.
– Yes, apprentice, there are no guarantees. There will always be forces one might not be able to defend against.
A tear formed in the corner of Alice's eye.
– But it hurts so much. Why, why must it hurt so much?
Afterglow knew she was not speaking about the physical pain, but about the brutality she was subjected to, what it did to her, how it hardened her.
– Pain is a good teacher, especially for a sweet thing like Alice in Wonderland. The best. Even though it can never prepare you fully for what might await you out there, for life itself, for the heart-wrenching pain that subjects you to.
– Like with big, bad Afterglow? Alice countered, in a moment of spite, her innocent expression cracking and exposing the hatred beneath.
Afterglow did not comment on it, but kept cracking and molding the clay in her hands.
– I am sorry. Alice is sorry.
– There is no need, Afterglow shrugged. – Never be sorry. Never!
Dreams were unending images and sensations of nightmares, of twisted features. Alice's body turned taut and muscular, and she moved with increasing confidence and lethal determination. Afterglow had to work harder to overpower her, and she did. Sweat began pouring from her skin as well. Alice began getting pointers, and even stinging strikes.
Afterglow struck her, making her fall, and hit her on her way down, in a whirlwind of movement. Alice lay still for a moment, too dizzy to move. Afterglow stepped back. Alice fought herself on her feet. Afterglow brought them back down into the aerie. The day of sleep felt like such a brief recess. It felt like seconds before they were back at it. The whirling wands distorted the air, the very reality once again.
– Feel! Afterglow hissed at her. – Go Deep! Draw strength from your very core, from what is making you breathe, play and live.
The words sounded strange in her ears, as if she had to taste them, consider them before speaking them.
Ever more powerful images, sensations caught them both and shook them, shook them hard, fading only with the greatest of efforts on Kathryn's part.
Time passed. Days and nights fled in blurs of red and mist. How many they could not say. Both lost all sense of time. Afterglow went outside now and then to fetch provisions, but the apprentice never did, not once.
The few trips outside felt like a dream, even more than the nights inside and she was never completely certain that the concrete under her feet and the stench of pollution in her nostrils were real.

She walked to the grocery store down the street. Usually it was the right one, the one Kathryn remembered fondly from her daily excursions, but sometime… sometimes…

It changed into something ugly and horrible. Everything looked wrong, everything felt bad.

She was heavy with child and it scratched her insides with cruel claws. Everybody she met looked at her with condemning eyes. Only her master looked at her with kind, encouraging eyes and that frightened her most of all.

The maze battered her, Malone battered her. He had bound her and made a noose that tightened around her neck. She frowned in despair. The maze, the maze he had made in her mind surrounded her and she could not find her way. His face had been concealed. She was unable to see its features, but she knew it was him. Every time he raised his stick and hit her skin she knew he held her reins. She begged him with a soundless voice to release her, but he never did.

Afterglow woke up one night, soaked in sweat. Her apprentice, being attuned to her did as well.

– What was that? Alice cried. – What is wrong?

– Nothing, nothing is wrong.

Afterglow sat there, with her legs pulled up, rocking back and forth, her long hair glued to her skin.

– Something is wrong, the girl insisted. – I felt it, I felt… you. I felt you. These things I see, this foul taste in my mouth…

There was no reply, no vocal response to Alice's statement.

– My Goddess, these are your memories, are they not? And I thought that *my* initiation was hard, something the Master did to punish me for my negligence. Afterglow was absolutely right. Alice is just a silly girl, pretending to be an adept.

– This should not have happened, the woman on the bed said, mumbled, with her head half turned away. – I have let it slide lately, have not kept myself in shape and I have lost my edge.

She rose. Alice rose, too, standing straight. Afterglow once more turned hard and distant.

– I came by my power naturally. Without yours you are even more vulnerable out there. My Master did not have to probe very hard for me to access it. Yours are buried deeper and does indeed need to be pulled out of you, like a heart.

Alice shivered when she followed the ominous figure. They sat down on the floor, opposite each other.

– You are ready. You will never be more ready. Are you ready, little sweet girl?

– Yes, Alice is ready, ready for whatever Afterglow desires of her.

– Focus then. A sorcerer brings out what is within. Do so!

They both sat there, with their feet crossed in front. Alice started breathing, breathing more evenly as the seconds passed. She had learned meditation at an early age. Going deep within herself was second nature to her.

Afterglow slapped her on her cheek. Alice froze and stared at the other with shock and incredulity in her eyes.

– Go *deep!*

Alice attempted to gather herself, to start breathing again. Afterglow gave her another stinging slap on her cheek. Tears sprung from Alice's eyes, not so much in pain, as in humiliation and despair.

– You do not have to do this. I will do it, will go deep.

Afterglow slapped her, again and again, at uneven intervals, as the minutes and hours passed by. At some point the girl got a distant look in her eyes, and just sat there, hardly even reacting anymore when the open hand hit her cheek.

She blinked once, twice, slowly, slowing down, as the world stopped around them. Afterglow found water and gave her, but Afterglow did not move.

But yet she did.

It was not mere water, but a bitter elixir burning like acid on Alice's lips and tongue and throat, and in her stomach, as it heated her veins, and numbed her body.

They sat there naked, exposed.

– The invisible blade cuts us, Afterglow intoned.

– The invisible blade cuts us, Alice repeated drowsily.

Afterglow felt the girl slip away and she followed her.

– It is us. We open ourselves, and the world fills the Void.

And the echo echoed the words in the Void.

Afterglow followed the neophyte there, re-experiencing what was so familiar and yet so different from the path she had once walked. The bluish glow surrounded them, as they walked through a dark cave. Light blue turned dark. Alice moaned.

They had walked forever. They walked forever.

The girl crouched on her side in a stupor, moaning and writhing on the cold carpet.

– I found this after I had been initiated.

(Afterglow cried in the Void)

– I found truth, but I also found deceit and horror, and did not realize what

I had found until it was too late.

– But *she* knew, Alice said in a dead voice. – You had two teachers, and they both betrayed you. He taught you the bitter taste of ambition and she of malicious pleasure.

Kathryn shook, and could not stop shaking.

– Should we not eat soon? The girl whined. – I am hungry, so very hungry.

The cruel creature slapped her. She felt the slap's sting a thousand times, and she cried out in despair.

– You do not have to do this. Please do not do this.

– What are you talking about? The nourishment, the table filled with the most delicious nourishment is right there, at your fingertips. Replenish yourself or *die,* silly girl.

Alice blinked, ever so slowly. The moon… the moon rose inside a cave, opening it up to the world.

A woman stood there, radiant and joyful.

– Who is that? The girl wondered.

– That is sweet, lethal Beatrice. If you behold her pretty face run, run for your life and self.

Kathryn crouched in shame, in boundless indignity, her face changing, shifting.

Alice crouched on the carpet, spent, exhausted beyond belief.

– On your feet! Big, bad Afterglow bade her.

On shaky feet she stood, with shivering lips she attempted to speak.

– I am so tired, Alice whimpered. – I can not go on.

– You do not know what tired is, spoiled girl.

Sleep is not sleep, is not rest, until you have found the treasure of your soul. For you it is a spirit quest. For me a Journey, but it is basically the same, and it is different for each person, every time.

And then a draft pulled through the cave and sounds formed syllables, formed words.

The Nine were born in the land of the moon.

Both figures halted in their tracks and tilted their head, attempting to catch the voice in the wind.

Afterglow dragged Alice with her across the floor, into the concealed room at the center of the apartment. The door, the wall slammed shut.

– This is your prison, until you decide it is not. I will keep you here, keep my trophy forever. It is up to you, apprentice to free yourself from your chains.

Ropes appeared in Afterglow's hands. Alice gasped and wanted to run, crawl away, but she was frozen on her spot, tangled in a sticky web and could not move. Afterglow tightened a loop around her neck and fastened the rope to a ring on the wall. Alice wanted to remove it, but she could not raise her hands.

– You are weak as a newborn because you are a newborn, the voice in the darkness told her. – You must learn to walk on your own or stay forever a child. I can not carry you. No one can.

The fasting, the hunger made Afterglow, made them both lightheaded. Afterglow felt it, felt herself crumble, and she blinked slowly, like when falling asleep.

A figure appeared before them in the moonlit cave.

It is really quite simple, the apparition said. Release the hand around your throat. Pull out the dagger piercing your heart. It is that simple. Do this and you will no longer see the world through narrow chinks of your cavern, but as it truly is: *infinite.*

Alice reached for it, and it faded away.

– No, she cried. – NO!

She crumbled and collapsed in tears.

Afterglow sat there with an astounded look on her face.

Alice curled her left hand into a fist.

Afterglow was pulled away, like Alice was pulled away, pulled apart, and they were alone, the way they were supposed to be, and Kathryn felt the girl's apprehension, as familiar as her own. Blue lips glowed in the darkness. Afterglow saw her face appear slowly in the mirror image, pulled away from everything she had known.

Blue fire was reaching into the darkness. She felt it probe her, tear her apart. He had split her open and filled her with fire, and left only ashes. She fell and hit the floor hard. Her eyes split open. The cave was no longer a cave, but an open landscape, a yard outside an old house, and she recognized it, recognized the place like the back of her hand. The land of the moon filled her up and left a warm, warm stream of water inside, and she felt like crying.

She witnessed how the girl rose up, half on her knees, further, how she reached out with her hand, and how it glowed and how the glow expanded, and the sizzling energy surrounded everything in the room and slowly fried Afterglow in its beyond powerful blaze.

CHAPTER SEVEN

The excited, spirited girl moved easily and with newfound confidence with the wand in her hands.

– It feels so great, she cried, – so different from last time.

Her hands sparkled and the energy flowed into the wand and was released when the advance missed Afterglow and hit the brick wall behind. The power had manifested itself, and it was a sight to behold, but most of all it was visible in her eyes and stance. She looked so happy and carefree, so free of constraints.

Afterglow struck her down, pushing the waves at her, keeping her from using her energy power in a wide blast against the attacker.

She dried blood from her mouth, her eyes still bright and shiny.

– Alice has taken a major leap forward in her studies, Afterglow commented dryly, – but she should be aware that she still has a long way to go and before learning not to rely on her newfound power.

The girl rose, straightened and bowed her head in deference.

– Alice is so grateful for what Afterglow has taught her, and looks forward to learn far more of her wisdom.

She is overdoing it.

– It is time then, for the sorcerer and her apprentice to continue The Long Walk, Afterglow stated dryly.

She showered first, as always, and allowed Alice to do so afterwards.

They dressed, both in «formal» attire, the hood and cloak and robe of the sorcerer. Afterglow had not used it since the apprentice had begun her training and felt strange using it. Alice put it on with usual, youthful exuberance.

– Yes, Afterglow acknowledged to the other's silent query. – We will stand out, but it is far more important than not to stand out where we are going.

And it will hide the bruises, she thought.

She felt the building as they moved down it, as they moved outside, slipped from its grasp.

They walked the streets, leaving the harbor with its taverns and bards. The city after midnight was a more open, vibrant place, where people accepted more and stared less than they would do during daylight. Alice looked around her with wonder in her eyes, even more so than she usually did.

– It feels so strange, she said in awe. – It has not been that long since I have been outside, has it, even though I experienced it that way, but it sure comes off as different, so different from what I remember.

– The world has not changed, but you have.
And the kid ate it up.
Ivy Avenue seemed exactly as busy as it always did. They walked past the long, long row of sinister statues and dark art. It spoke to Afterglow and also to her clearly more timid apprentice.
They reached a corner where a powerful draft pushed and pulled in everybody passing by.
– The wind is blowing here, a woman said. – It is always blowing here.
The two in hood and cloak walked to the top of the slight rise, to the next corner, and as they passed a certain point the wind… stopped. Alice looked attentive at the sorcerer, fascinated beyond words.
– It is just a tiny opening we must fit through, Afterglow explained. – Walk directly in my path.
She walked back and the wind caught her, and she allowed herself to be pulled towards the faint glow. Alice, walking right behind her saw how she vanished into thin air, a moment before the girl, too was pulled inside the hole in the air.
There was a moment of darkness, of shadow, and they found themselves in a completely different setting, at a top of a mountain peak. A vast valley stretched out below. Alice swayed, overcome by momentary dizziness, and in the grip of the wind coming from all sides.
– Wow! She cried. – That was awesome. *Awesome!*
She hesitated a bit, before her thirst for knowledge got the best of her.
– Was that… the Crossroads? The sorcerer to be asked in awe.
– No, this is merely a local portal. Except by… beyond powerful beings the Crossroads can usually only be accessed at the edges of the nine realms, and very few can travel it without being ripped apart. It takes both power and skill and experience to navigate it with a modicum of control, without being… lost. These local portals take you to one set destination and no more. Of course people without knowledge of them being accidentally pulled trough will have no idea what happened and will be lost, too.
– We can not step back the way we came… can we?
She waved her hand in the air, at what to Afterglow was a pale glowing afterimage of the portal they had passed through, but except for that there was nothing there.
– No. A firm headshake. – That path is lost to us. These portals are, generally speaking one-way only. To return to the place fairly close to where we came from we must walk a completely different path.
Something, what looked like a large airship wreck burned some distance away. Wreckage had been unevenly distributed over a considerable area.

Smoke rose thick and black.

There was a trail, fairly visible, leading down the mountain. It was steep, but not inherently dangerous, at least not if one did not get distracted.

– So, where are we?

– What the books at school would tell you is the mythical land of Arubal, in the equally mythical realm of Balakor. You are welcome, I am sure…

– No real-estate developers have come this way and made an impression on anything, Alice grinned. – Thank the Goddess!

The ground of the trail was dry, in spite of the green grass and growth around them and all over the valley. Dust rose every time they took a step. Afterglow attempted to avoid whirling it up, but it was both on and off the trail, and she gave up and shrugged.

– This is of greatest importance, she impressed upon the other. – Sorcerers are feared here, but not respected. If we should encounter anyone, you will not speak, not a single word or syllable, and you will do exactly as I say, no matter what it is.

– It will be as Afterglow commands, the apprentice replied shaken.

They reached the valley below. The trail expanded and turned into a road. There was an intersection right ahead, the road going in both directions from there. It was narrow, clearly made for wagons, for coach and horses. There were no made roads or anything like that, but treks created by ongoing traveling. Afterglow turned left, and they headed what Alice surmised was north, based on the sun's position.

– So, how does Afterglow find the portals? Alice asked, still in her respectful mode.

– There are several ways. Others may guide you to them, of course, and you memorize their position, but eventually you learn to spot them by the slight glow they emanate, even in the brightest day.

The plane wreck burned on their right. They strayed off course a bit, to investigate. The crash had been «light». Most of the plane was still intact, even though some parts had split from the main body. There were mangled bodies all over the place, a lot of blood spread around. Alice pushed a hand at her mouth. Afterglow looked totally calm and unshaken.

– Are there any…

– No survivors, Afterglow confirmed.

The bodies were still warm, but rapidly cooling, creating clouds of mist in the completely still air.

– I do not understand. Where did it come from? It had to be a large portal.

– Another portal. Afterglow made an effort, somewhat, to ease the young one's distress. – And size does not really enter into it. Under the right

circumstances any object, no matter its size could pass through a portal.
She looked slightly to the south, and there the newly used portal glowed or rather glimmered under a sky covered in light clouds.
– The airship does not look like any I have ever seen before. Alice kept talking in a nervous, excited way. – It is mostly… metal is it not?
– It is from the Fifth Realm, Afterglow told her. – They have lots of metal airships there.
Alice smiled a bit then.
– Is there anything Afterglow does not know? She joked.
The reply came swiftly, after just a tiny bit of hesitation.
– Yes!
Dust rose in the horizon in the north. It started as a tiny disturbance, but as they waited it grew to a dustbin surrounding a coach and horses, and a number of riders. They heard its noise eventually, as it roared closer.
– The shadows of the dead linger in pain and confusion, Alice whimpered.
– They do, Afterglow confirmed. – They did not know themselves while they were coated in flesh, and have now woken up in completely unfamiliar surroundings. Without help they will linger for a long time.
Alice wanted to say more, but Afterglow stopped her with a movement of the hand.
The riders and the coach and horses stopped about twenty steps away, in a slowly dissipating cloud of dust.
– I know of the man inside, Afterglow said, – a so called «nobleman», one dabbling in magick and unknown phenomena such as this. He stays inside. How very sensible of him.
The eyes of the riders stared at them in cruelty and anticipation.
– Tell them that they are not wanted here, Afterglow told the apprentice.
– GO AWAY! Alice cried. – YOU ARE NOT WANTED HERE! MY GREAT MASTER AFTERGLOW WANTS YOU OUT OF HER SIGHT.
The name meant something to them. The riders hesitated even more and glanced at the man inside the wagon. There was a sharp command and they dismounted the horses.
– Point at them, Afterglow commanded.
Alice did not hesitate.
– Fire!
The air crackled with power, as the energy emanating from the girl's hand hit men and horses alike, and all living beings fell to the ground. Not everybody lost consciousness. Men writhed on the ground. Some horses ran off. Afterglow walked among the suffering men, and gave them brutal kicks.
– You did not listen. She spoke softly to them, whispering in their ears

with her dread voice. – You never listen. But know this: The next time you encounter Afterglow or even suspect you are doing so… you run. Do you understand?

She spoke to the man inside the wagon, the man mighty enough to make the ground shake under his feet.

– Y-yes, he gasped, hardly able to speak, the searing pain visible in his face.

– Run, now, all of you. Those of you able to walk will carry those who are not. I want you out of my sight.

He dried blood from his forehead, while desperately attempting to make his electrocuted body work. It took five, ten seconds, but he finally practically fell out and hit the ground.

– You will give this warning to everybody. Tell them to *stay away* from the relics of other worlds. They, like the forest are off-limits to you all.

They ran and stumbled away, reeling under the weight they were carrying, leaving behind horses and coach and horses, and stuff that would slow them down, like armor and weapons.

Alice fell to her knees.

– Mighty Afterglow, she whispered.

The other ignored her and began walking, began trailing, walking in the footsteps of the retreating party. Alice rose and hurried after her.

They walked in silence for a while, while the young girl attempted to work up the courage to speak.

– Afterglow handled them so easily. She did not even have to use her power.

– Sometimes not showing your hand, the power of persuasion, of intimidation is often the best power of all, even though one must be prepared to back it up with the real thing.

– I could have killed them, Alice said with numb lips.

– Yes, you could have, – but it was not very *likely*. Your power is still nebulous, still weak and unfocused. Eventually you *will* be able to kill with a wave of the hand.

It was a long trek across the valley. Afterglow's attention was mostly locked forward, but there were a few times, including when they passed a forest to the right that the apprentice saw her master become distracted. It did not last and Afterglow speeded up and Alice followed.

They walked to the end of the valley and beyond. Alice did not tire. She was trembling in excitement and general emotional turmoil. They could no longer see the others. The men's speed had increased significantly the moment the unconscious among them had started waking up and had been able to walk on their own.

– They know we are coming, Alice pointed out carefully.

– Precisely, Afterglow grinned, and it was the same, dangerous grin that Alice and many others had learned to fear.

The ground rose a bit as they left the valley. As they reached the top of the rise they could see the other valley below and the village and its preceding fortress, see people leaving both places in droves.

– They took your command… literally?

– Of course they did. In this realm people are still capable of *listening*.

There were other lone dwellings or group of dwellings fairly close to their path. They saw and sensed no people anywhere. Some animals grazed on smaller or bigger fields, but no visible humans warred for their attention.

One of the henchmen they had encountered earlier, unable to walk any longer kept crawling, his panic so evident that his lungs threatened to burst. Afterglow (and thereby Alice) ignored him as they walked past him.

Their walk had lasted for hours when they finally approached the village and the fortress, and its wide open gates. Alice felt the long walk in her bones. Afterglow did not. Not everyone had left when the two of them reached the first houses. They caught glimpses of terrified villagers as they fled.

– They fear the overlord in the fortress, Afterglow remarked, – and they have seen his fear, seen him be humiliated, be crushed to nothing.

– And perhaps they learned something, Alice said. – Perhaps they will not obey the overlord so easily anymore.

– Perhaps, Afterglow nodded, – but do not hope for too much. They are basically peasants, and they have been terrorized into submission for generations.

Fires still burned in the fortress' courtyard, but they saw no people, not even the hint of anyone. It looked like a ghost house, abandoned to the tender mercies of nature. Afterglow led them to the kitchen. The pots and kettles were still cocking, still boiling.

– Yummy, yummy, Afterglow hummed. – This is perfect, is it not? I think you may serve Afterglow her dinner, now, apprentice…

Alice rushed to check the kettles and pots. She frowned visibly by some of the smells and because of what she glimpsed in the kettles.

– This will do, she admitted grudgingly. – With a little picking and choosing this will do.

Afterglow's surprisingly carefree laughter echoed between the walls, and in her own, desolate heart.

The dining hall was large, fairly luxurious, with a long table. Afterglow and her apprentice dined there. Each sound echoed in the room, their voices seemingly amplified, to a sort of choir.

– Using my power feels… good, the girl mused. – It does not hurt at all, but is like an extension of myself, like the energy is a part of me reaching out and grabbing hold of anything I might desire.

– It gives you a rush, does it not?

– Yeah, that is it! Alice cried out excitedly. – How did you…

A somber expression overtook the flustered face.

– Oh…

Afterglow grabbed her hand, squeezing it softly, squeezing it hard. Alice whimpered.

– You should enjoy it, because it is a part of you, what makes you what you are, but also always stay aware of the possible pitfalls, where it may lead you.

– I know, I know, Alice nodded glumly. – I have read all those stories about sorcerers giving in to Power, all of them seeking ascension or some other lofty, stupid prize, and not letting anything or anyone stand in their way, no matter what they had to do, some vanishing completely, without ever being heard from again and others being glimpsed in the Wasteland, mere shells of a human being.

The words alone brought images and sensations bringing increased potency to her brief account. Afterglow - and thereby Alice - felt and experienced the truth of it.

They fed, gorging on a ten course dinner, and lots of refreshing drinks, taking their time, enjoying it deliberately. Afterglow did, so Alice did as well.

Dark music seemed to rise at them from the very bricks themselves, engulfing them, rattling their bones.

– Where does it come from? Alice wondered astounded. – I thought everybody had fled.

– They have. This is coming through a portal. There are both an outgoing and incoming here.

– Where? She looked around her with wide eyes.

– Right over… there. She indicated a direction with her hand.

They finished their dinner, and sat there burping and farting and really enjoying themselves.

Alice began packing some of the food, for the travels, and her mentor nodded in acknowledgment.

Afterglow frowned, and grew visibly troubled as the music grew louder, and created a rumble shaking the entire structure.

– Time for us to take our leave, she said hastily. – I suspected we would not be able to spend the night.

Alice had suspected that, too, attuned beyond attuned as she became to Afterglow's thoughts and moods, but still she spoke out:

– Why, what is wrong?
– That is not just music, Afterglow mumbled darkly.
She attempted to hide her concern for the young magick-wielder, but did not quite succeed.
Alice did not voice her distress over the other's reaction, but followed her without a word through the shimmering portal at the end of the hall. One blink of an eye, a brief, prolonged sense of being torn apart, and the terrifying music faded in their ears and
They stood on an icy path, and a cold draft struck them and made Alice whimper in discomfort, as she strived to breathe in the stale air. Afterglow kept walking without even pausing for an instant. Alice rushed after her, striving to keep an even footing on the treacherous trail.
– What was that? I felt something, I think, a dread, something…
Her voice hardly sounded like her voice at all, but as a distant echo not quite reaching her ears.
She strived to put names on her evoked emotions, but failed.
– It is called the Little Death. It temporarily paralyzes and drains sorcerers' powers and leaves them vulnerable to just about anything. Then the Dreadnaughts come and fetch them, and they are never seen again. It is a search and destroy spell occasionally roaming the Nine Realms and beyond.
– The… Dreadnoughts?
– The Dreadnoughts, a different kind of Wraith, they have many names depending on where they are spotted and bring dread and misery and horror to wherever they tread.
The air hardly carried voices in this realm. Alice spoke up, making en effort of every word she uttered.
– But why? Who would… and *could* make such a thing?
– No one knows. It is recent. No one I know of heard about it, until about ten years ago. I guess someone wishes to eliminate the competition or have other, sinister purposes in mind.
– But… that is *horrible!*
Afterglow stopped and turned towards the girl.
– It is just yet another reason for why you have to *learn,* learn the way of the warrior witch, why you have to be at your best and fiercest at all times.
– Alice understands, Afterglow, Alice replied with numb lips.
It was cold and getting colder, as they made their way through the icy, barren landscape. They were fairly well dressed, but the persistent draft in the air cut through them to the bones. Alice wanted to speak, to ask questions, and receive responses from the cold, hard creature in front of her, but the numbing cold sucked all initiative and strength from her, and it was all she

could do to keep moving, keep putting one foot in front of the other.

Breathing itself became difficult. The air smelled horrible of sulfur and other infernal fumes. Each breath burned. Time lost all meaning to the young girl. Only suffering existed to her senses, her increasingly numb mind. They rested, sort of slept in a derelict cabin, body to body under thick blankets Afterglow found under a ruined bed. Alice quickly wolfed down the more pleasant food supplies like the hungry child she was.

They slept, or what could go for sleep, one that brought little or no rest. Noise coming from walls, ceiling and floor surrounding them shook bodies and minds alike. They woke up several times, gasping, fearing there was no air to breathe.

The next morning the rest of the food, whatever there was of it, felt completely insufficient to the task of feeding them. Alice stared out the opening, staring blindly at the remote, hostile landscape where no visible daystar brightened the world.

They moved again and kept moving, and each step felt like an ordeal. Hours passed and felt like years.

The ground shook under their feet. Even the air itself seemed to push at them.

She fell. The sorcerer was at her again with her wand in an instant, striking at her most vulnerable spots, where it hurt the most.

– Do not, please do not! She begged.

She got on her feet and stood on shaky legs. Afterglow struck her again, and again.

– Do NOT! She shouted, and attacked with all the fierce anger she could muster.

Afterglow struck her down, and she crouched there, shaking in tears and fatigue.

– We have just walked for a few days and you *dare* exhibit weakness, you spoiled brat?

The apprentice fought herself up, and they kept walking, kept walking for days and nights in a place where minutes felt like hours. In many ways it was like sleep. Afterglow knew that, knew it well. Conscious thought seemed brief and rare. Existence was hardly anything except that crucial act of putting one foot in front of another. She forged an even deeper connection into the girl's fragile psyche, forming it to her preferences, dream to dream, nightmare to nightmare, sorcerer to apprentice.

The cold intensified, making even Afterglow gasp. They built an open fire, gathering in a frenzy the few fairly dry branches there were. The flames did not really seem to be that warm, except when they brought a hand close, and the skin felt like it was shriveling on the bone. They digested the last pieces of dry meat they had brought with them from the fortress, the last of their food. It tasted like leather, and they wanted to vomit, but kept chewing and swallowing the best they were able.

There was walking, sometimes, ever so rarely rest, a hardly believable mirage in the eternal twilight, walking, walking, walking, and that was all. Countless eons passed in the fever of their mind.

– What is this place? It is so difficult to breathe. It is not just the sulfur and shit, but as if there is almost no air. Is there any life anywhere?

As if on cue there was something resembling a shriek, a cruel shout that actually brought the slightest fringe of hope to Alice's drawn features.

– Welcome to Nispelheim, «the realm of ice and mist», Afterglow said dryly. – It has many names, among many people, names like Helheim, Hades, Manala and thousand others.

Those names meant something to the apprentice. She had heard terrifying tales about this place since she had been a little girl.

They reached a rise and Alice stopped again, staring with dull eyes at the amazing sight down below. Molten lava flowed from a hole in the mountain to the right. It burned and shriveled skin this far away. Further away a volcano spit ashes in an even stream. It made the air even more arid, made it even more difficult to breathe.

– This is the realm of ice and mist? She said incredulous.

Afterglow had just continued walking. Alice hurried after her, but her breathing problems quickly worsened and she had to slow down. For a long time she feared she would not catch up with the other woman and even lose sight of her.

– Yes, Afterglow replied, perhaps hours later. – What little water is here has frozen to ice long ago, and we would have, too, if we had stayed long enough. I have heard that people were brought here to work in the mines and that they died while they worked, the blood frozen to ice in their veins.

The shudder in the sorcerer's voice tripled in the apprentice's limbs and fevered mind.

It was so hard to think. Alice made a monumental effort.

– But what is the point in that? Is there a portal leading back to the… to Balakor from here?

– Not that I know of, Afterglow replied. – There might be, of course, one that is a well kept secret, used to extract precious metals and minerals. Or… one or several parties may have used it or use it as a penal colony to punish undesirables, to instill fear in the potential rebellious mind, a less than obedient given population. There is a reason this kingdom is known throughout the Nine Realms.

Alice wanted to say something more, but the ice just froze her heart and her vocal chords, numbed mind and bones to a point that she no longer feared freezing to death.

And after that they still kept walking for a long time. Sometimes there was a trail, sometimes there was not. The girl realized dimly that that should have worried her, and she should have been on the lookout for hostiles, but she was reduced to nothing more than putting one foot in front of the other.

They had left the valley with the lava flow and no longer had the volcano directly in sight. Holding on to the sight of the back ahead of her was the only somewhat voluntary act the tired to death human being was capable of.

Alice stopped, suddenly blinking astounded, frozen, like the arid ground. She looked around her, looked twice, and their surroundings had clearly changed. It was warmer, friendlier and they were surrounded by trees, *trees*. She looked behind her, and she saw the same, changed land. There were not that many trees. This was evidently not a dense part of the forest. Her footprints in the soft soil went backwards on a straight trail for as far as she could see. A choke escaped her sore throat.

– When did we…

– Not that long ago, Afterglow shrugged, having stopped and turned as well.

Alice shivered one more time to the bone.

– I am ready, Master, she mumbled. – Ready, ready, ready

– You better be, since I alone was able to scout for enemies most of the time we walked through what could have been extremely hostile territory.

Shame coursed through the girl.

- Alice will better herself, Master. She will make herself worthy of Afterglow's trust. So she *swears!*

The master snorted in contempt and walked on, and the apprentice trailed her.

Alice whimpered as sensation slowly returned to her body, as her mind awoke from the coma. She bit her lip in an effort to better stand the pain, but the lip was too numb for that to be of any use. It was only when she felt the taste of blood in her mouth that coherent thoughts returned.

The trail broadened a little. Tracks coming from all directions sought this single spot, this pinprick of reality. The first leaves had begun to drop from the branches. The even deeper part of the forest swallowed them, and when Alice briefly turned and looked back there was nothing but that kind of forest there.

– An enchanted…

A frown in place of a grin appeared in her fatigued features.

– Only the inept would call it an enchanted forest, Afterglow curtly cut her short.

The apprentice sniffed and bowed her head in despair and misery. Afterglow grabbed her jaw and smiled cruelly. Alice whimpered in pain. When Afterglow let go saliva flowed from the girl's mouth.

They walked the path, the sorcerer first and the apprentice second. From the right another trail appeared. People in hood and robe appeared on it from nowhere, through another portal.

A wolf howled, and its head, its steaming mouth was glimpsed between the trees, in a moment that was briefly night. Alice experienced it all, sick and repulsed, curious and terrified.

– This, or this part of it is an enchanted forest, Afterglow, her revered teacher revealed to her. – It is a place between worlds, a part of Avaldami - «the Realm in the far west», neither here nor there, between awake and dream, between the Wasteland and physical reality. The Wasteland is not a wasteland at all, but a shadow-realm of infinite possibilities. Everything is mixed here, revealing the truth.

They reached a bridge, the bridge Alice had glimpsed in her mind, in her fever dreams. The bridge was not long. It covered only a short divide to the other side, but in that, in the mist below Alice sensed all the fangs and claws of existence roam, reaching for her and cutting her vulnerable skin. To cross was like balancing on a tightrope. Alice sought closer to Afterglow. She wanted to grab the other and never let go.

Everybody crossed, and if anybody fell they did not see it, even though they heard the screams, the banshee wails every time they closed their eyes.

– I am so tired, Alice said sleepily.

– Good! Afterglow stated.

Their feet once more touched solid ground. The mist cleared slowly, revealing a rather large, rectangular building placed in a field covered by vapors, vapors not fading in the blinding white sunshine. Alice glanced back. The bridge was still there.

– Yes, that is correct, Afterglow confirmed. – That was not an inter-realm portal like the others, but a hole resembling a large, gushing wound. It is leaking back and forth, from both sides. They are rifts and the bridge is built, like one crossing any ravine or Abyss.

– What was down t-there? Alice asked numbly.

– You will find out.

They entered the large building through a wide, open entrance, crossing into a minor hall, leading into one much larger.

– We are no longer within the nine realms… are we?
– No, we have entered the vast reality beyond the rim. Picture the nine worlds as a wheel, a slow turning wheel. It is not really, but it is a useful analogy. A wheel where its individual parts are somewhat connected, a tiny pinprick of everything that is.
– Wow! The star eyed girl brightened visibly. – Wow!
– This is an intersection, a way station, Afterglow once more cautioned her. – There is one corresponding to each of the nine realms. Sorcerers gather here to contemplate and gloat in each other's company. They bring their apprentice, their trophies here.
Yet another chill surrounded Alice and her dull mind.
They reached a reception area, just at the beginning of the great hall. Afterglow walked to the desk, to the clerk behind it.
– I would like a room, please, she said.
– Very well, My Lady, he said, – there is actually one available right now.
There were always rooms available here.
– That will be fine, thank you, Afterglow acknowledged graciously. – Everything is well for the time being, I trust? There are no… troubles?
– No troubles registered today, My Lady, he assured her.
– Good, she nodded preoccupied. – Very good. I would be very displeased if there were, you know.
They walked to a table further into the hall. It was a kind of cafeteria, or not. It resembled one or had a few similarities, but this was a different, alien environment.
– It pleased you to scare him shitless, did it not, My Lady?
– It most certainly did, Afterglow shrugged, – but I was not really talking to him, anyway, but to his masters. They know I am quite capable of carrying out my threat, if things do not go according to plan.
– And what plan is that, My Lady?
Alice pushed her, still humbly, but with a distinct pride and self-determination not present in the desk clerk.
– To get you out of here alive, and in one piece, Afterglow shrugged. – You may not, anyway, but then it will be no one's fault but your own.
That shut up the apprentice.
There were not that many people here. The large hall seemed almost empty. They noticed a few solitary Travelers, but most of those present traveled in pairs. Most of those traveling alone were fidgeting and looked visibly nervous.
– They will lose themselves, will they not? Alice said unhappily.
She slowly, only slowly stopped the violent shaking, still anchored to her

experience in Nispelheim, but also to the dreaded visions of the immediate future her fevered visions has revealed.

– Everybody not fully initiated need an anchor, Afterglow nodded. – Even many full-fledged sorcerers have difficulties holding themselves steady in the Maelstrom without aid.

There was a queue, of sorts, a first arrived, first served system. Alice's eyes flickered constantly, in both endless curiosity and youthful uneasiness. Afterglow relaxed in a perfect calm, patient as death.

She watched the room, too, but Alice could not see her do it. Afterglow knew others could.

– So, there will be dusk soon? Alice asked casually, impatiently, eagerly.

– There is always dusk here, Afterglow replied absentmindedly.

She saw the room in a dark hue, saw the lights dance in the air, and vicious snarls pretending to be faces twist and turn at her.

There were various degrees of commotion, as the assorted parties started to arrive. They looked different, looked alike. Alice stared at them with awe and anxiety.

– Do not mind the sideshows, Afterglow shrugged.

– They look funny, do they not, the girl giggled, – in their colorful costumes and elevated self esteem.

Some of the arriving sorcerers did not wear exactly black, but had a few distinct alterations added to their costume.

– They do indeed, Afterglow nodded, – but do not ever tell them that, at least not until you are ready to trade them blow by blow, until you have become their equal.

Alice in wonderland shrunk in her seat again, brought high, brought low, as she kept experiencing a rollercoaster of emotions in Afterglow's service.

– Do not worry, My Lady, she said soberly. – Alice knows her place. She will be respectful and humble, and strive to not be noticed at all.

The apprentice was not generally noticed, not really, except like furniture or a pet. To be noticed was to be singled out, to have reason to fear what would happen next.

Alice would know this. Her basic education in the dark and mysterious arts was quite extensive.

There was more commotion by the entrance, true commotion, not just a ripple but a tall wave. Afterglow and practically everybody else in the room froze. Alice noticed and looked astounded at the older woman.

A tall and imposing woman entered the hall. Behind her walked two even taller figures, ethereal creatures that hardly seemed to be there at all.

– Are they… *wraiths?* Alice whispered.

Her voice seemed to carry across the room like a scream. She shuddered and shrank in her seat.

– Yes, Afterglow acknowledged, hardly voicing her reply at all, unable to keep herself from shivering.

The wraiths were a legend seen as a myth by most people in the Universe, an army of ghostlike, impervious and tireless beings waging war and wrecking destruction wherever they appeared.

And they served Florence, the tall woman, served her unconditionally.

Afterglow knew they were real, knew it with every fiber of her being. It radiated from them and hurt her physically.

She knew, beyond knowing that Florence and her entourage were on their way here.

The presence of Magick permeating everywhere in this place increased yet another notch. Afterglow knew Alice looked at her, knew beyond knowing that Florence studied her, and nausea rode her like a mare. The mere presence of the wraiths touched her and hurt her.

There was no sweat on her skin, cold or warm. Afterglow had descended into a deadly calm state to the point that she imagined she had died and been buried.

Florence came with a spade to dig her back up, from her watery grave.

A young boy entertained a part of the gathering with his dance. They marveled at his agility and ignored his empty mind.

– So Afterglow has finally taken on an apprentice, Florence mused.

Alice jumped to her feet and curtseyed deeply, shaking badly again.

– Poor dear, I seem to have frightened the poor thing with my unexpected attention.

– Do not worry, Afterglow shrugged, – she can handle herself.

– I am certain she can…

The regal woman sat down. The wraiths remained standing.

– She has come here, come this far on her perilous Journey to test herself, I gather?

Afterglow did not reply. Florence never took his eyes off her and Afterglow never looked away, but returned the stare, the meeting of eyes with intense calm.

– So, what has brought the great Florence here, to this outpost? Kathryn heard herself say.

Florence frowned, over the obvious irony in the other's voice, something that was akin to an insult in their circles. Then she shrugged, too. There was no love lost between any of the sorcerers gathering here. Their lives consisted of deadly rivalry that could erupt into open warfare at any time.

Usually it did not, though, since they were mostly too evenly matched. Any fight would only weaken both, and leave the path open for others to pick up the pieces.
– One is supposed to mingle, is one not? She grinned. – To meet and listen to fellow sorcerers' exciting experiences.
Pure malice rested beneath her pleasant exterior.
The puppet boy drew applause from the captive audience. Afterglow rubbed her brow and made no attempt at hiding it.
– It is quite exciting, she acknowledged.
She sensed, knew the dead tissue and mind in the two towering creatures guarding Florence like snarling dogs, ready to take action on her behalf on a moment's notice, and sweat and bouts of panic broke constantly behind her cool exterior.
There was some more commotion by the entrance and Florence shifted her attention there. Afterglow could not help feeling relief and fought to keep it contained where Florence, the mighty sorcerer would not notice it.
– An old acquaintance of mine just arrived, Florence said. – Protocol dictates that I greet him. Protocol is such a boring concept, is it not?
She rose, rustling her clothes, casting her eyes at Afterglow one final time.
– Have we met? She frowned. – Met before, except in passing?
– Not to my knowledge, Afterglow shrugged.
Florence left, without bothering with any formal goodbye. Afterglow was glad. She saw, without seeing the sorcerer and her two wraiths make their way towards the reception area.
Alice sat, as if on needles, before finally daring to speak.
– You are glowing, she said incredulous.
– I am absorbing far more than intended of the ambient energy at this place, Afterglow said, more than slightly troubled. – I did not even realize I was doing it.
Fear had done that to her, made her lose control, for the first time in ages, made her hunger for more power, power to make her burst.
– You… *know* her! The girl said with conviction in her voice and entire being.
– I know her.
Kathryn nodded, hardly able to speak.
The apprentice did not ask any questions. She did not dare.
Afterglow and her apprentice observed the hall and its ongoing activities as time slowly passed. Alice nodded off now and then, increasingly prepared for her Journey, her trial by fire and ashes, mist and shadow.
She had not fed and would not either, except the way her Master had fed,

from the nourishing ether. Her stomach had stopped rumbling ages ago.

The constant dusk in this place eventually turned a visible notch darker. A waiter, or a man closely resembling that of a waiter, stood still and looked at them for quite a while, before finally approaching.

He stopped and bowed deeply. Afterglow acknowledged him with a slight nod.

– The room is ready, My Lady, he informed her. – It will be *ripe* shortly. If it pleases My Lady we can be on our way within moments.

– Excellent, she said approvingly. – Lead on.

He had to help Alice on her feet. She walked at his insistence, stared at nothing, totally oblivious to her surroundings.

They walked into another hall in the back. It was difficult, really, to distinguish it from the outside. It was the same blue sky, the same ground and the same, misty air.

And yet it was not. There was a quality to the air, to the sense of it all that was not present outside.

Alice turned back and looked, and Afterglow knew she did not see the building any longer.

– You may leave us, Afterglow told the waiter.

He was disappointed. In fact the disappointment burned in him like a cancer, but he dared not give the slightest clue to his displeasure, knowing fully well that his very life and eternal existence would be in jeopardy if he did.

Kathryn and Alice walked the alien landscape. Afterglow recognized it, somehow, even though it was different now, as it was formed more by Alice's thoughts and dreams than hers.

– What do you see? Afterglow prompted her.

– Colors, shapes, shadows, Alice whispered.

– Soon you will see so much more…

Afterglow raised her hands, and suddenly walls grew on all sides. A ceiling closed off the sky. The bright light darkened to shadow. Alice shook in excitement and trepidation.

– This is your prison, apprentice. There is no door in this place. Without turning that crucial key within, you will never leave, and join the many lost banshees in the Wasteland.

Alice shook, but sat down on her ass on the flaky ground, crossing her legs in front of her and closing her eyes. She started breathing, approaching that state of being that was required to reach the deepest parts of herself. The poison in her body finally took complete hold. Her flesh became paralyzed, her mind was soaring the edge of reality. Afterglow faded from the room and reappeared outside. Alice knew she had left, but she also knew that her Guide was with her, and would remain with her on her Journey.

Wails and the sweetest music rose in her ears, and she could not tell which was which, or which was dangerous and which was a necessity. She saw, Afterglow knew what she saw, a wheel turning and turning, seafarers traveling the vast sea, nomads wandering the land, the fields, forests and mountains of existence, her ancestors and descendants backwards and forwards ad infinitum. Tall fires on a field reached towards the night sky. She was pulled towards one of them, pulled into it and screamed a silent scream, and the fire consumed her, and left her like ashes on the ground, and she nourished the land, and she became the land and she rose above the land, while never really leaving it, and the Path stretched out endlessly before her. When she woke up she rested on her back on a large field a bright day. Afterglow stood there, a few steps away, a strange gleam visible in her eyes.

Where are we? Alice wondered, feeling strangely light-headed and clarity beyond anything she had ever experienced before, but still there was a frown, still there was something… lacking.

Where? Her Guide teased her.

Alice turned and there, on her Path, unavoidable was the dark forest she had glimpsed in her nightmares.

I cannot follow you there, The Guide stated. The final stretch of a Vision Quest must always be traveled alone.

Afterglow knew what she experienced. She dived deep within what she saw as the most pleasant, the most worrying place she could imagine. At the final step there was resistance, was reluctance, but the pull was irresistible, and she took that crucial final step, and she saw a mirror, and what she saw in that mirror was herself.

A mighty sorcerer does not fear the dark forest, does not shy away from the dark mirror image, she called, her inner voice whispered, but embraces it with all her heart, and one heartbeat is a lifetime.

She opened her eyes. The walls faded before her, and infinity opened up to her. She met Afterglow's twinkling pair of wells, and knew that, in that tiny moment at least everything was all right with the world.

CHAPTER EIGHT

Afterglow lived the moment through the girl, her carefree laughter, her twinkling eyes and the sense of unequaled triumph.

Alice laughed in the wind in what felt like a warm summer's breeze. She floated on its current on their walk back to the strange building. It did not leave her, this feeling of boundless elation, of being able to do anything.

– Laugh, little sister, Kathryn said. – Laugh!

– Surely you must recall how it was like? Alice said incredulous. – It is not that long ago.

There was no need for Afterglow to voice her reply.

– You never experienced it like this, the girl whispered soberly. – Your initiation was… of quite the different nature. Forgive me, forgive stupid Alice.

Kathryn touched her cheek lightly, and that was that.

– That is not your concern. You should enjoy the moment, feel everything there is to feel.

And Alice did, in spite of the more than subtle reminder of what the world was like.

They reentered the great hall. Alice did, and it was not the same place she had left. Everything and everyone glowed in strange new lights and hues. She was still the apprentice, but a new and exciting layer had been added to her makeup. There was a depth in her eyes, in her behavior that had been absent, dormant before. Sorcerers and apprentices alike sensed that, and beheld her with different eyes.

It was tangible, like a storm, and Alice could not help the sense of uncontrollable elation making her cup fill and run over.

She laughed and hummed giddily, and all the condemning stares in the giant hall could not make her stop. Sorcerers and apprentices alike nodded to her, acknowledging her new, elevated status.

They sat down by a table. Male and female servants served food, stinking, foaming, delicious food and the sweetest drinks, and Alice wolfed it all down, her stomach a vast, black hole, fearing she would never be able to feed again.

– I am… full, she whispered in her euphoria, – filled to the brim with everything existence has to offer.

She leaned back in her chair, content, pleased beyond measure, basking in the both evident and obscure adulation and attention the stage offered.

Afterglow led the way to the reception. There was a new set of receptionists behind the desk. She chose one to the left, a young, nervous female.

– Good afternoon, My Lady, the tall, pale girl greeted them pleasantly.

– Good afternoon, Afterglow replied patiently.

– Was the arrangement to My Lady's satisfaction?

– Very much so, Afterglow nodded mercifully.

– Is there anything this girl can help My Lady with, anything at all?

– There is, Afterglow nodded. – We would like to leave now, and to that effect we require a carriage.

– A carriage will be ready shortly. If it pleases My Lady to wait outside, it will stop right by the stairs and we will be on our way instantly.

– That pleases me just fine, Kathryn nodded mercifully.

They walked outside, on what in Alice's eyes now had become golden and shadow stairs. The two of them did not talk, each lost in their own thoughts, but still speaking volumes.

The coach and horses appeared from around the corner, the receptionist sitting on the coach with a whip in her hand, dressed in a dark robe and hood.

It pulled to soft stop, as the woman made the horses halt with obvious skill. She jumped down and opened the door to the two of them, and they climbed inside. Alice looked around her with big eyes, at the luxurious interior.

– You should enjoy this, Afterglow told her apprentice. – It is a great ride, with breathtaking sights to more than stun your imagination.

Afterglow frowned, tilting her head, as if listening to something, to a possible echo.

– What is it? Alice asked. – What do you hear?

– Nothing, Afterglow brushed her off, forcing a smile. – Nothing important.

The horses cried out as the woman on the coach gave them their whipping. There was a slight pull, and they were on their way. Alice looked out through the window with the disposition of an eager child, constantly changing sides in the vain hope of catching every possible detail.

They traveled through darkness, shadow and bright day, everything simultaneously. One moment, when she fixed her attention on a given spot she saw one area bathed in sunlight, while the next brought a completely different landscape clothed in darkness, and only dispersed bonfires illuminated the land.

– The boundaries of reality are highly unstable in this place, on this entire route. Afterglow enlightened her tentatively, as if pondering the sound of her own voice. – We are not really moving through all the different realms, though, but only catching glimpses of what is far away, of places we may observe but not go, at least not from here.

She was about to say more, but held back, as a barrage of lightning inverted the landscape. Her best effort could not hide her sudden distress, how upset she was.

– What is it? Alice cried. – What is wrong?

Afterglow wanted to ignore the girl, ignore the silly question and her own, ravaging memories, but failed miserably in all three aspects.

– He… put me on display, my Master did, before his peers.

The voice was calm, even, with just the slightest shaking betraying the emotion behind it.

– I was a mere tool, a pet he took for a stroll, a demonstration of his prowess, his triumph.

She dried tears from her eyes, just once, twice and was done.

– I am sorry, Alice whispered, hardly audible. – Alice is sorry.

The girl grabbed the older woman's hands. Afterglow allowed it. They sat in silence for a long time after that.

People began appearing in the flashes. Both women, for their own reasons stared intently at the indistinct faces.

– It is… strange, Alice said slowly. – It is almost like I can make them out, like I *recognize* and know them.

– That is strange, Afterglow nodded.

Making Alice glance curiously at her yet again.

– Change is truly a constant here, Alice cried excitedly, – developing the mind, making it work better, encouraging growth and better thought-processes.

A dark structure appeared ahead. They both looked at it through the window when the carriage made a turn. It was a building, a castle, one ethereal sight in a jumble of ethereal sights, and as they looked at it, it turned tangible and true.

– Is it there? Alice wondered. – Is it *real?*

– To us and everyone desiring it, Afterglow replied, a happy glow in her voice. – We make it real.

The carriage stopped outside, among a row of carriages and various vehicles. It fit nicely, very nicely in the spot to the right. Alice looked further to the right, and it was as if there was nothing there, nothing there at all.

They stepped outside, onto the Roman stairs leading to the tall and wide entrance. The coach jumped down, bowing to Afterglow, and walked ahead.

– What is she doing? Alice whispered.

– Checking our reservations, of course, Kathryn replied lightly.

They entered a great hall, clothed in shadow and mist. There were no electric lights anywhere, only natural fires, illuminating, in thousand ways the vast complex.

– This is amazing, Alice cried. – What *is* it?

– There is one such place in every realm, perhaps even on every world where humans dwell, in the entire big, bad Universe, Afterglow said. – It is open to those who are *open*, to those seeking a place where the petty rivalry among sorcerers is… of less significance.

There were cubicles that were rooms that were hallways, an intricate network illuminated and dark, in warm and cold colors, beyond colors.

A woman met them at a juncture neither here nor there. They instantly noticed the presence she had about her.

– Greetings Kathryn and Alice, she said. – Greetings, seekers of the Winding Ways. Welcome to this place that is not a place, this Dark Lodge in the wilderness. My name is Horath. I am a caretaker and will see to your needs, modest or demanding, as they might be, while you are here.

– A… caretaker? Afterglow said nonplussed.

– Precisely, Horath confirmed pleasantly. – Will you come with me, please?

They followed her through what was a labyrinth of light and shadow and walls and mist. Their feet clearly touched the ground or a ground, though they did not feel confident that was always the case. They glanced around and marveled at the sights.

Horath walked through ancient streets. They saw her, observed her when she appeared young and ignorant and not in any way the all-seeing oracle she had eventually become.

They heard water hit the shore, long waves rolling across the sand. The sound of water was, all in all with them all the time. Sometimes it was the sound of the sea. Other times it could be a sighing of a pond in the late evening.

– I thought the Dark Lodge was only a house, Alice frowned, unable to keep her eyes from wandering. – I have also heard it can be nothing but a camp in the forest.

– It is, Horath replied.

– But this is a Dark Lodge? Alice asked, as her natural curiosity got the best of her.

– It is indeed, the tall woman nodded. – This is the Dark Lodge.

So, the other places are just smaller facsimiles, then?

– No, they are all the Dark Lodge, the same place occupying different spots on different worlds.

And before Alice could protest:

– This is the Dark Lodge, not as it is, but like it will be far into a distant future.

Alice frowned again, deeply.

– How do you *know* this? Who are you? When did you come here?

– I have always been here…

The three of them reached a room, seemingly an ordinary room, nicely furbished, with one large bed and plush chairs, decorated with discreet lighting and amazing art. It made Alice gasp in awe.

Horath turned to Afterglow.

– This will be your room while you are lodging here, Kathryn. The ceremony will begin in two hours. Fruit and oils will be made available to you in the interim.

– Thank you, Horath, Afterglow bowed. – You are most kind.

The tall woman returned the bow and then she turned towards Alice.

– Remember, young sister, remember that curiosity did not kill the cat.

She walked away, and melted into the mist reaching for her at the opening, at the door-less door. They heard no sound of steps from the hallway outside.

Alice turned to Afterglow immediately, not able to contain herself and her excitement for a second.

– So, what was that about?

There was no reply. Afterglow seemed lost in thought.

– You were *joking,* were you not, about the reservations?

– I was, Afterglow nodded, very thoughtful. – One does not make reservations here. One just shows up. One is always expected. Someone is always here to greet you.

– So, who *is* Horath?

– I would not know. Afterglow frowned. – I have never met her or heard about her. I have heard about a caretaker or even *the* Caretaker, but I have never met any of them.

Alice turned towards the table, looking at the fruit-basket there, unable to tell whether or not it had been there the entire time. She grabbed a fruit. It was an apple. She took a bite. It tasted juicy and full.

Afterglow took another item from the basket, a small bottle with transparent glass containing an oily substance.

– Undress! She commanded casually.

Alice obeyed. She did not hesitate or object in any way. It was quickly done, by loosening a few straps. Her robe and hood fell on the floor. She stood nude before the other woman.

Afterglow emptied a bit of oil in her palms, rubbed them at each other and began applying the oil on the girl's pale skin.

It was cold, very cold, even more so than the other oil she had enjoyed a lifetime ago. Alice shuddered a bit, even in the warm, pleasant air.

– What is it? She wondered, recalling Horath's word about curiosity and the cat.

– It is an ancient oil, Afterglow stated solemnly. – It is called the Sorcerer's Blossom, for obvious reasons.

This oil also turned warm, even hot after a while. It felt almost like it was burning her, but Alice was not worried. She looked at her teacher in complete trust, and as it slowly dawned on her what Afterglow was implying: growing excitement and joy.

– This night is one of joy. We give praise to the new sorcerers in our fold, our kin in spirit. We celebrate a bond stronger than blood.

Alice blushed in pride and awkwardness. She stood very still while Afterglow finished applying the lotion on every piece of her skin. Every piece of her skin burned and tingled, and she could swear she was able to see the flames lick her body hair.

More aware of herself she also noticed the other woman with a keener eye. Afterglow seemed different, slightly less guarded here, even though she never let down her guard.

– But I am horny, *horny*, Alice mumbled.

– Of course you are. You need to be pleasing, a beyond tempting sacrifice to whatever gods there might be, mighty beings gazing at us from above and below tonight.

A bell chimed somewhere. The sound echoed through walls and air of the ancient structure, growing stronger, not weaker.

– It is time. Come, little sister.

Afterglow grabbed her gently, nudged her, and led her off. They walked through more hallways and places of mist and shadow. The sound of the chimes grew louder the closer they came to their destination, naturally. It shifted and changed, until it had become something completely different from what it had been originally.

Sensations filled them, filled the human beings walking the ancient halls and hallways, until it was impossible to resist the imposing call rising from the depths.

Silence greeted them when they entered the great hall. There was a sea there, a pool big as an ocean, small as a pool, lit by warm sunlight coming from nowhere. Steam filled the fairly small room, bathed it in a pale green light. It was a pleasant steam, not invasive in any way, not impairing vision or breathing at all.

Other pairs filed in, one male or female naked, led by a clothed male or female. There were nine pairs all in all. All the other apprentices had the same hazy look in the eyes as Alice, but also the same sense of extreme awareness.

The females' nipples grew hard and their pubic hairs wet, and the males' cocks hardened and dangled between their thighs.

All eyes were drawn to Horath. She raised her hands.

– Welcome, young sisters, brothers to your night of initiation. You will experience its pleasures and revels, like so many before you. When you leave this place you will know what a pleasure witchcraft can be.

Her words, her smile created quite the added visceral reaction in everybody present, also in Afterglow and the other sorcerers.

– Alice of the realm of Montan, in the land of Arcadia step forward…

Alice did, slid forward, proud and eager, with the water splashing around her feet.

– Corda of the realm of Asgard, in the land of Valhalla, step forward…

The tall, very tall, strange creature stepped forward, with the water boiling around her feet.

The others were called forward, one by one. The nine met in a small circle at the center of the pool, of the sea, facing each other, standing with their backs to the rest of the room.

– Celebrate yourself, and each other. Let your passions run wild.

The touching began, hands on bodies, bodies on bodies. They danced in the water. The sea boiled and moved around their feet. Afterglow watched them, and began feeling the first stirrings beyond basic arousal. A man, one with more than a passing resemblance to Corda touched her. She turned towards him, and returned his caresses.

There were no words, no more words, or if there were, they were silent, spoken without lips and tongue. She knew his name and spoke it in a thousand ways, just like she heard her own in a million ways more.

Alice cried out in her joy, as did others, all the others, all the eighteen gathered on this shore by the vast sea. Nude, sweaty bodies were spread around on the soft sand, on the hard marble and soft ground in the ancient ruins. Afterglow writhed on her back, pushing at the body pushing at hers. She heard Alice's carefree laughter and it made her smile and cry out in delight, in an ecstasy even beyond the moment, the intense rapture riding her.

Kathryn smiled to the new man before her, a big man with dark eyes, long, dark hair and a darkness dancing around his muscular, very muscular body.

– Hello again, he whispered in her ear.

She looked at him, a little nonplussed, a little anxious.

– I know, he grinned, – I know you, but you don't know me.

She recognized his type of English accent, but not him.

He had several distinct tattoos engraved on his skin. She recognized those as well.

His cock pointed at her, at her pussy. She heard her own carefree laughter, her curiosity and slight worry melting away in the warm, warm pond. Alice rode another male, her face dissolved in lust and abandon. It went on and on, on this eternal night. The eighteen, all the nine times two touched every other person present. The nine, Afterglow frowned. The Nine.

The pleasant moments on the beach were followed by long walks on the shore of the green luminance. Sweet words and actions were followed by passionate exchange of thoughts. They laughed, chuckled maculate the eighteen people gathered on the thin raft walking between the flickering greenish bonfires.

They parted at some point, even if none of them could tell what that point was. Afterglow imagined she saw Horath observe them from several turns of the crooked path, but she could not say for sure if that was truly the case. The eighteen got to know each other, more with every intimate and passionate look and sweet words whispered in attentive ears.

The night fell when the night turned to dark or dawn arrived in the middle of the day, in a place where there was no day, no night.

Alice and Kathryn sat, supported by pillows on a large bed in the room, the compartment chosen for them. Nude males and females poured wine in their glasses and put large and juicy grapes in their open mouths. Someone played the flute somewhere, yet another haunting sound playing so pleasantly in their ears.

– I could get used to this, Alice giggled softly. – They treat us sweeter than they would gods.

Her eyes, her wide open eyes remained hazy after the fucking. Her pose was lazy and relaxed. Afterglow found herself mimic it, echoing her passionate sentiment.

– It can be so pleasant being a witch, can it not, in a place where we are appreciated and loved?

Kathryn nodded slowly, with eyes just as wide as her young companion.

A grape cracked in her mouth, releasing the tasty juice. She leaned back on the pillows, letting two young males and two young females massage her sore limbs.

– Why should you not be appreciated and loved? A young stud told Alice in a shocked and innocent manner. – You, knowing the secrets and workings of existence, having so much to teach others.

– That is so nice, Alice said sleepily, – tell me more, nice boy, much more.

He did, whispering more sweet words in her ears and she smiled in a joy much deeper than her face.

One of the girls kissed Afterglow on the earlobe, making her freeze, making the first trickles of cold sweat appear on her skin.

– Relax, mighty one, the girl said softly, – allow us to please you, to ease your pain.

The massage, slowly turning sexual was indeed pleasant. Afterglow closed her eyes briefly. Her excitement rose slowly, inevitably. She grabbed one of the girls, grabbed her hair and pulled her close, kissed her like the predator she was on the soft lips. The girl cried out in shock and rising joy, as Afterglow touched her in ever more invasive ways, making her moans of surrender and submission rise to the ephemeral ceiling above.

– I feel it, the girl whined, – your power… like a storm.

– And you will break at the first signs of wind, Afterglow cautioned her, before kissing her yet again, drawing blood.

Alice and Afterglow met at the center of the bed, surrounded by flimsy, pleasant creatures. The apprentice bolder, stronger, empowered, kissing Afterglow on the lips.

– Thank you, she cried. – Thank you.

She drank a lot of wine, emptying her chalice, tumbling into the welcoming arms of the two males. Nine embraced on the bed and made love together, fucked together. They were strong and robust these men and women of The Dark Lodge. Afterglow did not have to hold back, did not have to worry about harming them. The large cock moved hard and fast back and forth within her. She moaned in satisfaction, and when fulfillment came to her she cried out in joy, releasing every pent-up emotion she had ever carried. Kathryn fell, Alice fell and rested on the soft bed.

The room had turned darker later, the lights faded very close to virtual zero, but not quite. Invisible green flames seemed to dance on the walls, on sweaty skin, from the abyss of rumpled sheets. The two women rested there, on their backs, or half on their backs, surrounded by warm and comforting bodies.

Alice was dreaming. Kathryn knew that much. The girl's mouth was moving, humming a strange melody. Kathryn knew that the girl was sleeping. She just was not certain about herself. The waves of the room moved so pleasantly around her, touching her, playing with her and she let them. One of the boys remained inside her. She felt him there, like she felt his skin and pubic hairs on her butt. They were all sleeping soundly, totally spent after the night's revelry. Afterglow smiled, and allowed herself to drift off, into sleep and Morpheus' realm.

A cold draft filled the space of the room. Afterglow touched and shook Alice lightly. The girl woke up virtually instantaneously and looked wide eyed at her mentor. They saw well enough in the weak light. The room looked the same. Their playmates did not wake up or even stir.

The coach appeared in the doorway. Afterglow noticed the difference in her in an instant, a split second before she grew into a giant beast, thrusting herself onward with a thunderous snarl. Afterglow cast waves at her. It did work, but not sufficiently to stop her. Claws cut through the air. Afterglow jumped backwards. The razorblade claws cut her arm and made blood flow. The pain woke Kathryn brutally from the lethargy and indecision. Anger and fear made her focus her waves into a powerful thrust. The beast was thrown brutally backwards and hit the wall at the opposite side of the room. The sound of bones breaking was clearly audible. The boys and girls woke up, screaming in blind panic when they spotted the creature, and running off in all directions, making it impossible for Afterglow to do anything.

– Take it out, she shouted to Alice. – Kill it!

The creature almost cut one of the boys in half. Alice fired at it with her hands, but missed. She tried again just as the beast was jumping forward. Afterglow and Alice hit it simultaneously, practically disintegrating it. Its remains fell on the floor, smoking and hissing.

Blood flowed down her arm. Afterglow stared at it, distant, almost indifferent. The room was swirling with activity. Panic was close to the surface. Only the general serenity of this place kept it from escalating. Alice tied a torn cloth around the wound. The white fabric turned red instantly. Afterglow felt faint, and feared she would collapse. Somewhere within a cold, scared voice manifested itself.

– She was Wraith, she heard herself say. – An advanced kind I have never encountered before, but still unmistakable.

One of the boys turned pale. The others, including Alice, were even more shocked by the events.

– I have never even heard of such wraiths, Alice said incredulous, still shaking. – How did you…

– I was one, Afterglow replied curtly, – in a place far, far away. That was why my power was at least partly ineffective against it. Those sending it knew that. I knew it was something about her, but it was so long ago. I could not properly identify the danger.

Horath appeared in the doorway.

– I am sorry about this, Kathryn, she said softly. – There are things even we are not master of.

– Call me Afterglow, the tall woman said.

Horath acknowledged her words with a slight nod.

– I do not blame you, of course, Afterglow said. – I would be stupid if I did.

– And you are not stupid, are you, Afterglow?

Alice studied them both closely. Afterglow turned towards her with those dead eyes of hers, and at that point she resembled the Wraith, and Alice got goose bumps all over.

– Come, my apprentice, it is time we took our leave.

– Yes, My Lady, Alice curtseyed.

She went and picked up their clothes in the corner, and clothed first her Mistress, then herself.

– It was fun while it lasted, she giggled darkly. – It was even fun beyond that, a great lesson of caution. Is not that true, My Lady?

– That is true, Afterglow acknowledged.

She once again felt the familiar fabric flow and touch her skin, and felt slightly uncomfortable, as they followed Horath through the ever-changing hallways.

They felt the portal from far away, and realized before they saw it that it was considerable bigger than any other they had seen.

– This should take you where you want to go, Horath said.

– I imagine it would, Alice said amazed and apprehensive, – if we could *navigate* through something like that.

She turned to Afterglow.

– Can you…

– Yes, Afterglow stated calmly.

– The forces hunting you are powerful, Horath stated, giving them one final caution. – They have to be, to do what they did, here… Good luck!

Afterglow did not reply. Alice turned half around and waved, before taking the sorcerer's mighty hand, and they were off.

What they experienced, the brief, eternal moment in there could not possibly be conveyed in words. They floated in an endless, eternal sea of lights and shadows. Scales and measure of any kind were meaningless. They were lights, shadows floating, no, racing through a violent storm of energy and impressions. Alice lost herself immediately to the onslaught and would have been reduced to driftwood quickly if not for Afterglow holding on to her somehow, navigating, somehow through the insane multi-labyrinth so far removed from everything the apprentice had known. Alice imagined she glimpsed millions of tiny fireflies move far away in the multidimensional space surrounding them.

She was torn apart and reassembled a thousand times before she had thought the first thought.

A thousand shadows tore into them, as their physical bodies were riveted by the forces facing them.

They stood there, on the floor inside the small room, their ordeal ending ever so slowly, frozen in place, as the world returned to them.

– Wow! Alice cried. – *Wow!*

Afterglow stood there, frowning.

– That was different. Alice shook. – That was so very, very different. Was that… was that…

She crouched weakly, holding on to her knees, thus keeping herself from falling.

– That was the Crossroads, Afterglow stated. – An advanced version of it able to bridge the barrier between the outer territories and the Nine Realms and even time itself.

– I felt you, the girl said. – You protected me, kept me from… from falling. I could never do something like that, never Travel through there on my own. Never!

Afterglow silenced her with a gentle move of the hand. The girl took the cue immediately and fell silent and was battle ready only moments afterwards.

They heard loud, excited voices in the other room, the stress level evident for even the untrained ear. Everything turned to noise, to pain. It hurt all over.

Afterglow walked to the door, with a clear intention of opening it. Alice, in a sudden anxiety attack opened her mouth to warn her, but stopped, and followed her, apprehensive into the other room. The sight facing them there made her truly feel like her blood had frozen in her veins. It was not a mere expression anymore, but honest truth.

People, mostly magistrates turned and studied them, as they entered the room. Kathryn saw Harley and Lola through a shivering pale red mist.

They had been nailed to the wall, and bled dry through a series of beyond brutal incisions. Their naked bodies were one single area of cuts and carvings, a mass of ruined flesh. Their faces had been left intact. That fact made Kathryn sick to the bone. They had wanted her to see the death masks, the frozen expression of horror and inhuman pain.

It was funny. They, whoever had done this had left so little to the imagination, but even so, imagining was all Afterglow did. She re-experienced everything vividly in her mind, as if what had been done to the two heaps of human flesh emanated from them in waves.

And then she realized that it did. To her it did, because of her sensitivity to the waves. More hot rage and sick, cold fear ripped through her.

– Afterglow? The Chief Magistrate asked her. – You are Afterglow?

– I am, she replied, with a voice resembling calm. – This is my apprentice Alice.

His eyes, his entire demeanor told her he was a man familiar with the term she used and with her. She had always suspected she had a file somewhere in public offices, and now he had just confirmed it. That did not surprise her in any way.

It was the fact that her numb mind could still reason, correlate and analyze that stunned her.

She and Alice sat by a table later. Their «interviews» had gone pretty well. It had all been much easier by the foreknowledge of the Chief Magistrate. He had conducted the interviews himself, and Alice knew the score, like any magickian, and knew what to tell and what not to tell.

He had not asked them how they could enter the building through a fortified ring of magistrates. He knew! Or knew or realized enough for him to not share the disbelief of others.

Did you know the two decorating the wall? He had asked her, deliberately patronizing. How did you know them? Do you know who killed them? Do you know who may want to kill them, to dislike them enough to do something like that to them?

And then he began to truly interrogate her. She answered all questions truthfully and dutifully… to a point, never once even hinting at her involvement or anything even resembling it.

The magistrates left. The first guests of the day arrived not too long after that. They whispered among themselves. The help had begun cleaning the wall well before that. At first the cleaning did not seem to have any effect, but then one could eventually see the wall behind the red. The blood and remains of flesh slowly faded, but not in Kathryn's inner vision.

A waiter put two beers on the table before them.

– On the house, Forsaken, he said, actually with a bit of sympathy in his voice.

Kathryn spoke before Alice looked at her.

– It was my name before Afterglow, just after… after….

– I understand, Alice said hastily. – I know.

The room calmed fairly quickly. This place had seen its share of violence, though not anything as graphic as what had happened tonight.

It was as if something had invaded the place, something dark and vile beyond even these people's ken. The uncertainty and anxiety in everybody's eyes were a clear indication of that.

– It does not have any religious connotations, believe me. It has far darker significance than that.

– I know, Alice said somberly, fearfully, brightly, – you are a survivor of the Kal Chek, the Ascension… twice. There are rumors of such creatures walking the ancient lands.

There it was again, the hero worship and nosedive admiration and respect. Kathryn wanted to chastise the girl, but found herself unable to muster the necessary energy. Images and sensations and tales surviving from ancient times filled her mind, of blood and rage and terror beyond belief. She did not close her eyes. There was no need for that for her to see, to experience and be overwhelmed by the searing visions.

Afterglow sipped her ale. Alice did, too.

– I can deal with it, you know, the girl assured her mentor, putting up a brave front. – It did upset me, I will not pretend otherwise, but I can take it.

She took a rather large sip of ale.

Afterglow turned towards her, stared at her, freezing her in place.

– You are not stone, not a tin man, she told the girl, – but flesh and blood. Society and its servants want to turn you to stone. Do not let them. Do not ever let them!

– I will not, Afterglow! The girl stated solemnly, a little shaken again. – Not ever!

They sipped some more ale. It had a round, modest taste. They enjoyed it and wanted to drink more, but the level in the glasses hardly decreased.

– I sat there, in the corner, staring at the wall for hours… or what may have been years.

Alice did not say anything. She looked at where Afterglow pointed, and imagined she could glimpse the young, broken figure in the corner.

– He was the last, you know, the only survivor of the old gang. You are an orphan. You can understand, at least to a point.

– I do, Alice stated solemnly. – I do!

– They are going after anyone I have ever known or even have had remote contact with.

Afterglow closed and opened her eyes once, and not anymore.

– It is safe to conclude that those still alive are in grave danger.

– Is that why? Alice spoke up. – Why you made me your… why you accepted me?

Afterglow smiled a little, a sore and brittle grin.

– I did want to prepare you for future ordeals, but I would have done that anyway. You pointed to yourself, apprentice, and you may even have a chance when they do come for you, at least when I am done.

The girl shivered in joy and dread.

Afterglow rose and walked to the other side of the room. The girl followed her like an eager dog.

A man glared at them. He made no secret of his contempt, his full-blown hatred. They basically ignored him.

The shimmer around Afterglow's frame intensified, as she focused and amplified her energies, and what had been on the cleaned wall returned. Alice gasped as Harley and Lola's bloated faces reappeared. The girl stared at them with an expression of sick fascination in her pale face, unable to help herself.

Afterglow's machinations did more than reveal the bodies. It also highlighted certain areas, cuts and stabs, almost like a…

– It is a map, Alice cried.

– Or a part of one still incomplete, Afterglow nodded. – They are making Magick, and they will complete the painting with our ruined bodies and shadows.

Alice rolled her left hand into a fist, one tied into a hard and painful knot.

Most of the others in the room, both the hired hands and guests looked at them with a mix of pity and awe, but kept their distance, leaving them alone to do whatever they were doing.

Afterglow preferred it that way.

The two of them left. No one spoke out or marked their departure in any way.

They sensed how the door to the secret passageway slammed close behind them.

The narrow alleys appeared even more so to their keen eyes. Kathryn moved with grace, striving for perfect balance. Every movement flowed from one moment to the next. The apprentice strived even harder to emulate her.

There was nothing, no sign of an imminent attack, but Kathryn knew that from now on, more than ever before, she would always expect one.

– So, what do we know about the murders?

She asked her apprentice.

Alice straightened like a schoolgirl being asked about today's lesson.

– They know you, she replied slowly, shuddering, – know us, our whereabouts and our current location, at least to a degree. They have to. They wanted you, wanted us to know their work firsthand.

Kathryn nodded, touching the other's shaking figure, calming it and its equally edgy mind.

– They either knew the precise moment we were coming or at least that we were coming. Both alternatives are disturbing to contemplate.

– They are cruel, Alice cried out or practically shouted, – cruel beyond description.
– They have other priorities compared to most human beings, Afterglow said steadily, cruelly, – and we must never forget that.
Alice nodded, waited a little, failing to speak, before nodding again.
The singing, vibrations began well before they erupted into the central parts of the city, before the giant statues appeared in their vision, but when they did the metallic song almost overwhelmed Afterglow, almost cut her flesh in its beleaguering power. Her ability to sense them had increased since the last time she had walked these parts. It unnerved her further, kept her off balance when she desperately attempted to regain it. The song, the squeal… neither had *bothered* her before.
Alice focused, squinting her eyes at nothing, really, gathering her thoughts, her raging emotions.
– They are powerful, she both reasoned and stated. – They have the ability to track people, to one degree or another over great distances and even from one realm to another. At least they can track you or predict your movements, of sorts. And they can hurt people both close up and from a distance. It is not just the vengeful dead, but living creatures as well. They reach out for you, vengefully from their land of the moon.
Afterglow shook, no matter how much she attempted to hide it.
– I am right, am I not? Alice cried, with both pride and apprehension. – It is The Nine?
The mention of the unmentionable made the vibrations grow that much stronger.
– The Nine is a myth, Afterglow said curtly. – A story to scare children. There is no tangible evidence to even suggest their existence, except in people's overactive minds. No one I have ever met has had any contact with them.
– So they exist, as a presence in people's lives, but not as fact? Alice marveled. – That is amazing.
– Nine is an old number of power, Afterglow shrugged, – both in mathematics and magick. There are nine realms, nine groups of gods ruling them. It is even said that they aided Isis before her Ascension. It is not unprecedented that certain types of people or groups of people attempt to take advantage of all these awe-inspiring stories to serve their own interests.
The girl nodded and smiled, safe in her reality as the sorcerer's apprentice.
Then… something happened, changed. The girl's face lost all expression and she froze in her present position. Afterglow sensed its coming, something moving through the air and the ground and people's shadows, a

hand with fingers like claws, and uncertainty and paralysis ravaged her.
Alice began singing, uncertain at first, but then stronger. Afterglow stared at her, reaching out a hand, as if to stop her, but let it fall again.

There once were nine worlds
Nine giants walking their lands
One for each realm
Gathered by Mjolnir
United by him
Like the world-tree
Uniting the worlds
The Nine were born
In the land of the moon
I remember the nine worlds
Nine giants before the ground below existed

Alice stopped. Her voice began to fail just as she completed the verse, as the wind picked up, as a cold draft blew from the nearest portal.
– I am sorry, Alice gasped stricken. – I did not mean to… I do not know why I…
Afterglow felt it, a presence, old and vile in her bones, stronger than she had in years. The clouds stopped drifting in the sky and turned several shades darker.
Passing people cast uncertain glances at each other, as they stared, as did Kathryn and Alice at the nine giant statues dominating their perception, as a chill of atavistic fear far more powerful than any winter passed through them all.

CHAPTER NINE

The ground was covered in ashes. The forest had been cut in two. One half, a mass of burned down trees and stumps was covered by the gray and dry substance. The remaining half looked fresh and deep and inviting. Afterglow and Alice the nascent witch sensed its allure, its powerful call.

They had walked up the steep mountainside and were soaked in sweat.

– This is the walk I never completed as a girl, Afterglow mused. – I was too timid, too afraid of what I might find.

– The city council burned down all this? Alice wondered stricken.

– They certainly did. They saw a fortune in real estate development up here, ignoring the ancient legends and dangers posed by this place, ruining nature with impunity, with their greed and blatant ignorance and plain stupidity.

– But why did not the rest of the forest burn down?

They stood a few steps from the demarcation line. It was as if someone or something had cut a swath across the land, a line so straight, so precise that the deviation was hardly measurable.

A loud hiss rose from between the trees, imposing itself on their astute ears and senses. It spread from the still standing forest to the still seemingly steaming ashes.

– Do not pretend you are stupid, too, Afterglow commented dryly.

Alice looked across the line, into the forest. If she tilted her head she could hear the flapping of wings, if she squinted her eyes she could just about make out creatures flying between the tall trees, and settling on the thick branches.

– Are those birds?

– More like a kind of birds of prey you would not like to meet or be noticed by. The city people fear them with good reason, fear them *now*.

A creature with horns and long fangs and claws flew close enough for them to study more closely.

– Are they d-demons?

– C'mon, you know better than that.

Alice did not respond verbally to the snarling words. Afterglow, too, shuddered visibly.

When she spoke again, after a prolonged pause, there was a distinct shiver in her voice.

– They are human beings, or at least they were once. Now, they are trapped in the Wasteland, changed irrevocably by its sinister influence.

A couple of the winged creatures ventured closer to the line. They stared at the two on the other side with something close to empty eyes.

Suddenly one of them charged forward and hit the invisible wall. Dark sparks and flames flew and danced, as the creature made its mindless attempt at freedom. At first it seemed like the wall would repel it, but then it seemed to… slip through. Alice took one step back with fear in her eyes. The creature, exhausted fell to the ground.
– Quickly, Afterglow hissed, – zap it!
– What do you…
– Burn it. Teach it your power, your superiority.
The creature rose up on its legs. Alice shook it with her energy, energy making ashes dance in the air. The creature fell, but kept fighting to get back on its feet or flap its wings.
– Again! Afterglow snapped.
Alice obeyed. More ashes rose and danced around them. The charge hit the creature. It fell, squealed, and fell to its knees, bowing down before Alice, shaking in fright, its mighty wings pulled close to its body. Alice glanced at Afterglow.
– Congratulations, the mentor said dryly, – you have made a friend, taken yourself a loyal pet.
– But… what will I do with it?
– Collar him, and keep him, of course. He will recognize you and be devoted to you wherever he goes, and will serve you beyond loyalty.
Suddenly Alice was no longer afraid. She approached the imposing figure with a slight smile on her lips. Afterglow threw her a red ribbon with a heavy lining, and she caught it easily in the air, hesitating only slightly before tying it around the creature's neck. It glowed slightly, before once more appearing like an ordinary band.
– What you see is not truly the Wasteland, Afterglow taught her, – but a kind of borderline *branch* of it, a place where the walls between worlds have been weakened by human irresponsibility, weakened sufficiently for the occasional breakthrough.
– I remember when they burned it. Alice shook her head in despair and rage. – I felt it. It was not just ashes that rained over the city.
– No, it was not.
The entire area had been saturated with dark, eldritch energy. Afterglow and Stane, the «newspaperman» had both taken advantage of that.
Afterglow stepped forward, grabbed the beast and threw it at the wall. It yelped when it hit it, but slipped back on the same spot it had come through just a minute earlier. They watched, as the scar in the wall healed itself.
– Scat, Alice commanded him. – I will find you when I need you.
He understood, a deep, ugly wrinkle on his forehead, and took to the air

with a howl of despair giving both women the chills.

Other creatures lurked in the shadows, but made no attempt at breaking through the wall or even approach it.

A draft, stronger than a wind started blowing, started surrounding the two. The ashes floated and whirred around them, occasionally being pulled to exposed skin, where it glowed and burned.

- Its energies… are undiminished, Alice said astounded, – and some pieces even stronger charged than before.

Afterglow bit her lip as a dark leaf was transformed into a blue flame.

– Yes, she affirmed. – If anyone attempted to weaken the power resident in the forest, they failed miserably and caused the exact opposite to occur.

They stood there for a while, practically soaking up the resident energies, feeling the pain and pleasure, the full impact of the remains of what had once been.

– Afterglow is saturating herself, empowering herself wherever she goes, is she not?

– She is.

All the dark fireflies, animated remains of the recent fire returned slowly to the ground. The wind from nowhere rested. Sighs slipped from open mouths and dazed eyes.

The two left the ashes of the forest and made their way back down the mountainside, back to the seemingly so distant city below.

– It feels good to stretch my legs, Alice said, a little subdued, but yet energized way beyond her youthful excitement. – Too few people move hard enough to make the sweat flow, and even fewer dare to venture into the wild. And behold, I say this even after our recent prolonged walk through Nispelheim. Alice amazes herself…

– It is a gathering sickness in parts of the population, Afterglow acknowledged. – They are taught to fear and stay away from the unknown and the wild, both so precious and so essential in human life.

– And being in good shape enhances your Magick, too.

– It does indeed, as working the craft can be very taxing to your system. If your heart starts hammering in your chest at the first hurdle you will not achieve much.

They reached the first homes in the mountainside. The houses were mostly empty, since very few had the stomach to stay there for very long, no matter how inexpensive the property.

The city of Talaho was a narrow line stretching far in both directions at the base of the mountain. It did not take long to cross it, to reach the bridge crossing the canal to Howell. Basically, Talaho was the old Roman settlement, and Howell was the newer, English additions. Only at the fairly recent settlements on The Island did the two and also several other origins mix.

Right by the river and the Appalon Bridge rested the fairly large estate of Lucius Flavicus. It wasn't as extensive as it had once been, when his ancestors had lived there, but was still one of the largest in the triple cities and surrounding area.

Afterglow stopped, just outside the gate, where the sentries stood straight as poles.

– Do you hear that?

She held up a flat hand, crouching slightly.

– I am not certain what «that» is, Alice said, shaking her head in apprehension, – but I do hear it.

It was a mix of a low rumble and a hiss, and came from several different directions, changing position rapidly and abruptly.

Afterglow rushed forward to the two sentries, making sure she did not step to close.

– Pleasant day to you, good people, she said, speaking in Roman. – I would like to visit Lucius Flavicus, please. I have been assured that he; in his generosity always keep his home open for me.

They recognized her, but still shone the magickal Shadow of Revelation on both her and Alice. The women felt it invade them, turning them inside out. The sentries nodded, before stepping aside and letting them pass.

– They actually used it on us? Alice shook her head distraught, and in disbelief. – They actually used it, one of the most expensive magickal gadgets there is.

It was a rare metal alloy, treated with even rarer magickal properties, and could only be used once.

– That tells us he does not let many guests in these days, Afterglow noted dryly, anxiously. – It also tells us that he feels jumpy as hell.

– He has certainly put up enough protection spells and watchdogs…

The apprentice spoke with both reverence and excitement in her voice and stance.

They could not run because of that, but had to move cautiously, deliberately down the broad, torch-lit road. Snarling creatures and wisps of air snapped at them.

A set of smoky teeth settled in Alice's sleeve before she gave it a hearty dose of her power and it pulled back, yelping in shock.

A giant statue representing Isis guarded the entrance. Its face was one of the more popular variations, one found in many homes, from many

nationalities.
The large doors stood open, as was the custom.
A servant met them right inside.
– Pleasant day, good people, she greeted them. – On behalf of my master, Lucius Flavicus I wish you welcome to his house.
When she said «house», she meant the entire estate. It was a common practice. Afterglow nodded graciously.
– Please, she said impatiently, foregoing the usual bowing and scraping, – it is imperative that we meet with the master of the house immediately.
A number of guards, both seen and unseen waited in the wings if that was not acceptable.
– My master agrees, the servant said, – please follow me.
Flavicus and family and circle of close allies observed the old ways of conduct, even to the point of risking their own lives, and it was virtually a miracle when Afterglow and apprentice were let into the inner chambers as fast as they were.
Oil lamps lit the house inside, too. Flavicus detested electricity.
He waited for them in his study, not in his formal, very formal reception room and the herald at the door did not cry out their names, facts that Afterglow was twice grateful for. She detested formalities.
– You are in immediate danger, Lucius Flavicus, she stated, straight to the point.
– So you graciously informed me about days ago, he nodded, – but nothing has happened since then.
He was dressed in a fairly modern version of a toga, something that would have scandalized his ancestors, but still looked out of place in the present.
– I do not know why our common enemies have not struck yet, she acknowledged, – but they are right at your gates, now. I sincerely hope you have strengthened the wards and Magickal defenses as I suggested.
– You aided me years ago, he said. – I will always be grateful for your timely assistance, even though, as you so kindly advised me about it is that kindness of yours that is now returning to haunt me and my family.
It had been a little more than «timely assistance», like it usually was when it came to Afterglow's services. She kept her silence.
The rumble and hisses… approached. She noticed her own restlessness, a constant itching under the skin. Howls and screams followed, as the attackers made mincemeat of the protection and wards on the estate. She frowned. They had reached him in time, it seemed. She felt reasonably certain they would be able to protect him. The frown turned deeper.
– Your family, she said abruptly, – where are…

He ran, foregoing any formality, and they followed him, into another room heavy with the scent of Magick. Afterglow felt it brush against her and her ward. They were let off easy because the spells could, to a certain extent determine intent, but they still had to be cautious, to not be ripped to pieces.

The vicious attack made no qualms about its intentions, made no effort to conceal them. Women and children knelt terrified at the center of the room. The air turned heavy with menace. Alice froze, her face a study in shock, and for a moment Afterglow feared she was paralyzed, but she grabbed Afterglow's hand and they charged forward. The defenses, even the strongest of defenses here broke down, were ripped to pieces like paper. Afterglow and Alice saw the creatures, saw what they had become, and even the others could glimpse them, glimpse what would haunt their nightmares in the years to come. They saw what was both human and not identify the weakest spot of the defense, and charging along that path. Someone had done a sloppy job, even worse than someone like Cochran would have done, and the attackers charged the defenseless humans at Magick's center… where Afterglow and Alice met them head on, and they were dissolved in screams of hatred and pain. The two women sent wave after wave of their combined power at them, and it worked, effectively ending the threat in seconds. The room turned dark, turned shadow, and then silent. Through a rift in reality itself Afterglow glimpsed a thousand eyes.

A mist and sparkling shadow slowly fading hovered in the air. Afterglow touched her earlobe. It was bleeding.

We take your blood little by little, sweet Kathryn, the thousand eyes hissed. One time, soon we will come for it all.

Unable to sustain itself any longer the attack ended.

– It is done, Afterglow said to Flavicus. – The immediate threat is ended. With the level of power they are using they will not be back for a while. But they will be back.

– The gods will protect us, Livia, Flavicus' mate said, deeply shaken.

– Forgive me, My Lady, Alice said, – but it is well known that the gods, in their wisdom never interfere or intervene in the affairs of men, or men and spirits. They leave it to us to fight our own battles.

Clever girl, Afterglow acknowledged with a nod, acting and wording worthy of a bard.

– I am afraid my apprentice is quite correct, she said. – The gods have not made their presence known since ancient times.

– Not everybody would agree with such a sweeping statement, a man, Lucius' brother said angrily, as he entered the room, deliberately foregoing any polite and formal wording.

Lucius stopped him from coming with further outbursts with a cold stare.
The situation slowly calmed down and normalized itself. After a round with his family Lucius retreated back to his study with his two guests and saviors.
– We did not get to agree to a fee this time, he said. – Name any price and it is yours.
– I do not want your gold, Lucius Flavicus. It will be either too much or too little. Once, sometimes in our future I will ask a favor of you, one that will not be impossible for you to grant.
He did not voice any further comment, but nodded, looking at them with a touch of smile.
– Then do me the service of attending our late dining, he insisted. – It is the least Lucius Flavicus can do for you and your brave apprentice.
Alice beamed at him and then at Afterglow. Kathryn nodded.
– We are honored by your hospitality, she said, - and we accept.
The household gathered in the great hall, Afterglow and Alice, and the Flavicus extended family and allies.
Kathryn studied the table with an amusement and interest that did not reveal itself. All cutleries were fully metal, including the handles. The forks, spoons and knives showed the centuries' old design and art of the clan. Everything here exposed age-old tradition.
Gathered were Lucius and Livia, his brother Tonacy and mate Ariel, and a host of children of both couples. And several associates with flickering eyes, some of them casting angry stares at the present sorcerer.
Servants put food on the table. The «modest» meal began.
– To Afterglow and her brave apprentice, Flavicus boasted, raising his glass of twinkling wine, - for their selfless services. Let it be known that I, Lucius Flavicus is in their debt and will be happy to settle it when the time comes and that the two warrior witches will always be welcome in my house.
Afterglow raised her glass as well.
– Kathryn Caldwell is honored beyond words by Lucius Flavicus' kindness, she acknowledged, - and will always consider him and his clan her allies.
Smooth, she kicked herself, very smooth. She avoided Alice's amused glance.
The somewhat humble banquet continued leisurely, like a slow-moving wave. Afterglow enjoyed herself and made no attempt at hiding it. Alice, like a good apprentice kept herself in the background of everybody's attention, but an easy smile played on her lips.
– So, you are a sorcerer, a genuine magick-wielder, Afterglow? Livia asked, clearly not just making conversation. – A proud, but alas so rare tie these days to another of our age-old traditions?

– I am, madam, Kathryn replied. – And so is my apprentice. We are both the last of our respective lines and sole heirs to vast powers.
– That is a lot of responsibility, Ariel remarked. – You must be eager to restore your lineage to the proper power and glory.
There was a hint of sarcasm and accusation in her voice. Afterglow ignored it, as she took another sip of the tasty wine.
– I guess I am, she replied casually.
Ariel did not push the issue and from that point on, when she spoke, she hardly uttered more than pleasantries. Tonacy, having been chastised by his older brother and overlord earlier mostly kept his mouth shut.
– The reason I am inquiring about your gifts, Livia said, striving to sound respectful, – is that I see some signs in our children that they might be heirs to that ancient power as well, and I would certainly appreciate it if you… if you probe the matter when the time comes.
– I will certainly do so at your prompting, Afterglow said unconcerned.
And that was how far the kindness between the two women went.
Tonacy snorted, in a subdued but more than evident manner.
Lucius made an effort at portraying harmony, to make the guests feel welcomed, but it was clear and would have been clear to even the most casual observer that all was not well in the house of Flavicus.
The meal ended, the company ended, and it was a relief.
– Thank you again for your kind hospitality, Lucius Flavicus, Afterglow said, once again making the effort. – I am afraid we must take our leave, but we should do this again sometime.
– We should, he nodded. – Your visit brightened our house and as stated: you may return at any time, at your convenience.
They stood in the entrance hall. Lucius and Livia saw them off.
– It is imperative that you strengthen your defenses, Kathryn told them, – that you realign them to the best possible strength.
He knew what she was talking about, what she conveyed behind veiled words. She saw that. They both nodded.
The two magick-wielders, the sorcerer and the sorcerer-to-be bowed and took their leave, departing as swiftly as they had come. Everything seemed… normal outside, as if nothing had really happened. They sensed the turmoil lingering in the air and the ether, but very few others would.
There was no more rumble or hisses.
– I like that he does not hold it against you that you are, at least in part the source of his woes, Alice pondered. – Many others would.
– In spite of the other faults he may have, he is an honorable man, Kathryn agreed. – One of the few left.

– You fancy him, the young girl giggled. – I saw that immediately. You enjoyed yourself in his company, and even strived to not ruin the mood, the already ruined mood…

Afterglow scowled at her. Damn her power of observation.

And more, something making the older woman frown.

– He is attractive, the girl shrugged, – in a kind of aloof, non-striking way.

They crossed the bridge. Alice, still excited, still worked up after the brief and intense battle, and the subsequent expressive party turned to her mentor.

– So, why do they not attack with greater frequency?

Afterglow smiled, a snarl of a smile.

– They will either torture me slowly, or they lack the power to finish it quickly, or both. It is fairly evident it takes an enormous amount of raw power to sustain the sort of attacks they perform. They need to rest. It also seems clear that they, for some reason were unable to track us this time, which is or can be useful information. All this gives us slightly improved changes to save the people on the list.

At the middle of the bridge, at the darkest spot between the lights of the twin cities she stopped. The darkness seemed to envelop her, to devour her, and Alice gasped, until she realized that Afterglow was in control, commanding the dark waves around her.

She stood by the rail. Alice stood a few steps behind her, lost in wonder.

– Come here.

Alice hardly heard what seemed to be a distant voice. She rushed forward in a mix of bravery and curiosity.

– Look down.

She obeyed. It was pitch black down there, nothing to se or even glimpse.

Afterglow found a few bigger rocks from the shingle at her feet and threw into the darkness. They hit the surface of the ebony waters. A world without form and substance suddenly changed and the apprentice gained a measure of the distance between them and down there.

– When you look down like this you can not truly be certain there is a surface down there, even though your memory tells you there is. In the endless time before the rocks hit the water we might just as well be looking at open air, a bottomless pit where the stones will fall forever. Do you understand?

– I think so, Alice whispered. – I do not know.

– You will!

Slowly, only slowly they reached the light at the other end of the bridge and solid ground under their feet. Alice felt like she was the rocks, falling forever through the darkness.

They headed north east, crossing the south-eastern parts of Howell to Afterglow's home at one of the two southern harbors. They approached the neighborhood with a certain apprehension, with their guard up, but nothing happened and they did not sense any immediate danger.

That did not mean there was not any, just that it was less likely.

They rode the elevator to the top. The door slid open to the quiet apartment. The two of them probed the air and found it untouched. They moved through the place and confirmed to their satisfaction that it was empty of people and threats. Both fell into a relatively relaxed mood. They undressed. It made their sore limbs ache. Kathryn rubbed the bandage on her arm. The wound did not feel too bad. She had practically forgotten about it again not that long afterwards.

The two women showered together. There was more than enough room and they used all four hoses.

– It feels good, does it not?

The apprentice lit up in a smile behind all the water and vapor dividing them.

Afterglow allowed herself to close her eyes briefly. The water cleansed them, both physically and spiritually. Their mental state improved somewhat. Kathryn watched Alice as she cleaned herself, the shifting shadow, the lines of her jaw, the lips bathing in water.

Alice looked at her with lowered eyes.

– May this apprentice serve you, Master?

Afterglow frowned, noticing the strange infliction in the girl's voice, but nodding, a little distracted.

Alice grabbed a cloth and a sponge from the compartment in the wall and dipped them in soap.

– Please step forward, Master.

Afterglow did, the constant pressure on her skin from the falling water vanishing.

Alice began soaping her in, quite skilled with the cloth and sponge. Afterglow began relaxing almost immediately. It felt so pleasant, so good.

– The Master has traveled far, Alice said softly. – She is weary and tired, and needs to unwind, to let go of her burden, at least for a while.

The treatment began on the shoulders, cautiously, tenderly, applying the cloth and sponge like soft petals, or so Afterglow felt the hardest rub. Alice moved down and back and front. She did the breasts. Afterglow felt the nipples rise, hard and sore. Alice crouched, doing the thighs and back, and between the thighs. Afterglow shifted her position.

– Step back into the flow, please.

Once again the falling water hit the sore skin. The cloth and the sponge removed what soap the water did not. Alice stepped into the falling water, too, pushing herself at the other body, kissing it on the lips. Afterglow froze.
– Please, Alice whispered. – Please, Master! This woman is not Beatrice, is not a vile creature with a desire to sacrifice her beloved Master to the ancient gods.
– No, Afterglow remarked, – but she is sly bitch eagerly resorting to deception to achieve her objective.
– This woman has had a good teacher…
She looked down, reddening, with shivering lips. Afterglow grabbed her and pulled her close, and kissed her brutally on the lips. Alice moaned, and turned limp in the other woman's arms.
– Alice is sly, clever and skilled, Master. Please let her work her Magick.
Afterglow touched the other's cheek, before letting her arms fall. Alice stepped close, and began touching and fondling and caressing the other. With a shy smile she pushed the bigger figure at the wall. She cupped a breast in her hand, kissed the skin on a shoulder and rubbed her body like she would a cloth or a sponge at the other's skin. Afterglow began breathing faster, hardly feeling the hard wall at her back. She bit her lip, or tried to, but she feared she could not get enough air and her mouth stayed open. Alice kissed her. Tongue met tongue and caressed each other. Water fizzled and burned both before and when it hit the two hides. Alice turned it off and they stood in a steam of lingering warm moisture and mist. The fairly small room suddenly looked so much bigger. They walked outside. The apprentice grabbed a towel and began rubbing the Master slowly and sensually. Afterglow grabbed another towel and began drying her.
– Beautiful Afterglow, Alice whispered.
They took their time, savoring the experience, the sweetest of sensation and exquisite sweet pain. Afterglow rubbed her own breasts hard and brutal, squeezing them, shouting short and sharp. She pushed Alice at the wall and used her power on her, attacked her with a soft wave again and again. Alice moaned in ecstasy. They walked to the bed, kissing and fondling, fearing they would never reach it.
Both crawled onto the bed. It looked coordinated, simultaneous, but was just a rush of motion. They knelt face to face.
– I know Afterglow can crush little me in her mighty hands, Alice whispered some more. – Do not worry about it. Alice will take care of everything.
Afterglow held her hands on her back, exercising a limited form of self control she had been forced to teach herself. She pushed her lips at the other

girl, playing with the other playful tongue. Alice bent down a little and began licking the large breasts, sucking on and biting the nipples. Afterglow let her, let her lead.

A hand sought between her thighs. The gasp filled the room with the unending waves emanating from her body.

– I feel it, Alice cried. – I feel you.

They fell on the bed, their already hard sweat mingling, as they clinched. Hair came in the way of their sight, and their chuckles chimed like a pond in spring.

– Your skin is so soft, Alice mumbled. – But once pressure is applied it turns hard as wood, tough as leather.

She rubbed it, ever so softly. Afterglow moaned, and stretched her body the entire length of the bed with the beginning of a happy grin on her lips.

– Alice is good, yes?

– Very… good, Afterglow gasped.

The first droplets of sweat began forming on her brow. Skin turned flushed and red. Alice, using both palms and fingers on both hands rubbed her skin ever so skillfully, seemingly not touching it at all. She kissed sore lips, licking them lightly. Kathryn choked and wanted to touch the other back, but Alice stopped her gently and decisively, pushing back down arms with no strength. A roaming hand re-entered the wet place between the thighs.

– And you are soft on the inside…

She moved aside the skin down there, between Afterglows's spread thighs, using both hands, and having done that pushed her face at the moist place exposed. Afterglow felt her tongue, an instrument she used with great skill. The large body shook a bit, as Afterglow did bit her lip, as the pain of that did not truly register anymore, and everything turned into the pleasant haze slowly turning unbearable.

It exploded, and she did, too, inward, outward, softly bathing the other girl in her power, making her, too shake in powerful lust and satisfaction.

They crouched in each other's arms afterwards, enjoying the moments ticking away. Afterglow chuckled quietly while listening to the quiet darkness surrounding them.

– So Alice spent some time as an intern at a pleasure dome, did she?

– Yes, Alice replied. – Her uncle sent Alice there in a moment of spite because he saw her as willful and undesirable, and she trained hard with other boys and girls to learn good behavior. She returned to him attentive and pleasing.

– It is all right, Afterglow comforted the shaking girl. – Perfectly all right.

She kissed Alice on the forehead, as if to drive the point home.

– I can not believe they have not shut those places down long ago.
– It is a century-old tradition, Alice said in a small voice, – well established.
Afterglow wanted to vent her irritation, her rage, but smiled to the girl, petting her cheek.
– Those are the hardest to break, she acknowledged.
– I am just happy uncle felt he had to pull me out when he did, Alice said, shivering when she shook her head. – It is said that those completing the training, no matter where they go and what they do belong to the dome body and soul.
– I do know how that is, Afterglow said.
Alice looked curious at her.
– As you know, I was a Wraith, Afterglow said. – A mighty sorcerer fooled us, a bunch of children, of hopeful apprentices into following her to her land, to a place where she ruled supreme. She broke us and transformed us into her mindless soldiers to be used as her enforcers, her terror regime. On her orders we did horrible things, atrocities to beat the worst you can imagine. We knew what we were doing, but it did not seem to matter, you know. I ran away, leaving all my brothers and sisters behind, and I'm so *ashamed.*
She wanted to say more, to keep talking, but her voice failed her, and she began shaking badly.
Alice took her in her arms and began comforting her, and the girl's feather-light touches felt so good.
– Poor Afterglow.
– No, no, the big woman shook her head, – it is not me you should pity, but those that was left behind.
– Hush, Alice whispered. – Hush. You were just a wee child, crushed to dust by a mighty sorcerer. It is a good thing that you got away, against all odds. That was the only thing you could do, and a small miracle that says a lot about your will and ability to endure. Perhaps you even inspired others to follow you, even though you may never know that. This was far away, was it not?
– Yes, Kathryn choked, – far beyond the Nine Realms. I was terrified for a long time that she would find me, before the logic of the truth overwhelmed my irrational terror: that I had changed way too much for her to recognize the girl she subverted, even if she through extreme chance would manage to track me.
– It was the woman we met at the crossroads station. Alice nodded to herself. – You did meet, like you probably have several times, but she sees Afterglow, the mighty sorcerer, not the defenseless girl she enslaved and

hardly knew except as a passing ghost in her service. Yes, what you have just told me, and everything else happening to you is more than suggesting that you do know how «it» is. Alice is grateful to Afterglow for having shared her tale with her. Now, she knows more about Afterglow than anybody else in existence, perhaps with the exception of…

– Yes, Afterglow said hastily, and Alice fell silent.

They both did, as they rested some more in each other's arms.

Time passed practically unnoticed, there, in the soft shadows. They let it, alone, or perhaps alone together with their thoughts.

The bright lights in the darkness danced behind Afterglow's eyelids, like they always did, whispering secrets and shameful truths. She could never forget.

She awoke abruptly and Alice was right behind her, as the girl was practically thrown half across the large bed.

– Sorry, she whimpered.

– It is all right, Alice assured her, repeating it in an even softer voice, rubbing a sore shoulder. – It is all right.

Afterglow rose from the bed, and reached out a hand.

– Come, she said.

Alice reached out her hand and allowed Afterglow to catch it. They had had not slept for long, but long enough for the two moons, Big Moon and Little Moon to rise above the horizon.

– Does Alice feel tired?

– Not really, I…

– Does she feel sharp and ready for everything that might come her way?

– She does, Alice replied. – She feels beyond ready and is pleased to join Afterglow on her prowl in the wretched night.

They showered again, slowly, uneventful, with only a few touches of affection. The moonlight had only moved a little on the floor when they returned to the living room. No electrical lights had been lit. They dried each other again, rough and soft and everything between. There was some kissing and fondling. Afterglow grabbed Alice's arms and held them, held them hard.

– Tonight was an exception, Afterglow said softly. – It can not be allowed to continue.

– Alice understands, the girl acknowledged, sniffing a bit. – Do not worry, Master. She knows her place.

Afterglow changed the bandage on her arm on her own. It had turned wet and practically been torn off during the recent energized activities. The wound itself looked fine. It had closed okay, and was not infected.

– Does it hurt? Alice asked hesitatingly.

– No!

It burned a bit, and there was pain when Afterglow moved the arm too abruptly. She had not really noticed earlier, but now she did, when there were no more distractions.

They dressed up. Afterglow added a few items, and seeing that Alice did, too. There was quite the varied and numerous items in the arsenal gathered in the apartment, on walls and in drawers, including knives, swords and even crossbows. Afterglow sensed the poignancy of the girl's excitement and anxiety.

– Afterglow prepares for… for war, does she not?

– She does, Kathryn confirmed.

She fastened straps various places around her body. The process felt instinctive, casual, as if there had not been years since she had worn the set up.

– You were a mercenary, were you not, in the far lands?

– Yes, Afterglow said, – it felt like the right thing to do, to follow… my apathy. I believed it would help me get back on my feet, and it did. It got me up and then almost down for good. It was very liberating to see blood fly all over the places, though, over all the places.

The laughter was short, with sharp edges and free of happiness. Afterglow easily caught the chill passing down the girl's spine.

She walked to a special compartment at the opposite side of the room. There was no hesitation, no delay. She opened the doors. There were only a few, very distinctive objects in there, more space than anything else, really. Afterglow heard Alice gasp behind her.

– The Bands of Kordon, the girl said. – The Cup of Wines and…

She had to strain herself to continue.

– … the Black Blade of Oradecht.

Afterglow picked up the black blade. It hurt her, like it always did when she held it, just a small knife, but pulsing with energies to potentially lay waste to the world.

– May I hold it?

The voice came from far behind her, hardly audible. She turned and saw the girl stand just a few steps away.

– No, it's mine, only mine, for as long as I endure.

She put it back at its spot in the closet. The sensation of it lingered in her hand, as if it had been born there, as if it belonged there, and she knew it did.

There were a few more objects there, stones twinkling in eerie light, a crystal ball, and other items Alice did not recognize, but they all had one thing in common: they glowed to her inner eye, as all things of power did.

– Afterglow has such a great collection of precious objects, she said formally, – worthy of her stature.

The older woman nodded curtly, with a slight, spiteful smile. She had become distant again, the cold mask Alice recalled from the first time they had met.

Afterglow closed the compartment. She walked to the wall and grabbed a sword, and put it in the sheath on her back.

– The final part on your path to become a warrior witch begins, now, she declared. – You have already tasted blood, a few drops that will eventually grow to a sea.

Alice swallowed hard, as she willingly and even eagerly accepted the straps and light body armor Afterglow handed her.

– You will learn to dress yourself without conscious thought. It will become second nature to you… like it has for me. The sword is not that difficult to handle compared to the wand. It is mostly about a shift in balance and attitude. We do not have time for much training anymore. You will learn as you go, as you cut and stab and draw the blood of your enemies. When your kill instinct has been awakened fully, your education will be complete.

Alice picked, unprompted a sword from the wall. She swung it a little. It felt awkward, but good in her hand.

– You chose well. This blade will speak to you and howl for the blood of your opponents. It will extend the reach of your arms, add to the power within you already possess.

Afterglow drew her sword, and swung at her. Alice blocked the advance without thinking.

– And sometimes, when the power within is gone or useless, which may happen in a number of different situations it will be your last line of defense against what threatens you.

They parried for a few minutes. Afterglow slowly increased the pace as Alice got the hang of it a little.

– Yours is a light sword, useable for women of average or just above average strength. A man, a sword-maker from the East in the realm of Earth coming here a few decades ago calls it a Katana. You do not need a lot of strength to use it if you do it correctly. As you have already surmised its strong part is for defense, the weak part for offense. You can cut through anything with a well used sword.

– And yours?

It was Katana-like, but bigger, heavier.

– He made it for me.
That was yet another of her curtly responses that told Alice so much.
Alice tested out Afterglow's instructions, not really doubting her. The «strong» part, close to the handle could catch even Afterglow's strongest blow, if done right. The weak part, close to the point achieved an enormous speed and power when swung right.
As the icing of the cake they wore coats hiding well the special-made sheet on their backs. It did not show, even upon closer scrutiny, but seemed to be an integral part of the back.
– The body armor makes us both seem a little bigger, but only people that know about such things will be able to recognize it.
She walked to the large window. Alice followed in her shadow, striving to walk and stand straight. They stood there for a while, pondering the sight of the town below stretching across the land.
It was kind of peaceful, even to them, listening to their own, churning insides.
The distant noise of engines hardly reached them at all. Mother Moon and Daughter Moon kept rising on the night sky, bathing night owls in their silver light.
– Listen, Afterglow said, – with your mind, not only your ears.
Alice closed her eyes.
– Open your eyes, Afterglow chastised her. – Do not use cheap tricks to more easily achieve your objective.
Alice felt anger, very aware of how easily her mentor had pushed her buttons. She focused, like she had learned, striving to keep her eyes open, to allow that distraction. And then, suddenly it was distraction no longer, but just a part of the picture, the image she was weaving in her mind, and a smile formed on her lips, as the expanded surroundings were born inside her.
– You laughed, Afterglow said.
Alice turned, a little dizzy, apprehensive, looking at her teacher and friend and terror.
– You giggled darkly after you had killed the Wraith, after you had tasted blood for the first time. It was not shock, was not how most children react upon facing Death for the first time, but savage triumph to celebrate your accomplishment, your victory.
– My Lady, I…
– That is good, Afterglow said.
Alice bowed her head in deference and acknowledgement.
They headed for the elevator. The sorcerer walked first, and the apprentice in her shadow. The doors slid open, and they stepped inside. A slight pull,

and they were on their way down.

– It is so quiet, Alice said.

– Yes, this is a fairly new building, endowed with recent technology, Afterglow shrugged.

They met Mrs. Galbraith on their way down the stairs. To Kathryn's amazement the woman grunted a greeting. Afterglow returned the greeting in a similar way.

– She is the landlord? Alice wondered.

– No, I have never met them, him, her or it, Afterglow replied. – She hinted that she was not the owner when I leased the apartment, but was not forthcoming in explaining herself.

– If she is an intermediate she is close to a perfect such, Alice grinned.

Afterglow had to grin, too, unable to help herself. The girl's fairly light mood was inevitably contagious.

Alice turned serious, changing to her curious mode. It happened so quickly that Afterglow knew this was not a spur of the moment fling. The girl had prepared herself for it.

– Afterglow…

The teacher looked patiently and patronizingly at the student.

– What do you think happened to the ancient gods?

They stepped onto the streets, the noise of the city reaching them undiluted.

– I do not know. No one I know of does. It is a riddle to compare to the Great Mystery. They were present in humanity's life for so long, but then they suddenly vanished without warning or explanation.

There were not that many people out this late at night, and not many cars either. Just a few individuals sat outside the taverns and had beer and stronger stuff.

The silence lasted a few seconds longer than it should, which certainly told the youngster a lot.

– I have met a man that fit well the description of the old gods, surpassing them by far, a walking dark fire in human guise. Anything I tell you about him would be insufficient, unsatisfactory.

– He is your lover, is he not?

Afterglow sighed. The girl no longer hid her pleasure dome training.

– I knew it, Alice chuckled

They passed the big clock on the wall. Afterglow did not bother to compare the time, did not bother at all.

– I am not certain he has my best interest in mind…

– Has any guy? The youngster chided.

Has any gal? Afterglow thought.

The partly light mood changed, into something poignant and frantic.

The girl touched the older woman's cheek, and wanted to do more, but was kept at an arm's length by an invisible wall. The young face turned sad and filled with longing.

– What do you need, Kathryn? Alice pleaded with her. – Please tell me and I will get it for you.

A car passed them, with a low sound, no louder than the flapping of distant wings. It was just a passing roar, a single loud noise before the silence reasserted itself.

– I need nothing, Afterglow said, – nothing at all.

CHAPTER TEN

The walk felt long and strenuous at first, every single step like an ordeal.

The streets, the city, the immediate surroundings expanded through their senses, without them even trying. Afterglow, pondering the issue, herself and the surroundings knew her senses had improved, and she was able to actually feel, in a tangible way how Alice had grown, had taken yet another quantum leap forward in her education.

Kathryn, in a spur of the moment so unlike her grabbed the other, held her and kissed her on the lips. Alice froze a little at first, but then she smiled happily and turned limp in the strong arms holding her in their grip.

The girl laughed, a happy little laughter, before they disengaged and walked on.

Other couples, too, fondled and kissed and caressed each other, nothing out of the ordinary. Afterglow kept an eye on them, on every single human being on their path, doing so in an experienced, non-obtrusive way, striving to keep her focus, distracted by a thousand stormy thoughts.

People had their beer on the broad sidewalk taverns by the pier. Others, drinking harder swallowed their liquor in single turns. Afterglow and Alice passed by it all, pushing deeper into the city night.

They took left on the corner. Onion Square, as always beckoned them to the right, but they chose to ignore it.

– Can you still hear it? Afterglow asked.

– I can, Alice replied. – I think any sensitive can. It is the sound, but it is more than that, so compelling and intimidating. Looking at the faces of the statues… They are so majestic, so serene. I want to kneel in their presence.

They pressed deeper into the city, heading east, towards the mountains rising between the cities and the sea. There were fever people here, at this time, during the night. The neighborhood was not exactly the best. The two women did not care about that. They shrugged off pointed stares from the local clientele.

Alice returned the stares on occasion, also making threatening gestures.

– I suspect you are provoking our fellow humans on this place, my apprentice, Afterglow said lightly. – You want to prove yourself, but should not bother. There are no challenges for you here.

– There are not? A dark giggle escaped the girl. – That pleases Afterglow's apprentice a lot.

They entered a dark alley. Alice's hand never strayed long from the sword.

There was a suction here, too, making their fingertips tingle.
– Is that a portal? Alice asked, frowning, squinting her eyes in uncertainty.
– It is, Afterglow replied, – sort of. It is fading, and will be useless soon.
It pulsed and waned. Images danced around it. They heard sounds and caught scents and taste.
- Is that blood I imagine in my mouth? The apprentice wondered.
- It is, the sorcerer confirmed.
The area was clearly unstable. Reality itself bounced and bounced back in its surroundings.
They heard the sound of a coach and horses. The girl, even though her attention was drawn to the impressions noticed that Afterglow froze, that unpleasant thoughts visited her.
Newfound clarity brought further awareness to the girl.
- This is a rather rare experience, is it not?
Afterglow nodded and Alice's eyes glowed even stronger in unambiguous curiosity.
– What are they, the various portals and pathways? Who made them?
– The way I heard it, and I believe that to be true is that no one made them. They are natural rifts between realms. As you known, there are manmade bridges and passages in appropriate places, though. This *is* a rare occasion, making the nature of the portal an even deeper mystery.
They passed the unstable spot, cautiously avoiding its center. The rest of the walk through the dark alley remained uneventful. At least nothing substantial happened. They suddenly heard louder sounds, insistent whispers. A flicker of evident concern was lit in Afterglow's violet eyes. She signed for the apprentice to be on her guard, and Alice's jittery increased by a mile.
They appeared at a rather large square, with a tall, imposing old building on its opposite side. Afterglow raised a hand. She did not have to point or anything.
A little to the left of the building, in front of what clearly was a more modern structure hummed a car. It had its engine on. An unusual amount of smoke flowed from its engine. Its front lights burned across the square.
Afterglow stood still, alert, frozen in her blazing thought.
The car showed in both the window and on the street, but the red lights in the window reminded her of eyes, and they glared at her with a vicious glow.
She stood still, grabbing her sword hilt, readying herself, and Alice, taking her cue from her, as always did as well.
The car drove away. The red lights in the window seemed to linger well after the vehicle had left its spot, but faded eventually.

– What was that? Alice wondered. – A mouth?
– No. Afterglow shook her head. – Not a mouth.
– Alice would guess that the car belongs to certain families, even though it did not had the usual markings and that its passenger did as well. She would also venture that they had nothing good in mind.
She did not really expect an answer and she was proven correct.
They crossed the square with caution, walking to the large door at the front of the old building. It seemed to expand as they approached, making Alice shrink in her tracks. But nothing more happened. The car did not return and the square remained empty.
Afterglow knocked on the door.
– What is our purpose here, if Afterglow's humble apprentice may ask? Alice asked, beside herself with curiosity, one once again overcoming her apprehension.
– You may ask, Afterglow shrugged, before continuing, replying to the actual question. – We are going to invite ourselves to a dinner,
– At this hour? Must be quite a gentleman, then, having dinner guests in the middle of night, even though his earlier choice of guests rather contradicts that.
She was loyal and dedicated. Afterglow nodded in acknowledgement.
– So, you know it is a man? I cannot say I am surprised…
– Alice studied Magick and its users long before she sought out Afterglow, the apprentice stated proudly. – And among them, even among the mightiest of them Afterglow stands out. It is said she is *ancient* and has been born and has died a million times. But there are not that many candidates among her recent associates still among the living… in the Triple Cities.
Afterglow shivered, and through her open eyes a million glimpses revealed themselves.
The door opened. Susan Howard greeted them with a dark, dark smile.
– Surprise! She grinned.
– It certainly is, Afterglow conceded willingly. – What are you doing here, if I may ask?
– Of course Mighty Afterglow may ask this woman whatever she wants, Susan curtseyed. – Stane the Sorcerer has granted this woman the honor of becoming his apprentice. She sought him out after her previous encounter with Afterglow, eager to learn the secrets.
She sounded much very like Alice, very much like the polite, humble apprentice she was supposed to sound like.
A subtle change had come over her. She was an apprentice, lower than the ground Afterglow walked.

– I would like to see Stane, Afterglow said brusquely. – I have urgent business to discuss with him.

– Of course, Susan said. – Please enter, and this apprentice will take Afterglow to the Master. The other guests have already arrived. The Master will be with all of you shortly.

– By all means, Afterglow shrugged, deliberately, – my guess is that I would want to speak to them as well.

They stepped inside, clearly crossing a barrier as they did so. Both Afterglow and Alice noticed it like a slight pressure on the skin, very aware that the contact would have been far more brutal if they had been unwelcome.

The light contact still brought unpleasant sensations more than resembling warnings.

Susan brought them through the entrance hall. The house hissed at them and watched them with cruel eyes. They could not keep themselves from shivering a bit. Susan led them to the rather large dining hall, before she faded back into the background, devoured by the hungry house in which she resided.

Most of the seats around the long table were empty. Two sorcerers had sat down. One paced the floor. Two of them had an apprentice. Afterglow knew two of the sorcerers, the man and the female couple, but not the scowling man finally sitting down at one end of the table. The apprentices were new to her. Afterglow nodded to her colleagues, and they returned their greeting.

– Well met, Afterglow, the woman said, sounding like something was stuck in her throat.

– Well met, Lenore of Lambruia, Afterglow greeted her in a similar fashion.

– Well met, Afterglow, the man said.

– Well met, Rowan of Lambruia, Afterglow said sweetly, giving him a dazzling smile.

The apprentices were, as usual ignored.

The pacing man did not invite a traditional greeting at all.

Alice changed, to become servile like the other youths, a customary apprentice. When Afterglow sat down, Alice took her place behind her Master, standing, like the other two.

All the sorcerers had sat down by the time Stane arrived. He made an entrance, even though it was not evident, his hawkish face a study in lack of expression. Afterglow and the other three rose, paying tribute to the house master.

– Unexpected guests? He raised an eyebrow. – What a pleasant surprise.

– You love pleasant surprises, Afterglow commented dryly.

The other three sorcerers glanced stunned at her, no doubt because she dared talk back to the great Stane. She sensed both shock and joy from Alice.

Stane sat down in chair at the end of the table. The four visiting sorcerers sat back down.

– I love having dinner guests, Stane remarked. – I get lonely in this big house.

No one commented on that. Afterglow wanted very much to do so, but held her tongue.

He clapped his hands once. His servants, Susan and four others entered the hall virtually instantaneously. They served dinner, food and wine with lowered eyes. Afterglow sensed how her apprentice, like the other two visiting began shaking in apprehension behind her, an event neither unexpected nor unusual. Stane was not known for his kindness when it came to apprentices, his own as well as others'.

– Cheers.

The house master raised his glass, and his fellow sorcerers did the same. They did not say anything. He drank. They drank as well.

The dinner began. Afterglow and the others took the first bite of the steak. They took their second bite, and had some more wine.

– An excellent steak, as usual, Stane, Afterglow said, praising the master.

– Thank you, Afterglow, he beamed (not beaming). – I appreciate that.

The meal, at least its first few minutes proceeded in relative silence. The scowling man at the other end of the table almost jumped out of his seat, but kept his mouth shut.

– So, ladies and gentlemen, Stane finally said, drying his lips and surrounding skin with a napkin. – What brings you here tonight?

No one, or very few, visited Stane without wanting something from him, a service or more. Afterglow recalled her own previous visit not that long ago.

It was very subtle, really. He looked across the table at the scowling guy.

– My name is Uther, the other man began. – I am from the Aswanian territories, and I heard about the great Stane… the barterer, the aid of sorcerers… in need.

Afterglow kept her face impassive through the initial bootlicking approach.

– You have traveled far, Uther, Stane nodded. – May we inquire why?

The other three sorcerers looked closer at the far traveler, as if to stress Stane's words.

– I believe… I am convinced my life is in grave danger, Uther said.

A stunned silence followed his words. Such blunt speech was quite unusual among sorcerers, where hints and subterfuge were the general rule.

– That is… unfortunate, Stane said, looking at the angry, fuming and desperate man across the table.

– I need a protection, Uther stated firmly, suddenly quite calm, deadly calm. – I need Ra's Razor or its equal.

There was a collective gasp around the table. Even the apprentices could not keep themselves from releasing a sound of astonishment and fright.

– You have unforgivable and mighty enemies, Uther, Stane said, pausing at least twice. – Who are they?

– I do not know, the big man said, frustration very evident in his voice and stance. – It started off as a minor skirmish at the borders several years ago, and I believed that to be the *end* of it…

Uther was a monarch, not only a sorcerer.

– But such was not the case I trust?

Stane rubbed it in, deliberately, remaining the barterer, even though the frown did not fade from his brow.

– I believed it was, for a long time, Uther said. – The army, when it eventually arrived was far greater in numbers than before, and it had among them strange and mighty creatures, almost untouchable and each strong as ten ordinary men. They reduced my city to rubble, and I and my most trusted apprentice barely escaped with our lives. He was killed on its way here, by one of those very creatures, by a… a…

– A Wraith, Afterglow whispered.

Everybody looked stunned at her. Stane and the couple shifted in their chairs, as if to jump out of the way of… of a *skirmish*.

– Forgive me, great Uther, she added, hastily, deliberately humbly, – but I know quite a bit about these creatures. I used to be one of them.

Several seconds passed, before Uther decided to let mercy overcome his sense of pride.

– Please, proceed! Uther grunted.

– A mighty sorcerer captured me and other apprentices in my youth, Afterglow said, – transforming us into her mindless soldiers. But we were only raiding small villages bordering her kingdom, nothing like this. I guess my former brief Master's obvious ambitions have been realized or others have… profited from her knowledge. This was very far away, even compared to the Territories, so far away that I do not know how far away it was.

– And you escaped her bondage? Uther growled. – I have heard about you…

Everybody has, Alice would have said, if she had been allowed.

– We, I and my apprentice recently encountered one that could change shape. I do not believe or rather I am fairly certain they cannot all do that, if it is not their power to begin with.

Afterglow turned to Stane, abruptly.

– I believe your life may be in danger as well, she said. – That was my initial purpose with my visit tonight, to warn you.
– There are things brewing, Rowan of Lambruia said, totally out of character. – I believed it was a mere personal matter, but now I am not so certain anymore.
– I believed that as well, Afterglow said. – It might be several matters, not necessarily related. Lately, sorcerers or associates of mine have been attacked and also killed, but there have also been other incidents, clearly not directly related to me.
– There have been noticeable distant rumblings, Stane mused admittedly.
– I guess this night has turned out quite differently from what we all expected, Uther stated, not at all so embarrassed anymore.
His bargaining power had been increased tenfold.
– Existence is vast, Lenore of Lambruia said. – We have always known that it one night would pay us a visit. The legends…
Alice opened her mouth to speak. She did not, catching herself, but the damage had been done.
Afterglow jumped to her feet, and struck her down, almost severing her head from her shoulders. The girl hit the floor like a rag doll, still conscious somewhat, shaking in terror. Afterglow kicked her brutally in the ribs, kicking her several times, punishing her in a fit of rage, without a single sign of remorse, making sure the object of her contempt stayed awake while doing so.
The girl still moved, somewhat when her master was done. Afterglow stepped back. There was blood on her boots. Nobody moved or said anything. The apprentice crawled towards Stane, forcing herself to her knees, putting her head to the ground.
Stane did not say anything or even do anything outright, but the girl still sensed his approval.
– Forgive this lowly apprentice, Master, she whimpered, awaiting her fate.
Stane did not say anything, did not even visibly acknowledge her words or even her presence.
– So, Afterglow has finally taken herself an apprentice, he remarked.
The moment passed. Alice pulled back, her head and knees never separated from the ground, resting at Afterglow's feet, like a dog.
– Several of more… local sorcerers had… a working relationship with the sorcerer in question, Afterglow said, a twinge of acid in her voice. – They are more or less directly responsible for her increase in stature.
– Yes, yes, Lenore nodded, – the rather… unfortunate treatment of apprentices. That particular practice has been suspended for quite some time,

now.

– But the damage has been done, Uther snarled. – That bunch of dogs fed her power for decades. In an effort to eliminate potential competition they aided in the creation of their own certain future doom. They could just as well have knelt before her like the lowest of creatures. What were they thinking?

– I do not think they were thinking.

Afterglow shrugged.

– They let their ambition think for them.

– Never a good idea, Stane said, noncommittal.

– But Afterglow returned to her Master afterwards, Lenore said, pointedly at Afterglow, but careful not to issue a challenge.

– My Master was being kind to me, Afterglow said. – He prepared me, wanted me to return, strong of will and soaked in power. I would not be worthy if I did not.

– And he did an excellent job, did he not?

– Ladies… Stane implored them.

And yet again the four stared astounded at him.

– I seem to have come to the right place, Uther said, after more uncomfortable silence, – unwittingly, but still. I salute you all!

– It seems like you have, Stane acknowledged.

– Our common interests are unquestionable, Rowan agreed, glancing cautiously at Lenore.

She ignored him.

– We also came here seeking needed aid, he added, his wording still cautious.

Afterglow felt a flare of contempt, keeping it in check with an effort.

– I did not, she stressed. – I came here to deliver a warning. I need no favor.

The subtle change in language was, as always very telling.

She stared at Stane. He shrugged again.

– I acknowledge our common plight, he said, – but I am a barterer. I have a reputation to uphold.

Afterglow grinned without grinning, in spite of the chaotic cauldron and sick relief churning through her.

– Uther came here seeking assistance, seeking aid, Uther said, bowing to Stane. – He will be happy to honor his initial intention.

Rowan deferred to Lenore, deliberately.

– Lenore and Rowan will, too, she said, bowing slightly.

Afterglow waited.

– Stane will be delighted if Afterglow will be kind enough to return a favor,

Stane said. – Please stay.

– Afterglow will stay, she replied. – She has always intended to return the favor she owes Stane and thanks him for his generosity, for the opportunity to do that.

And then she bowed.

Things slowly returned to a semblance of normality.

– Please follow me, Stane bid them curtly.

They did. The shaking, suffering figure on the floor remained in the same, totally uncomfortable position. She did not move or move her eyes the slightest. It was as if they were not working anymore, as if nothing was working, except the need to cringe on the floor. Afterglow pretended to ignore her, to forget her, but just as she left the hall, she signed for her apprentice to rise, to follow her.

Alice rose, on shaking feet, and began stumbling after the group of sorcerers and apprentices. She walked fast, almost falling every time she took a step forward, but she stayed on her feet somehow.

There was still blood on her face. She made no attempt at wiping it off, none at all.

They entered a smaller room, one where the very air itself seemed to glow in deep, dark red. Stane himself seemed to shift and change slightly. It resembled an alchemist's laboratory, with its rising fumes and flaring fluids, but anybody even remotely sensitive would sense the power here. This was not just his sanctum, but his inner sanctum, his Place of Power, where he was at his strongest.

Afterglow noticed another shift, sensed movement, something making her frown she was unable to identify and quantify, and could not keep the slight sense of apprehension from manifesting within.

There was a lot of apparatus here, even a few more machines she had not seen before.

– My, oh, my, you have expanded, she whistled. – And upgraded, too, I wager.

– The life of the inquisitive mind never stands still, he replied lightly.

She fought, fought hard to not let a deep frown display itself on her brow.

– We are all in luck, Stane said. – I happen to have Ra's Razor, one of the most devastating weapons in existence in my possession. I assume Uther is familiar with its quirks, its dangers and pitfalls?

– Uther has indeed studied ancient history extensively, Uther said. – He is ready for the task.

– Very well then. Stane began pushing buttons and making preparations. – We will need one apprentice each as conduits. I will provide Uther with his.

– Stane is most kind, Uther said politely.

Stane raised his arms and began speaking his curses, incantations, whispering instructions, spells in everybody's ears. Afterglow sensed how they influenced her, inevitably, but sensed no malice, no foul play, confident that she would if they should manifest.

The machinery started humming, turning to life around them. Energy traveled through thick, transparent wires. Afterglow felt it as it moved, as her power practically turned itself on without her prompting and made her aware of everything happening in the space between the walls and floor and ceiling. Her attention even pushed itself to the rest of house and to the streets outside.

The spells filled the room, caressing the people inside it, as the lesser among them began showing signs of becoming entranced. The intrusion shook them and froze them in place.

Alice staring straight forward with empty eyes, totally taken over by the spells climbed into one of the pods. Susan and three other apprentices equally mesmerized were designated one each as well. The moment their backs pushed at the wall straps tied their ankles and wrists. Afterglow took her place in front of Alice. The other sorcerers took their place. Stane opened a compartment. A metal glove that had already started glowing rose into the air. He grabbed it, holding onto it, even as it attempted to escape his grip.

Archaic words flowed from his mouth as he struggled with the device. He was sweating hard, as he carried the glove across the floor to Uther. The sorcerer monarch was bathed in arcane energies, and so was Susan in the pod behind him.

Afterglow once again found herself impressed by the ease in which Stane worked his Magick. It was both casual and powerful. She felt how it cut into her, felt pain ravage her, release the power resting inside. Alice and the other apprentices moaned. Energies flowed from Alice and into Afterglow, startling Kathryn with their potency, making her blink uncontrollably and gasping for breath. The room started to shake in her vision, fields of shadows, holes in reality started appearing, and she was not certain if she saw less or more.

– Your left hand, sir, Stane shouted to Uther.

Clearly straining Uther of Aswania raised his left hand until its fingers pointed forwards, matching the holes in the glove. His pain already severe, he strived to not cry out. Stane pushed the glove onto his hand, and then Uther crouched and screamed, his mighty voice making the walls tremble.

The energies subsided. Afterglow could breathe again. Her vision was still impaired, but righted itself slowly, and she could not tell whether or not she felt relief or disappointment.

The room and its apparatus… settled. It sighed like an entity might do after holding its breath.

Afterglow looked casually at her hands. They were glowing in ghostly blue fire, and she could not stop it from happening, no matter how hard she tried.

– That was amazing, Lenore gasped. –What *happened?* The energies were far more potent than one would expect and what was necessary for the procedure.

– A procedure so brief and eloquently simple, Uther said in appreciation to Stane.

– It is a fairly simple set of spells, Stane shrugged, – but not without its potential pitfalls, carrying with it the risk of something unexpected and dangerous.

Afterglow watched Stane and now she could not keep the frown from manifesting.

The blue fire faded slowly, only slowly from her hands.

Their restraints removed the apprentices, clearly dizzy and weakened climbed out of the pods. Alice took her place close to her Master. Afterglow sensed her, did not have to look at her to know she was there, sensed her, how she strived to submerge herself, to become a part of Afterglow's shadow, a part of Afterglow.

– Now, test it! Stane told Uther.

– On what, my good man? Uther wondered, clearly hesitant. – I can feel its energies. I fear they are so vast that they will lay waste to anything they are tested on.

– On whatever you desire. Stane replied.

Uther pondered a bit before pointing his left hand at the wall. Then there was something resembling a mighty roar. Energies flared and the wall disappeared and left a giant hole in its wake.

The hole was pitch-black. There did not seem to be anything there at all. When Afterglow studied it she imagined it was totally empty, not even the blackness it had appeared as at first, but a huge hole of Nothing.

– My study has inbuilt safeguards, Stane said, once again explaining himself. – If they had not been there, the firing of the weapon would have destroyed most of the house.

– There was no sense of being drained, Uther said puzzled.

– It will drain you, Stane said, – but only after repeated use, and you will recover quickly. It is not merely one of the most powerful arms in existence, but also one of the most effective. It should put quite a dent in your enemy's wraith army.

– It will lay waste to it, Uther said, his voice thick in triumph. – Their master may still win, but she will have to change tactics dramatically. You have given me a fighting chance. Thank you, all of you. I will repay you all one day, if the fates are kind.

He bowed, and his fellow sorcerers did, too. Then he swept his cloak around him and strode out of there.

– The wraiths may not be possible to kill, Afterglow told him. – Not even with Ra's Razor, not outside their master's realm and with the magicks she has placed on them. They can only be contained or the razor will destroy their ability to move around in our realms, destroy the metals they are wearing on their hands and feet.

– Thank you, Uther said briskly, – I will remember that.

And he was gone.

The remaining four glanced at each other.

– It will be interesting, Rowan remarked.

Stane turned towards the couple.

– So, what can Stane do for Rowan and Lenore?

– We came here for two reasons, great Stane, Rowan said. – To possibly find out what was going on and to gain allies. We have succeeded in both and are beholden to you, to both of you.

He and eventually Lenore bowed.

– The tale of our meeting will spread, and will in itself contribute to our cause. I imagine our enemy or at least one of them will meet with quite a bit of… trouble in Uther's kingdom, and give us time to consolidate our forces.

There was more quick bowing, and then Rowan and Lenore took their leave as well.

Afterglow and Stane stood by the exit, front to front, face to face.

– The extra energy… he said slowly, he acknowledged. – That was yours. My guess is that the bitch Lenore eventually realized that, too, and stopped challenging you out of self-preservation.

– I guess she did, Afterglow did. – I think she might have been one of the apprentices listening in when Malone bragged about me… just like you were.

– You are leaving, I trust?

– Not very far, she grinned. – You just need to shout very loud, and I will rush to your aid. I trust you will manage to hold off invading forces until the reinforcements arrive?

This time there was no bowing. Afterglow stepped outside, through the shield and her apprentice followed right behind her.

She tensed, preparing for a possible attack, but there was none. The streets were fairly quiet, unassuming, not posing any instant threat.

Filled with energy as she was, cut open as she was, she sensed more than she usually did. Sensations reached her from all sides, from the fortress behind her, from the streets ahead, the air above and the ground beneath her feet. It was like a map, a labyrinth she had to navigate, but not that different from her existence as it had been for a long time.

Different enough. The waves emanated constantly from her body. That was not new. But right now, in bursts and protrusions the texture and movement of her surroundings, even her far surroundings were briefly known to her.

She began walking, the shade trailing her like a leaf in her slipstream.

There was a slight tug to mark its presence and nothing more.

She took to the left, to the center of the city, further away from her comforting home, the sanctuary on the southeastern harbor. There was a nervous rattle in the streets she had trouble noticing, something growing in complexity and gaining strength from day to day, night to night. The sword hilt quivered close to her hand. She felt it in her fingertips.

Steam flowed from a nearby coffee shop. People's scents and voices flowed. The feeling of being many places simultaneously persisted and even spiked further. A man passed them. He was staring, even if he was not looking at them directly. She recognized one of the Maximus clan's henchmen.

He faded away, his mission just to be seen, to convey the ongoing message, not to take action or aggravate.

They reached the unsavory part of the town, where the streets turned narrow like alleys and alleys turned narrow, where people living on the edge of society thrived or at least could gather quietly and with lesser risk of being bothered.

But even here, especially here there were clear signs of the ripples surging in this realm. Afterglow would have sensed that without trying, without any prior knowledge of the gathering forces.

She glanced at Big Moon, imagining that it had grown distinctly in brilliance.

The unsavory brick building with no visible door had not changed, not physically, but Afterglow had no trouble sensing the changes inside.

The old key, the brick she moved first did not work. She let out a snort of contempt. It took her less than five try-outs to gauge the new, slightly more complex code. The door opened and they stepped into the hissing darkness, the brief passage touching the Wasteland. Alice shivered under the onslaught of the creatures hiding there, and would have, in her poor state of mind been consumed instantly if Afterglow, with her potent presence had not prevented that.

They reached the tavern. There were not that many guests, not compared to what would usually be a busy evening, but they all stared without staring at the two new arrivals.

– We will stay here for the night, Afterglow told her apprentice, her squire.

Afterglow sat down by a table close to the entrance, while Alice approached the desk and the man behind it, the man serving anybody.

– My Master requires a room.

The sound of the apprentice's voice made Kathryn wonder a bit. It sounded different, changed, like her appearance, her changed bearing.

The man serving anybody hesitated only briefly before handing the woman at the other side of the desk a key.

– First floor, he mumbled sourly.

Alice nodded to herself. It was a good room, one fitting of Afterglow's standing.

– My Master requires her Glenmorangie.

The barkeep filled the tiny glass.

Alice returned to the table. She put the glass down and knelt by the chair.

Afterglow drank slowly, savoring the taste more than usual, sensing how the burning sensation spread in her body and mind. The strong liquor did not really affect her that much, but it brushed off briefly what long ago had permanently unsettled inside her.

She emptied the glass and rose.

– A bottle, she told the barkeep.

He put one on the desk. Alice grabbed it.

The two of them left the room. Alice walked first up the stairs, braving the way, as the eager-serving apprentice she was.

The room was fairly nice, clean and comfy, one of the best the place had to offer. Afterglow nodded pleased to herself.

– This will do, she conveyed to her humble and beyond humbled apprentice.

Alice put the bottle on the night table. She did not react, did not make any sign that she had heard her Master speak, but silently continued with her tasks, preparing the room for Master's use.

Her movements were precise, meticulous. She searched for magickal traps. There were none. She searched for poisonous animals. There were none. She remade the bed, preparing it for Afterglow's pleasure, in small and big things changing the room to suit Afterglow. When she was done she knelt before her Master, her eyes cast to the floor, her entire demeanor that of a dedicated and humble apprentice.

– Come, Afterglow bade her, smiling sternly, – sit with me.

There were two chairs facing each other. Afterglow sat down in one, Alice in the other. The girl's eyes remained cast to the floor, even her thoughts staying bland and mute. She was attentive, but showed no active self what so ever.

– He spared your life, Afterglow mused amused. – I did not think he would. It does whet my curiosity.

Alice shivered under the onslaught of the cruel voice and spiteful nature of her Master.

– The reason is far from apparent. It can not be because I will owe him any favor. He is not that stupid. He knows or should know that I do not care about a lowly apprentice's fate. Perhaps it amused him? Perhaps it was because the insult was on me and not really on him? I do not *know*. That fact bothers me a bit, it does.

She clapped her hands together, just as sorcerers often did to call an apprentice. Alice straightened in the chair, even more attentive.

– Make some tea, apprentice, she commanded casually, with an implied chill in her voice cold enough to freeze the other's blood in her veins.

Alice jumped on her feet, and rushed to the kitchen. Not long after that the scent of heated water filled the room.

– He was lying, there, at the end, too, or at least not telling the entire truth, which amounts to pretty much the same thing. The fact that he bothered to explain himself when I prodded him about the expansion and upgrade of his laboratory is also a tell-tale sign. He has an agenda of some kind, one beyond the obvious and one he does not bother to explain.

Alice did not react or made any sign that she even heard the Master's voice. She kept doing her chores, as the sorcerer had ordained.

Afterglow listened to the sounds from the outside, both from the streets and those the Wasteland imposed on them.

Alice returned with the tray and cup and smoking brew. She put it on the table on Afterglow's right. There was hardly any sound as she put the china down.

She proceeded to return to the chair. Then the sorcerer signed to her, the sign of submission. The girl froze and quickly knelt down before the stern woman.

Afterglow sipped the tea. It was hot and strong.

– You failed me, apprentice, she said, – disappointed me.

Alice did not move. Her lower lip shivered hard.

– You knew well the etiquette guiding the conduct between sorcerers and apprentices and still you failed them, insulting me most gravely.

The apprentice made no attempt at speaking or moving or defending herself in any way.

– I could not and can not allow such a transgression to go unpunished, of

course.
The woman in the chair drew a golden collar from her coat. Alice's shivering turned even more pronounced.
– This was made from a teacher of apprentices when he transgressed against the royalty of the land. He was a stern teacher and still is. He will guide you in correct behavior and will be very cross if you are stupid enough to break the code of conduct ruling an apprentice.
She rubbed the metal against the half-dried blood on Alice's skin. Alice bared her neck and Afterglow slipped the collar on her.
The whispers began almost immediately. Afterglow heard it, too, through the girl. Alice shook in a moment's defiance. The current flowed through her instantly. She screamed and fell to the floor. Afterglow studied the effect with keen interest.
The punishment finally let up, after a series of moments Afterglow knew that Alice had imagined was forever.
– A stern teacher indeed. He will not accept the slightest opposition. You will learn very fast, I believe, to obey his kind guidance.
Alice remained unmoving on the floor, making no attempt at drying her tears. Afterglow did, in a fashion, speaking softly to her, comforting the girl somewhat.
– I and Karmak together will teach you everything you need to know, on the last stretch on your path to become a full-fledged sorcerer.
On an impulse she showed kindness and gave the apprentice the sign, and allowed her to kneel on the floor.
Afterglow rose and walked to the night table. She grabbed the bottle, opened it with a slight push of her thumb and took her first huge swallow.
Kathryn Caldwell welcomed the burn, the fire flowing down her throat, to her stomach, spreading from there to encompass her entire body and mind.
She fell on the bed, hitting it with her butt and back and head, pulling her legs after the rest of the body.
– You may serve your Master, she snarled to the subdued girl, – when the proper time comes.
Her head rested on the high pillow. The numbness spread with the liquor in her body and created a pleasant haze in her mind. The shadows and the waves imposed themselves on her and she let them. The pleasant haze made her lose control and she let it. The bed and the room and even, by default the building shook noticeably now and then, as Afterglow indulged herself and imposed herself on the world.
Dead, she thought. Everybody is dead.
So alone, Alice said without speaking, sighing in the wind. You are so alone.

Afterglow took another huge gulp. The liquor burned all over her, as if she had spilled it on her skin. The bottle seemed to be just as full.

She turned it in her hand, making its fluid flow into her mouth, down her throat. She swallowed it without tasting it.

Images began appearing before her eyes. It always amazed and horrified her how Beatrice dominated in her mind's eye, obscuring the others.

And then the others, for the first time in a long time demanded her attention, and the horror grew.

The metallic song of The Nine coursed through her and she could not stop it.

– I am falling, Afterglow mumbled, – falling without end.

There was no more sound, no more faces or smells or taste or sensations. Everything was just turned off, and she fell into the beyond deep Abyss awaiting her.

The bottle fell from her hand, empty and filled with mist. It hit the floor without a sound. She saw it without seeing it, even as she knew it kept falling, and she kept falling with it, caught by the heavy mist inside.

The maid walked to her, began undressing her limp body. It was an easy task. The big woman did not even stir. The girl covered the body with a blanket. Then she stood there, stood there for a long time, looking down on the half sleeping, half unconscious woman, before finally pulling back.

– I have died a million times, a voice originating from Afterglow's throat said.

The girl shook in fright.

She found another blanket in the closet. It was dark in there, and scary. She still moved in the same puppet-like manner. The shiver of her lips and flickering of her eyes did not translate to the rest of the body.

Alice, the apprentice rested on the floor, receiving words and prodding and instructions and teachings from the Voice in her head, and also from Afterglow's muddled mind.

She moaned in her sleep.

An eternity passed in her dreams.

They both moaned in their sleep, writhing and sighing endlessly on the bed and thin carpet.

CHAPTER ELEVEN

Dawn arrived somewhat. The light from the daystar shone hard in Afterglow's eyes.

It scorched her, turning her exposed skin to a crisp.

Alice knelt behind her, with the breakfast tray in her hands. Afterglow nodded. The maid put the tray on the table in front of her Master. Afterglow sat down in the chair and began feeding. Everything was off center, like she knew it would be.

She looked down on the streets. There were no sentient beings moving close to the tavern. Most stayed away from there. But she had no difficulty watching closely those passing by in a wider circle around the building, those still casting cautious glances at what was hiding in their midst, from their flickering eyes.

– Watch, my apprentice, study, and tell your Master what you see.

Alice obeyed unresistingly, rushed to the window and to Afterglow's side with glimmers of her old enthusiasm.

– Alice sees mundane people, master, going about their mundane tasks. They have limited awareness of both themselves and the world. Many do not know that something is missing and quite a few of those who do, do not seek to broaden their knowledge.

The girl waited in breathless anticipation for her teacher's judgment. She kept doing it, without daring to speak, until Afterglow eventually once again spoke and demanded her attention.

– Is that how you will live your life, be like them, with no influence over your own life?

The girl shook her head vehemently, curling her hands into fists.

– NO, Master! They are dry leaves blowing in the wind. Alice is not!

The collar hurt, not enough to make her cry out, but sufficient to notice. She fell on her knees.

– Karmak is such a wily and cruel teacher, Afterglow chuckled, looking at her apprentice with disdain. – You are too independent for him, but I do want that, so you have to stand up to him a bit, I'm afraid.

Alice glanced at her with tears in her eyes.

– The collar stays on. Pain is a good teacher. Do you understand, little bitch?

– Yes, Afterglow, Alice whispered. – Alice understands.

She rose and stood on shaking feet.

– You will now commence your morning workout, Afterglow commanded.

The apprentice obeyed instantly, drawing her sword, began moving, cutting the air with the whirling blade. Very soon she was covered in sweat, a sharp, dull expression brightening her eyes. Afterglow spoke to her, whispered softly, cruelly in her ears.

– Your surroundings, the reach of your sword are your friend. It is your enemy, where you slash and cut, or being cut or stabbed in turn.

Karmak spoke to her, hissed at her, curses and insults, and gave her affectionate pain whenever he felt like it.

Every word was hammered into the mind and instincts of the creature flowing with increasing ease across the floor. More than one ghostly voice spoke directly to Alice Thornbridge's core, shaking and burning it.

Afterglow bent down and picked up her sword from the floor. One step, two forward and she was out there, on the floor with her student. Swords flashed in fire and shadow as they sliced the air and screeched like banshees as metal hit metal.

The walls dissolved around them. They imagined they did, at least, imagined their sudden, brief surroundings of forest and fields and mountains, before it faded and Afterglow disarmed her squire with a slight twist of her wrist. The sword hit the floor with its tip first and stood there, shaking, as if alive. Afterglow pushed the sharp side of the blade at Alice's throat. Alice froze with misty eyes.

– Just a little added push and you would have been dead.

Afterglow lowered the sword. Alice remained in place, like a statue. Afterglow struck her, slapped her hard with her left hand, and she fell to the floor. She remained there, gasping, her eyes staying lowered.

– You are being born, Afterglow snarled. – Tell your Master what birth is.

– Birth is pain, the apprentice gasped. – Alice knows this and is prepared for it. She is fierce and strong and eager to learn the secrets.

A snort and Afterglow turned her back to her and walked to the window, ignoring her. Alice rose to her knees and made the tiny move with her little finger, signaling that she begged for permission to speak. Afterglow ignored her for a long time, watching many people cross each other's path on the far away street before acknowledging her.

– Alice improves… does she not?

– In a fashion, but so agonizingly slow. At this pace you may become a sorcerer at your death bed, if you are lucky.

Alice did not react to the cruel, patronizing snarl in any overt way, but to Afterglow the further devolving of stature was quite evident, and she laughed contemptuously.

Afterglow undressed casually and walked to the shower. She turned on the water. It hit her heated skin ever so pleasantly. The workout had made her sweat, but there was no sense of fatigue. The water still felt pleasant against her skin.

It touched her, ever so briefly, before moving on. She felt it spread and herself spreading with it. When it flowed in the sewer below the building and below the street, she flowed with it.

She dried herself, as Alice walked into the cubicle and had her shower. Her skin and hair dried quickly, both with and without the use of the towel. The air in the room was warm and pleasant. She found her spare set of clothes in her bag and dressed. That, too, felt like quite a satisfying task.

Alice appeared from the bathroom.

– You are so beautiful, the girl said.

Afterglow looked at her.

– I do not care if you p-punish me. I love it every time you t-touch me, anyway.

She knelt, preparing herself for the worst, the voice in her head coughing a warning.

– I have no desire to punish you, Kathryn said softly. – You are just a wide-eyed, unruly child, that is all, and like all such you need to learn the way of the world, its pitfalls and abysses.

Alice crawled to her, a happy sound slipping between her lips.

Afterglow petted her on the head, and as she pulled her on her feet she kissed her on her brow.

They walked downstairs, to the dining area and had breakfast. It looked very much like the breakfast room of any tavern. Afterglow and Alice would have known better, even if they did not know where they were. Those present were mostly low-keyed magick-users, but it was still obvious, very much visible to those able to see.

They glared at the two with hostile and scared glances. Some left the room with fast steps. Others reluctantly remained.

The two ignored them, like Kathryn had always done and sat down on seats recently vacated, the best available.

Afterglow noticed something new among the guests before it turned evident.

There was a restless mood in the room, even more, far more than it usually was in such way-stations between average people and the hidden world. There were whispers, and not only with glances directed at the two most recently arrived but a general, increased… excitement.

– Another big ship has entered our waters, a man insisted as he spoke to a man enjoying his company. – People at the Observatory spoke rather excitedly about it, the way I heard. I am willing to bet it has come through the portal…

– *The* portal?

The other man paled.

- Jupiter's Cauldron, aye, the first man confirmed. – The ship is on its way and its vile stench will reach us in a few hours.

Almost everybody nodded, Afterglow, too.

– Why? A young male asked. – Why does it stink so much?

Others looked at it him with forbearance.

– Engines from that other realm use a kind of oil-based, antiquarian fuel system, a man replied. – It stinks like week-old dung.

– Or worse, another insisted. – People say it is nothing nature made.

The conversation continued on the various tables, clearly louder and with a higher intensity than before. Alice studied it with the same unrelenting curiosity she studied everything, everything she deemed interesting.

She bowed her head before turning back towards Afterglow, before speaking.

– I have never understood it, she said, – the excitement, I mean. Those coming through that particular portal are a rather sorry lot, most of them hardly able to tie their shoelaces, as independent as sheep.

– The ships or boats or airships usually bring something. Afterglow shrugged. – Technicians or some new and even viable knowledge easily applied to various communities in our realm, variations of music, of the arts we would not otherwise enjoy. And news from Rome and England and other places besides, and about relatives thought long lost.

– The old Roman Empire has been in ruins for centuries, Alice pointed out, – and England has also fallen on hard times. The Realm of Earth has changed beyond recognition from how history books and the old tales describe it.

– But the insanity the old settlers fled from has grown and multiplied, Afterglow mused. – It has spread like a plague. Many of those coming through the portal bring with them dogmatic religions, rigid ways of living alien to most of us.

– Fortunately it loses much of its bite in our realm, Alice stated happily. – Even most of the newcomers quickly realize how ridiculous and horrible their beliefs are. The ancients created a resilient and strong foundation for our society easily able to defend against an invasion based on fear and discord.

Afterglow and others, at the neighboring tables listening in nodded.

– But it is like a poison, the girl added abruptly, – one of the mind, virulent and bitter, like a rattlesnake before it strikes.

A shudder passed through the assembly.

A woman glared at them, glared even harder than some of the others had done before their attention had been directed in a more mutual agreeable direction.

She stood up, shaking in outrage and righteousness.

– There is only one God, she shouted, – and you should all fear him, because he will surely punish you for your heathen and satanic ways.

Most of those present shrugged. Some laughed outright.

– Thus a point well made is further proven, a man said, nodding in deference to Afterglow and her apprentice. – Even here, among the enlightened the madness is present.

The woman set forth towards the exit, turning towards Alice just before she vanished through the door.

– You will die, the disturbed woman shrieked, pointing a bony finger towards Alice, – like all the rest she has touched with her death.

The bony finger turned and pointed at Afterglow.

Everybody breathed a sigh of relief when she was gone.

There were a few, though, giving credit to her words, at the very least to her parting words by their uneasy glances.

The buzz on the streets outside and the market at the Square had grown even stronger when they approached it a few hours later. The crowd whirled and whizzed around them. The woman's eyes haunted Afterglow.

– She scared me, Alice said. – Not because of what she said, but the way she said it. I know it is foolish, but I can not help it.

– People like her are disturbing, Afterglow acknowledged.

The icy claw had settled in their guts once again, pulling and tearing, eliciting pain and an anxiety they could not name.

They drifted like wood with the crowd towards the harbor, but could not quite share in the general anticipation.

– Afterglow and Alice are like specters moving through the world, the girl said softly, – belonging everywhere, nowhere.

The older woman nodded in acknowledgment to her, with a both sad and joy-filled, inevitable catching in her throat.

There was no sign of the ship or boat yet, but quite a few spectators had already gathered on the quay. Magistrates were out in force, too, forming a chain, keeping people from pushing past them and to the edge of the quay, the large or rather gigantic spot designed for what had to be quite a big-sized ship.

– There are procedures for this, ladies and gentlemen, a self-appointed speaker for the event cried. – Right now there are support-vessels approaching the foreign ship. They are used for all known ships coming to our shores and can easily be adapted to this task. This is a rare occasion, an event. It does not happen that often, hardly more than every second generation or so that something this big and noteworthy comes through the portal, and no one alive today has experienced the kind of passenger liner the gossip tells about today.

People had started up with entertainment on several spots, jugglers, fire-breathers and various performance acts. Afterglow heard the brittle strings of a guitar vibrate somewhere. She glanced around, unable to determine its location.

– One of the fire-breathers is quite good, Alice mused. – One might suspect that he is one in fact.

– One might, Afterglow agreed.

– I know it does not matter, the girl said, – that it is a false distinction, but you know I talk a lot, especially when I am nervous… or excited.

She giggled.

– Begging My Lady's forgiveness…

Her giggle rose to the level before full-blown laughter.

The giggle stopped abruptly. Stricken, she curtseyed and bowed her head.

– Alice knows she is trying Afterglow's patience and will strive once again to improve herself, to be worthy of the honor Afterglow has bestowed upon her.

Afterglow nodded, clearly distracted. Alice noticed, of course, and was neither annoyed nor relieved. She was very aware of and familiar with the cruel and casual treatment a sorcerer gave a given apprentice.

The ferry arrived from the Island, its departing passengers looking wide-eyed at the commotion, eagerly seeking the relevant news among the crowd. They did not leave, but joined the rare gathering. No one entered the ferry. Its captain rang the bell, the final sign of departure. It brought no more passengers. The captain shrugged. The door closed and the ferry left empty-handed.

– We will wait inside, Afterglow decided. – There will be hours before anything substantial happens here. Alice, the wily apprentice will secure a table for her sorcerer and better be skilled in the venture.

– At once, My Lady.

Alice straightened momentarily, before rushing off towards the large, square green-painted house across the open space.

When Afterglow entered the place ten minutes later Wily Alice stood by the table and on the table waited two large glasses of ale.

Candles lit each table and together the room. There was an intimate, warm mood obscuring, in a way the size of the rather large hall appealing to Afterglow. She sat down and tasted the ale. Alice stood straight by her chair. Afterglow nodded imperceptible and Alice sat down, too, tasted the ale, too.

Kathryn stared at the shimmering candle flame, for a moment imagining that it shifted into blue. It sang to her. She knew she was not imaging that.

The vibrations of the room, and the surrounding areas outside spoke to her, and she could not help but listen.

Glasses met and parted over tables. People toasted and drank. They raised their glass high and drank deep. Kathryn sensed their hunger, the yearning to let go.

– Cheers, she said to her apprentice.

– Cheers! Alice replied.

They both heard the loud, high-octave sound when their glasses met and parted. Alice drank and glanced at the sorcerer with a cautious hope in her pretty eyes.

One man played the violin and another the piano, playing a haunting, strangely uplifting tune. Several people began dancing, alone and as pairs. The music and the intense mood seemed to fill the hall, the entire guest house. Afterglow noticed without trying the increased activity among the employees, as every possible guestroom was made ready for the added influx. Even the empty neighboring storage building was prepared. She sensed their low-keyed panic and eager anticipation.

– This is a special day, is it not? Alice mused. – The man outside was correct. This is a rare occasion, one people will use for a variety of purposes.

– All kinds of greedy and adventurous and curious spirits may be sated today, Afterglow nodded.

She watched the dancers with a distant look in her eyes. For a brief moment, through Alice's eyes she looked young and vulnerable. She shivered visibly.

– Afterglow remembers another occasion similar to this, does she not?

– She does, Afterglow acknowledged. – It was one of the last nights before… before…

Alice grabbed one of her hands and caressed it in a way clearly meant to be comforting, and Afterglow felt comforted, felt the poignant mood between them.

A smile crossed her lips. She seized it and held on to it one moment, two, until it slipped her grasp like grains of sand between fingers.

– The Enlightened seems to be here in force, too, Alice said, slightly ironic, grinning, hungering, like she always did, as she let go of the hand.

– They sure are.

The girl waited a bit, before continuing.

– They have never seemed that impressive to Alice, most of them, not before she started on her training in Afterglow's service, and certainly not now, when she has gained a slice of the knowledge beyond comprehension she has always yearned for.

Kathryn masked her emotions, her slight apprehension.

– Let us say that The Enlightened has never been very enlightened.

And she felt even closer to the girl, as the bond of minds forged between a sorcerer and her apprentice grew further.

A flock of birds flew by outside. Their loud, human-like cries echoed in everybody's mind. The flapping of wings created a vibration everybody close by seemed to sense, at least on a subconscious level. When the flock had passed by the harbor and people breathed in relief it turned and made another flyby. Kathryn and Alice watched as people writhed uncomfortably in their seat, as those standing outside crouched slightly in the shadow of the flock.

The cries seemed to grow louder, more insistent, as if they attempted to convey something, something important.

– It does not *stop*, a man shouted in distress.

Others threw rocks at the birds, to no avail. They continued to circle. The shadow on the ground below their path turned a darker hue.

– Is that… is that an omen? Alice wondered.

– I believe so, Afterglow shrugged. – The question is what it concerns.

The girl leaned forward, cautious but unable to hold back her… her excitement.

– But there is more, is it not, or you would not be so… interested?

Afterglow closed her eyes ever so briefly, and reopened them as quickly as she was physically able.

– When I was younger, in one flash of a moment, wrecked by horrible pain I was assaulted with imagery, with sensations beyond powerful, she said. – I saw myself on other worlds, saw myself *die* there, an endless row of unfamiliar faces and bodies I knew, I know to be mine. Since then the visions have revisited me infrequently, in times of heightened emotion and tension.

– I… understand, Alice said. – You seek a unique experience you are both dreading and longing for. Alice always knew you were a true Seeker.

There were both innocence and cunning in the girl's eyes.

Afterglow grabbed her, her hand chasing forward with fingers formed like claws. Alice froze, the pain making her numb and dull, but even though she bowed her head in submission, she kept glancing at her mentor, kept meeting her eyes.

– My… Master knew, knew that about me before I did, and he *exploited* it. He knew beyond knowing that my desire to learn, to find what is hidden would make me do anything, make me follow any path and that he could easily steer me in the direction he desired.

There was hatred here, thinly veiled, just below the surface, so much stronger than the earlier despair. Alice shivered.

Kathryn let go of the hand, but to Alice it felt like she was still in its grip, like its claws were buried deep in her flesh, and she knew, knew they would never let go.

– You begin to understand, apprentice, finally begin to grasp deeper hidden truths…

Slowly, slowly the world beyond the table began reasserting itself in their reality.

They drank deep, both briefly lost in the mire of their own thoughts. A loud lure sounded from the tower in the bay, the signal that a ship was on its way in. They emptied their glasses.

– Alice may now fetch two more glasses of ale, Afterglow said.

Alice did, rushing off like a roe before the predator, the excited smile never straying from her features.

Kathryn watched her dance towards the bar, sneak past people in front of her in the queues as if she was born to it. The pain of another memory touched Afterglow.

She returned in what was practically a whiff with two glasses filled with foaming fluid.

– You are a natural at this, Afterglow remarked.

– Thank you, My Lady, Alice giggled happily.

They drank. Time passed.

Sometimes people around them seemed to move faster than normal, sometimes slowing down to a crawl. The entire room and its every angle was Afterglow's to enjoy.

– … swords, a voice said incredulous. – Every single one of them had swords and according to my friend the blades were covered in blood. They were not your typical fencing club members.

She pushed it deliberately a bit further for once, straining to pick up more, to catch something important in the massive amounts of dialogue and speculation surrounding them, but she did not. When she rose she did so in a seemingly calm manner. She walked to the lavatory, looking for the two men, but she did not see anyone fitting her somewhat vague impression of them and did not hear their very distinct voices.

The trip to the stall, to the toilet bowl brought sweet relief, but no illumination. She made a quick, unsuccessful sweep of the Gentlemen room. One more foggy mirror greeted her and dismissed her. The many voices and impressions of the tavern assaulted her when she emerged from the hallway and she was forced to dampen her awareness. She walked to the bar and picked up two more glasses of ale. Alice welcomed her with her open smile. The sorcerer and her apprentice kept consuming alcohol at a fairly relaxed pace.

The girl got drunk, slightly more so than Afterglow did. She opened up further to the sorcerer's invasive scrutiny. The dam leaked further.

And the trickle the other way increased as well, becoming a flow.

– … and my cousins that were pretty much my siblings were hardly more than wailing gnomes. They were always wooing uncle for attention, attempting to be first in his eyes. I can not say I miss them much.

A pale smile accompanied the girl's dark giggle.

– I know you were a lone child, that you can not know how it is to have tiny ogres constantly dogging your tail…

She yelped. Pain wrecked her features as the collar sent a charge through her. She had been disrespectful and her long dead teacher was not pleased.

Karmak had been quite fond of regimentation when alive and death had not lessened that.

More ale found its way down her aching throat. She sniffed, but kept talking, but clearly more measured, her eyes once more cast down.

Afterglow listened to her, and to the place and its people, to everything with equal measure.

The waves of the world flooded her.

A male, a young boy danced, attempting to entice a girl to join him on the floor. She rejected his advances with a contemptuous shrug.

Afterglow sat still, but she reached out for something, something she grabbed right out of the air.

Alice began rocking sideways in her chair. Her eyes remained open, but did not seem to see anything, at least not in her immediate surroundings. She looked at something far away, rocking sideways on her chair.

And then she stopped.

– You stood in the schoolyard, she said with a voice hardly resembling her own, – so hungry for what was hidden, for what he offered, and he came and plucked you, like he would a ripe fruit from a tree.

A chill trickled down Kathryn's spine.

– It was like the Fates themselves had grabbed you. From that day on, no matter what you did they shook you until you hung in their strings like a ragged doll, unable to escape their cruel machinations.

They stopped drinking long before darkness fell. The intoxication wore off fairly quickly. They were only slightly unsteady on their feet when they rose and walked outside with the others, with all others present, greeting the twilight, and the ship approaching the still distant harbor.

The ship looked like one giant lamp, its thousand tiny lights illuminating the shores long before it sailed close to land. It maneuvered the unknown waters with the help of the small boats surrounding it. People noticed the stench and the loud noise from its engine and shook their head.

A special impromptu system had been put in place for what was clearly a passenger liner. The quay did not really have proper facilities for it and had to be modified for the task. The small boats were not made for aiding such large ships, and it was clearly putting a strain on them.

– I am reminded of a large bull and its poor handlers, a girl giggled.

A bit of laughter echoed her words, but most of those present were too taken by the moment to join in.

The ship lit the harbor from far away, even when there was still fairly bright twilight. At least it seemed to be. It was clearly a fast ship for its size and even at reduced speed it seemed to be fired at the onlookers at the harbor with the momentum of an arrow.

All kinds of people, young and old and in-between had lined up on both sides of the cove, and on The Island to witness the rare occasion. The triple cities and surrounding areas had come to a standstill. The waves of the realm and those inhabiting it mixed and joined in anticipation. In the Wasteland, on the mountain and beyond the realm the lost hissed and burned.

– Something is happening, is it not, something significant beyond the excitement of the moment?

Afterglow nodded distracted, in response to the coherence formed by Alice's childish voice.

– Something in the very air, both threatening and not.

– Alice is very perceptive.

And Alice beamed.

– The Dark River itself is bringing that ship.

Alice turned to ice.

The entertainment slowly ended. The dancers, musicians, actors and fire-breathers joined the others as the ship grew in everybody's vision.

It had been only a pinprick in the horizon. Now, it dominated everybody's attention.

Afterglow saw it as one side bright and one side dark, and the shadow at the center grew by the second.

It came in fast, too fast, it seemed, on its way to one of the piers.

People pulled back, or tried to, from the point where it seemed likely that the bow would hit land.

The handlers managed to stop it from doing that, and before it ran afoul the sandbanks flanking the harbor, the danger that no local ship needed to care about.

– It is ugly, is it not? A man shook his head.

The large, bulky ship shivered in the water. Kathryn noticed its waves. She rubbed her temples. The waves changed, turning solid in her eyes, changing into wings dark and red.

Alice whimpered. Kathryn heard that, as if from far away.

– I am there, she heard herself say, not realizing immediately that she had spoken aloud.

It dawned on her slowly, as she briefly saw the harbor from the ship, as she faded back into herself.

– M'Lady, Alice said, striving to speak, to master her fear, the same fear the sorcerer felt deep in her gut.

– Alice should not worry, Afterglow soothed her charge. – There is nothing to be worried about.

– Of course not, My Lady.

Alice straightened, pulling herself together.

– Afterglow's power is growing, she said with a proud stance, – making her even more a force to be feared.

The girl's words thrilled Afterglow, as she sensed the truth in them. Unable to help herself, she found herself pleased and a triumphant joy filled her being.

Floating quays were put on the water. They were usually used during celebrations and as a ramp for fireworks. It seemed strange to see them used for purely practical purposes.

They were heavy and solid, able to take quite a bit of weight and high seas. The only problem with some relevance tonight was to make them stay in place. It did take a bit of trial and error, until there was a path from the ship all the way to land.

Communication had clearly started early. There was not that much of it, now. Passengers stood on the deck by one of the emergency stairs and waited impatiently. Their fidgeting was visible from far away, to everybody. The high stress level onboard was quite evident. Voices rose and faded in uneven intervals.

– They have no idea where they are, a sympathetic voice on land said. –

Poor souls.

More voices rose to offer their sympathies. There were snorts and snarls of contempt, too, but they were a minority.

– Lost at sea, with bubble water in abundance at their disposal, one voice rose over the murmur.

Unanimous contemptuous laughter.

– Do they come from…

Another cried out with a voice that faltered before he could finish the sentence.

And the mood changed yet again. A sudden curiosity grabbed many men, women and children.

– A friend of mine is in the coast menagerie, a man said. – He pretty much confirms they were spit out of Jupiter's Cauldron.

A chilly draft seemed to come from nowhere. Suddenly he appeared to stand completely alone. Those finding themselves anywhere close to him visibly pulled away. His statement made most of the people present fall silent momentarily. Some of those present did not understand, but those who did glanced uneasily at each other.

– Almost every single soul that has ever come here lost was spit out of Jupiter's cauldron, a woman said, – including our ancestors.

That silenced them all for minutes. Only small talk, excited but low-keyed persisted in clusters.

– There will be a performance at the Town Hall tonight to showcase it all, the woman declared. – Everybody is welcome to attend.

Some stared angrily at her, others nodded to themselves, while others again did not react in any discernible way to her words.

– Most citizens are still very much in the dark about it all, are they not? Alice said. – In spite of it being pretty much public knowledge.

– It is one of the best kept publicly known secrets there are, Afterglow acknowledged. – I guess a certain kind of people, no matter how «enlightened» does not want to think too much about certain things.

The process of helping the travelers the final distance to shore progressed in pushes and pulls. The first began descending the stairs, halted occasionally by screams of madness and despair.

The stairs shook violently and many stopped stricken, doing their best to calm those refusing to reduce the output of their fears.

– The Council has chosen to be very open about this, a woman remarked.

– Of course they have. What choice is there? To bring in the ship in the middle of the night, to close off the entire harbor and attempt to keep it a secret? Forget it!

The first travelers reached the shore. Members of the Council and a few others met the ship's captain and some of the officers.

– Welcome, Ronald Porter, one of the current council members said and reached out a hand.

– Is that the Queen's English? Samuel Robbins, the captain bristled.

Porter looked a little baffled, but kept it together.

– You said that before, earlier today, too, old man, another in the welcoming committee, cried. – That's the Queen's English exactly.

Robbins blinked, then frowned and blinked again, when he looked at the man who had spoken last.

– Davis Fremantle, he cried, – as I live and breathe…

He blinked yet again, and then he stopped.

– But you disappeared, he said, clearly both moved and distressed. – You disappeared in the…

He looked astounded at the other man.

– I found myself here, the other man said, – found aid and support to survive and thrive, just like you and your crew and passengers will, like people have for centuries.

– We were off course, the captain pondered, – and none of our instruments were working, but I didn't see the connection, I just didn't…

– Nonetheless, you and your people are welcome here, captain, Porter said, – to the triple cities of Talaho and Howell, and Auburn in the land of Arcadia.

– We *are* glad to be here, Councilmember Porter… We're just rattled, that's all…

– Perfectly understandable.

Their English was different. Robbins' was smooth, seemed to flow more, more polished, and some words and phrases varied, but they easily understood each other. It was a difference in dialect, not language.

– Shall we…

Porter indicated the path with his hand.

Magistrates were out in force providing a path for them to the guesthouse and to the storage building, with its added, impromptu facilities not far away, but it was not truly necessary. People pulled back, making their walk more comfortable, less stressful. The sympathy in people's eyes was evident even to most of the anxious of the new arrivals. They read curiosity in people's eyes, but not one excessive and bordering on cruel.

– They do not expect… kindness? Alice wondered. – And not compassion either?

– No, they do not, Afterglow said. – They are not exactly used to that.

Alice looked at her, as curious as ever. Afterglow ignored her and closed her eyes, and concentrated, and suddenly she was among the people in the long line, hearing them speak, somewhat, and sensing their mood.

It was garbled, much of it, but she managed to pick up a few things here and there.

A tall dark man spoke to a tall dark woman. They held hands. A woman with black skin walked behind them. Afterglow found herself pulled towards them all.

– The Forsaken disappeared for years, did she not, Alice said, – and returned as Afterglow.

– That she did, Kathryn confirmed, as the familiar scythe of pain cut her.

Alice wanted to say more, to ask more, much more, but Afterglow stopped her with an abrupt move with the finger freezing the girl in her place.

Afterglow listened in, as crew and passengers of the lost ship was led into the storage building. A giant hall appeared to them. There were beds there, and the simplest of conveniences.

– We need to put most of you here for a few nights, Fremantle said, – in order to better organize everything. It isn't much, but…

– This is fine, Robbins said. – Thank you, thank you so much for your kindness.

– I found myself well here, Fremantle said. – You will, too, giving time.

– Where *are* we? One of the passengers spoke up. – There's no fucking land called Arcadia, nowhere on…

His eyes widened, as if something obvious finally dawned on him.

– Nowhere on Earth, Fremantle completed for him, speaking very loud, making sure everybody heard it.

And then the man, and many others paled, and others started crying, and only a few were positively amazed.

– Go to the Town Hall meeting later tonight, Fremantle urged them. – You will be met with curiosity, but most of all with kindness. They treat foreigners well here.

But many would stay behind, crawl into the mire of their anxieties. That was clear to everybody.

A baby whimpered in the mother's arms, echoing her silent wails of despair.

Afterglow heard them. She sensed bodies sharp as blades move through the approaching darkness. A surge of expectation burned her insides.

Alice noticed. The girl whimpered in what were clearly the modest beginnings of rapture.

A shadow passed before her young and shiny face.

– Alice would ask a boon of her creator.

Afterglow looked at her. As always it was sufficient.

– Allow her the honor of channeling you, to be your vessel, filled with your essence. Travel on her wings to the Other World.

Afterglow hesitated, musing momentarily.

– But Alice is aware of the risk involved, is she not, the danger of losing herself completely.

– She is, and she remains dedicated beyond measure.

Kathryn smelled the stench of blood in her nostrils. A shadow passed before the mature and experienced face already cast in shadow.

– Afterglow will consider her request.

The girl's joy and gratitude washed over her like lukewarm water, as she more than sensed the quiet acceptance in her mentor's seething, whirling thoughts and insides.

Those on the outside watched as the few remaining passengers disappeared into the large storage building. The door closed, and Afterglow allowed her awareness, her focus to shift, too, letting go of those inside. People began to leave the harbor, even though the buzz lingered in the various groups returning to the triple cities. Some walked home. Most did not.

Afterglow and her ward set course directly for the Town Hall.

– We need to be early for the good seats, Afterglow said, without Alice saying anything.

The special mood prevailed. The two women noticed that everywhere they looked and walked. People stared at them, even more than usual. They whispered among themselves and cast long, dark curious looks at the rather large huddle of travelers traversing the sidewalk towards the cluster of buildings ahead.

Afterglow studied the newcomers, studied each and every one of them. Some of the faces stood out to her like lighthouses in a storm, and she realized startled that that was a more than correct analogy. The cityscape, the labyrinth changed in her mind. Those new faces imposed themselves on her. Suddenly she was back in the Dark Lodge and rows of people paraded before her in the steaming, steaming pond that was the sea.

Alice noticed, as always. She wanted to speak, to inquire, but Alice the apprentice wisely kept her mouth shut.

The hall of the central community house could host lots of guests. Its construction reminded of the old Roman amphitheatre, but had some additions and modifications that were clearly a more modern take on the ancient structure.

Its system of «stairs» was not so steep and the stairs were actually broader. There were tables and chairs on each level, where people could dine and still enjoy the performance at the center below. Afterglow and ward sat down at an empty table on the ninth row from the inner circle, where they had a fair view both up and down and sideways. No one of the townspeople sat down in the empty seats, as the hall filled itself to the brim. Alice grinned at everybody staring at the two with anxious eyes.

She put a triangle flag on their table, signaling that they also had come here to eat. It was an excellent system that had worked great on previous occasions, but tonight the waiters and the kitchen really strained to get the food to the guests within a reasonable time-frame.

On the stone walls there were paintings of travelers, clearly fleeing from something. There was fear and determination in their eyes. The people depicted seemed quite normal, even at a closer range.

But if you looked closely and paid attention, you would see that some of them had pointed ears, and also what would be considered deformities.

The place affected the two women and also others profoundly. The waves and whirling energy of the room gathered and was resubmitted, inevitably, subconsciously by Afterglow and Alice in Wonderland.

– We must go here more often, Alice whispered cautiously.

And realized that her master hardly noticed. Afterglow was preoccupied and irritable and Alice wisely stayed silent and humble.

Several groups of people from the boat entered the amphitheatre, drawing many a curious glance or stare. Afterglow did not look at them. She did not have to. One group of five in particular made its way down one of the aisles, searching for a table, its members straining their eyes for a considerable time surveying the vast sea of people before finally spotting a tiny break in the pattern.

– Excuse me, ladies, the man in front said politely, but with a certain flair, – are these seat available?

– They are indeed, Lester, Afterglow greeted them, greeted him. – Make yourself at home.

He frowned, then shaking his head and choosing the first available chair.

– My name is Lester Brown, he said. – This is my wife Martha.

He reached across the table to shake hands with the enigmatic woman.

– Call me Afterglow. This is my apprentice Alice.

Alice did not say anything.

– The phrase «make yourself at home» has certainly gained quite the poignancy for us lately, Martha said both nervously and brightly, – as you can imagine.

– I can imagine, Afterglow said.

The others presented themselves, giving their names and uncertain smiles.

All the last arrivals sat down in their chairs.
Lester tried to avoid looking at her… too much, bursting with curiosity and a nagging doubt.
– Nine seats, he said. – Is that common?
Afterglow referred to Alice. The other five did not notice but Alice did, of course.
– As you probably have noticed, all the tables in the theater have nine seats, she said. – The number or constellation nine is fairly common in our society. So is also what is dividable with nine, or other similar mathematical configurations. There are triple cities, here and elsewhere. There are nine statues, nine cities, eighty-one national council members, and nine from each city within the country of Arcadia, nine realms where humans and creatures roam…
– That's so fascinating, Leila Osborne said. – I study foreign cultures for a living and it's pretty unique. My curiosity for the evening, I admit is peaked.
– The paintings here are unique, too, Stuart Bainbridge whistled. – They remind me of…
The waiter arrived with a smile and an incomparable eagerness.
– Hi, my name is Betty, she greeted them. – What can I do you for?
– I will have the veal and the root beer, Afterglow said. – So will my apprentice.
Betty's features darkened just a bit, but the smile stayed in place.
– I'm afraid we have to sit this one out, Lester said. – We have no cash, no… funds viable here.
– That is no problem, Betty grinned. – You will all, as you get assigned in the days to come be given considerable funds to start your life here in Howell or in the other two triple cities. We will simply subtract a modest charge from that amount.
– It is quite inexpensive compared to what you are used to, Afterglow shrugged. – Food and necessities are mostly free here. There are exceptions to that rule, among them dining out and similar.
And Alice looked at her again.
– That's certainly something to be thankful for, Martha cried.
She and Lester squeezed hands.
– Your accent is slightly different from most of the other people here… Afterglow, Leila said pleasantly. – I didn't really notice it at first, but it's quite pronounced as one hears you speak.
– I spent years abroad, Afterglow shrugged again.
– Afterglow has traveled all the nine realms and even beyond, Alice stated proudly.

– I'll have the same as our generous… host, Lester told the waiter.
– I will, too, Martha said.
Everyone but Leila picked the veal and the root beer.
– I'll have the duck mashed in vegetables, the… Kar'an, she said
She almost pronounced it correctly as well, drawing nods of acknowledgement from the crowd.
– I've always loved trying out exotic fruits and dishes, she said excitedly.
Martha shivered as she glanced down at the center stage clothed in darkness.
– I am afraid there will be some waiting tonight, Betty said, her smile in place. – Enjoy yourselves in the meantime, okay?
– We will, Leila said. – Thank you very much for your kindness and hospitability.
Betty looked a little nonplussed at her, but returned the smile, before she took off in a whirl of motion.
– I guess you guys take such things for granted, Leila said amazed.
– «A stranger is a friend in need», Alice quoted.
– That's what I figured, Leila nodded.
There was some delay, and a few people grumbled about it, but tonight at least, the waiting was not really waiting. The theater buzzed with expectation and a growing excitement. Everybody noticed, even the grumblers. It was impossible not to, really. Afterglow and Alice and several others present easily identified the energy circling the tables of nine. It was palatable, like a seething presence in the very air.
When the food arrived Lester and the other four looked baffled at it.
– Is that what goes for late here, Leila chuckled.
– The performance will begin when people have finished their dining, Betty informed them cheerfully.
They ate, they fed, accompanied by low-keyed conversation. The buzz of voices filled the room like a thousand echoes. Afterglow strained herself a bit in order to listen, like she always did, behind the noise.
– That storm, Joshua Mendelssohn said, shaking his head, – it was awful, an electrical barrage I've hardly even heard about before and certainly not experienced. It's amazing that we survived it, and in one piece, but we did. And when we came here… no one really knew what to expect. But that, too, seems to have worked out well, hasn't it?
– You will feel welcome here, Afterglow said. – People are friendly and accessible, and they will teach you what you need to exist and perhaps even thrive. But you should acknowledge what you already know: that any world is a vast entity of great and dangerous unknowns, where any wayward

unprepared individual or group is virtually defenseless.

She noticed the chill in their eyes and veins and nodded in satisfaction.

People completed their meal. The conversation faded to an absolute minimum. Kathryn noticed that Alice's heart skipped a beat. That, too, was noticeable to her, like an absence of thunder in her ears.

When Afterglow accessed the labyrinth of the mind deliberately she instantly knew more about what had spooked both her and her apprentice. Something was chasing through the streets, something unseen, a dark shape out of sync with the realm, but no less tangible and threatening. It rose, rose, rose through non-existing space.

Alice wanted to speak again, but Afterglow stopped her with am almost invisible move of her hand.

Karmak looked very displeased. Alice wanted to gasp, but could not even do that.

A few more knives and forks were put down, some more bones pushed to the end of the plate. Then the entire theater turned quiet and silence fell as all light was dimmed, and everything turned dark around them.

The performance was about to begin.

CHAPTER TWELVE

A figure only hinted at in the shadow played the guitar, played it alternately low-keyed and hard. All chords, every touch of the fingers above the natural sound enhancer box rode the waves to the farthest reaches of the theater. Other sounds, down there on the darkened stage did as well.

There were beastly snarls, loud wolf howls and things that went bump in the night. They seemed to be coming from everywhere, creating a chilling, startling effect.

Whatever happened on the stage was not quite visible or did not seem to be, but concealed in shadows, in apparent mist and invisible curtains. All of it put together like this, created a startling effect.

The playing was not that rough, but still carried an intensity borrowing deep into everyone present.

There was no applause during the performance, but occasional gasps of awe and expectation as it affected those watching and listening and sensing.

It did not drag on, but set up the mood, pulling people onto the stage, the sense of the distant past shared among the audience enhanced by the performance.

The music stopped and the figure and the bumps in the night faded away.

A man seemed to grow out of the shadows, until he had become fully visible. He was dressed in traditional roman attire and had a way about him, one making everybody pay attention.

– Good evening, good people, he cried, and his voice echoed between the walls, – and welcome to this evening of revelations and mystery. I am Victor Lucius Corbin. I am one of several residents in this house of history and seeking. Allow me to present the gifted Cindy Patterson. She is a Storyteller in a long line of storytellers, a thespian and teacher at our school of art and antiquity.

There was more quiet applause, as the man faded out of everybody's attention and a woman faded in.

She stood there for a while, the red hair twinkling in fire. The fairly young face looked smooth but ancient in the special light, her eyes pools of dark water. A few drums beat now and then, adding to the already deep frame of mind.

A loud and powerful voice filled the theater.

– Sometimes, out there on the Foggy Banks an eerie mist forms out of nothing, she began. – Dark clouds explode out of thin air and there is a storm, one to end all storms.

Something aided the voice during the presentation, a potentially invasive power of the mind gently charging the spectators. Afterglow felt her presence within, but one did not need to be a sensitive to do that.

They imagined they saw that particular spot of ocean as she invoked it. She did invoke it. It was as if it was there, with them.

– The name «Foggy Banks» is a contradiction in terms. Most of the times there is no fog out there. It is in fact one of the most tranquil seas in this realm, with what seems to be an eternal and endless blue sky and blinding white daystar light. Its secrets keep confounding those seeking them. Representatives for the sciences, the alchemists, and the Wise alike have frustrated themselves in an effort to solve this riddle, and some of them have been lost out there, never to reappear.

Those present imagined it and imagined they even experienced it, as if they were actually There.

– People have discovered wreckage… not from here, since before the first days of the cities. Strangers and ships have appeared from the Foggy Banks, seemingly from nowhere… like the firstcomers, the founders of our community themselves.

There were murmurs and incredulity and anger among the gathering.

– Cindy and her theories have always brought anger and recrimination, Alice told the others around the table in a pleased tone of voice, – even before she took them that much further, until she began gathering evidence.

– Ours are a multicultural community, Cindy continued. – Our first ancestors fled the Roman Empire right after the beyond brutal and cruel murder of Hypatia and the burning of the library in Alexandria in order to escape the wrath of the ascending power of the followers of the One God, those today known as christians. They crossed the sea with great danger to themselves and founded this community, its first city after living through the worst storm in living memory.

There were a few angry cries by now, but most still listened politely and fascinated.

– After centuries had passed people sailed around this globe, searching for the place of their origin and found no trace of the Empire, and thus the quandary of The Great Mystery was presented to us for the first time.

– Later the English arrived here, and the Brown and the Yellow, presenting more clues to the riddle, bringing news of the Empire and its demise in the world, more than suggesting that these two mysteries are linked. Recently most of us studying them realized the stunning truth: that both the firstcomers and almost everybody arriving here later had been cast out of the foggy banks, through what is clearly a portal through space and perhaps also time.

There was some more unrest among the gathering, as people looked stunned at each other.

A man, one of the newly arrived travelers was chuckling to himself. It sounded more like crying.

His friends looked at him, at each other, in ridicule, amazement and fear.

– The Bermuda Triangle, he mumbled. – The god damn Bermuda Triangle.

Cindy Patterson raised her right index finger, drawing further people's attention.

– 1: Rome is clearly not anywhere in this Realm and never has been. None of the places and cities known to the Romans is. 2: Quite a few people being spit out of the Foggy Banks know about the Empire and its history and its demise. They are clearly from the Realm now known as Earth. Thus the Great Mystery is solved. The Mystery lives on.

Afterglow sensed something move in the shadows, a… charge given form, one further agitated and empowered by the angry individuals among the audience.

Thoughts and apprehension and action were one, as she signed to Alice, as the apprentice followed her on her jump from the chair and her run down the aisles. A wall of sort rose in front of the two. They grabbed hands and with an energy beam flowing forward they smashed the attempt at keeping them off the stage.

There was more pronounced unrest as some people stared angrily at the two and others noticed the snarls and hisses growing out of the shadows. Cindy looked astounded at Kathryn and Alice as they made their way to her.

The sudden chill in the air was felt by all. It assaulted them, like something tangible, and, as many with at least a minimum of awareness realized with paralyzing shock; a potent and present danger.

– Kathryn, what…

A loud sound, tearing at everybody stopped her from completing her question. Afterglow and the apprentice surrounded her, quickly drawing symbols in the air. First they were not visible, but soon they turned into mist and shadow and pale fire, observable to all, first forming a circle around the three, and then a protective cone surrounding them on all sides and at all angles. A man cried out in pain and grabbed his earlobe. His hand turned wet with blood. Others experienced similar or worse wounds. A woman screamed. Blood flowed between her thighs.

– Blood… Afterglow breathed.

Something hit the cone and some of the force pushed itself inside it, ripping into Afterglow. She crouched, drying her bloody lips, but standing her ground.

Another directed force, clearly resembling a blow hit Alice's side of the barrier. She was pushed backwards, into Cindy.

A gasp rose from everybody present, as the invisible entity turned visible, a giant man clothed in shadow, made of mist. Its eyes looked like pools of water and smoky hands hardened to solid claws.

– Assimilation spell, Afterglow hissed.

– Assimi… Alice blinked stunned. – Is that w-wise?

– The barrier will collapse. Be ready when it does.

The two of them began the incantation. Cindy joined in. An ancient language, hardly even words filled the cone of power. Cindy cried out in pain, but kept chanting. They fixed their attention at the entity outside, as it kept renewing and increasing the strength of its attack. Afterglow wondered if there was intelligence there, a glimmer of understanding, but there was not, or that very intelligence would have understood what was happening and at least attempted a withdrawal.

There was nothing but directed rage there.

The barrier broke and one moment later it was over. The directed energy was split in three, split between those it had been aimed at. All three screamed in pain and rage and Cindy in boundless terror, as impressions of what she had not dreamed existed filled her consciousness.

Afterglow's violet eyes glowed that much stronger. Alice gasped in awe as her strength increased significantly and the spirit locked in her collar cried out in dismay.

And Cindy felt the first major stirrings of what she had only imagined earlier in life.

– Congratulations, Afterglow bowed to her, – you are now a truly magickal creature, like you always wanted, irreversible and inevitable. The rest of your life will be a continuous effort to master it.

Cindy Patterson looked stunned at her, at herself. Afterglow sensed how the energies changed her, changed herself.

– A spirit drawing strength from contradicting emotions, Afterglow mused. – So insidious. Or it would have been if only people lacking the necessary defensive capabilities had been present. A bungling sorcerer, for instance would have taken everything, not only the energies, and thereby become the purpose of the spell, destroying himself or herself in the process.

– Afterglow is wise and powerful and crafty beyond words, Alice breathed with an even stronger worship in her twinkling eyes, striving to handle the influx of power ravaging her.

She did not overdo it, not in full public view, but in her mind she curtseyed deeply before her teacher.

– You saved my life, Cindy cried, – thank you, both of you.

– We need to leave, Afterglow said, as people slowly recovered, somewhat from what they had experienced, recovered their bearings. – Come!

They left through the back of the stage, passing empty dressing rooms and hallways, until they emerged in the back alley, where steam and mist lingered in the air. Afterglow and Alice drew their swords in preparation for what might wait for them, but there was nothing, no people, no entities, nothing but the charged air, an ongoing invasion of their being.

Afterglow did not stop, but did slow down a bit. Alice noticed. She knew.

There were sounds, very distinct of running and feet hammering wooden floor, but the loudest noise rummaged their minds. All their senses lit up in anticipation of what was coming.

Lester Brown and his fellow travelers rushed through the theater backdoor, out of breath, both because of the quick intense run and what buzzed in their insides.

Afterglow stopped and turned and looked at them.

– What was that? He gasped.

– You know what it was, she replied, – you do not need a crystal ball to understand the obvious.

Lester, Martha, Joshua, Leila and Stuart glanced puzzled at each other.

– That was a magical design, Alice added, very helpful, – a mindless entity emulating human life, created to execute our friend Cindy and generate as much havoc and suffering and death in our world as it possible was able to before burning itself out.

Afterglow felt the city move around her, felt the creatures of flesh and metal roam the space between quiet buildings.

– Come, she told the six, the five travelers and Cindy, – there is not much time.

Lester looked like he wanted to say more, but he held his tongue. He frowned again, but followed Afterglow and the two others into the city night.

Leila hurried to Afterglow's side.

– What we just witnessed isn't uncommon in this realm, I take it?

– It is not uncommon anywhere, but most people here are more receptacle to it than on current Earth.

– Is it… magic, truly and undeniably *magic?*

– Magick, sorcery, witchcraft, Afterglow shrugged. – The true power of the Universe, knowledge far beyond mere information. It moves and touches all things and every being in existence.

– Can it be… learned? Can I learn it?
– Yes, you could.
She moved, and they all moved in her slipstream. Leila kept close to her, as if she wanted to stay in her shadow.
– It was the… the Bermuda Triangle? Stuart asked out of breath.
– Aye, the Abyss, the Bermuda Triangle, Jupiter's Cauldron, the Foggy Banks, Afterglow confirmed. – It is an anomaly to end all anomalies, not like the other portals or even the Crossroads at all, but a maw, an access way into all space and time. It has a far more random, dangerous, even deadly quality and could have sent you anywhere. You were lucky.
– «Lucky»! Joshua snorted.
Sounds and voices imposed themselves on them, giving the travelers an illusion of close proximity. Leila clearly pondered something.
– So, she mused, - refugees from the Roman Empire, the christian Roman Empire arrived here sixteen-hundred years ago?
– We believe so, Cindy agreed. – At least most of the historians agree on that by now, even though that certainty has been muddled through the centuries and not everybody is ready to state their opinion in public about the particulars you heard me state quite brazenly...
– I've heard three names, Leila persisted, – Talaho, Howell and Auburn. They aren't Roman names at all, are they?
– Talaho is the Roman city.
– But that's my point. Many Roman cities had a rather elaborate naming. Shouldn't that be reflected?
– Congratulations, Cindy grinned, - you have touched upon another subject of great controversy. Most of the records from the first couple of centuries have been lost, so we do not know for sure. One school says the early settlers called it *Talahobatum* or something similarly elaborate and unknown. Another says it had its current name from the start.
It looked like she would say more, but then she stopped, clearly taken aback, almost embarrassed.
- Yes, congratulations, Afterglow chuckled. – It is not often Cindy has such an appreciative audience and as you can see it clearly has an impact on her.
The group did exchange the start of smiles, the most brittle amusement.
They kept walking or rather rushing through what the travelers could not help but see as unfamiliar, even alien surroundings.
Afterglow speeded up slightly more. There was still not running, but a fast stride making the travelers equally breathless.
Leila kept looking around her with excited eyes, as they moved through the darkened city streets.

– All this is so interesting, she cried excited, – the architecture, the similarities and differences of it all, so familiar and so wonderfully *alien*. At first glance the houses and streets and stuff don't look so different at all. Even though the composite puzzle doesn't fit it could have been anywhere on Earth. But then you begin noticing the details...

She was a tall and big woman and seemed to fill out her surroundings in a way Afterglow easily recognized.

All five did. It was palpable to her. They all wore the subtle glow of the twilight like a cloak around their body.

– And your clothes are *amazing*. Everybody wears tailor-made fabrics here, don't they? There is no mass-produced stuff.

– No mass-produced... anything, Afterglow stated. – We go to tailors and similar to cover our needs.

Communication was... difficult. Even though the English-English language gap was fairly easy to bridge, there was the even harder struggle to make contact across cultural boundaries. Alice clearly struggled, even though she managed.

A heartbreaking scream from a street to the right cut through the five newcomers. Afterglow and Alice hardly reacted at all, except by growing even more alert.

Afterglow watched the five, studied them with more than a few casual glances.

Alice wanted to give in to her curious nature, wanted it badly, and was about to ask the question several times, but she had learned her lesson and stayed silent.

– Is there a bed where we are going? Lester yawned. – I feel like I haven't slept for nights.

He frowned and caught himself.

– And we haven't, really, have we now?

– There is, Afterglow acknowledged, – but there will not be any sleep for any of us tonight. Far more crucial acts beckon.

– I don't think I can sleep again, ever, Leila brightened. – There is so much to experience, to... embrace.

– I can not either, Cindy shuddered. – I do not dare close my eyes. You do not want to know what I see, what I feel every time I close my eyes.

Afterglow did not say more. She left that to Alice, who was more than happy to oblige.

– You have all left your old lives behind, she stated with the pointed stare. – You will never be able to return to what and who you were.

Those words shocked them. They were not unexpected, in any way, but they still shocked them.

The two women moved in a certain manner through the darkened streets, one the six following them inadvertently made an effort to duplicate. Lester yawned again or stifled another yawn, fighting to keep his wavering eyes open.

– What's that *smell?*

It was a rhetorical question, really. Moments later he stopped expecting an answer.

The odd group charged through the early Howell evening. The twilight was not quite gone yet. It lingered, in a way the five travelers were unaccustomed to. The walk turned fairly long, with too many steps to count. They removed themselves from the Talaho Mountains and approached the Howell Hills in the east.

The two moons rose, within minutes of each other above the horizon. The five stopped briefly and stared at the, to them startling sight.

The other four looked at Leila.

– The star constellations are different, of course, she mused. – I can see that without batting an eye. I don't really recognize any of them, but if I should guess I would say we are still in the same spiral arm of the Milky Way Galaxy. With access to a telescope I could…

– This is the Milky Way Galaxy, Cindy confirmed. – At least we call it that, too.

– It's an old name, Leila said, – very much ingrained in our collective consciousness and common ancestry. When we look up we all see the milk of Hera spread across the sky, at least those of us with a Greek wiring.

She exhaled with a huge smile on her face.

– I'm *so* glad we came here.

They reached a non-descript house in a non-descript street on the first step of the first hill.

– Wild growing gardens, Lester said, – homegrown food and forests in the middle of the city. I just love that.

His wife looked at him. He did not seem to notice.

– Many people prefer being self-sufficient, Cindy said. – And the forests are so peaceful compared to the noisy city center.

– You call your city center noisy? Leila chuckled. – That's a good one.

Afterglow raised a hand. They understood and froze immediately. She stopped outside a gate. Leila wanted to ask something, but the sound stuck in her open mouth.

– You are lucky to have Afterglow's protection in this to you strange new land, Alice said in her solemn, sinister manner, – but she has gained many enemies as well and they have targeted her friends and allies lately.

The door to the house opened. Fremantle opened it in a calm and measured manner.

– It's safe, he called.

Afterglow moved in. The others followed her anxiously. Alice covered their rear. She was the last charging through the door before Fremantle slammed it shut and locked it.

Big Moon and Lesser Moon cast two pale shadows the moment she crossed the threshold of the living room, the moment Davis Fremantle greeted her with an embrace and a kiss on her lips. She responded somewhat favorably.

He was a big man, also bigger and taller than her, which was rare around here. She had always found it refreshing.

– I think I recognize you, now, Lester frowned, clearly pulling forward a distant memory. – You fought for the right to meet the boxing heavyweight champion of the world once, didn't you?

– That was a long time ago, Fremantle mused, shaking his head.

– All the kids in the neighborhood, me included wondered what happened to you… after your defeat.

– My world had crumbled. I did what was very popular at the time. I set out on a journey of «self-discovery» and eventually ended up here.

Fremantle shrugged.

– I found far more than I could ever have imagined, found life and challenges, awareness and a fire beyond my wildest dreams.

He and Afterglow and Alice moved in accordance with each other. The others did not notice at first, but then, slowly, they did.

– You have come here, to this place, of all places, Afterglow declared, – to one better in many ways compared to your point of departure, but with its own dangers. We appreciate true self-reliance here, and achieving that might, if one is lucky or unlucky also be a matter of life and death.

The room, the house seemed to isolate them. The outside world brought no sound or impression at all.

Fremantle removed the rug on the floor, revealing a trapdoor. The hatch was heavy. They easily saw that, when Afterglow grabbed the ring and opened the gateway to the cellar, but she handled it without effort. Suddenly the initially cozy surroundings had turned into something else altogether.

Stairs appeared, seemingly from nowhere. The procedure was repeated. Afterglow moved down first, followed by the six, and with Fremantle joining Alice in covering the rear.

The stairs clearly brought them deep into the ground, far below what they would deem an ordinary basement.

A rather large space came to their attention, more than large enough to roam below several of the neighboring houses, but there were no other doors the six could spot.

They stepped down into a world of deep darkness. Only the light from above brought illumination. When Afterglow lit flickering gaslights, and the world above faded away the shadows remained. The moment Fremantle closed the hatch it felt like a mere formality of facts.

Afterglow walked to a heap of wands and picked one, swinging it with a skill that made the others gasp in awe.

– No guns? Joshua wondered.

– Guns and bullets are handmade, Cindy said. – They are scarce and expensive. A group of magistrates have them, by the decree of the Council, and sentinels of the wealthy, and a few others, but that is all.

– Besides, a gun, even though it has its advantages should not really be the weapon of choice for a human being, a warrior witch, Afterglow shrugged. – You learn only scant skill and balance with it and hardly anything else. A wand, a sword becomes a part of your body, a true extended reach.

Fremantle and Alice picked their wand.

– This or a sword is your reach, she told them. – This is your world.

Afterglow, Fremantle and Alice moved and startled the others realized they were included, that they were a part of the pattern being weaved.

Suddenly a revolver, a model some of them recognized as a Smith & Wesson '44 Automatic appeared in Fremantle's hand. They gasped some more as he directed it at Afterglow and fired.

She raised a hand and the bullet lost all momentum, fell harmlessly to the floor in front of her.

– And against a certain kind of very dangerous foes a gun is usually completely useless.

They gaped. They stared.

And then they started shivering all over.

– I can fight with a wand, Leila cried.

She rushed to the heap and picked it up, swinging it in a seemingly fast and skilled manner.

– In many places and situations such an empty boast would have cost you dearly, Afterglow stated calmly. – Fortunately for you this is not one of them…

She attacked and Leila could hardly do more than defending herself. In a time-span covering no more than five seconds her wand was struck out of her hand. The next strikes hit her body and head and she fell beaten bloody and dizzy to the ground.

– On your feet! The woman towering above her snarled.

But nothing worked.

Afterglow struck her on the thigh. It hurt terribly. Leila jumped on her feet and stayed there, swaying hard, staring hurting and enraged at the other woman.

– Take off your high heels, Kathryn commanded her and Martha. – You would be dead in a few seconds during a true battle with such horribly impractical footwear.

They obeyed her in rushed, frantic movements.

– You've been to Earth. Lester took one step forward, fighting hard to keep his voice from trembling. – You can take us home.

– I could, Afterglow shrugged, – if that is your desire. But it is a rough journey. You are all fairly well trained and would probably survive if nothing happened, but if something did, you would not last more than moments.

– You will be warriors, Alice told them, – by the spilling of blood, both yours and others.

– Will we be… apprentices? Leila asked Afterglow.

– No. Afterglow replied. – An extensive previous knowledge of Magick is a prerequisite for that and you are more clueless than the smallest child of sorcerers.

She frowned, but they did not notice. Alice, however, did.

The three teachers moved and the students, picking up wands moved with them.

– We do not have much time tonight, Afterglow said, – but a half an hour crash course is better than nothing.

Martha looked like she wanted to ask another question, but she held her tongue.

The five and Cindy were all fairly athletic. They prepared themselves or made the attempt at doing so without further incitement.

– We're all into… sports, Lester remarked. – A part of a rather large continent of people on the ship was. We were on our way to the Triathlon championship in Sao Paulo.

He was indeed a big man, even though he could not compare to Fremantle.

– You're correct in your assumption that most people here wouldn't know what you're talking about, Fremantle chuckled. – They don't do dangerously silly things like sports here. Any sort of competition is rare.

– The firstcomers were so disgusted with the games in Rome that they vowed to keep such acts out of public life forever, Cindy said. – And that, like most other customs was respected and even adhered to by those following them through Jupiter's Cauldron. Many of them also fled from persecution and oppression and easily acknowledged the firstcomers' points about many things. It was a very healthy and encouraging environment for human creativity and freedom and still is.

Fremantle began swinging the wand. He did it so fast and with such force that they felt the wind against their skin. The two women did, too, and even though there was no wind from them, there was a kind of shimmer in the air they felt as a distinct pressure the moment they came close enough.

They all began swinging their wand, taking instructions, started doing their best at imitating the whirling movement.

– Feel your reach, Afterglow said. – Touch it with your mind. When you strike something or someone, you do it with the entire force in that tiny point contracting the wood. Like with a sword you defend with the strong part close to your hands and attack with the weak far reach. Open up the closed casket within and pull everything outside, to grab hold of and know.

Cindy moved and blinked, and moved and blinked, attempting to clear her vision, shaking her head.

– This is indeed about control, like most masters preach Martial Arts, Fremantle said, a little amazed, – but it's also about letting go and find the point beyond the box of your own mind. It's a discipline no longer learned on Earth and you're all so very lucky to have the change of learning it. Eventually it will set free everything you are and then you will discover what you're *truly* made of.

They listened to his words. They were a warm breeze compared to those spoken by Afterglow, but they still hammered all those «in training».

– Attack us, Afterglow told them.

They glanced uncertain and anxious at each other.

– *Attack!* She commanded them.

Her voice shattered their hide and bared their insides, and they obeyed.

Cindy's vision shifted in red, in blue. Afterglow saw it through her eyes and Alice did, too. Claws roamed the three of them. The soundless growl shook their gates, shook Cindy's walls.

– What *is* this? She wailed.

– You are struggling to adapt to the energies of the invader. Alice cautioned her, talking while she moved. – There is no mind there, no matter how much you fear there is. There are only you. Everything is blown wide open in you, without preparation and groundwork, and you must learn to master it, master yourself.

The growl manifested like a headless beast in the air. Cindy screamed. Her sweat turned into ice cold drops not melting on her skin.

The others stared at her, but Afterglow quickly steered them back on track.

– Do not bother with her. Attend to yourself.

They did, with an effort. The wands began making contact. The sound of wood against wood cast brittle echoes in the undetermined size of the room. Sometimes, though not often, the teacher's attack point would make contact with the students' bodies and jaws.

– Savor the taste of blood, Alice shouted harshly. – Let it linger and grow.

They were brought to the point of exhaustion, or at least what they imagined was fairly close to it.

– You think this is your threshold? It is not even close. It is a mere snack of the delight of fatigue.

– That's a good one, Leila gasped, heaved, joked. – Poetry of the highest order, without… without…

She trailed off, lost in deep concentration. When she, the next moment wielded her wand she did so with all the force she could muster. The stroke, when it hit her opponent, her invisible antagonist and rocked the room made her shout in joy.

It was intense, in spite of the seemingly low key exercise, clearly beyond the six's previous level.

Whirls of wands and bodies turned into one, indistinguishable movement.

The workout, when it was done felt both brief and long, as if time itself turned immaterial within the sphere of their reach. Afterglow stopped moving and the others did as well.

– I thought I was in good shape, Lester gasped, heaving for breath, for oxygen he feared just was not there.

Only painfully slow their heartbeat slowed down.

– I feel it, Martha insisted. – I felt it!

– You do not want to know what I felt, Cindy snarled.

She dried saliva from her jaw. It did not quite work. She had to do it twice, thrice.

– It moved within me, she frowned. – It…

Suddenly Afterglow was at her side. Cindy gasped.

– GODDESS!

– Breathe, Kathryn hissed at her. – Focus on the stream. Let it flow, but do not submit to it.

Cindy whimpered, but… settled. The snarl distorting her face faded away. She gasped and looked at Afterglow with blind eyes.

– Thank you, she panted. – It was so horrible, so overwhelming. It was as if I was fading, going away, but you *saved* me. Oh, thank you.

She kissed the other woman on the lips, several times, in excessive gratitude. Afterglow let her, but did not respond. They disentangled.

– I didn't notice anything special, Lester frowned.

– None of you did, Afterglow said. – Even if you were prime sorcerer material it would take longer than a brief training session for you to bring out what is inside, especially when you have denied it for so long.

Once again Martha looked like she wanted to say something, like she wanted it very much, but held her tongue.

– I am going to show you the Universe, now, Kathryn Caldwell told them, placing herself before them, still moving. – Give you a taste of it, show at least a tiny bit of what your lack of awareness has concealed from you.

She put down her wand. Everybody else did the same.

– Come, she said, – it is almost time.

– Time for what? Leila wondered.

The female foreigners grabbed their high-heeled shoes and put them on. The group moved back up, reappearing into what seemed to the newcomers as a sparse living room.

– You know, I didn't really expect a reply to my silly query, Leila grinned, bowing in deference. – It just slipped out of me, like days' old stomach gas. Forgive me, Afterglow, for my ignorance.

She was joking, but was also respectful.

There had been a subtle change in the way the newcomers acted during their fairly brief time in the basement. Everybody moved in accordance with Afterglow, now.

– I like your place, Davis, Lester said to Fremantle. – It's very much lacking in electronics and similar, but I understand that that isn't unusual in these parts.

– It isn't, Fremantle said.

– But your level of technology is clearly on par with Earth, and even superior in some ways. Your cars… I've never seen an engine like that before.

– The Science Advisory Board inspects every new invention and prospect, deciding, often with the citizens' aid what is useful and truly needed, Cindy said. – The kind of portable phones you carry, for instance was banned because its radiation is damaging and lethal, slowly ruining a body and brain close to it.

– They missed out on the Dark Ages here, Fremantle grumbled. – A fact that led to a number of good things, both to a scientific head-start compared to Earth, and to a more cautious approach. There's no idiot box either, or even long-range radio broadcasts. We like it live here. The little mass communication there is, is done through the stationary phones.

– To endless frustration, Alice grinned.

– I have threatened to kill people calling me without a valid reason,

Afterglow said, a bit preoccupied.

They exchanged worried glances and they believed her.

– Tomorrow you will all register your citizenship at the immigration office, she told them, – but tonight you will learn to know your new home in all its wonder and horror.

They moved outside. Alice was point sword. She moved with the blade in a way that took their breath away. When she made a swing with the forged metal they imagined that she was probing with it, not only the air right in front of her, but a considerable distance of their upcoming path. There were no words or even a nod, but somehow they knew when Afterglow gave them her go ahead.

– This *is* a special night, Afterglow acknowledged. – What we do tonight carries great weight, both symbolic and actual. That you and your ship arrived tonight, of all nights is seen as a potentially potent sign for quite a few parties.

– And my guess is that that puts us in danger, Lester said.

– It does, she replied, – for no other reason than that they believe in your special status.

– Do you believe it? He asked.

– Yes.

She said.

He shook his head and kept shaking his head long after that.

– But… how could you? He wondered. – Unless you have a reason, something solid that convinces you of…

He trailed off.

– Someone just stepped on your grave, she said. – I know that feeling.

They moved on, back towards the city center. The direction and also the destination quickly became evident. It dawned on them that they were on their way to the harbor. Anxiety struck their hearts, and even more so as they observed the subtle signs of Afterglow and Alice preparing themselves.

– You take us back to where all the passengers are gathered, where the chances of us being attacked is at the highest?

Martha asked enraged.

– Yes.

Kathryn glanced at the rooftops. Ravens flew along their path. There were nine of them. The sight made her shudder so hard that she was unable to keep it from the others.

– You will all grow this night. We will all grow, but there must be blood, must be sacrifice and lots are coming up. There must always be death.

She felt them move, once again approaching her through dim streets, the stealthy swordsmen already dead.

The sorcerer and her apprentice tensed and moved with their swords as if they were a part of them.

– One hundred years ago, to this night a ship like yours arrived here, Alice stated, anxious but measured, like they had learned to know her. – Certain parties, and it was never revealed who was behind it sent a group of swordsmen to attack the passengers, and those swordsmen killed every single woman, man and child that had been on that ship.

A chill passed through them all, also Alice and Afterglow. Kathryn frowned. There was something here, something…

– But that's… horrible, Leila gasped. – Why?

The harbor was flooded. The high tide reached them half to their knees in some places. After a moment or two of hesitation they followed the sorcerer and her apprentice further along the new, temporary shore.

They reached the building harboring the passengers from the ship. A group of magistrates guarded the entrances. Afterglow and Alice froze slightly, even as their eyes never rested.

– I do not know, Cindy said, shaking her head. – I do not know about any who does. But it is not unlikely that they will want to repeat it tonight.

Leila and several of the others wanted to say something, ask the obvious question burning in their gut, but then they, too, stopped in their tracks.

Afterglow cautiously approached the closest magistrates.

– Are you guarding all the access ways? She asked them from a non-threatening distance. – Even seaside?

The magistrates all carried heavy firearms. A woman nodded. Afterglow was clearly known to her. The respectful conduct was more than evident. She signaled for the others to stay calm.

– Trouble is coming, Afterglow stated. – Big trouble.

The sound of many light steps coming from the dark alleys they had just left turned louder.

And then…

Big Moon turned blood red.

It was not gradual, but abrupt and decisive, from one moment to the next, without any obvious forewarning, and everything below was cast in the same, sinister light.

Silver moonlight changed into slivers of blood. People and surroundings transformed into something new and different.

Afterglow looked at Lester from the corner of her eye.

The sword-wielding women and men dressed in black advanced across the harbor plaza. One moment there had been no one there, the next one, two, three, four, five, six, seven, eight, nine and many more had appeared from dark alleys and shimmering ruby air.

– Your weapons will not be totally useless, she told the female magistrate leader, – but you need to fire them at close range. Understand? It is crucial that you understand this.

– I do, Afterglow, the chief magistrate replied with lowered eyes. – It will be as you have ordained.

The woman spoke fast and excited into the radio.

Afterglow hardly heard her speak and the other woman's words lost all meaning.

– *Pe a pe a peo pe y ye fo…*

The song, the ancient and terrible chant rose from Kathryn Caldwell's throat. It continued with seemingly subtle variations, rolled off her tongue like the sea water surrounding them rolled on and off the shore.

Alice's eyes turned huge and scared.

– I can understand you, she cried startled.

She translated continuously for the others.

– «The Nine were born in the land of the moon. They came from nowhere and everywhere across the nine realms and their destiny is to transform all they survey. Human beings live apart from each other. They are spread across many a distant land like grains of sand on a thousand beaches, but the Nine will rule them all».

The same chant rose from the throat of the attacking swordsmen and women, joining with that of the woman blocking their path. They hesitated momentarily when Afterglow stepped forward and challenged them.

– I can not die, she shouted. – Kill me a million times and I will rise again.

They charged and the chant became the shouts of pain and blood it had always been.

She attempted to freeze them, to catch them in her waves, like she had done the last time she had faced them, but they had prepared for her, and the irritating, painful voice in her ear told her that she was not quite as powerful as she had been then.

Three of them holding hands deflected her attack. Two and two of them protected themselves from the rays Alice fired from her hands. A shotgun went off. The hail lost all momentum long before reaching anyone.

Everything happened so fast, like a whirl of motion towards the travelers from another realm. There was not any pull/release, push release, but what seemed like an even, unending flow.

Afterglow focused her waves and hit one attacker with it, piercing his skin and very body. He expired in a brief, muted howl of pain.

Then she was distracted again. In the unending flow of attack and defense it was hard to gain the focus needed to use her power effectively.

Except through the sword. The blade, enhanced by the energies burning within her burned through anything. Enemies fell left and right, above and below, in front and behind. She and Alice moved as one, one single being of fluid motion and death.

And blood filled the air. She was able to taste it, like milk from a warm nipple, corrupted, tainted with the sinister Magick that had transformed these creatures. They had been human once, and now, even though they still looked like flesh and blood and bone they were nothing but puppets dancing to another's wicked tune.

Afterglow's blood boiled in her veins. She noticed it the second the elevated movement began and every moment since, the moment she began straining, began exerting herself beyond the familiar critical point.

Alice noticed it, too, inevitably. She lit up like the fire she was. Her smile heated every point of air, mixing with Afterglow's pyroclastic flow.

Her focus sharpened to a razor's edge.

A Ka, a short swinging blade sharp on all sides rushed through the air towards them. They avoided it by twisting their body just right, and still remaining in balance, ready and able to fight on. Afterglow checked to see if the blade would hit anybody else, but it would not.

She cut off the head of the nearest attacker. The woman's body crumbled into dust and pus, the only thing left of her. Kathryn shouted in rage and even sorrow, and her howl froze everybody present, harming beyond harming those who were nothing but dust and pus. She cut them down, one by one, two by two.

One slipped past her, past the defense line towards its intended victims, one step, two, three, four steps. Afterglow sent forward her waves and severed the man's head from his body. Lester shook as the form dissolved just two steps away from him.

She felt it, as she was soaked in the blood filling the air, with her content smile turned towards the others.

It lingered within her, the rush of blood and power did, and she realized, she knew then, even more than before that it always would. They stared at her in shock, in awe and terror and a thousand not easily identifiable emotions.

She rushed seaside, saw the first swordsmen appear from the ocean, intending to take advantage of the decoys' action, their intended diversion.

They turned and rushed back towards the sea the moment they spotted her. The surface boiled as they vanished below the surface.

Afterglow sent her waves at them. The boiling sea became steam and mist, and she heard the screams, even if no one else did.

She beheld herself from a thousand points in space and time.

Alice rushed forward and knelt before her.

– Do *anything* to me.

Blurring blobs of blue danced in the air around Afterglow, briefly challenging the pervasive red glare, before seemingly being pulled back into the seething, powerful form of flesh and blood.

Kathryn bent down and removed the collar.

– There must be nothing between us.

Alice gasped, her face transformed by joy and gratitude.

– Thank you, My Lady, she said, rising, but keeping her head bowed. – Thank you, o' kind and cruel Queen, beloved and dreaded Master.

The others looked frowning, uncomprehending at the two.

Lester sort of stepped forward, even though observers could not quite decide if he truly moved.

– Who were they after?

Afterglow did not look at him, as she spoke to the air.

– They were after you.

The word «you» was a deceptive word in all variations of English. It was often hard to know if it was meant as plural or singular and this time, even if the enigmatic woman clearly emphasized the word, it was even harder.

– Either they, the forces behind the attackers wanted to crush the prophecy or to segment it or possibly bend it to their will. They seem quite the ambitious bunch, do you not think?

– But we aren't important, Martha objected.

Afterglow did not hear her or ignored her. It was difficult to tell.

– This is not suitable, she said. – We will need another place of sacrifice and blood.

– Alice has the perfect place available for Afterglow, Alice said.

Afterglow nodded.

– Yes, she agreed, – that will be very suitable.

She turned towards the others and now she gave them her full attention. It shocked them, like electricity, but far deeper, more pronounced.

– You will come with us, she told them.

And protest did not occur to them.

– You will, too, Afterglow told the female magistrate. – Your old life is over. Soon, it will be no more than a distant memory, like your earliest childhood.

Caroline Tsjekov's lips shivered and she walked to the imposing woman's side, her eyes cast down.

– Good girl, Alice acknowledged. – You know your family history, know what Afterglow is.

– You have trained hard? Afterglow asked casually. – You have kept yourself fit?

– Yes, o'kind and cruel Queen, beloved and dreaded Master.

– We require transportation. I am afraid our bloodstained bodies will not go far on the public buses.

– At once, My Lady.

Caroline ignored her fellow magistrates. It was truly as if she had already forgotten them, her old life.

– This is an age-old… arrangement of sort, isn't it? Leila mused. – A generational thing centuries old. People may be handpicked, even from birth to serve the… the sorcerers. How very interesting.

The fight had clearly shaken her, but she had kept her composure and relative aloofness, the burning passion lurking just below the surface.

Afterglow appraised her, grabbed her jaw and studied her, deliberately patronizing. She wanted to break free, but was frozen in place by the very air itself.

The hand, the vice let go. Leila sagged and almost fell. Afterglow directed her attention to all her surroundings once more. Leila glanced at the magistrates, as they were scurrying around, talking to people flowing from the boarding house, calming them down.

– Won't they… will they not want to talk to us as well, take our statement?

A haze appeared in her eyes, as she made the change in her speech in an effort to fit the local dialect and custom.

– They know there are vast forces beyond their ken, Alice snorted, – know enough to keep their noses out of it, as much as possible. At least their bosses, key people within their ranks do.

Afterglow smeared blood from her hands and body and sword on Leila and the others. Alice joined her. Leila stood still with a rigid expression in her face. The others squirmed uncomfortably, but did not attempt to move away.

The battle, the images and sensations of blood and pain stayed with them, more so every time they blinked.

– Yes, Alice stated, – you are all a part of this, not only by the blood and sacrifice, but by the ancient magick penetrating all realms, all people.

And she bristled as Afterglow granted her a glance of approval, and heat surged through her like the light of Big Moon.

And drops of blood almost turned to steam still fell slowly to the ground.

CHAPTER THIRTEEN

Restlessness prevailed, the unrelenting pressure in the back persisted. The scene and event at the Howell western harbor stayed at the forefront of their consciousness.

Blood covered them. They smelled and breathed it.

The bus raged through the night. It moved slowly, surely through the urban landscape, on the northern occasionally bumpy main road.

Caroline drove. The others sat facing each other in comfortable seats right around a round table behind her.

– God, Stuart said, – that was…

He tried several times to express himself, in vain.

– You have no words, Afterglow told him. – You have never stared Death in the eyes before.

– But I have, he protested. – I was in the army. I fought and killed in Afghanistan.

– That boy-army of yours? She grinned. – Where you kill your enemies from a distance? Do not be ridiculous…

She leaned back a little, briefly closing her eyes.

– When you have cut hundreds of enemies with your sword and can not help swallowing their blood, when you have fought close up, for days and nights without pause… then you know war.

And it was as if they could see, see the battlefield or at least glimpse it, in prolonged flashes, as if the stench of the red fluid and sweat and rotting bodies made their nostrils twitch.

– The world has opened its eyes to us, Lester whispered. – The entire world.

– The entire Universe, Leila breathed.

Silence fell again. Afterglow and Alice communicated without words, preparing for what was to come. It was subtle. It remained a powerful sensation. The boiling blood from the fight stayed with them, sharpening their senses to a razor's edge.

The windows appeared to them like true windows to the world, to the extended reality. Afterglow saw more, but everybody present saw glimpses of existence beyond the streets they passed by.

Lester shook behind the haze of his eyes, clearly seeing something shaking him up, shaking him up bad.

– I don't see many cars, he said, clearly attempting to pull himself together, to distract himself from whatever haunted him, – haven't really since we came here.

– Private cars are not that popular, but many people have the technical know-how to make one, Cindy said. – Cars are not manufactured, but usually made in a person's garage with various parts that might have been made elsewhere. It is more like a technical… hobby than for transport. There are no factories like you know them.

– But what about railroads? You would think that would make a given population choose railroads.

– The triple cities up north have pulled their resources into a railroad system. Other triple cities have chosen different solutions. There are very few standards on Montan.

– Montan?

– This Realm…

– This planet, you mean?

– That designation may or may not be accurate. It varies from realm to realm. One realm may consist of several balls floating in the spheres, and another of only a part of one.

He looked up on that giant sphere hovering above them.

– That isn't really a moon, of course. We are on a moon of that planet.

No one contradicted him. He had clearly half expected someone to do so.

– I remain amazed, Leila sighed entranced. – All this is… is so…

She just trailed off, bathing, shivering in the crimson light of Big Moon, glancing in deference at Afterglow.

– We are on our way to something, Cindy said with a thin, thin voice. – I can feel it moving inside.

– I can feel it, too, Alice grinned. – It is so powerful, so great.

– And it is just the beginning, Afterglow mused, – the beginning of everything.

She frowned, pondered it and frowned again.

The bus moved, its tires turned and turned through the mist of the night, all blanketed by the crimson glow of Big Moon in both air and mind.

And then, as they drove on a rise they saw cars, a long row of them stuck in congestion ahead. There had been an accident and several vehicles blocked both directions.

The bus avoided it by taking off from the main road and drive on one of the bumpier access roads to the house on the hill. It took some time, as Caroline maneuvered between the numerous holes, until they finally reached their destination. The fairly silent engine stopped and the loud sounds of bumps kept shaking their aching ears. They stepped off the vehicle. The sound of shoes against the shingle echoed in the silence of the blood red night.

– The color doesn't go away, Martha complained, glancing at Big Moon, – like it will stay this way *forever*.

Nobody replied to her. She stared distressed at them.

– There has been a lot of traffic here recently, Lester remarked.

He had noticed the many tire marks.

Afterglow studied Alice, but the young girl did not seem too anxious.

– I was wondering… Martha said. – I've seen no… is there a church nearby?

Cindy shook her head, slightly surprised when considering the perceived peculiarity in the other's question.

– I understand your request, she said. – I mean, being a scholar and all I understand its motivation, but I doubt many others would. There are no public houses for prayer or worship anywhere in these parts and no tradition for such. Communion with the gods or its vain attempts is considered a private matter.

– Oh, Martha mumbled sullenly, with more than a stint of despair in her voice and stance.

– At… home… on *Earth* there is a church or similar in every single village, Fremantle grumbled. – I'm pleased they've avoided that trap here.

– In every single village? Cindy wondered astounded.

– Every fucking one, Fremantle confirmed. – Often there is even more than one.

– Amazing. Cindy shook her head in disbelief.

The house loomed above them, its energies and true face tangible. Afterglow nodded pleased to herself.

They walked up the shingle road. The walk seemed very steep and very hard. Several of them had to make an effort to keep moving forward. Only Afterglow and Alice remained unaffected.

– Welcome, travelers to my humble abode, Alice declared, as she unlocked the heavy door and entered the hall.

Everybody stopped there for a while, in various ways taking in the sights, as the house inevitably imposed itself on them all.

– You have such a nice home, Alice, Leila said, striving to keep her breathing even.

– It has been bathed in blood and death, Alice stated with a grim smile. – It is perfect for our purpose.

– Of course, Leila mumbled.

It was big, far bigger and more spacious than Fremantle's modest digs.

– It has belonged to powerful sorcerers and leaders for centuries, Alice told them. – Alice is the last in her line. All their might is congregated in her.

She went straight for a concealed door, one not visible even to a thorough investigation of the wall and opened it. Her traveling guests imagined that they heard a sigh descending from above and a growl shaking the house.

– Her kind master Afterglow has granted her servant the joy of aiding her in her craft.

There were marble stairs leading upwards, a fairly narrow rise in the walls.

– Alice's great grandfather made this secret passageway one hundred years ago to this day. He was one of the last well known seers and foresaw that one of his descendants in the service of a mighty sorcerer would use it the night when the Blood Red Big Moon would return.

The travelers glanced at her, unused as they were to people speaking about themselves in such terms.

– Her speech pattern is a sign of humility in this realm, Cindy enlightened them, – not of bluster and arrogance.

They nodded, very enlightened, nodding to themselves.

– You have been thrust into extraordinary circumstances, she added. – You have been given a change to enjoy life at its most basic level and should grab the opportunity by the tail.

She was clearly sincere and that confused them further.

– She speaks the truth, Fremantle nodded. – You should embrace your new circumstances. That's how life should be lived, how it is lived by many here and in the territories.

They ascended into an attic, a loft, where huge windows made out most of the walls and ceiling. A pentacle covered most of the floor. The powerful glow from Big Moon once more filled their vision, their being.

Leila walked to the south wall, casting her eyes and attention towards the land below, towards the distant Triple Cities. She turned towards the east. Dancing red mist rose from the sea, flowing slowly towards the cities, towards them from Jupiter's Cauldron.

– Beautiful, she mumbled. – I feel such joy, such terror.

The pentacle on the floor began glowing, weak, almost imperceptible at first, then strong and steady. The big candles on each of the five points and the lamps and torches on the walls lit themselves.

The floor seemed to briefly disappear beneath them and everybody except Afterglow and Alice staggered.

– This place of mist and Shadow recognizes our power, Alice beamed, – acknowledges our right of access and use and mastery.

Her words made Lester frown, made him shake his head.

There was a giant wheel on the floor in one of the corners. Alice loosened a harness on it and began turning it. She had to pull hard. The windows opened, opened wide, letting in air from the outside, the first few dots of the red-colored mist. She completed the process and locked the harness again.

– Cindy, Lester, Martha, Leila, Joshua and Stuart, Afterglow bade them, – step into the circle and stand on each of the pentacle points. Martha and Lester together. Caroline and Fremantle, stay alert, prepare to defend us against any undue intrusion.

There was that something in her voice making them obey her without protest or even consideration. They stepped into the circle. There was a slight tingle and discharge. The six took their designated places at the points. Afterglow and Alice, with coagulated blood on much of their skin and clothes stepped inside right after them. There were more discharges. They walked to the center of the pentacle.

The others stared astounded at how the mist began dancing around them, forming patterns and waves.

Sorcerer and apprentice faced each other, palms against palms.

They seemed to breathe it in, the red, the mist, the night and the approaching, shimmering twilight. It glowed within them. Those standing in the circle could almost see their insides, their bones and red-glowing veins and what was dancing in their eyes.

– I am open, Afterglow cried. – I call Selene, the Goddess of the moon, its red and silver shadows. I glimpse the waves of the night. I want to see them clearly.

– I am open, Alice stated. – I open myself to the forces of the realm, to my mentor, my teacher, the terrible and cruel Afterglow, to her cuts and strikes. She will see through my eyes. I am her vessel, traveling the Other World.

Voices, singular and plural echoed in the void between moments, moments approaching like the breath of wind, the draft shaking their bones.

The added glow from the candles, torches and lamps intensified.

A door slammed open, quietly, imperceptible, there was no door. The waves danced in the mist. Afterglow and Alice clutched hands. They stood still. Everybody else shook in the wind. The mist kept drifting, dancing, not blowing. There was no wind, only what was shaking the air. Nothing moved the flames rising from the candles and the torches.

The blood burned the faces of those standing at the points. Its stench once again turned pervasive and strong.

The voice rose above the silent roar.

– By the tome and tomb of my ancestors, by those closest to the waves of the realm, I, Afterglow take possession of this girl, this vessel and use her as I see fit.

The words changed, turning foreign and incomprehensible. Cindy shook her head in amazement, shivering in anticipation. The red mist turned partly bright blue and dark violet around the two. Each of the figures present cast five shadows, in five different directions.

Afterglow stopped talking, stopped chanting. Deep shadows and a dim blue light connected the two. Alice opened her mouth. She frowned and strained to speak.

– I can see you…

See you.

Her voice turned deeper, more invasive, more Afterglow than Alice.

– I can see me.

See me.

– Death keeps chasing Afterglow, but even though it is catching up to her now and then, it can not truly touch her. She keeps escaping its dark touch. We have danced to our tune of blood and resurrection for time immemorial, beyond time itself. It catches her in her unprepared youth, but then she once more slips away. Afterglow knew Death early, but slipped away, marked for life. The bard of the world is taunting her, singing her praise, visiting her in her dark and gloomy hours, bringing her cold and warm comfort and illumination haunting her all her days and nights. She feels a hand reaching for her, feels its flesh as hers and his connect and let go, and she falls, falls from the highest mountain, the tallest building. She is falling still…

Alice shook, trembling like the shifting air surrounding her. Gasps escaped her between the spoken words. Afterglow's lips trembled.

– She is drifting through the realms, through existence like a mote of dust, reaching out with her claws in an effort to anchor herself from the onslaught of reality constantly slamming her. The Nine is hunting her, The Nine will catch her. The nine realms and beyond are her playground, where she will wither and rise.

Blood flowed from Lester's open mouth. He could not close the gap. Leila rolled her head left to right, right to left in a perpetual, unending movement. She was humming and moaning. Martha screamed, but no one heard anything.

Her scream reached across the realms, heard by no one, felt by all.

Fremantle and Caroline crouched by the window, by the cold draft resembling a portal.

Afterglow and Alice squeezed each other's hands. Facial skin turned pale and gray. Pain ravaged their features. They held on.

All eight gasped. The other two outside the pentacle felt it as well. It was as if the very act of breathing hurt.

Afterglow's eyes closed, closed hard. Blood flowed from the slits.

– He told her she was destined for greatness and left her in the dirt...

Kathryn Caldwell shook and the air shook with her. She studied herself through Alice's eyes, Alice's extended awareness.

– There is a nexus in all realms, lighthouses of shadows attracting all sorcerers, all wielders of magick. Afterglow is called to those hot and cold spots, like they are all called. She swore she would never return to the island of her birth and adolescence, the place where she found love and betrayal and awareness beyond belief, but she is pulled back there by a force beyond comprehension.

The force, she imagined she could actually see it, see it in the mist, see features appearing on the indistinct face in the mist.

Visions of the old and empty house and its cave, its basement shook in her, in their vision, and then the quality and the quantity of the vision changed, showing more than one ancient and empty house and place: a cave inside a high mountain, an eerie, transparent building levitating in the air and the mist, a castle and a garden bathed in moonlight. And then the nature of the visions shifted again. There were nine, nine sites standing out from the rest, solidifying in the minds of everybody present.

It started raining, the blood red rain, and yet somehow Big Moon remained visible and potent through the clouds and mist.

Then Alice's voice, its very nature changed again.

– I feel very small, I feel dead, nothing but a tiny speck drifting in the wind.

It still sounded like Afterglow's voice, but childlike, a whimper more than actual speech.

– I hurt, *hurt,* HURT

Fear touched them all, like something tangible, visible in their stricken faces.

A figure formed in the red mist. Kathryn recognized it immediately.

The mist turned a sickly brown, like puss flowing from an infected wound.

Hands attempted to let go, in vain.

– We are coming, Beatrice grinned viciously. – If you surrender now we might go easy on you.

She faded away again, just a glimpse, but one burning into their retina forever.

– I am like a wet blanket covering you. The ghoulish voice reached them from the mist. – I keep you down, down, down...

The blood red color returned. Moans filled the mist.

– It must run its course, Alice gasped. – It can not be stopped.

The sight and sense of a barren land invaded them, the sulfur from the volcano tearing into their nostrils. The very air burned and froze their skin.

They walked through a vast forest surrounded by bloodthirsty beasts on two and four legs and vicious eyes studying them like they would prey.

One blink and Kathryn glimpsed a hand, no, two hands bloody and slippery clutching each other, one vision she was unsure she shared with the others. Two hands slipped, as they could no longer hold on and she fell, fell.

– Falling, Alice whimpered. – I am falling. I have always been falling, falling, falling…

Afterglow heard her own voice, a multitude choiring in the mist and shadows of the realms.

A sea, a vast ocean, a small pond twinkled in green and twilight. The Dark Lodge, foreboding and infinitely attractive glowed in shadow.

The red glow faded with the onset of dawn. Hands clutching hands let go. The spell ended, burning itself out.

They collapsed there, on the floor. They blinked a few times, before eyes closed and they stopped moving and fell asleep.

Dreams potent and vivid rose within them all and everybody squirmed and moaned on the hard and cruel bed. They saw more of themselves together, saw and felt blood and death and power unbound.

In far away realms humans lived and died and thrived, on beaches without end.

Martha screamed, far louder than before. She did not wake up, but whined loud enough to shake everybody present and the very foundation of the house. The others did not wake up either, but this time they heard her and saw her and experienced her. In a flash of a moment her howl gave birth to what would come and they saw themselves changed, before everything turned pitch black around them and they slept without dreams, without thought.

Fremantle took one step forward. Caroline stopped him from intervening.

– I have seen this before, she said softly. – The apprentice was correct. It must run its course, even in Morpheus' realm. They will awake rested and somewhat enlightened. We can only guard them, do our best to protect the sanctity of their circle, as Afterglow bade us.

She sat down, her feet crossed in front of her, her eyes half closed, half open. Fremantle hesitated a bit, before joining her on the floor. He took longer to reach her state of sleepy wakefulness, but eventually he also got there and two sentries watched over those in the circle.

Blood Red Big Moon kept casting Arcadia and Montan in its crimson light, one, though weakened in the white glow of the daystar still very much notable.

Cars and vehicles passed by outside, the congestion cleared. People passed by, but there were no sounds of anyone stepping on the shingle, no alarming sounds disturbing the wake. No one approached the ominous house on the hill.

At midday the mist had dispersed in full. The eighth inside the circle began stirring and moving.

They sat up, slowly returning to the room, awarcncss oncc morc brightening their eyes.

Caroline walked to them carrying a tray with eighth glasses. Afterglow and Alice grabbed theirs, and the others, having hesitated joined in. Everybody drank. Martha coughed and shook hard, the others less so.

Unable to sit more than a little at a time they crouched on the floor, drinking the refreshing potion.

– I feel… Cindy breathed. – I feel pretty good.

She and the other novices stared astounded at each other.

– Thank you, Alice said, grabbing Afterglow's hands. – Thank you.

They noticed the ambiguity in her voice and nodded to themselves.

Leila stood up, fighting herself on her feet.

– This is… truth, isn't it? She frowned. – This is the world, life as it truly is?

– It is as if I have been asleep my entire life, Lester breathed, – never truly experiencing anything of consequence until this very night.

A distant banshee sound rose from the pentacle and even though it quickly faded away, it lingered in their mind.

Afterglow walked to one of the windows, one of the walls, She saw a superimposed image of the distant cities, all three of them, the triangle, saw all nine cities and the bigger triangle, saw it in a blur, in a confused imagery mixed in with all the others racing through her mind.

And then…

During the course of a few heartbeats she saw the nine realms, the wheel of fire and shadow turn and heave, and glimpsed beyond that… a thousand worlds, the stars and empty space of her most vivid dreams.

They walked the long path down the stairs, back to the place they hardly remembered.

– Everything feels… recent, Leila mused. – I see everything through new eyes.

Her words made even Afterglow smile, but her frown did not let up. She masked her concern, her raging emotions from them.

Alice exhaled slowly. She seemed upbeat, free and downright euphoric.

Afterglow felt a tingle in her toes, felt it increase as she descended the old and clearly enchanted house.

– The big, bad wolf of the Wasteland is screaming in my gut, Alice declared boldly.

She embraced Joshua and granted him a long, sultry kiss on the lips. Her intent, her desire could not be misunderstood, in any way.

– Females are not timid here, she practically hissed at him. – We know what we want and do not hide ourselves.

– At least you declared your intentions honorably, he joked.

He looked very intimidated. Uncertain laughter whispered in the room, as she stepped backwards and reached out a hand to him. He grabbed it and pulled her to him. They saw how he had to crouch because of his visible hard-on, what had been there before she made any overt move towards him.

She willingly allowed him to fondle her, roam her, enticing, encouraging the fumbling boy. He growled and pushed her at the wall, and she chuckled pleased. She slipped out of his arms and walked to the lush carpet at the center of the living room, where she proceeded to undress. It was clear that she did not really display herself to them, in spite of the fact that everyone was studying her.

But she was displaying herself to him, with every tiny move she made.

He tore off his clothes as he approached her. His cock grew in the blink of an eye to its full size and pointed straight at her. He reached for her. She grabbed him and used the force of his own movement to put him down on his back. It stunned him and allowed her to do as she pleased. She jumped him, quite simply jumped him and pushed him into her and began riding him, as he began pushing against her.

The others began shifting their feet and bodies as the growls, moans and horny shouts filled the room and their ears and being. Afterglow gave Lester a hot look. He pretended he did not see it. She shrugged and left the low-level arousal to burn itself out within her.

The two lovers crumbled on the floor, a big, content grin spreading on Alice's face.

A phone started ringing somewhere not far away, shaking eardrums and minds alike, pulling them all out of their feverish thoughts.

Alice kissed Joshua on the cheek and rose, picking up her clothes, taking her time dressing as she headed for the other part of the house.

– Alice will make breakfast, she said. – Please join her in the dining room.

The phone kept ringing. She let it. When she finally picked up the receiver more than a minute had passed.

Afterglow studied Lester as he came to rest before her, the dark shimmer dancing around his body. To her he seemed to be dancing, moving even when standing still.

– The Thornbridge residence, you are speaking to Alice.
There was a very excited voice at the other end. The others could almost make out the words.
– Yes, I have inherited the… firm, and we are very much still in business, Mr. Hornsby. We are, in fact in better shape than ever. You want a commission?
More talk, less excited erupted from the receiver.
– We have several groups, at various stages of skill you may hire.
More talk, clearly more exited flowed from the receiver and into her ear, into the room itself and almost everyone present.
– You are in luck, Mr. Hornsby. That can be arranged… for the right price, of course.
The buzz on the phone echoed several times in Afterglow's ears.
– Then we will see you then, Alice said graciously.
She returned the receiver to its spot on the table. The smile vanished. She ran to Afterglow and stopped before her with lowered eyes.
– Alice has accepted a commission on Afterglow's behalf, she said humbly. – Alice is sorry if she was presumptuous.
– She was not, Afterglow replied casually.
The girl relaxed and the smile returned to her sweet and innocent face.
She rushed off to the kitchen. They sat down around the table and not long afterwards they heard her scramble around out there, and then the smell of warm food reached their nostrils.
– So, what happens now? Lester wondered.
Afterglow felt the depth of his dark eyes on her.
– As stated, you must claim your citizenship.
– But do we have any claim, any at all?
– All human beings are citizens of Arcadia.
She shrugged.
– At least that is how the pompous council speeches go.
– There are those moving on, Cindy said, – to the other triple cities and even the territories. This realm is still rare of humans and there is plenty of room to those desiring it. There are hunter-gatherer societies and quite a few others, smaller cities and even villages.
– And… portals to other realms? Martha stated eagerly.
– And portals, Afterglow nodded.
– How many must we pass through to get to Earth?
– Four, if you are lucky. It is about half through the wheel of fire and shadow comprising the nine realms.
– How can there be a *wheel?* Martha wondered. – It's just a bunch of

randomly interconnected planets.
– It is not random, Afterglow said. – It probably started out that way, according to older sorcerers, but now it is not anymore. The wheel may be a metaphor for something else and similar or it may not.
– This is *so* interesting, Leila bristled. – So beyond *exciting!*
Martha scowled at her.
Alice appeared from the kitchen with plates of bread and butter in her hands.
– This is the first time I entertain guests since… since I inherited the house, she said, both anxious and subdued. – Please enjoy the food and eat until your heart and mind and stomach are full.
– Thank you, Alice, Lester said. – That's very kind of you and we will.
– It is kind, Fremantle said, – but seen as common courtesy in the realm. In ancient times humans never rejected a stranger his or her a place around your campfire, and that tradition has been kept here.
Alice raced back and forth, putting glasses, milk, juices, hams, vegetables, eggs and even some warm dishes on the table. In an amazingly brief time span she had completed her task.
– That is everything, isn't it? Leila joked. – I don't believe there is a single available spot left on the table…
They all chuckled. It was a great joke.
The travelers sat there, in the light of the glaring moon and enjoyed their meal. Afterglow found herself drawn into their circle.
– This tastes absolutely phenomenal, Stuart declared. – I know it's just breakfast, but my senses tell me that I've never enjoyed a meal quite like this before.
– They don't use poisons when they produce food here, Fremantle grumbled. – No pesticides or shit whatsoever, not even preservatives to prolong its usefulness.
– That must be it, Stuart marveled. – It tastes like heaven.
– Earth is the insane asylum of the Universe, Fremantle practically shouted. – It is not the only place where insanity runs rampant, but it is certainly high on the list. And very few people do anything to correct that.
– Perhaps it is a good thing that the Bermuda Triangle is such a dangerous passage, Lester nodded. – It makes it hard for Earth's malignant forces to reach this place.
He looked stunned as he pondered his own words.
Cindy hesitated, glancing at Afterglow, which nodded.
– There was a submarine, USS Scorpion, with the classification number SSN-589 that came through several decades ago, Cindy said. – The

aggression of those aboard created a hostility towards travelers that is almost unprecedented. Dozens of people had been killed when those maniacs were finally subdued. Some of the surviving crew-members ran off into the territories and the mere thought of them returning is still causing anxiety among the population of all the Triple Cities.

– Ninety-nine, only ninety-nine people with dangerous weapons. Fremantle shook his head in disgust. – And the result was a massacre.

– The Triple Cities were unprepared, Afterglow stated slowly, – but even though they are less so today, they are still vulnerable to a massive invasion force, inevitably.

– We will never tell, Leila swore, – never tell anyone, not in a million years.

Echoes of agreement sounded around the table, from all the travelers.

The light mood, turned heavy, slowly turned light again.

The memory of their time around the breakfast table that morning would always stand out to them, perhaps even more than all the incredible events they experienced. The easy laughter echoed in their minds.

Afterglow knew Alice studied her, but kept up an impassive expression. Kathryn looked at everybody gathered here, and saw them in a different light. They all appeared older, with drawn faces and eyes filled with experience, and some of them hardly seemed to be present at all. She saw Lester's unease, saw what he was not aware of himself.

Fremantle caught her glance. She changed, practically transformed on the spot and smiled sweetly to him. That act alone made him frown and stare at her with an astounded and suspicious glare that in turn made her smile that much broader.

– Afterglow and her apprentice need a shower and a change of clothes, she declared with her usual dry flair. – Public tolerance goes far, but will not accept us walking around covered in blood in broad daylight. Feel free to join us.

The two of them undressed, clearly not shy or anything. The travelers could not help but staring. The room was fairly large with five hoses. Afterglow and Alice did not get any company there. They washed and cleaned each other, but did not move beyond that, even though the temptation, the low-burning desire was always there.

The others cleaned their faces in the sink and washed a spot here and there from their clothes.

– Do not worry, Cindy told them. – It does not show, at least not much, not to most people.

There was something in her voice, something making them look closer at her, making them want her to explain herself, but she did not do so.

Afterglow had to use Alice's clothes. They did not fit her well, but well enough.

Every time she took a step forward her belly showed. She smiled to the creature with violet eyes and twisted face in the mirror.

They departed the house. Alice locked the door behind them.

– I mean it, Martha declared. – I will call on private and public organizations to invest heavily in organic farming the very moment we return.

– That will be the day, Leila grinned wickedly.

They walked to the bus. During the short distance all eyes were inevitably drawn up, towards the towering globe in the sky.

– This city is not that different from my hometown, Leila said. – I can, when I'm distracted forget that we're on another planet, until I look up at *that.*

Everybody shuddered and shared a sense of foreboding when they looked at the ominous Big Red Moon.

– The light of the sun, the daystar, she mused, – will be blocked during the day… won't it?

– It will! Cindy confirmed with gloomy eyes.

Then she brightened.

– It will spice up the celebration considerably. They can not possibly get away with the usual boring shit.

They entered the bus. Not long afterwards they were headed back to town.

– It's funny, Leila said abruptly. – We didn't sleep that long tonight, did we? But I don't feel tired at all. On the contrary I feel great, feel… awake. I didn't think it was possible to feel this great, this… aware.

– The deep sleep prompted by the Ceremony of the Hollow often brings powerful emotions and awareness, Cindy remarked. – I have read about it and thought I understood it, its textures and connotations, but I did not, of course. I was not even close.

– We saw so much? Leila nodded. – So much strange. I saw it, but it didn't make any sense. I saw me, in places I've never been. What does it mean?

– It means that when we part we will meet again, Afterglow said. – You saw places you will go to and glimpses of your fate.

– We saw the future? The woman gasped. – That is what you are saying, right? But I saw us together and it's only a coincidence that we came to this place and encountered you guys at all.

Afterglow turned towards her and the violet eyes twinkled in a cold light.

– We were fated to meet long before you came here.

The sense of foreboding grew stronger and they all shivered in the heat of the warm day.

Afterglow shivered, too, as Beatrice's hateful stare flashed before her eyes.

– But that's *impossible!* Lester practically shouted.

She grinned cruelly at him, making him pull back in… making him pull back.

Eyes were drawn to the naked, burned-out part of the mountain. Minds asked the silent question.

– They burned it, burned as much of the forest as they possibly could. The city council gave in to an enterprise lobbying for the forest's demise and that was their downfall. It takes a lot of dismay to get rid of an elected council before its time is out, but this in all likelihood did it.

– The point was hammered into everybody when they had to spend days to clean streets and houses, and the sight of the ruined forest keeps staring at us like sore eyes, Cindy spat.

Afterglow and Alice cleaned and oiled the swords, sharpened slightly dulled edges. They did it with dedication and also with an ease that turned the others silent. They found themselves staring again.

Blades covered with what seemed like rust once more turned shiny and oily.

The bus approached the inner city, driving through remains of the red mist. It made its way to the magistrate parking lot. They left it there and walked through streets increasingly crowded. People were out in force today, some curious, taking a look at the newcomers gathering at the Council Hall Plaza, the *Agora,* others shouting angry words at the council members brave enough to show their mugs.

– This… place looks familiar somehow, Leila frowned.

– It is quite the correct representation, replica of the agora in Alexandria, where Hypatia spoke and taught, Cindy said proudly. – The firstcomers made it to honor her and all unafraid speech and acts, started making it the moment they decided to settle here.

– But the statue wasn't there.

– No, it was not.

The statue represented a woman in Roman attire. At its base there was a Latin inscription:

HYPATIA - OCCIDIT PER CHRISTIANIS

Right below it a newer, not quite correct English translation:

HYPATIA - SLAUGHTERED BY THE CHRISTIANS

– I take it christians aren't very popular here, Lester chuckled, drawing a hurt look from his wife.

– Nor should they be, Fremantle grumbled. – They've fostered a nightmare society through 2000 years. The visions of insane men have become the norm wherever they have trodden.

– They cut her flesh with shells, Cindy cried, – practically flaying it from her bones. And that is what they have done mentally and often also physically to everybody unfortunate enough to suffer their presence all the time since. Alexandria had an ethnically and religiously diverse population giving rise to a great exchange of ideas, belief and culture, until the rise of Christianity.

People heard her and nodded excited and shouted their words of agreement. Passions already running high ran even higher.

A queue was lining up before the stall outside the Hall. The stranded people from the ship glanced around them with anxiety and hope.

– You should join them, Afterglow said. – You will want to get the registration over with well before the festivities begin.

– Festivities? Lester gawked.

She grinned lewd at him. He turned a deep shade of red.

– The arrival of travelers, of new blood is celebrated here, she told him, – even if it does not always bring joy.

And he strived, strived hard to pull himself away from those deep, violet eyes.

– I'll help you get settled, Fremantle murmured. – It can be a drag going through it all without someone who knows the drill.

– I will, too, Cindy said.

And Caroline nodded.

The travelers walked to join their fellows.

Afterglow and Alice remained on the spot.

– They don't recognize us? Alice said, finally bursting aloud with the thoughts that had been on her mind for many hours. – Why don't they?

– Because they have yet to meet us where we first met them.

Clarity and astonishment brightened Alice's eyes.

– It is *fate,* then, the girl half whispered. – I never understood that before, but I do, now.

The line began to move faster, as the travelers were admitted into the Council Hall, as the daystar moved closer to the edge of Big Red Moon.

Alice held her tongue, even though she had wanted to speak. There were no outward signs of her hesitation, but Afterglow caught it still.

– Forgive Alice, the girl said, suddenly visibly anxious.

Afterglow did not speak, hardly reprimanding her in any way.

– Our commission… it is Ironwood.

– Of course it is.

Kathryn closed and opened her eyes.

– I wanted to wait, Alice cried softly. – I did not want to be the bearer of bad news, wanted you… to enjoy yourself tonight without thoughts of tomorrow and yesterday. *She* brought you there the first time you… Your exploits are legendary, especially in the magickal community, you know that. We know everything or at least almost everything about them and I wanted to… wanted to…

Kathryn touched her cheek.

– You wanted to serve me, to protect me to the best of your ability. Thank you.

The girl choked in relief and joy and grabbed her Master's hand and kissed it.

They watched, watched the proceedings, as they listened to the excited chatter among those appearing from the Hall. Leila was the first of their new companions approaching them. She was light on her feet, visibly so.

– That was… weird, she said, frowning. – I had visualized an *interrogation,* like it would have been in my country… my land, but I was called in to a nice, young woman asking me about my skills and interests and desires. It was such a thrill to encounter a public official that actually wants to *help* you.

She embraced the two women in a bout of euphoria.

– I *knew* I would like it here!

The others appeared and returned to the sorcerer as well. Afterglow noticed that Martha practically clung to Lester.

All of them shared Leila's puzzlement and happiness.

A horn was blowing somewhere, a loud, prolonged sound stirring the gathering.

It made everybody pay attention to what was happening on the stairs of the Hall, where the final preparations had been made.

But they were distracted, glancing up, not glancing up. The sound, or rather its distinct echo seemed to herald something far more sinister.

– I feel such a chill, Martha said and shivered visibly. – I can feel the shadow move across the ground towards us like a hungry beast.

– You all feel it, do you not, Afterglow said quietly. – I, on the other hand am uneasy in the bright light of the daystar and my eyes see so much better in the dark.

They finally looked up, at the daystar, as its disk, on its travel across the sky touched the far bigger disk of Big Moon and the hours-long event's first impact began revealing itself. Leila nodded. The others did as well. A mood clearly more somber spread through the gathering of the agora.

All small talk ended and only the occasional anxious voice was heard, a state of being growing far more pronounced during the next minutes, as the bright day turned dark, dark as night and Big Red Moon reigned supreme.

Torches were lit and the fireplace at the center of the square turned far more visible. Its flames seemed to reach for everybody present, in ever wider sweeps. Everybody pulled closer together, turning towards the stairs, where a woman appeared in front of several other well dressed people.

Afterglow felt the heat of the fire and a smile grew on her lips.

A man stepped forward.

– Welcome, citizens, he cried, – to this gathering, this celebration. Please give heed to Councilor Adira Alura.

The anxious, restless mood lightened a little, but persisted, inevitably.

– Look at them all, Cindy said softly. – All people's deeper emotions have been roused since yesterday.

Councilor Alura raised her hands above her head.

– DESPOILER, someone spat.

A lot of angry cries followed, flowing towards the people at the top of the stairs.

Alura let her hands fall and waited.

Silence eventually returned, even though seething anger remained in parts of the gathering.

Alura raised her hands again. This time no one spoke up.

The sun shrieked behind Big Red Moon, writhing in its cruel maw.

– Dear friends and newly arrived friends to be, Alura cried, her voice echoing through the agora and beyond. – We have something to celebrate today, a dance, a feast welcoming all newcomers to our extended community.

She went on and on. Quite a few people, both old and new citizens of Arcadia listened with wet eyes.

– Is she serious, sincere? Stuart asked sheepishly.

Afterglow shook her head, rejecting the very notion.

– No, but as you can observe, she is quite clever. She waited until the eclipse appeared, stopping the discontent she and her fellow council members have experienced lately from growing further, stopping today's protests before they began.

Fremantle snorted in disgust.

– Politicians and the filthy rich, they are the same everywhere…

– And she's both I take it, Leila stated more than asked, her ample power of observation making it easy for her to see through the woman on the stairs.

– Daylight is deceptive, treasonous, Afterglow said, – while everything or close to everything appears as it is in the night. In the darkness of the Shadow you can not hide your true self.

The speech ended, blissfully early. The chords of the fiddle and the beat of the drums rose from the ground and filled everybody's ears. The tables for nine were brought outside. Mead and ale and beer and drinks abundant were put before thirsty and anxious people, all fluid colored in red and fire. People began the process of selecting their spots. There was no rush, no competition to reach an available seat, the fact that there was more than enough for all those present evident to everyone.

People from the ship called to Lester and the others. They heeded the call, a bit reluctantly.

– Join us, Afterglow, Leila called. – Honor us with your company.

And Afterglow and her envoy did.

They joined a cacophony of voices and emotions threatening to confuse the most confident of minds, but Afterglow and Alice were used to navigate in such stormy waters, and handled it in stride. Cindy's anxiety increased almost immediately, but she was handling it and her special troubles with an effort.

– It is as if I can see… see the Other World beyond the veil, glimpse it with both open and closed eyes, in visions and not.

– You always will, Afterglow stated.

Many groups of nine sat down around the special tables. There were exceptions, but not that many. People, also those from the stranded passenger liner had clearly been caught in the prevalent mood. Leila studied it all with her big eyes and when she blinked it was as if there was a distinct glow behind the lids. Martha sat in Lester's lap, proudly displaying her position.

Air and scents and emotion seemed to whirl around them. Afterglow and Alice bathed deliberately in the free-floating energies, the others did not. Lester kept rubbing his arms.

A man's familiar face and stance appeared before her.

– Salve Amicus, Kathryn Caldwell, Lucius Flavicus greeted her.

– Salve Amicus, Lucius Flavicus, Afterglow greeted him in return.

It dawned on her that he treated her with something resembling respect for the first time and not with the old anxiety and disregard. She masked her happiness carefully, as she presented him to the others.

– More foreigners, he bristled, reminding her more of his old, conceited self. – I can not say I am overly happy about that.

The travelers were inadvertently taken aback, of course, but Leila still gave him a dazzling smile.

– We will all strive to be worthy of your hospitality and great society, sire, she said.

– Of course. He seemed to catch himself a little. – Forgive me, I meant no offense.

– No offense taken, sire…

– You will have to visit my dwelling as honored guests at a day or night of your convenience.

– That's not necessary, sire, Lester protested.

– I insist. I am confident Afterglow will be pleased to make the arrangements and I will make sure my household is prepared for your visit.

– I will, Lucius Flavicus, she said, bowing slightly. – Salve Amicus.

– Salve Amicus, he replied.

He bowed, to her, to them all and was off, leading his considerable entourage to another table several rows from theirs.

A little stunned they sat down.

– Quite a character, isn't he? Stuart said, shaking his head.

– He is a Roman, Leila countered him, slightly agitated, – a dying breed, I suspect.

– If you think he is aloof and arrogant now, you should have seen him when he and I first crossed paths, Afterglow joked, surprising herself with her laughter and the warmth she sensed coming at her from around the table.

A feeling increasing further as she was pulled further into the festivities, into the conversation with surrounding tables filled with other travelers from the ship.

– Where do you guys get your clothes? A woman asked scandalized. – I would love to wear threads like that.

– Most tailors in the Triple Cities will be more than happy to fit them for you, Alice replied generously. – And people will be equally happy to point you in the correct direction.

– Thank you, the woman babbled, overflowing with gratitude, embarrassing Alice to no end. – Thank you so much.

The consummation of food and drink began in earnest. The celebration took off, like a fallen dry leaf rising in the wind. Countless loud cheers echoed on the agora, between the tall fires and torches in the day turned night.

– When a new ship arrived in Alexandria their scrolls were copied and placed in the library, confiscated if necessary and then returned.

Cindy weaved her tale with passion between the intakes of hot food and chilled drinks. Everybody within hearing distance listened eagerly.

– Knowledge, knowledge without slant or dogmatism was favored above all else, and thus the library and its proponents were among the biggest threats to the emerging christian hierarchy.

– To free exchange of information and opinion, Fremantle cried and raised his glass. – To the agora.

– HEAR, HEAR, the tables of nine within hearing distance responded.

– The Roman Empire was bad, was oppressive also before the christians took over, Cindy related, – but when they did, it took a major turn for the worse. Those of our forefathers and mothers fleeing from the new cult had learned an important, even crucial lesson, however. They rejected slavery in all forms, of both mind and body and cried NO MORE!

The clinking of glasses changed into a choir of the multitudes gathered at the plaza.

Cindy clearly enjoyed herself. She evidently had few opportunities to flex her knowledge of ancient times outside the theater.

The euphoria… took of.

The dance began. The space not taken by the tables filled up with celebrating people. Seconds stretched into minutes and an hour lasting forever.

Afterglow and Lester had stood up from the table. She led him away with a hot stare in her eyes.

Fire mixed with shadow, turning into one undiluted flow.

Cindy blinked and blinked again, as she began seeing what was not instantly apparent to most others, as the celebration was joined by transparent figures appearing from what seemed like nowhere.

– What is happening? Cindy whispered to no one in particular.

– The agora, the very agora itself is a crossroads of sorts, inevitably, Alice said happily, – having gained a position in the spirit world akin to its physical reality. People and spirits both seek this place not a place, its vast dangers and rewards.

– Goddess, Cindy breathed in awe and fear, as that reality imposed itself on her, on her newfound sensitivity. – Holy Goddess!

Similar emotions tickled pleasantly Afterglow's more experienced and cynical bones. She danced with Lester, pulling him closer, enticing him with her powerful wiles.

Some people began leaving, fleeing from the passion. Those remaining began seeking close to each other all over the plaza. The mood turned sweaty and beyond intense.

– You pull me to you, she whispered in his ear.

He froze slightly.

– You do not look as impressive as the last time I saw you, but you will do.

She ignored the puzzled look he sent her, and kissed him, wet his lips with hers, with her tongue, as she pushed him to a wall, at the back of the base of the Hypatia statue, briefly concealing them from the crowd.

It did not matter anyway. Everybody had their attention elsewhere, at some more or less exposed skin in front of them.

– I don't understand, he breathed. – I don't understand any of this.

– You will! She snarled thrilled, exposing her fangs to him.

A bell tolled somewhere, from a direction no one could identify.

– We shouldn't do this, he breathed. – I want to do right by Martha.

– You are not doing wrong by her, she breathed passionately, – and you should not worry about the rest. I certainly am not.

She fumbled with his belt, with his zipper. He yelped as she pulled too hard.

– Can you feel them? She hissed in his ear. – Can you feel the spirits, how they observe us with gleeful anticipation? I know you can!

– No, I can't, he protested. – I…

She pulled down his pants, revealing his erected cock. The expectant smile transformed her face. She let go of him, switching position with him, leaning towards the statue, displaying herself to him.

– I know you want me…

An unmistakable haze of desire clouded her eyes.

– I know you want to possess me, ravage me. It is alright, it is alright, alright, alright…

Everything closed in on them, isolating them. Lester Brown heard his own breath, truly heard his own breath, for the very first time in his life.

– All this… happening totally in the open, no modesty or anything?

– This is how we PARTY in Arcadia, she grinned, shouting her words across the agora and beyond.

He stepped close to her, moving feverishly, his hands acting of their own accord, tearing at her clothes. She released a content sigh.

Quite a few across and just outside the agora had gotten the same idea. He heard moans from the other side of the statue, heard it rise into the air, the ether and join with it. His hands exposed her hips, her groin. She grabbed one of his hands and pulled it down there. His skin turned wet and warm. He gasped, unable to keep himself from doing so. It was as if the skin on his hand burned. He rubbed her and she cried out, mewing in anticipation.

Seconds had passed. Moments had faded away in the gathering fervor. They were fucking. He pushed her hard at the cold marble, held her hips as he pushed back and forth inside her. She chuckled pleased. He grunted content as her muscular thighs and big lips squeezed him. Thoughts dwindled, fading into nothing.

He imagined he glimpsed several people dancing nude not far from there, with swinging hips and dangling breasts and cocks, but it seemed more like a fever vision than actual reality, even though it was a good bet that the festivities were about to take off everywhere within the range of his suddenly so very acute senses. The tall flames of the torches rose yet another notch, as even the surface of the red moon far away seemed to mirror the dancing fire.

They were alone. The square was empty in all directions, for as far as they could see. Nothing or no one distracted them anywhere.

Her wet hair whipped his skin as she shook her head in uncontrolled cramps. He hardly noticed. The increased pain only added to his pleasure.

– Yes, she mumbled, her face and very being dissolved in passion and need.
– Yes, yes, yes, yes, yes, yes…

Voices echoed her mumbles, mumbles surrounding them, penetrating deep within them.

A choir rose in his ears as he pumped into her and she cried out in undulated pleasure.

They collapsed in each other's embrace and drowned the other in kisses, as all loud sounds faded and the silence of their surroundings slowly imposed itself on them both.

CHAPTER FOURTEEN

Almost at dusk the sun briefly reappeared in the western sky, a sky turning as red as the moon and the realm. Those watching imagined that the very atmosphere sizzled and burned, and all kinds of emotions ravaged them. It was an amazing spectacle making an impression on everybody present, but most of all on those coming to Montan from elsewhere. If they had not realized fully that they were in a completely different place before, they did now.

The Blood Red Big Moon faded with the night, faded as it slowly fell in the horizon.

Afterglow had been dozing off. She knew that by the brief touch of dreams, of stars and imposing images and infinite space in her mind.

Lester had disappeared. She rested on the ground, with her back to the base of the statue.

Alice approached her. Afterglow rose. She pulled up her pants and faced her apprentice. Alice stepped close and kissed her lips, a lingering, passionate kiss.

– Is Afterglow okay? Does Afterglow feel good?

– Afterglow feels great, Kathryn replied softly.

The fires still burned tall. Their scent tore into her nostrils. People slept or relaxed across the plaza. Some had engaged in passionate discussions. Bottles and glasses and scraps of food were dispersed everywhere.

– A great party for sure.

Fremantle called to them from the nearest corner, his black skin covered in sweat. He had a large grin painted on his mug.

– Indeed, Afterglow agreed.

Cindy walked with fast steps towards them from the opposite side, clearly determined, driven, her red hair dancing like flames on her head.

– Come with me, she bade them.

Afterglow and Alice did not move, but received her good-humored and curious.

– I saw something, she said, – something… I can show you. I can…

– Very well, Afterglow acknowledged with light teasing. – Lead on, sorcerer to be.

Cindy giggled uneasily. She rushed ahead, around the corner of the building. The rest of the group stood there, talking, not really talking or interacting much. They were all there, glancing, not really looking at each other.

– Come, Cindy urged them. – Come with me, all of you.

They followed her, hesitant, apprehensive. She brought them inside, to the theater, to the stage and into the dressing rooms, and all the time Afterglow and Alice easily caught the emotions and sensations emanating from her.

Dark shadows danced around them, as they walked through the hallways, as they passed the long row of original paintings, as they ended up in one of the exhibition halls, and she stopped.

She turned towards the uncanny group and indicated, included the room as she moved her hands.

– I dreamed about this place, she said. – I imagine you did as well.

– Afterglow and Alice did, Alice said, – since we shared the alien energies with you. The three of us clearly became connected from that very moment.

Afterglow blinked, and this place added itself, like it had during her sleep earlier to the stars and dark space in her vision.

In an exhibition surrounding them nine elaborate masks imposed themselves on them. They hung on display in a circle, seemingly staring at those within it.

– They are beautiful, Leila marveled, with just a touch of shiver in her voice. – Do they… do they have *eyes?*

She stepped closer to one, and could ascertain that they had not.

– No, the holes are just holes, empty holes, but so deep, oh, so dark and deep.

Afterglow sensed the shiver, sensed it in the very air, unable to tell if it was real, whether or not she created it, if it emanated from her or if it flowed at her, sought her.

– These are the Masks of The Nine, Cindy stated empathically. – They count among our most cherished relics. No one knows their origin, neither the place nor the date. Speculations claim that they were found in one of the many caves surrounding the Triple Cities in the year 623, but no one has been able to uncover which cave, no one we are aware of. They were brought here and have stayed here since. No one has ever attempted to remove them from this place, none that we know of. They are said to be cursed. According to folklore no one «unworthy» can wear them for long and live.

– Superstition, Stuart bristled.

– Perhaps, but are you not reaching, now, reaching far more than those seeing the masks as sacred?

He did not reply, lost in the murky images filling his vision, shaking under their onslaught.

- When you say the year 623 I presume you don't mean the western, christian Earth calendar? Leila mused in her unique way.

- It is the year 623 after the founders' arrival, Cindy confirmed. – That is our «official» calendar.
She chose one mask, the red one.
– Many try them on, she said, – to see if they fit.
It did fit her, was indeed snug on her face and head.
The fire color, the shades of red and orange and even the black spots of the mask matched that of her hair perfectly, the green emerald at the center matching that of her eyes. It was not merely a mask but an arrangement circling her neck and upper body. Two more emeralds resembling eyes fell on her chest. Caroline helped her fasten the straps. One Mask of the Nine stood there, glaring at them. Afterglow felt dizzy when facing her.
– What do you feel? She heard herself ask.
– Nothing noticeable. Cindy frowned, – nothing beyond wearing a piece of cloth. It does fit me, though, does it not?
It was a half mask, with bird feathers and other decorative arrangements, reaching out horizontally beyond the head. The lower part of the face, like the mouth and jaw was exposed, but looking strangely different, not like her face or part of her face at all.
She rushed out of the room. The others rushed after her, gave chase as best they could, clearly out of breath almost immediately. She stood before a mirror, the full-figured mirror in the hall, stunned.
– It does look quite striking, does it not? She marveled.
She turned around, sighing, as she faced them, as she unfastened the straps and removed the mask.
– But it does not really look like what I saw in my dream at all. In my dream the person, the *entity* wearing the mask and a lot more besides, of clothes and paraphernalia looked far more imposing, more like a goddess than a human being.
They returned to the masks. She returned the one in her hands to the empty display.
– I saw it, she mumbled subdued. – And I wanted you to see it, too.
She crouched and released a low sound.
– Are you alright? Afterglow asked cautiously.
– I am fine, Cindy replied, a little defensive. – I just have some trouble dealing with all those new sensations, that is all.
– You are waking up. What you could not do on your own fate took care of for you.
– The three Fates weaving human life? Leila joked lightly.
– Some make that claim, Afterglow shrugged.
– It's quite interesting, Leila said solemnly. – I almost missed the boat. They

were about to close the door when I arrived.

– Life is full of such coincidences, Stuart pointed out.

– It is indeed…

They returned to the outside, from the chill inside to the warm and dry Arcadia dusk. Flickering eyes met and parted.

– What now? Lester asked.

– Now, the female travelers need new, fitting shoes, Afterglow stated, – and you all need traveling gear. There is an excellent store selling such not far away.

Once again, for perhaps the thousandth time they looked startled at her.

– We do, Leila acknowledged. – We need to be practical and dangerous. Thank you, My Lady.

She bowed.

The others, hesitating just a bit did, too.

As they made their way through the streets it became very clear to the travelers that the celebration had not ended. They encountered nude and drinking and fornicating people in smaller and bigger groups on several spots along the way, some very public.

– Public drunkenness and nudity are obviously not illegal here, Martha mumbled.

Then she started laughing, laughing hard and everybody joined her.

– You are free, Leila stated, – you can do what you want.

A shiver passed through Martha, one of both pain and pleasure.

The store was at a corner by a coffee house, slightly hidden in the intersection of two alleys. The coffee house was closed. A message on the door told them why:

JOINING THE FESTIVITIES - DO NOT EXPECT US

The store was open. At least it was lit. Alice tried the handle. The door slid open. They walked inside.

A man met them at the center of the floor.

– Fair evening, good people, he greeted them. – Is there anything I can do to help you?

– Fair evening, Afterglow replied. – These weary travelers are in need of some useful shoes and gear. Time is of essence, I am afraid, so it can not be made to fit. I trust you have merchandise they can try on?

– I am happy to confirm that we have, My Lady, he said pleasantly.

Kathryn recalled another store many years ago. She knew Alice studied her and felt her slightly more volatile emotions.

Both watched their new friends while they tried on clothes, shoes and gear. Lester caught her stare and a wide smile spread on his face. She felt how the blush extended all over her body. It was impossible to control it, no matter how much she tried.

The five changed with the clothes. It was tangible, unmistakable.

– These are *clothes,* Leila mused, as realization hit and a taint of fear reached her eyes. – It feels like… like putting on another *skin.*

Her own words stunned her.

Afterglow tried on and bought new clothes as well, discarding those borrowed from Alice. She, too, traced parts of the fabric with her fingers, mirroring the action of her novel friends.

– Any change contains potential magick, she stated. – Believe that!

Time hardly passed between those unknown walls. It certainly did not feel like it did. There was no rush, only the pleasure of discovery.

A memory made Kathryn smile and then it made her sad. She knew it was visible on her face, but did not care, though she allowed Alice to comfort her, to gently rub her back and head.

They were done. The four natives looked amused at the travelers.

– Will that be all, My Lady? The salesman inquired, directing his question at Afterglow. – Is everything to My Lady's satisfaction?

– I do not know, Kathryn grinned, turning towards the five. – Is it?

– Hell, yeah! Leila said, still dazed. – This is… this is groovy beyond words.

She walked to the nearest dumpster and dumped her high heels there.

– It feels so good to be rid of the shit, she declared. – I can't imagine why I held on to social conventions for so long and fucking harmed myself doing so.

Their change was visible in the way they walked and looked at the world afterwards. The streets had turned both more familiar and different.

Lester took a slow, deep breath. They had stopped on the corner of some non-descript street. There was nothing special about it, nothing at all.

– The ocean of mankind is present in your eyes, Cindy said, a catching audible in her voice.

The others looked at her, swallowed hard and in the subsequent emotional turmoil they missed Afterglow's subtle but visible reaction.

They walked a little longer, not saying much, taking in the scenery and mood instead. It was a casual walk, not really going anywhere, hardly directed by the conscious mind at all.

Joshua stifled a yawn and shook his head, giving the others an apologetic look. He yawned again and this time he did not hide himself at all, this time the yawn was loud and deep.

The laughter came easy once again, though the travelers began casting reluctant glances towards the harbor.

– You're welcome to stay at my place for the night, of course, Fremantle offered. – It might be more accessible and preferable to the more noisy alternatives.

Shouts still reached them from all directions and what they knew was all the way from the temporary quarters by the quay.

– I appreciate that, Joshua said. – I'm quite tired. God, how tired I am. I can't remember the last time I slept properly, and I would like to do so tonight, more than anything.

Everybody consented by more or less quiet and happy agreement. They followed Fremantle through busy streets, backtracking yesterday's path.

– Where do you... where does Afterglow live? Leila asked, approaching her with the usual reverence.

– Close to the harbor, Afterglow replied. – The chances of us being... found there are bigger than at Fremantle's place.

They heard the sounds in the dark, the flapping of wings and the sinister whispers. None of them could avoid hearing any of it, and the travelers were once more reminded of the undeniable uncertainty that had entered their lives.

– That is only ambient noise, Alice grinned. – Sorcerers live with that every night of their life.

– Is there danger? Stuart asked.

– There is, Alice replied, – but not much to speak of, not compared to the true danger awaiting us.

– Thank you, Stuart mumbled, – that was quite helpful...

Brittle laughter eased the tension without being close to ending it. The powerful, newfound emotions kept bringing them both high and low.

The others saw easily, with their equally newfound power of observation that Alice and Afterglow and Caroline and Fremantle had placed themselves at defensive positions on their flanks.

A car approached them. In the ambient silence they noticed it from far away. Its noise thundered in Afterglow's ears.

– Stand back, Afterglow advised calmly. – You too, apprentice.

She stopped and drew her sword. The others stopped as well and pulled back to the wayside. The car approached fast, or so it seemed. When it appeared they could see that it moved slow, far slower than the travelers were used to see a car move. It had dark windows. They could not penetrate the darkness and peek inside.

It passed them in a totally non-threatening way. Everybody, except Afterglow released a sigh of relief. It turned in the next junction and was gone.

– Its eyes, Cindy moaned. – Its eyes stared at us.
– I didn't see anything, Leila said. – Where were they?
– You did not? They glared at us through the rear window. They burned my very bones.
The travelers now knew, knew beyond conviction that the woman with red hair and green eyes saw more than they did.
Afterglow left fast, walking off in a blur of motion. The others rushed after her, struggling to keep up.
They reached Fremantle's abode. It felt more than a little comforting in their tired, even exhausted minds and bodies, but they still approached it with caution, even after Fremantle had given Afterglow his nod.
– Is this our lives from now on? Joshua wondered. – A state of mind constantly on guard?
– This is nothing, Fremantle said brightly, – compared to a few months down the road. By then you will look back at this with a patronizing snarl on your lips.
They entered the house and sat course straight for the basement. Everybody seemed to know that that would be the safest place to crash. Fremantle found sleeping mats from a locker and spread them evenly on the floor.
– By then you will prefer sleeping on the hard floor and look with unease at most soft beds.
The travelers glanced at each other and shook their heads in distress. They realized that he was joking, *joking*.
Afterglow and all the others from the realm, including Fremantle undressed. It happened casually, without such things as modesty or the opposite entering into it. After some hesitation the travelers joined them. Fremantle put out all the lamps, except two in the far corner of the room. Everybody stretched out on the pleasant mats, pulling blankets up to their shoulders.
– No… guards tonight? Lester queried.
– No. Afterglow shook her head. – We all need sleep, need rest. That is worth the risk of leaving ourselves open for attack, and we are fairly safe here anyway. The wards around Fremantle's home are quite effective, at least against the casual intruder.
She was quite pleased by the fact that he did not push the subject further, that he did not ask the next, logical question, and she once again found herself smiling sweetly to him.
There was something in the air, something impossible to grasp properly, something ongoing and multifaceted she was unable to pinpoint. It had not vanished after the attack at the harbor and showed no sign of doing so.

Martha pushed herself at Lester, lifting the two blankets separating them. She began kissing him, clearly more than a little aroused and determined. When he looked at her, a little startled and opened his mouth to speak she put a finger on his lips. She did not glance around her once, evidently deliberating ignoring the others' presence.

The low moans and groans of their fucking filled the room. Their movements grew more excessive. The sounds and visuals haunted the others as they closed their eyes and consciousness faded.

Afterglow writhed on the mat long after the others had fallen asleep.

She dreamed, in a sleep she could not quite gain about the masks. And it was not like she remembered it. For one thing they floated in the air, not even close to any attachment. They hovered in front of her, offering themselves to her, and they were all seductive, all tempting, but most of all she was pulled to the one with dark raven feathers and light blue jewels.

One time during the night everybody woke to a loud, sharp crack, as if somebody had struck the wall outside. Afterglow and Alice had drawn their sword before the others had opened their eyes. Everybody stared at them, very attentive. Afterglow shook her head. She sheathed the sword and returned to the mat. It did not take long before both she and her apprentice once more were sleeping soundly.

All the others shook their heads in amazement and attempted to get back to sleep. The mere attempt at closing their eyes proved trying.

Kathryn knew she was sleeping, but the unrest did not end. It remained, like rain on the ground on moist days. She heard Lester groan in the midst of light snoring, saw a shiver pass through the large frame. The sensation of falling gripped her, something that had not happened for years. The anxious moan rising from her open mouth made her feel like a young girl again. She slept and could not wake up, no matter how much the gathering giant shadows scared her.

And only with the first dim light outside she was able to fall into a deep sleep.

They had, some time ago reached the mountain plains above the triple cities. The sight of the eagles - the natural feel of the wilderness appeared in their line of vision, the disheartening walk through the burned down forest behind them. They stopped there, on the rise, shaking their heads in wonder.

– The landscape is so great, Martha said. – It's imposing itself on you.

– So different and so similar to Earth, Joshua nodded.

– And even though we are so close to the cities, there is hardly any rural area at all, Leila marveled. – It's like we took one single step and ended up in the wilderness. It's easy to imagine that the nearest building is far from here.

– There are no settlements here, Cindy said, – even though there have been quite a few attempts at founding them. The lessons of previous generations are quickly forgotten.

They knew a bit by now about those lessons.

– We have far to go, haven't we? Leila said excited.

– There is quite a stretch…

– Then what are we *waiting* for?

She reminded Afterglow of a young deer learning to run. Kathleen swallowed hard, the catching in her throat impossible to contain and so she held her tongue.

– YAAHH

Leila's barbaric yelp lingered in their ears as they ran westward, ran like the wind through the uneven terrain. There were places and stretches with many roots where they had to slow down, but they still kept going at a fairly high speed.

Their backpacks felt snug on their body and did not slow them down much. Neither, evidently did the bows, arrows and swords Afterglow, Alice, Caroline and Fremantle carried.

Theirs were clearly a playful mood, as the run turned into some kind of competition. The sun raced across the sky, as they raced across the land. The others attempted to take the lead, but Afterglow and the apprentice easily kept their position in front. It was clear to the rest that they could easily have taken a bigger lead, if they desired, but they stayed a certain length ahead most of the time, and only speeded up each time anyone tried to catch up.

They finally took a break by a large pond, drinking from the well stemming from a hill.

– I thought I was in good shape, Lester gasped, hardly able to articulate himself.

Hearty laughter echoed in the wilderness. Afterglow laughed with them, the sound coming from her reminding her of her young, carefree self so very long ago.

– I mean, I can accept that the two of you can easily outdistance us, he said to Kathleen and Alice, but Cindy easily kept up with us and she's an… an *academic,* for God's sake.

More laughter, even less malice.

– Children learn to move every day, as a natural part of their existence from an early age in this realm, Fremantle explained. – There is no television or extensive education allowed to distract them from that crucial need. They are taught that physical prowess saved the firstcomers and that it one day may save them. Basic self defense is mastered by almost everybody.

They relaxed a bit, stretching and softening limbs, enjoying the heat of the daystar, the scent and taste of the fresh and clean water.

– Big Moon is… moving on? Leila queried.

It was still visible in the horizon, but it was evidently about to return to its more predictable «orbit».

– It will take months before it blocks the daystar again, Cindy nodded. – And when or if it turns red again is anybody's guess.

Afterglow stood up.

– Time to move on. We still have far to go. But in order for you to still be alive when we get there, I suggest we exert ourselves less the rest of the way.

Joking, she was *joking*.

They proceeded at a slower pace. It was still a hard run, approaching brutal, but the travelers persevered without completely draining themselves of strength. The landscape imposed itself on them again, and they were able to enjoy it more, to catch more of its character.

– It feels so strange, Stuart breathed, – both familiar and not simultaneously. In a moment of distraction I imagine I'm back on Earth, but then I know that I'm not.

He frowned, pondering the issue.

– The vegetation is all wrong, and the sounds…

They heard the many animals, but did not see them, at least not those on the ground. The birds in the sky, their very flight created an eerie sensation at the deeper parts of their mind.

Night came, with only Little Moon illuminating their path. Afterglow made them run a little beyond that. There was a bit of stumbling in roots and awkward movement, until they reached another pond with flowing water and she signaled for them to stop.

Alice drew her bow and put an arrow on it, and vanished into the deep darkness.

– She's gonna hunt with… that? Joshua wondered.

– Or with the sword, if that is called for, I guess, Lester said cheerfully.

He took a deep breath.

– The air is *pure,* he marveled. – I never could imagine what that truly felt like before.

He filled his flask with water and drank, drank so much that he had to make a conscious effort to stop.

Caroline began building a fire. It took less than ten minutes until it burned, and the flames stretched into the dark sky and danced on everybody's skin, as they gathered around the heat.

A roar loud enough to shake the ground startled the travelers.

– I should be scared, Leila said, – but I'm n-not.

Not even when Afterglow and the others drew their swords and put arrows on their bows did they feel overwhelmed by the anxiety boiling within.

Alice returned with a deer on her shoulder. The travelers slowly relaxed. She started preparing it without delay, and not long afterwards she was turning it in the metal harness above the fire, roasting it slowly until the skin turned burned and crispy.

They writhed out of the soaking wet clothes and sought closer against the chill imposing itself on the part of their bodies not facing the fire. Alice cut the roasted deer in pieces and put them on a loose, flat rock clearly put there for that purpose.

– Careful, it is hot, she said, clearly patronizing.

Impatience ruled them, but it was a good one, the anticipation only adding to the moment, to the mood charging through the circle, doing so repeatedly. They fed, and as they did that, it was as if they re-experienced the moment the feeding started. Hands reached out and grabbed the meat and they ate like that, fat and pieces clinging to skin on fingers, hands, lips and cheeks.

Afterglow felt the potency of something changing within them, within her. Alice did, too, and squirmed on her spot. The effect was tangible, almost physical. Alice mouthed a word. Heat from nowhere passed through Kathryn. She attempted to catch it, catch its breath, but was too late.

Memory hit her again and it lingered and burned.

– You will learn, Afterglow said. – For the sake of yourself and for your tribe you will learn everything there is to learn, and you will be good at it, better than almost everybody.

They stared incredulous at her, unable to meet her pointed stare.

– You were shaken by the events bringing you here and continued to be shaken after your arrival, but that is not a bad thing. Changes lead to spiritual growth and ultimately to bigger awareness.

– It's funny, Martha said cheerfully, high strung. – I feel like I almost know what you're talking about…

She seemed high strung as a kite, a bundle of nerves and exhilaration and fright.

– This is the beginning of Magick 101, isn't it? Leila stated.

Afterglow looked blank at her. She did not get the reference, even if the setting implied much, just like one could understand one unknown word in combination with a given sentence.

– You said we wouldn't be your apprentices, Leila clarified, – but you are still teaching us the basics.

– The basics, yes…
Afterglow closed and opened her eyes, and in that blink was an eternity. It truly felt like that. One moment the circle formed around the campfire felt far away, the next uncomfortably close.
– Afterglow has sort of taken us all under her wings, Cindy said. – Such and act is not unheard of here, especially during unusual circumstances, even though sorcerers tend to be reclusive.
– How does it work, the apprenticeship, I mean?
– The apprentice serves the sorcerer, Alice said. – The sorcerer can do whatever he or she wants with the apprentice.
– That sounds so…
– It is a great honor, Alice said brightly. – And the potential rewards are staggering, *staggering*.
– You will become a sorcerer yourself, Stuart nodded.
– If Afterglow, in her wisdom finds me worthy, yes.
Afterglow sat there, listening to them. They and the surroundings, the fire and the darkness moved in her vision, like a three-dimensional painting shifting and burning.
Everybody present looked at her, doing so often, practically in a constant flow. She found it both unnerving and pleasant, both right and wrong, but most of all so very familiar.
The deep night and dreams arrived. Stuart moved in on Afterglow and she allowed it. He was skilled and persistent and made her cry out in need and lust and joy. They slept close together, his body warming her back, his breath wetting the skin of her neck.
The foreign sky and its stars shadowed the travelers, making them squirm and toss and turn. Travelers and residents alike shared or seemed to share each other's dreams and sensations, in a dreamscape of one room or a number of interconnected rooms or realms. Worlds, they dreamed entire worlds. In their deepest, feverish thoughts they witnessed how the wheel of fire and shadow turned and turned without end.
Afterglow woke Stuart up the next morning, at the advent of light. She covered his mouth with a hand and put her free index finger on her lips.
What's up? He mouthed with his lips when she removed her hand, the art of silent speech not unknown to him from his military service.
She signed for him to stay put and roused the others the same way, signing for them to follow her.
They did, beyond curious, fighting to free themselves from the cobwebs of sleep, noticing that she brought her sword and bow.
There was a rise not far off. She led them almost to its top, before falling

down on all fours and cautiously moving like that the rest of the way.

First they did not get it. They watched a herd of four-legged animals grass at the far side of the field. Then their eyes grew big and they all stared at Afterglow, almost crying out in incredulity.

Afterglow let them watch for a while, making sure the sight was imprinted on their consciousness and then signed for them to pull back, doing so very decisively, and they did. They returned to the camp and dressed in their now almost dry clothes, and rushed off, choosing a detour, a route taking them far from the herd's position.

They moved fast for several minutes before Afterglow slowed down, signaling for them to relax, or relax more, they could not quite tell which.

Leila could not stay silent anymore, anyway.

– Was that, she gasped quietly, or as quietly as she was able, – were those *unicorns?*

The other travelers gasped, too, as if the very word she spoke stunned them.

– It was indeed, Afterglow replied.

– But that's…

– Impossible, Lester completed in a very lame expression of disbelief.

– I knew it when I saw them, Martha said, – knew something was not… right.

– I see them, Leila said with closed eyes. – They are so beautiful. Why couldn't we stay longer and watch the herd, or even approach it?

– You do not want to do that, Kathryn cautioned her. – They are nasty buggers, especially if they feel like they are disturbed or even bothered.

– Nasty, huh? Leila sighed in despair. – Nothing like in the fairy tales in this case either, then.

– They were hunted almost to extinction in many realms, and developed a rather nasty disposition because of that.

– You speak of them as if they are…

– Intelligent? They definitely are, and very warlike if they are provoked. I have seen those horns feast on human flesh and blood quite a few times.

– Horses can hardly be said to be their distant cousins, Cindy said, – not even like apes are compared to us.

The recollection of a female stabbing the air with her horn and crying out in a powerful whinny, not really a whinny at all sent more shivers through the travelers.

– Do you have more surprises for us, dear Kathryn, Stuart asked, in both awe and scorn. – Is there no end to them?

– There is not, Afterglow stated.

She could have added a lot to that brief, cryptic statement, and did, without doing so, with subconscious gestures and body language.

– We will never return to our life, the way it was, will we? Joshua spoke in a choke and a whisper, as if exposing some great secret.

He received no vocal reply. They moved on.

More than one whinny or their echoes kept touching their ears.

The landscape changed some more, as it started descending and they finally reached the western mountain ridge, and a vast valley appeared below.

They stood there, staring at it for while. Afterglow let them, let more of it, the enormity of it all sink in.

– The mountains… Lester shook his head. – It is as if some great force has carved them out of the land with a giant spade or something and discarded the giant landmass… not there anymore. It's quite the amazing scenery.

The small group of human beings stood between the sharp rocks and looked across the vast valley at the significantly taller mountains in the west.

– The shadows... they look like teeth, Martha said, very timid.

They did, an effect that became even more pronounced as the wanderers descended the steep ground.

– According to ancient folklore, told by the local population preceding the firstcomers a giant died here long ago and became the very land, Cindy said. – Another giant took a bite of him, leaving the low-elevation valley.

– Right now, that doesn't sound too far fetched, Leila mumbled. – Brrr.

And even less so later, much later, when they glanced back at them from afar.

The valley seemed even vaster as they crossed it. At one point the shadow from the jagged mountains in the east seemed to double back and... chase them. But that seeming illusion faded quickly, as the daystar rose in the blue sky.

– So, the firstcomers weren't truly the firstcomers? Lester more stated than asked.

– No, the deeper you delve into the material, into writings and legends it becomes more and more clear that they were merely one of several groups creating what would become Arcadia, no matter how much they ignore that in party speeches. We are indeed a people of many births and origins.

Then the daystar fell behind the range in the west and the shadow enclosed them, and in certain moments, when they feared they glimpsed something at the edge of their vision, they felt like turning around and return faster… much faster to where they had come from not that long ago.

Lester frowned a bit, as they reached a natural, lower area in the terrain.

– I thought I saw something, he said slowly, attempting to hide his evident apprehension.

Something stuck up from the ground around the next turn.

They stopped there, the travelers, startled.

– It's funny. He shook his head. – For a moment there I thought…

He did not complete the sentence, clearly flustered, embarrassed.

– We know what you thought, Stuart stated.

Before them was a chaotic collection of more or less overgrown iron poles stuck in the ground.

– What's this? Joshua asked. – Another version of what you guys deem modern art, like those horrible statues in Howell?

– They brought construction materials with airships, Alice explained, good-humored. – These particular poles were not properly secured and fell from high up, penetrating the ground like arrows would flesh.

– I knew that, Lester mumbled, – knew it had to be something like that.

Martha smiled and kissed him on the cheek, clearly intent on comforting him, alleviating his distress.

Afterglow looked at him, demanding his attention. He met her eyes.

– The jaws are always there, you know, she said softly, – here, on Earth, everywhere, its teeth ready to bite.

The trickle flowed down his spine, she knew it did, feeling it as she would if it had been her spine.

Long after they had left the strange sight behind, all of them, travelers and locals alike turned and glanced at it, even when they could no longer see it.

They reached the end of the valley and began ascending the western mountains.

The travelers stopped walking the moment they reached the forest about halfway up the steep climb. Something clearly dawned on them.

– There was no big vegetation in the entire valley, Martha said. – Except for the grass and similar there wasn't a single tree or bush anywhere.

– No, there is not, Afterglow said. – They have tried to grow food there for quite some time, in vain.

– It's like one giant cemetery, Martha shuddered, – a valley in the shadow of Death.

The land rose around them, and they rose with it. They reached the end of the forest and continued upwards on the steep path, their breathing constantly labored. There was not a single moment of rest in the cruel terrain, no break from the relentless onslaught of the mountain imposing itself on the creatures climbing it.

When the terrain finally flattened around them, they hardly noticed. Only later did they realize that the walk had become lighter and that they, relatively speaking could rest more.

The plain stretched out before them. They saw the cloud, a kind of mirror move in the sky first, before the structure, visible from far away revealed itself. It was not just the imposing sight, but something deeper, eliciting all kinds of emotion from every member of the group.

– There it is, Maximus' Folly, as it is affectionately called, Alice said with expectation in her pretty eyes.

– Maximus, he's some kind of big shot in Arcadia, isn't he? Stuart stated more than asked.

– They. They are… big shots, an entire extended family of power-hungry thugs. Afterglow has had a feud with them since her youth, one that grew significantly more serious when she eviscerated old man Maximus' favorite son recently.

– But they own this?

– Not anymore. After attempting to make it work for years, they sold it to a competitor, even an unfriendly one. If they had not Afterglow would never have accepted this commission. It was a major loss of prestige to them.

– It's… pulling at me. Leila shook her head in more disbelief. – I can actually feel the physical tug in my gut.

The ancient stones washed with dusk blinded them in their brilliance and they had to look away.

– It's great architecture, Joshua sniffed, – but still fairly mundane.

– You should have seen it in its heyday, Kathryn said with distant eyes.

– It is not the building itself, the way I have heard it, Cindy said, – but what it contains. It is built on an old pre-settler spot of burial and sacrifice. The lore describes how a Seer attempting to make sense of it all went raving insane.

It was as if they could see her, every time they blinked. One blink was a scream, not exactly scary, but clearly unnerving.

They walked the long stretch of uneven terrain. Sometimes the building was visible and sometimes not. There was no lack of small growth here. It took time, but they felt strangely… patient, not in a hurry at all, as if enjoying the scenery and the thrilling expectation and growing horror in their hearts.

Then the construct towered above them, even from fairly far away. The travelers studied curiously the desolation and entropy of the made materials and what had been the rural surrounding area. Former lush lawns and well-prepared landing sites for the airships were covered in wild growth. Bushes and grass and heather had long since invaded the incomplete road. Vines had reached the lower part of the front wall. On other parts of the building it had reached significantly higher.

The rather big marble front door had broken in two pieces. It was easy to pass through the crack and enter the place.

She noticed it the moment she crossed the threshold, the nausea swelling her throat and quickly spreading throughout her being, making her feel weak and washed out. She fought it for a few seconds before she relented and accepted what was happening.

They stopped right inside. The first thing they noticed was the special light. Then all of them, without exception realized that the visual impression was only the tiny start of what the entrance hall and the entire place… conveyed to them.

It hammered Kathryn Caldwell, and there was no escape from the memories and the pain.

– The past is coming back in full force to haunt Afterglow, is it not?

– It is, Kathryn nodded.

– But Leila's guess is that Afterglow wants it to happen, that she has been seeking it for quite some time, even though she was not aware of it at first.

The black woman spoke formally and respectful to the sorcerer, as if she was a native.

Afterglow shrugged and tilted her head, forcing herself to focus on the here and now, ignoring the moving images of young Kathryn and Beatrice holding hands as they progressed to the desk at the depth of the hall.

– It feels right coming here. All this feels so very right.

She touched the thick layer of dust on the reception desk. It rose into the air and danced before her, performing enthusiastically in her honor.

– This is a fucking hotel, Martha said incredulous, – but a vast overkill, if I have ever seen one.

– Yes, a hotel, a guesthouse, and filled with excessive splendor, an overkill to end all overkills.

– Now, it's only a ruin, Lester said.

Afterglow studied the dust, as it floated off, as it joined the flow, the draft, the slow-floating stream at the center of the building.

– My… master planned on using this place, its untapped energies, residing here like a king.

She opened the two giant doors to a giant hall. The windows covered most of the walls on both sides. The travelers gasped in awe.

– And this is his throne-hall? Leila asked/stated.

– Your awareness serves you well, young sorcerer to be, Afterglow nodded.

– Thank you, Leila grinned, – but that was a big giveaway. Your master was a prick of the first order, methinks.

– He was an arrogant bastard, a beyond wicked shithead, but his power gave him access to space and time, and he spoke enough of the future to reveal that the coming years are crucial when it comes to human development. We live in a time that will decide what will dominate our lives for thousands of years.

They felt the potency of her words and shivered under her stare.

– «Our» lives?

Afterglow did not voice any direct reply to her inquiry.

– My master planned on being at the top of that heap, but we will beat him to it, and anyone else going for that prize and take their place.

Fremantle frowned, too. She practically saw him do so, even while standing with her back to him.

– Cathy, baby, he whistled, – I rather thought you were more than you let on, but I had truly no idea how much was hidden in that rather pleasant hide of yours.

He was, when you reduced everything to its basics, a rather traditional male. She ignored him, but the name he used did affect her, did push her waves inward, shaking her bones.

When Afterglow turned towards them, she gathered them in the heat of her vision, and they froze in place, awaiting her word.

– Humanity's path is a dark river, with many brutal twists and turns. All the talk about the light you hear is just party speeches and hypocrisy and hardly even that. We need to prepare ourselves for everything that may come our way. We need to harden ourselves against the rising tide.

– And cleansing an old spook house of malevolent spirits is a good way to do that? Lester wondered, keeping it light.

Afterglow shook her head, as the visions kept assaulting her.

– You have no idea…

But you will!

– It is a maelstrom, a veritable flow almost unprecedented in my line of work, so potentially deadly that I just can not use my usual approach. It is not dangerous at the moment, but that might change at any time. We must not dawdle.

Alice stepped forward, finding her tools and powders and stuff in her pouch. She showed great skill and efficiency in every little move she made. The travelers and the dabblers among them studied her with unadulterated admiration.

– Dust is like fire, like Shadow, she said aloud.

And the words themselves seemed to confirm that, to enhance the truth to a point that they could actually see it.

– Dust, not dust, but Dust is what all human beings leave behind when they depart the flesh. It is the true, glorious ashes of mankind.

She began painting the pentacle on the floor, continuing to show great skill and confidence.

– You're doing this by *hand?* Leila cried. – How can you make the form so… perfect?

– I have been doing this since I was five, Alice shrugged.

When she had completed the five-pointed star and its surrounding circle she found the special red ocher powder mix and covered the lines of the symbol with it.

– Martha, come with me, Afterglow bade her.

Martha looked incredulous at her, but obeyed the bidding without further hesitation when the tall woman left the room. The others remained, glancing puzzled at each other. Afterglow led on, back into the reception area, moving beyond it, to the north wall, where she without delay began constructing another pentacle.

– There are ghosts? Martha asked with numb lips. – You said that much.

– Yes, there are, but they are not here right now.

It was not difficult sensing them, even from afar. Kathryn knew Martha did, knew it the way she fidgeted and scratched the nude skin on her arms and by the fact that she could not stop turning her head.

Martha glared at her.

– Don't think I don't know what you're doing? I'm not stupid.

Afterglow turned towards her with a pointed stare.

– And why do you think I picked you to accompany me here, sweet witch to be?

Cat got Martha's tongue.

– So you could get that off your chest, of course.

Afterglow distributed the powder on the lines, the lines of power, doing so with an ease even rivaling her apprentice. But there was a recklessness, a bravado in the manner she did it, absent in Alice.

– Witches are the servants of Satan, Martha finally said.

Afterglow scorned her with the dark chuckle.

– Do not be silly. We can not allow silly tonight, if we are to survive and do so with ourselves intact.

She produced her pocket knife and waved Martha to join her at the center of the pentacle.

Martha did. Afterglow grabbed her arm and cut the meaty side of her palm. Martha gasped in pain and shock. Her blood flowed down on the floor, and she imagined how everything turned ruby red.

Alice completed the distribution of the powder and put all gear at the center.

– We may stay here a long time, she instructed them, – and we need to be prepared for that, for that, too.

They watched her work, Fremantle and those native to this realm with certain admiring distance, the travelers with something very close to awe.

Dust whirled in the air by the edge of one of the windows. Lester saw it with his back turned and his eyes grew even wider. He blinked, he kept his eyes shut. It did him no good. He still saw.

They turned to Alice again, as if in sole agreement.

– Please tell us about her, Leila begged her. – Please!

Alice seemed to consider the request carefully.

– They say no one is safe for Afterglow, the apprentice said. – She has already become a modern legend, a tale to scare young children. They tell us to beware when her wind blows in the quiet air and in the night outside people's door. Something happened to her once, something terrible scarring her for all time. If there were scary legends with true substance in the distant past, and *there were,* she rivals them all.

No one asked more questions.

Afterglow returned with Martha in tow. Martha's left hand was covered by a red-stained bandage. She looked pale and drawn.

Shadows within shadows shifted and sizzled in the air. The corners burned with a dark flame.

Afterglow did not look exactly as they remembered her from most of the time they had known her either. She noticed their looks, their worry, well before she crouched and vomited the moment she breached the circle.

Wet and swollen eyes still looked at them with the steady gaze they knew so well.

– I have been swept with dizziness since we arrived here. It is one occasional result of heightened awareness. It takes time to adapt to changing conditions.

A door slammed shut somewhere. At least that was how it sounded to them. The entire building and the ground below shook.

High-strung as they were, everybody jumped in their tracks, including Alice and Kathryn. Afterglow's waves and Alice's energies moved around their bodies, becoming visible and more distinct.

– I feel bloated, Cindy whined, crouching, clutching her belly.

– It is your power, striving to assert itself, Alice explained.

– I feel BLOATED, Cindy complained, as if the other had not spoken at all, her hair flowing around her like blood. – Like I am pumped up and ready to pop.

One mighty hiss rose from below and into the charged air, from the ground, one voice sounding like many, many voices sounding like one.

– We can not visit the Wasteland this time and we do not need to, she explained, attempting somewhat, to alleviate their fears, not really succeeding. – It is here, with us already.

The hiss sounded like it originated close to their ears.

– All of us need to be in the circle this time, Afterglow stated calmly. – There is no way around that, no room outside. Take your position like last time, Fremantle and Caroline between Stuart and Joshua.

They joined her there. It happened quickly, without the awkwardness of the previous time in Alice's attic.

– I feel like I am waking up from a dream.

She shook her head, speaking with a dreamy quality in her voice.

Alice found the small bottles. Their content, the brew already mixed twinkled even weirder in the eerie glow illuminating the very air.

Afterglow spoke. There was no sound when she did that. The others felt only the impact of her action. Alice smiled in something resembling ecstasy.

– The Curse of Silence, she cried. – THE FUCKING CURSE OF SILENCE

– To the ancients I present your daughters and sons, Afterglow spoke in a ghostly voice, and now they could hear her. – They are choosing your craft, and one night they will join you in eternity. Join with them, if you so desire. Share yourself with them, as they will share themselves with you.

Eight bottles were passed to those placed at the corners of the pentacle. Afterglow drank, Alice drank and seven of the others drank. Fremantle stood still and frozen. The rest started shaking in heat and wind. Cindy looked at her arm and hand. The veins started glowing, long before the content could possibly reach them. They crouched, feeling the brew in their stomach, felt it settle there…

Then it was like fired from that point and into their body at large.

They began seeing things. The building revealed itself to them.

And there was movement outside, shapes they imagined transformed into creatures, snarls filling the night.

Afterglow drew the attention of everybody within the pentacle. She filled their consciousness. Alice shook her head in delight.

– *Feel,* Kathryn told them, – feel yourself, your surroundings, your vast depths.

– I do, Leila, shouted. – I DO!

– My God, what are those things? Joshua cried.

– What are you doing? Lester asked, besieged Afterglow.

She turned to him, facing him, making him face her.

– You told me to make haste, she replied, – and I am doing that, speeding up the momentum of events.

– I… told you? He said incredulous.

– Yes, she breathed, – not as you are now, but *as you will become*.

He stared openmouthed at her. She reached out her hands, taking his in a surprisingly gentle grip, catching her eyes in his, sending a thousand charges of scintillating energy through him.

– Trust me?

He nodded, too numb to speak.

Martha blinked and snarled at her in disbelief. Afterglow just grinned.

She pulled back, continuing her spell.

– I had a long morning tonight. It lasted twelve hours and was filled with midnight.

Memory assaulted her.

– The day burned one hour in the heat of the eternal daystar. Rivers flowed like sand.

Memory overwhelmed her.

– It is word association. Alice spoke in a hushed whisper, translating, explaining Afterglow's spell when the others sent worried glances in her direction. – There is a double, triple depth to the words.

– The dance of swords begins. I can see it, see the blades cutting us.

And with the change in her voice and the literal words

Cuts appeared on everybody's skin. Blood flowed like geysers from deep wounds. Sounds of gasps and pain filled the space between those gathered in the circle. Blood drew lines in the air, mirroring those on the ground.

And then another glowing pentacle formed in the air above.

Leila bit off a piece of her tongue. It fell on the floor and dissolved in a hiss of fire.

The bell struck midnight, twelve heavy strokes of memory and thunder, each evoking another powerful sensation.

An energy cone formed around the ten. One of the giant windows broke. There was no accompanying sound. It broke in a thousand pieces and fell silently to the floor. Afterglow kept chanting, kept spitting silent curses. The other window broke. An army of creatures entered the hall from both sides, drawn by the scent of those inside. A creature with a giant wingspan reached the barrier first…

And disintegrated upon impact.

A few more mindlessly hit the energy wall. Their ashes spread in the wind. Then even the most dull-witted of the invaders got the message and stopped at a distance perceived as safe.

– BURN! Afterglow cried with a mighty shout.

She and all within the cone screamed in pain. The energy field extended to the entire hall, burning to cinder everybody there. It reached outside, in rays of light and heat. Blood splattered the land and the walls. It filled all the floors of the building, pushing at its walls. Dead and dying dropped to the ground. Those not grievously wounded fled in nameless terror from the deadly onslaught. They did not look back.

– THAT WILL TEACH YA! Afterglow chuckled darkly.

The energy, pulling back brought with it the Dust of the dead, bathing those within the protective cone in its power. Thought joined Dust, joined air, joined fire, joined shadow in the circle, sizzling like something tangible,, almost visible, crashing and burning a thousand times.

She gasped, like an echo of the other nine, as she watched them collapse, as she herself collapsed and joined the writhing shadows on the floor, on the ground of soil and stone and wood.

They fell and kept falling, drowning, spiraling down into a vast well without any bottom in sight, assaulted by horrible fever dreams without end.

CHAPTER FIFTEEN

The twelve strokes of midnight kept repeating themselves, kept evoking memories. Each stroke brought new thoughts, new vibrations. They walked through a thousand caves, an invisible labyrinth to beat all labyrinths. Stroke six made them gasp and heave. Stroke nine made them smile. Stroke ten shook them hard. They stood in a circle, gathering around one single, imposing figure.

Nine walked through the burning waste of a desert in blazing daylight. The twelve strokes of midnight kept repeating themselves.

They shared each other's burning dreams, the feverish visions, jigsaws of a puzzle turning into a jumble of horrible impressions and sensations.

The place had no name, not anymore. Thousands of skulls had been placed on poles. The sight filled the entire valley. The poles stood so tight that there was no spot you could stand and not be able to reach out and touch two simultaneously.

Some of the mangled skeletons on the ground still wore clothes, wore rags, but they had all been picked clean of flesh. They created a sea of bones covering the ground as far as eyes could see. The ground was still wet. The heat from the burning daystar could not dry the blood-soaked land.

The little brown-skinned girl ran from something or someone she could not see. Fear and tears burned her eyes and cheeks. She fled from whatever was chasing her through a forest, a dark forest.

Lester was a young man, hardly more than a teenager. He entered a room at the local museum, one with a circle of masks placed in a circle. The masks and their eyes drew him in, pulled him into the dark wells revealed to him. He recalled that the moment had impressed itself on him even then, but not even remotely as much as it did now, when he re-experienced it.

Martha stood at the top of a hill. She looked down at the crowd gathered below with a big smile on her lips.

Eagles circled the mountain, the tall, pointed aerie. And sometimes there were winged creatures that were not eagles, but human-like, with what seemed like an impossible wingspan.

A waterfall vanished into thin air. Almost all the water fell through what had to be a crack in the very fabric of reality.

A stone bridge with elaborate gates and statues of grotesque creatures seemed to lead to a giant moon hovering in the sky.

People walked coughing through a city covered in fog, through a street where four-wheeled vehicles constantly spat poison. Every time the humans breathed they coughed some more, and they did not stop. There was no escape from it.

In the fog appeared a house shining in a radiant glow. The house seemed to change, turning into different buildings, different shapes. And eagles circled it in the twilight, circled a place that certainly was not in any thriving city, but one left in ruins and partly overgrown long ago.

The dark towers hovered in the air, or rather in the ether, in the void. There was no staircase leading up there. The towers were virtually indistinguishable from the surrounding night.

Vultures picked the flesh of those fallen, devoured the hot, oozing flesh and chuckled pleased for every new tasty bite making spittle flow from their beak.

The Valley of Skulls… grew from its fairly humble origin to cover a vast expanse. Some of the bodies were still alive, writhing and kicking in the relentless heat. They felt the beaks pick, pick, pick…

The ten within the circle writhed and moaned. Pain assaulted them in waves. They cried out in their discomfort and horror.

They floated in an endless sea, floated upwards towards the surface in an endless warm stream. Everybody held their breath, desperate to breathe, to feel air in their strained lungs.

Leila sat up, her eyes opening wide. The others did as well. Images repeated themselves endlessly in those wide open eyes.

Dust and fire and shadow and everything rushed back in, bathing the residents of the dissolving pentacle.

An echo of silence reigned in the great hall.

– It's cold, Leila said with shivering lips.

– It is always cold, Afterglow shrugged.

– What was that, Leila cried subdued and frightened. – What the fuck was all that?

– That was the spirit world and the Wasteland combined imposing on the material world, Afterglow explained with disdain. – That was reality invading your very being. It still is. *That* was our combined power, a force to be reckoned with in any realm.

Afterglow's dark, ecstatic laughter made air and skin shake.

All the powerful sensations kept assaulting Leila, assaulting them all.

– That little girl was me… wasn't it? She said. – But I can't remember it. Why can't I remember?

Afterglow did not reply. She studied the others. They rose, as she rose.

– Our protection is… gone? Lester wondered.

– It is. Afterglow confirmed. – But we do not need it anymore, at least not

for the time being.
If that was meant to be reassuring, it clearly was not…
Alice approached her, awaiting instructions, using yet another opportunity to demonstrate her awe, her nosedive admiration.
Everybody stood before Afterglow on shaky legs.
– Come, she bade them.
She drew her sword and left the hall in a casual walk. She heard Alice draw her sword behind her.
They walked through the reception area, to the broad staircase leading upstairs. Limbs and pieces of flesh covered substantial parts of the floor and they had to tread carefully to not step on any of it. It was not a major problem, but always There, not letting go. The travelers took great care to avoid the warm body parts steaming in the chilled air.
The upper floor looked distinctly different. Afterglow shook her head.
– This place is truly remarkable, almost unheard of. It is not just the burials or even the sacrifices, but far more, layers upon layers of complexity and magick.
– What does that mean, mean for *us?*
Leila's voice had turned whiny and that whiny voice once more filled whatever space surrounded them.
– Nothing good, Afterglow replied casually.
The black woman shrunk in her tracks.
– I don't get it, Fremantle mused. – I don't know if you have noticed, but the walls, even if they look solid enough seem like they aren't really there. We move through what seem like a narrow hallway, but the echo makes it sound like a much bigger space.
– What looks like a small, contained room can contain infinite space, Cindy said. – I have researched tales about the Wasteland. Standard physical laws do not apply here.
She looked pale, and vomit had spoiled her clothes, but she basically looked okay.
– The term «standard physical laws» is an oxymoron, anyway, she said brightly and those among the others able to see such things spotted hunger in her eyes.
The truth of her words was illustrated in excellent ways as they moved down the dark corridor. They walked quite fast, but never seemed to get anywhere, at least not getting closer to the hallway end.
Stuart grabbed Afterglow's shoulder, a light touch not really impeding on her movements.
– What… what is our objective here?

– The first is to survive until dawn, she replied without sounding too concerned, without slowing down. – The other, if possible is to cleanse the place of the Wasteland infection. If we attain one, we probably attain the other.

– That is comforting.

He said, not very comforted.

But he did smile when the other travelers laughed their brittle laughter.

Paintings on the walls did not look like paintings at all, but like windows, glimpses of vastly different realities. One was of a bridge covered in mist, one where winged creatures flew and snarled below and occasionally above. Another was a street where dry leaves blew in the wind, one where skeletons walked. The others, at least in those particular glimpses defied description. They reminded of realms of dreams, where nothing was solid or real or permanent.

Beatrice sat in a room of mist, with her brushes, making her strokes on a large white canvas, a vast tapestry. Characters and places shifted and burned under her cruel direction. Her sinister hum filled the halls and hallways of her castle.

They approached an intersection, where two hallways crossed each other. Two bodies had been smeared against the ceiling there. One other hung suspended in the air, as if from invisible threads. Reality shifted and burned at that spot. The very air seemed to shimmer. A loud, enraged roar shook material and flesh alike.

A creature with wings suddenly rushed towards them. Alice aimed her hand and fired an energy-beam at it. It cut its body in two.

A choir of roars echoed the one of rage and subsequent pain.

– Damn! Afterglow muttered.

Then she waved them with her and ran off. They followed with labored breathing. It was as if every breath here, every step was a strain. The cold sweat started running on their skin and flushed faces.

They reached another intersection and this one was filled with creatures.

Afterglow immediately hit one of them with her waves, not allowing them time to even consider an attack, deliberately using non-lethal force.

– AFTERGLOW IS MERCIFUL, she cried. – PLEASE DO NOT MISTAKE HER MERCY FOR WEAKNESS.

They folded their wings, kneeling before her, shaking hard.

– You will convey this message from me: we do not seek your destruction. Allow us to do what we came here to do, and we will leave the rest of you in peace, not in pieces.

The male she had hit growled something the travelers did not understand, but Afterglow evidently did. She nodded, and the kneeling creatures pulled back and fled down yet another shadowy hallway.

– They were scared out of their wits, Leila said, – scared of you. I take it that Afterglow is well known in the Other World as well?

She received no reply.

They kept charging forward. The paths, the number of intersections seemed to grow, to multiply before them. No matter what direction they chose, everything looked the same. Time passed horribly slow, and there was no end to their surroundings.

– Have we moved for hours, or nights in here? Caroline whimpered, dead-tired and out of it.

HERE HERE HERE the echo hit them from everywhere, from close and far away and all possible angles.

– One hour is far away and a day is an eternity.

Alice looked harried, her voice strained.

Afterglow stopped, they all did. They watched her while she stood there, concentrating, focusing on truly seeing what was around them. Everybody saw it through her eyes, how the path painfully but distinctly re-revealed itself.

The vast labyrinth dissolved around them, lost coherence, but it did not disappear. They imagined that it was alive, a living entity waiting for them to offer themselves to the gnawing maws.

There was another stairwell. They ran up there in three and three steps. They heard a loud sound, one stemming from one single heavy step.

And then there was more of the same.

They reached a bedroom, a luxurious suite, one with an open door. The air above the bed… leaked in all directions.

Caroline, Alice and Cindy looked at Afterglow, but did not speak.

A loud crack from below shook everything and everyone.

– What *is* that?

Stuart shook his head. Afterglow noticed how he moved, with constantly flickering eyes. He had returned to the war. She recognized that feeling easily.

– Giants attacking the protective circle.

– But the circle is gone.

– I made another, Afterglow explained. – We might see ourselves here, but they see us there. The dog will always go where it smells blood and Martha's is potent beyond belief. Its stench leaks through the mirage, the fake circle.

– That's an excellent tactic, Stuart acknowledged. – How long will it last?

– Not long…

She started the preparations, working fast and confident. Alice joined her, and their cooperation was as efficient as ever. They poured red ochre on the bed and through the large room, poured it on each other and everybody. It stuck to the skin, burrowed its way into it like living creatures. It burned and everybody crouched.

– This is… fantastic, Fremantle gasped. – I feel so strong, like I can take on anything and anyone. Even if this doesn't end well, I will almost be happy that I experienced it.

He looked alive, as if life itself was burning inside of him.

– Is there something we can use, anything? Stuart asked.

– Break off the feet of the furniture, use anything you can get your hands on, Afterglow said. – The creatures that will be with us shortly are solid, are mortal. They are vulnerable. You can kill them. Do so, kill as many as you can until you no longer can. Fight and kill for as long as you breathe and for as long as you endure afterwards.

They saw the anxiety in her features. They stared open-mouthed at her.

– You… underestimated the danger? Lester said astonished.

– I did, she confirmed. – Whatever resides here has grown far beyond the possibility and even probability of containment.

Towering creatures hammered at the barrier circle where the ten seemed to be crouching, the barrier leaking and breaking.

Afterglow… growled. Once again they stared astonished at her. She growled in rage.

– I feel it, Alice cried in excitement. – I FEEL IT!

– They will not get us, Kathryn Caldwell growled. – No one will!

She practically jumped to Alice, grabbing her in mind and body.

The barrier cracked, cracked open like an eggshell. The creatures rushed inside and found only blood and death. The shards of the barrier, suddenly solid and deadly reattached themselves to themselves and imploded, squeezing all the living beings within, squeezing them to a pulp. The new barrier exploded and gutted the rest of the creatures in a wide circle, no dome, as it expanded to all sides, all angles. A roar of rage rose from everywhere. Afterglow and her companions heard it.

– You are destroying them all, Cindy whimpered. – It is remarkable, *remarkable*.

Afterglow spoke fast and intense to Alice, while handing her a tiny bottle filled with the twinkling, light blue fluid.

– Drink it when I say so or if you feel there is no other recourse, but not before. Drink it all.

Alice stared at her, stunned.

– But you said… you said we should never…

– There are risks and concerns, even grave risks and concerns, but now those are outweighed by those stemming from not drinking it.

The walls dissolved around them and it no longer felt like their imagination or only that. Those among them unused to extended realities realized that this was indeed happening. Afterglow and Alice stepped in front of the others, as much as they possibly could. They were only two and could not form a proper perimeter. Stuart stepped forward, too, breaking off a foot of the bed.

– What do we *do?* Leila cried.

– Fight! Afterglow growled. – Go deep within yourself. Find the cold hard place and use it, use it to kill, to survive.

Lester, in a sudden fever pitch of action broke off all the three other legs of the bed and handed two of them to Leila and Joshua. Fremantle had his wand. He pulled it from the sheet on his back. Caroline's feet shook, but she remained standing.

The floor and ceiling faded away as well. The entire building disappeared around them. They stood outdoors, on a low rise in what resembled a basin. The creatures, those unable to fly flowed down the terrain towards them. Those with wings large enough to fly attacked in steep dives. Afterglow and Alice began firing at them the moment they became close enough. Blood dark like night jumped from torn-apart forms and filled the air, slowly falling in the flickering, hazy twilight.

The noise started as a low hiss, but rose to a loud, ongoing growl.

– Everything is so… clear, Leila muttered. – My Goddess, all my senses are *screaming* at me.

– Your own senses can't be screaming at you, Joshua pointed out with impeccable logic. – Your senses are receptors and…

The number of creatures charging them grew to a wave and words failed him.

Some of them, struck with fear bolted or attempted to bolt, but they were blocked by the approaching wave rolling across the landscape. Heaps of dead carcasses were piling up and actually briefly halting and delaying the onslaught.

– P-PAIN, Cindy wailed.

They all felt it, felt it pound in their veins, but whatever the reason she felt it far more pronounced. Blood flowed from her nostrils and covered her nose.

– You are all being born this day, Afterglow cried, cried louder than the noise and scream and everything around them, – born in pain, like all beings. Accept it and know thyself.

A hissing nightmare charged her with all its claws out, avoiding her focused wave. She practically split it in two with her sword. Alice dealt with two foes quickly and efficiently.

Then everything turned into one unrelenting melee, the brittle defense perimeter collapsing completely. Stuart swept the piece of wood in front of him and froze stunned when a… beam seemed to be fired from it and into the air. The noise around them rose to an onslaught of disruptive and violent sound. Stuart struck at a creature, but missed, but the focused beam hit the tough skin and cut a deep rift. The demonic face twisted in pain and screamed. Afterglow and Alice swung their swords like they moved, in a constant, unending flow. Lester struck at the piece of flesh in front of him, bashing in its head. An attacker grabbed Cindy in the arm, raising his other clawed hand ready to strike. He gasped, shook and was dead before he hit the ground. Cindy stopped screaming that very moment and looked astonished at the dead body by her feet. The others stayed away from her, their eyes suddenly wary and apprehensive. The attack itself halted for a second and two. Cindy moved her hand with a nasty grin. All the entities catching that pulled back in horror. Afterglow and Alice attacked viciously. Lester and Stuart followed them. They cut into the enemy like a swath of blades and moving shrapnel. Whatever glowed like light in Stuart's hand flickered on and off, but cut and bled those it struck just as well as Afterglow and Alice and their blades did. Fremantle swung his wand left and right, up and down, back and forth. Afterglow pulled Joshua down, saving him from a savage swing of claws. They scratched his thigh and blood flowed. Leila kicked a male in the ribs, making him suffocate on his lung's blood. Lester struck a female in the head with the tip of the «club», breaking her skull. Martha was grabbed from behind, pulled into a merciless grip. Alice cleaved the male's back with her sword, her blade drowning in red and ruby.

Afterglow was struck with long claws tearing into her shoulder. She fell back, ignoring the searing pain, her charging foe being roasted by her waves, even as more pain and pronounced dizziness assaulted her.

– Drink! She shouted to Alice. – DRINK DEEP!

Alice heard, even though there was no visible or evident reaction in her moves. She kept flowing, kept hacking at those threatening her. Afterglow's left arm did not work, but hung useless down. She let go of the sword and in a swift move drew the tiny bottle from its hiding place in the pocket of her jacket. The pain turned to red spots in her vision. She drank, they drank deep. The light blue, shimmering fluid flowed into her mouth and down her throat, spreading almost before it reached the stomach.

She blinked, once, twice, the second time the sorcerer and the apprentice blinked in tandem. They saw, saw it all like in slow motion. It was not, they knew that, but they imagined the figures moving and fighting around them hardly were in motion at all.

They saw their hands move through the air, leaving a trace of the blue flame, a ghost of skin and bone. Even their hair left pieces of itself as it danced on their head. Eyes burned as perception changed, changed forever.

And then reality and its speed and insane throes returned. They both shook, even as they fought to shake it off, to embrace it. Alice smiled in prevailing and mounting ecstasy. Afterglow laughed hard enough to shake everything and everyone.

The two of them began glowing in blue flame and it spread. It stretched and flowed around their body. They moved at the attackers and brushed them aside as if they were paper, as if they were nothing. Claws directed at them in horror and desperation dissolved with contact, instantly followed by the sturdy bodies themselves.

The two of them held hands, standing at the top of the rise, the light spreading from the center point they had become like circles in the water.

The attackers froze one moment, pointed in distress at the two the next and fled in panic, in absolute horror the next after that. Afterglow's laughter thundered even as she spoke:

– AFTERGLOW WARNED YOU, she shouted, – BUT YOU DID NOT HEED AFTERGLOW'S WARNING. THUS YOUR VERY EXISTENCE IS FORFEIT

The tattoos, usually invisible suddenly appeared and burned in her face.

The light turned practically solid. Their companions felt it like a blow as it passed them, without harming them that much, shocking them to the core. With the solid light came emotions, visions, sounds, taste and smell, a stench of rotten flesh.

Flesh, blood and bones jumped and sizzled in the air, as if it was all ripped apart. Five steps, ten steps, fifty steps away all the close creatures of the realm were carved to pieces and most of their flesh turned to dust, their blood transformed to acid howling more than hissing in the thick, almost fluid air.

The blood dropping from Afterglow's arm resembled the blue flame, even as the ecstasy slowly faded.

– The *Destroyer,* the smart, still living among the creatures cried out in multiple voices and hissed in infinite hatred and fear, crouching behind rocks and whatever hiding spots there were, even as some of them still was hit by the shockwave and died in agony.

Before the survivors pulled back into the shadows, fleeing to the far lands beyond this limbo between realms.

Alice stumbled and would have fallen if Afterglow had not held her in her firm grip. Afterglow was unsteady on her feet as well. They stood there looking at their comrades in arms with a cold stare, the blue flames slowly fading in their eyes.

The walls reappeared around them.

The dark, bluish light in the air faded as well, until they found themselves in what seemed like a somewhat ordinary guesthouse room, with ordinary light passing through the window and brightening the twilight dawn. Dark clouds covered the sky outside. The morning resembled the night.

There was no longer a hole in reality above the bed.

– Death closed the rift, even as death opened it, Alice explained to them.

They nodded slowly, as if that made some sort of sense.

Alice started tending the wounds, sewing and bandaging shredded skin. No one released any sound of pain or even a whimper while she did. The numbness kept them all in its grip. Afterglow made no attempt at treating her wound. Alice took care of her last. The floor and the dusty carpet had started to turn red and slippery. Dust twirled everything gray.

– You expected to encounter Beatrice here, did you not? Alice stated, not really asking a question.

– I did, but she was not present. She has passed beyond these near far lands, or she would have been here, free and beyond dangerous already.

– Congratulations, Leila told Kathryn with an unfamiliar, uncanny ogle.

Kathryn did not respond.

– You succeeded did you not, Leila persisted. – You completed your assignment.

– We have all traveled a long, long time and way to finally reach this junction, Afterglow shrugged. – We have all succeeded and are better off because of it.

– We weren't here, but there? Lester said slowly. – Really there!

– Oh, yes, Afterglow said, – and we would have stayed there forever and eventually, if we had not persevered become like those we fought. If we had died we would have been lucky.

Loud cries of small and big birds sounded from both inside and outside the building. Alice tightened the bandage around the sorcerer's shoulder, making the arm difficult to move.

– The eagles have their nest in the tower, Afterglow hummed with closed lids. – They will be gone by the time humans return to this place.

They all turned more aware of their surroundings, of this room, as the light blue fluid on the floor slowly turned to ruby once more.

The stench of blood and guts had become a constant in their senses.

– We should leave, Afterglow said. – There is nothing for us here anymore.
– There was something for us… before? Joshua wondered, not really expecting an answer.
The room faded behind them. The hallways and halls did as well. Dead bodies still decorated the place here and there, but the eerie quality in the air had vanished.
– The various refurbishing crews will get shivers down their spine, Fremantle chuckled pleased, shaking like a leaf.
The reception area still looked foreboding, somewhat, even though they saw no bodies there. The stench still ripped their nostrils.
– What happened in there? Lester asked. – Where… were we?
– The Wasteland, Alice replied brightly. – Or at least a tiny part of it, one «near» our world. The dead and near dead are stuck there, not able or willing to move on to the Spirit World. It is not exactly a realm like we understand it, but a completely different plane of reality, one of many touching what we call the material plane. And the accounts differ and are conflicting and even contradictory on many levels. One school says that the Spirit World is a part of the Wasteland. Another says that the Wasteland is part of the spirit world. A third or ten says something completely different.
– Thanks for clearing that up, Lester mumbled.
They laughed with him, not of him.
Afterglow stumbled.
– Are you okay? Stuart was there in an instant with his sweet, worried expression.
– I… burn, Kathryn replied weakly. – I will be okay.
During what Afterglow suspected was the first throes of fever visions she saw the reception area filled with people, including a younger version of herself and what had been her companions.
They walked outside. The first rays of the daystar split the twilight. Cindy crouched and released a gasp, a gasp turning into a whimper as she straightened, as blood flowed from her nostrils.
– What is it, NOW? Martha cried out in boundless frustration and apprehension.
– I… do not know…
Cindy frowned.
She screamed, her shrieking voice sending ripples through the air and the very reality around them. They saw it.
Everybody noticed the stirring in the air and the ground, noticed before they actually saw it. They realized that their senses had become extremely acute. The scream hurt their ears.

When it stopped abruptly the silence bore down on them like a downpour of chilled rain. Even though they did not turn wet, they really felt like they did. The trickle down their spine turned ongoing and spread to their entire back.

There was movement to the left, and then to the right and right in front of them. An arm stuck up from the ground, then another. Then they saw heads, skulls, bones and skull and bones partly covered with flesh.

– It is the cemetery, Caroline gasped, – the ancient cemetery.

They heard sounds from the inside as well and saw a few skeletons break through weak spots of the floor. The same thing happened all around them, except on the extended spot of their position.

– THE BLOOD, Cindy whimpered. – THE BLOOD

Afterglow turned to her, grabbing her arm, feeling the energy charge through it.

– They are yours, she told the shaking woman.

Cindy looked incredulous at her.

– They are yours to command. You are a necromancer, a mage of the dead.

– They are? I am?

– Can you not feel it, in your flesh, in your bones?

The redhead nodded, slowly calming down.

– What do I do?

Afterglow spoke to her in an intense, but relaxed manner.

– They are nothing to you, nothing but… Dust.

The skeletons and figures that could stand took one step forward.

Cindy snickered.

Then they took one step backwards.

– I could do a lot with this at festivities…

Then they collapsed, virtually dissolving on the spot, reduced not long after that to heaps of bones and whatever flesh remained on the ground.

None of the living moved, as if they were momentarily caught in the field of the dead, unable to escape it.

Then Cindy collapsed, too, a quick moan being released from her slack mouth on her way down. Afterglow, suddenly overwhelmed with lethargy followed her a few seconds later. She tried to speak, to communicate to the others, but was unable to do so.

Alice fell a moment or two before the rest, before all the others fell unconscious on the soft and almost malleable ground.

And it was as if they never actually lost consciousness, as if everybody was swept into a twilight pit, down the dark river surrounding them.

The visions began, first as tiny fluctuations hardly touching their feet, then as a mighty wave hitting them head on.

There was a pressure behind their eyelids, as if they were nothing but those eyelids, that pressure, and then they were elsewhere, floating through a void of mist and shadow. Flashes and sensations assaulted the tiny figures in the vast ether, touching their skin and senses light as feathers.

Lips moved, but there were no words in the empty space, only indistinct imprcssions and sensations burning with both clarity and confusion, forgotten as the moments raced by them and through them.

This is random, chaotic, like a journey through the Crossroads, Afterglow told them, and suddenly they heard her, wondering how she could speak (how they could hear her) while unconscious. Learn from it. Pick up whatever you can from the experience. Teach yourself startling truths.

They glimpsed something, glimpsed many things, also what they imagined was the Crossroads, a place where everything speeded up and all impressions shook them like leaves.

The movement slowed down, for one second, ten, and in this space moments were an eternity and they were elsewhere, a place they could not in any way fathom.

In a somewhat higher realm above this one a row of frozen, flesh-like statues stood unmoving. A flaky substance seemed to cover them and occasionally fall off and hit the ground with a soft thud. If they blinked, if they moved at all it was so slow that no one catching only a glimpse of this place could discern it. The flaky stuff had hardened around the oldest and still had not completely formed around the newest, but no one moved. They stared straight ahead with blind eyes.

Afterglow was there, or someone they knew to be her, and a man, hardly a man at all. Both of them moved. The flaky pieces attempted to attach themselves to them, but failed. There was a dreamlike quality to it all, as if it happened below a water surface, or in the thickest air. They spoke, exchanging words, excited, anxious words, but there were no sounds, only moving lips, and the buzzing of what resembled angry wasps.

Read my lips, Afterglow said.

This is the Ascension, a place, a «higher» realm sought by sorcerers for thousands of years. There is nothing those seeking it will not do to achieve their goals and what makes that twice ironic and horrible is that it is all a trap, a honey trap specifically designed to keep these assholes off the board. They languish here, suffering a fate worse than death because of their sick ambition to conquer and dominate us all, revealing themselves to be hardly more than fools.

She/they focused on the last statue in the row, the most recent arrival.

Malone, Alice enlightened them. Afterglow's cruel mentor and destroyer. Pay attention!

And they did.

He succeeded, Kathryn chuckled, Afterglow spat, succeeded beyond expectation, against impossible odds and «here» he is, nothing but yet another victim of an entity far crueler and far more powerful than him.

She raised her fist to the statue, the form that might still be able to catch her presence.

You succeeded Peter, in punishing yourself in ways far worse than I could have ever designed for you. You put me on display before your peers, but it was you that ended up on a cruel pedestal.

But what about…

Leila wanted to ask a question, but was cut off by a roar, a powerful pull.

Ten seconds going on hundred ended, and they were whisked away, if it could be said that they were ever here.

Young Cindy entered the place of advanced learning in Howell for the first time. Her big green eyes were filled with an expectation she could not contain and a burning curiosity that could not be denied.

Her fast heart-rhythm accompanied them on their Journey, becoming something different. Young Cindy entered the room of the nine masks and she smiled. Older Cindy writhed and moaned on the ground outside a building that looked even more like a ruin than they remembered. They saw her, even though they realized there was no way they could actually see her.

The wheel, the burning wheel was turning.

Is this the beginning, or the end or somewhere in-between? A woman asked.

Afterglow and Alice recognized Horath, the caretaker of the Dark Lodge, but the others did not.

Even though the two facing her when she spoke were Lester and Leila, a Lester and Leila a far cry from the two writhing in cramps outside Maximus' Folly.

It's all of the above, Lester, older and bigger Lester replied.

Afterglow and Alice prepared for tonight's ceremony, for the Sorcerer's Blossom in their quarters. Kathryn applied the lotion on every part of the girl's skin, and she shook in heat.

A bell chimed somewhere. The sound echoed through walls and air of the ancient structure, growing stronger, not weaker.

– It is time. Come, little sister.

Suddenly Afterglow's voice was loud, as if she was really speaking, and not recalling a memory.

They walked through the long and dark and bright and familiar and unfamiliar corridor of light and shadow. The sound of the chimes and of the heartbeats mixed and turned into one, poignant sound.

Silence greeted them when they entered the great hall. There was a sea there, a pool big as an ocean, small as a pool, lit by warm sunlight coming from nowhere. Steam filled the fairly small room, bathed it in a pale green light. It was a pleasant steam, not invasive in any way, not impairing vision or breathing at all.

Nine sorcerers, nine apprentices approached the twinkling waters, submitting themselves to its certain delights.

All eyes, hazy and not were drawn to the lone imposing woman raising her hands.

– Welcome, young sisters, brothers to your night of initiation. You will experience its pleasures and revels, like so many before you. When you leave this place you will know what a pleasure witchcraft can be. This is your night, young sorcerers to be.

The nine glanced shyly at the other nude bodies, seeking comfort with their sorcerers.

– Alice of the realm of Montan, in the land of Arcadia step forward…

Alice did, slid forward, proud and eager, with the water splashing around her feet.

– Corda of the realm of Asgard, in the land of Valhalla, step forward…

The tall, strange creature stepped forward, with the water boiling around her feet.

– Martin of the realm of Earth, in the land of Canada, step forward…

He looked strange, even compared to the others, like he was not there.

Everybody else looked very much present. All of this seemed real, very real.

– Coltrane of the realm of Balakor, in the land of Arubal.

– Lola of the realm of Nispelheim, in the land of Avalon.

– Trom of the forest people, in the realm of Avaldami.

– Shani of the desert, in the realm of Muspelheim.

– Leshi of the realm of Darkland, in the Land of the Moon.

– Chi Wo of the realm of Palobi, in the land of Kanchenyounga.

The walk forward seemed to last forever. The youths' eyes were glazed, their skin covered in sweat adding to the lotion. The nine met in the small circle at the center of the pool, of the sea, facing each other, standing with their backs to the rest of the hall. The other nine, gathered at the edge of the pool, at the shore of the sea looked patronizingly at them, as their eyes, too glazed over, and their bodies also began heating up.

– Celebrate yourself, and each other. Let your passions run wild.

The touching began, hands on bodies, bodies on bodies. They danced in the water. The sea boiled and moved around their feet. Afterglow watched them, and began feeling the first stirrings beyond basic arousal. A man, one with more than a passing similarity to Corda touched her. She turned towards him, and returned his caresses, writhing in his strong arms.

There was something, something in his eyes.

– You look at me, she said. – Why waste time looking at me? I know you, do I not?

She realized she did, in a thousand ways, even if the knowledge was dim, distant, distant no more.

– I know everyone, he said hoarsely, clearly caught up in the moment, – but I know you better than most. I am Odin. From my point of view we have already met many times, Cathy of Arcadia. I know your name, know all your names.

That startled her, as she saw the truth of his words in his eyes. It had seemed on occasion like he was not there, but now he clearly was, as he embraced her, as he touched her and made her cry out in pleasure, as the others gathered around the two.

They spoke with lips and tongue and fingers and toes. She gasped. He could rouse her, he could excite her and she marveled at the experience of him, total and all-encompassing.

The build up was slow, but inevitable. She smiled. Distracted and oblivious to her further surroundings she hardly concerned herself with Alice at all anymore.

They were nine, nine people moving closer, pulled towards each other. Two other males and three females studied her with a strange smile on their lips.

– This is Lester of Earth, Odin presented.

Kathleen smiled to the new man before her, a big man with dark eyes, long, dark hair and a darkness dancing around his muscular, very muscular body.

– Hello again, he whispered in her ear.

She looked at him, a little nonplussed, a little anxious.

– I know, he grinned, – I know you, but you don't know me.

She recognized his type of English accent, but not him.

He had several distinct tattoos engraved on his skin. She recognized those as well, recognized the tattoos, but not on him.

When he kissed her, it was very possessive and powerful, much more… personal and intimate compared to Odin's more distant touch.

– Look at you, a tall, dark-skinned woman mused, kissing her as well. – I hardly remember you as you are now. You have so much ahead of you, do you know that? So much bad shit you can't imagine.

– This is Leila of Darkland…

There was a red-haired woman there. Afterglow dimly recognized Cindy, but she looked very different compared to the woman Kathleen had known for years and last seen just a few weeks ago. She realized that Death danced in the green eyes and that her skull showed in glimpses behind the sinister expression.

– This is Martha, Queen of Avaldami.

Kathleen could not look directly at the beyond imposing entity. She radiated power in a disturbing way Afterglow had never quite experienced and she wanted to bow down to her. It was clear that Martha could command armies without batting an eye.

– We all know you, the beastly woman with the ebony skin stated, with something resembling a low growl.

– Then you have me at a disadvantage.

– It's only fair, Leila said, flashing her fangs. – When next we meet you will know us, and we won't know you or even ourselves.

– I do not understand.

She knew she sounded like the young girl she had once been and hated it.

– You don't need to understand yet, only to know that you one night will, will understand everything. Knowledge, as much knowledge as one consciousness may contain will fill you and you will become our equal.

Lester grabbed her. They all grabbed her, with hands and mind and powers that shook her like a rattle. She heard her own carefree laughter and wondered how she could face beings such as these with such abandon. The festivities reached its peak. Eighteen minds and bodies filled with desire touched and mingled, floating from one partner to the next in the endless sea making up the center hall of the Dark Lodge. Alice rode yet another male. Afterglow did, too. The skull only partly coated in flesh caressed her neck with lips and tongue and bone. It went on and on and on and Kathleen's slight remaining, fading apprehension dissolved into the water of the warm, warm pond.

And the dancing skull burning in dark flame burned in her eyes, even when she had her back turned. A black panther growled from the shadows and its claws scratched and cracked hard skin. Hair like blood flowed between them all and Cindy's unfamiliar face was brightened by eyes burning in green flame.

They were all pulled into the air, even as they fell on soft pillows and the Dark Lodge celebrations continued into the night, and reality dissolved around them all.

I will speak to her first, Odin said to the others just before the ceremony. I will prepare her.

She faced him, in yet another dark room filled with shadows.

– I know you are not fond of Seers, Kathryn.

Lester of Earth grabbed her, grabbed her again and the scene earlier repeated itself, but this time he spoke to her, really spoke to her in an insistent voice.

– You need to make haste, to speed up the process of our ascension.

That was all. Screeches of ravens filled her ears.

And both men were just voices in the void again, nothing but specters haunting everybody's dreams.

Cindy, the Cindy writhing on the soft ground outside the ancient ruin stood in front of the masks, the pieces of cloth staring at her with empty eyes, admiring the one, when she suddenly gasped in pain and crouched. The room turned dark. A figure stood before her, wearing the mask, the entire stunning and disquieting costume, carrying a scythe. The wraith-like creature looked indistinct framed by the shadowy portal glimpsed behind it.

It looked at her, with the dancing green flames in its eyes, its beyond deep eyes.

– I know what this is, she replied to the unspoken question, striving to breathe where there was no air, where one fill of the lungs was a lifetime. – I understand, I… accept.

The scythe flashed in dark, transparent and ethereal lighting.

She took one step forward, and so did the figure holding the scythe, and they merged, and then she, the only one there, was holding the scythe. Her eyes glowed briefly before a chilling smile transformed her half concealed face.

They sat up with a loud, collective gasp, and opened their eyes wide as they returned to the world.

CHAPTER SIXTEEN

Skies changed above them, land around them. Their surroundings shifted and rocked until everything slowly returned to a semblance of their distant memory.

The warm, warm night imposed itself on them, on their bodies, leaking through what felt like liquid eyes to their very core somewhere inside, outside their shaking bodies, the outline of the building towering above them just about visible to their senses.

– It was… morning, Martha said weakly.

– Now, it's n-night, Joshua stuttered.

– We spent an eternity on the edge of the Wasteland, Alice said brightly. – What a blast!

She stared at them with eyes staying wide, wide open.

Her eyes met Afterglow's and conveyed an astonishment and reverence even greater than before. She could not steady her eyes on any of them. Every time she tried she had to blink and look away. It was as if the very sight of them blinded her.

Only Fremantle and Caroline seemed somewhat ordinary.

– I had some idea, she mumbled, – some notion of what this was, but in truth I did not know *anything*. My lords, my ladies, I am at your bid. I am yours to command.

It was as if they did not hear her. Bewilderment and shock dominated their features and conscious thought.

Hers and Afterglow's eyes were drawn to Cindy. Cindy sat there with her arms around her raised knees. They had no trouble spotting the scythe in her hand, her left hand whitening around the strange-looking wood. Joshua and Leila, those sitting closest to her jumped away in horror. Cindy smiled, but that did nothing for them, except making them even more scared.

Afterglow reached out a hand to her. Cindy hesitated a moment, two before grabbing it. Nothing happened. She pulled herself up.

– I am more than I was. She shook her head in wonder and inevitable apprehension. – I do not even have any idea how much more I am.

Afterglow did not comment on her words. She looked fairly relaxed, even though the shivering had not stopped completely.

Leila kept shaking violently.

– We should go home, she whimpered like a very young child. – I want to go home.

– Very good, Afterglow said unmoved. – It does not truly matter. You will find yourself, no matter where you happen to be or go. Life will find you, wherever you run. Contact with the spirit realms will transform you, strengthen or weaken you in body and mind according to your strength of spirit and your potential.

She spat, as an afterthought:

– Females are quite the frail creatures in your realm, are they not? Perhaps it was not you we all encountered and experienced in the dreamscape at all, but another spirit that had overtaken yours, grabbed your spot in destiny's scheme? Or perhaps we saw nothing but lies, deception, our own fears and hopes and longing reflected back at us? Destiny is a fickle companion, after all. Nothing is certain and life's flame can be extinguished by the softest of drafts.

– You callous BITCH! Leila shouted at her.

She rolled her right hand into a fist, before relenting and collapsing on the ground.

Afterglow looked unimpressed at her.

– You will find no relief, wherever you go, until you acknowledge yourself. And what makes you think a frail creature like you can handle the rigors of the Journey through the realms anyway? Can you breathe where there is no air to breathe? Can you move when you can no longer feel your legs?

She returned her attention to Cindy. The scythe faded. It was as if Cindy put it away inside herself with a wave of a hand.

The redhead met her eyes with an excited expression all over her face.

– I felt her, felt myself through you. Thank you!

The eyes, all the difference was in the eyes.

Most of the others nodded to themselves, as if they understood something.

– I can sense so much more of the world, now. My impression of it is changed beyond imagining, transformed like I am transformed. It is so amazing, so beyond amazing.

She drew one short, deep breath.

– I can see even beyond the boundaries of this world, do so without trying. It is like I can reach out and touch what is not there and certainly not here.

The others did not share her enthusiasm. They still looked haggard, shaken. A strange and bitter smile crossed Afterglow's lips.

– It is time to go, she declared.

She turned and walked away, and the others followed her. Cindy and Alice did on light feet and with bright eyes. The group left the obvious sore in the landscape and returned to the practically untouched wilderness just beyond the rise. The dim glow of Little Moon occasionally cast shadows in the night through drifting dark clouds. Kathryn, everybody really saw the place in their blurry vision, the inner eye without looking. They knew well what they would see if they turned their head and looked back, but no one did.

And then, after more time not measurable, when they did turn and stare, it was not there.

– This, all this feels like a dream, Cindy mused happily, – but I know it is not.

No one replied to her or commented on her words.

Alice kept her eyes on Afterglow, doing so almost constantly, except when she occasionally did a sweep of the others with aware and steady eyes.

The trees and bushes around them… breathed. That evident truth had become so beyond clear to them. Cindy's green gaze twinkled with the leaves she cast her eyes at. She walked with light steps in the fairly hard-walking terrain.

They reached the end of the plain, the edge of the mountain and the terrain started descending. Leila was the first to stop not long after that. They all did. She crouched and vomited. It flowed from her mouth in an even, prolonged stream. Everybody else, except Fremantle and Caroline repeated her ordeal no more than thirty seconds later. They stood there, swaying, glimpsing each other through eyes filled with tears. Afterglow walked on. The others followed her.

The forest seemed even more foreboding, the walk-through, eerily taking longer than it had done on their way up, the recollection of them having entered it dim in their minds. They heard loud sounds behind them, weaker sounds ahead and on their sides. Then everything turned loud.

An owl hooted aloud, making Martha and Joshua jump in their tracks.

A wolf howled somewhere to the left. The sound joined with the silver slivers of Little Moon, making goose bumps appear on all uncovered skin.

– My Goddess, that's beautiful, Leila choked, filled to the brim with emotion.

The trees and its branches swayed in this night without wind.

Wary eyes glanced up at Little Moon, imagining that it did not move an inch on the unruly sky.

– Has the forest… grown? Lester wondered, looking at his watch, pushing a button, lighting the numbers.

– No. Afterglow shook her head. – The forest is without beginning or end. It is exactly the same size it has always been.

It seemed to burn around them, burn in shadow. They caught glimpses of what they had not glimpsed on their way up, what they had only seen in deep dreams earlier in life.

– You see more, because you are more.

They reached its other side and the travelers breathed in brief relief. The downward path became even steeper, the pressure on different parts of the muscles than it had been on their way up. They had to be cautious to not stumble and fall and thereby tumble down the slope in a more than hazardous way.

The valley stretched out before them, but they felt no relief when they reached its more or less flat ground.

– My skin itches, Lester complained.

– It is the Dust, My Lord, Alice told him with a sweet smile, very helpful. – It is drawn to and attaches itself to powerful hosts, becoming a part of them, aiding them on their path to power.

Then it was as if she caught herself, as if something dawned on her and she pulled back.

– What is it? He wondered. – What is wrong?

She did not reply, but kept pulling back until she walked in Afterglow's shadow. Afterglow shook her head in irritation and kept walking. Alice released a hardly audible gasp of sick relief.

– The apprentice was presumptuous, Cindy explained to the others. – She forgot herself, reached above her station and is sorry beyond belief, presenting herself to her master for punishment.

– Because the sorcerer can do with the apprentice whatever the sorcerer pleases? Leila said.

– Precisely. She was fortunate that her master decided to show lenience and that Lester is not a sorcerer. If he had been, her act would have been one of unforgivable disrespect and he would have been within his right to eviscerate her on the spot.

They continued on their trek. The fatigue and nausea, present in waves since they woke up kept them from running or running for long. There was more vomiting and dread.

– When will it let up? Stuart cried, clearly irritable, cranky and not quite himself, in any stretch of the word.

– Take comfort in the fact that it eventually will, Afterglow replied, the touch of cruelty very much present in her voice and demeanor. – Every ascending wielder of Magick suffers it from time to time.

– I've read that only neophytes do.

She gave him her sweetest smile.

– I suspected you guys, at least some of you, had studied available lore…

She sniffed a bit, drying more vomit from her jaw, pausing a bit before truly replying to him.

– That is true, as far as it goes, but it is also true that every new level a sorcerer reaches brings new dangers and travails.

They walked on in silence, all kinds of confusing thoughts churning through their consciousness. Their return-path clearly deviated from their original route, but not that much. The landmarks and their position, when they checked were not changed enough to notice without consciously considering it. The valley was an endless path of sameness giving the emotionally charged people traveling through it deep, dull chills. No one spoke anymore, lost in their thoughts, in their chaotic inner realm.

– I can feel the wrongness here, now, Stuart mumbled, – feel it so much stronger, doubting it no more.

Afterglow moved closer to him, as if actually touching him physically, not only mentally, adding her awareness to his.

– The wrongness may be stronger in some places, but it is widespread.

Everybody suddenly looked very skittish. Their senses, their enhanced senses told them that there was more happening than what they could observe in their direct line of sight.

– Don't tell me that the ghosts and demons have followed us in order to get a reckoning, Martha said, timid as usual, but also with a growing irritation.

– This is not a wrongness, Afterglow said. – It is worse!

– What do you mean? Martha growled. – What can possibly be…

Even as she finished or did not finish speaking, she frowned, a frown deepening when she saw that Afterglow had stopped. They all did, a rising anxiety manifesting in everybody. Afterglow put an index finger to her lips.

– Stand still, she told them. – Do not move, and by that I mean do not *move*.

They had become so very sensitive to her and to each other. The anxiety increased as they watched everybody else closely.

The sound started like a low rumble. They did not really feel threatened at first, but then, as the sound turned louder, it took on a distinct, sinister meaning.

– It is the herd, Afterglow stated. – It is on the move and we are close to its migratory route.

No one asked which herd. They turned cold.

– How close? Joshua whispered.

– I do not know, she replied. – I guess we will find out.

The sound of dozens of hooves hammering against the ground filled their ears, their entire consciousness. Then the dark mass entered their line of sight from the other end of the field. The direction was impossible to ascertain. It quickly became clear that it would pass not far away.

Afterglow stood relaxed on her spot. All her companions tensed to the point where their legs suffered from sudden cramps and had trouble standing still.

The unicorn herd passed them with only a dozen steps to spare. The humans were able to study them in full in the light from Little Moon. They imagined they were able to actually reach out and touch the four-legged creatures. The metallic-like horns flashed to the point of almost blinding the frozen people.

Beyond violent noise assaulted all their senses, and it lasted long, much longer than they had anticipated it would.

Slowly, only slowly the sight and sound faded from their senses. They had expected relief to flood them as they saw the herd vanish at the other end of the field, but it did not. Anxiety kept holding them in its grip.

– Let us get away from here, Afterglow said.

– Do you think they might come back? Stuart wondered stricken.

– They might.

– So they saw us, noticed we were here?

– Most certainly. Lucky for us they were in a generous mood, also because we probably did not block their path. They have been known to change their mind, though.

– You *are* funny, Leila said, looking very pale in the moonlight. – Your gallows humor is just…

She relented and stopped speaking even before her lips stopped moving, so dizzy and drained mentally that it affected her balance.

The group ran off and speeded up after just a few dozen's steps. They did not slow down, not when the Little Moon hid completely from them and not when dark clouds rolled in and the sky did not give them a single slice of light. Their feet moved and kept moving, even as dawn arrived and at least some of them felt gratitude for that small favor. They climbed the teeth, the jaws, and kept moving east. Hooves shook the ground and their nerves, but they did not actually see any more four-legged creatures.

Afterglow stopped for a moment, with her head tilted, clearly listening, before moving on. Several of them looked back, at the valley, taking comfort in the fact that it was empty or at least looked the part.

Not long after that the fatigue grabbed them again, and as the daystar appeared in the east they had to stop completely.

– The daystar is rising. Time to go to bed and dream dark passions, riding the Dark River.

Afterglow's voice sounded weak in their ears, as if reaching them from far away, but they still heard her well enough.

They found a shelter, a natural fortress, a set of rough edges of tall rocks where the daystar did not shine and they could enjoy its deep shadow and also where they were able to scout far in all directions.

Fremantle and Caroline did not sleep. They guarded the sleepers. Afterglow saw their eyes far into dream, as they constantly scouted the terrain and their ears listened for distant sounds.

She fell, and there was no end to her fall. Sometimes there was a ground somewhere far down. Other times there was nothing but darkness.

In her dreamscape, a dark land with a different moon they were not there. She caught glimpses of herself and some of the others while they slept, while they walked in a strange garden without visible light, with the occasional glow from the hovering moon.

The sleep hardly felt relaxing at all, but more like a pitiful dormancy she could not escape.

There was a long march. She was surrounded by hundreds, perhaps thousands of others clothed in arms, dressed in armor. They walked through a desolate landscape, under a burning daystar giving them no mercy. She shook her head. There was no danger, no imminent threat, but she kept shaking her head in distress.

She awoke soaked in sweat, to a soft scent of burned meat. Fremantle and Caroline had prepared a meal from a buck they had killed and roots and berries they had gathered.

The others woke up, too. They looked as out of it as she felt, but like her, there was a sense of renewal in their eyes and demeanor.

They fed, greedily, like wild beasts. The food energized them, even as the fear of the wretched nausea kept hunting them, even as the hunger made them ignore it, ignore anything but the need to feed.

– I'm so hungry, Leila munched. – I'm willing to bet I've never felt hungrier in my entire life.

It was more mumbling than speech, more sounds than words, but they had no trouble understanding her.

– There is a vast void within me waiting to be filled, Stuart said.

– It's dawn again, isn't it? Leila wondered. – I firmly believed it was dusk, but the bright light is in the east… isn't it?

– It is, Caroline confirmed. – You have slept and dreamed and rested and replenished yourselves.

– I feel good, Cindy said. – I feel great.

– In my dream the sun… the daystar raced across the sky. Leila spoke fast. It was if she could not speak fast enough. – The shadows moved like lightning on the ground and every single angle flashed with images and sensations I could not catch.

She shook her head in wonder, in horror.

– Existence is so much, so big. I always knew that, of course, but I still had no idea…

She rubbed her face in her palms, inadvertently slightly scratching herself without noticing.

– This meat has an incredible flavor, Lester shook his head. – Yesterday I would never have been able to imagine such a taste even existed.

They sat there and kept feeding, long after they should have been full. It was as if both their bodies and minds had become supercharged, hyperactive. Afterglow felt it just as potent as the rest. She felt its rise and experienced each breath as a gasp. And she noticed instantly when it turned, when exhaustion reclaimed them. She tried to rise, but failed. The others did not even try. They became sleepy again, tired again. Afterglow kept trying to resist it, to fight off the lethargy, but was unable to do so.

– It can not be stopped, she mumbled more than spoke, – but has to run its course.

She turned towards Fremantle and Caroline, half into sleep.

– Guard us, protect us.

– Of course, Caroline assured her. – Have no fear.

But suddenly the sorcerer had fear. She had known there was something out there, more than one force directed at them, and now, for some reason it was closer than ever.

Faceless shadows marched against them across vast plains, and Kathryn Caldwell could no longer tell if she slept or stayed awake somehow. Her body rested on the ground. She stood upright and so did Cindy, new, improved Cindy with the scythe in her hand.

– This is so new to me, the redhead stated calmly. – I know things I could not imagine yesterday and it does not feel new at all, but like something I have always known. Does that make sense?

Yes, Afterglow heard herself reply, knowing beyond knowing that she did not move her lips.

– They are not ready, the familiar/unfamiliar woman said and indicated the bodies with the scythe. – And neither are we. Certainly not I, and not even you. We have come further than them, but not in any way far enough. We need more… need… time.

– Time, Afterglow echoed.

And now her hollow voice joined that of her old acquaintance on the vast plains.

The arm holding the scythe moved and reality itself seemed to dissolve in the air around it.

– I am here, there and everywhere, Cindy hummed. – Do I qualify to be your apprentice, now, Janet Kathryn Caldwell of the Blue Flame, Scion of the Bone People?

Kathryn shivered all over her body, the chill long since having spread beyond her spine.

The already ethereal figure seemed to vanish altogether for a while, while Afterglow stood there sweating and staring, and a thousand winged creatures took its place, but then it returned with a vengeance and blinded Afterglow with its dark brilliance.

Horses, no unicorns thundered across vast fields, their hooves thundering far more than the ground. Nine houses in nine realms revealed themselves to the woman looking at them, being there, until Kathryn, after what felt like forever opened her eyes.

– The trials of the ages are upon us, and we have so very far to go.

Afterglow heard the echo of the last sentence as she looked around, at her companions writhing on the ground, waking up from their slumber.

She focused on Cindy, on the disoriented woman attempting to get her bearings, a far cry from the creature she had encountered in the Dreamscape.

– Are you well? She asked.

– Yes, Cindy replied. – Yes, I am.

– How much do you remember?

– Remember? There was a frown and a smile. – Quite a bit actually, but not everything. I remember the overwhelming sense of *power*.

– I do, too, Afterglow said.

The others rose around them, everybody clearly well rested and with their strength returned.

– Five hours, Fremantle informed her, almost before she had cast her eyes on him.

Kathryn noticed that Lester and Leila glanced at each other, as if sharing a secret. They had communicated in the Dreamscape as well.

Alice was there, standing straight in front of her, bright, energetic, attentive.

– Is there anything you require, Master?

– Not right now, thank you, Afterglow replied, slightly distracted, still caught in the Dreamscape, in the wasteland of her dream.

Speaking almost politely, an act making Alice study her closely.

They had another, light meal, all of them ready for departure before everything had been devoured. There was no need for words, not right now. Not many minutes later they were on their way.

The wind started blowing. It did not seem hard enough to rock them at first, but then, suddenly it did, briefly, before stopping.

The ground moved under their feet.
Fire sizzled in the grass.
Water flowed between rocks, like the blood in their veins.
It turned when they reached the watershed half into the plain, flowing with them, no longer against them, and they felt it, felt its tides and eddies…
(Like the blood in their veins).
Out there, in and around Jupiter's Cauldron something unspeakable twisted and turned.
They felt it.
It reached for them, with claws far sharper than they could muster. Swirling mists formed hands, feet and bodies, eyes big as the sky gazing at the ten chasing the wind eastward.
All of them noticed when they approached the rural and urban areas. There were no visible signs, nothing in the terrain even suggesting that they should, but they did. Afterglow spotted the signs with a few casual glances.
They felt it before they reached the edge of the burned-down forest at early dusk. And here there were signs, whirls in the air of what resembled smoke and ash. Leila bit her lip, but forced herself to bend down and touch the black wood.
– It is cold, she said. – It was cold when we left and is cold now, and has been for a long time. Why, then do I get the feeling that it is still burning?
– Because it is, Alice stated condescending, only a little worried about the consequences of her impudence, clearly feeling that Leila, as she was now was not worthy of her respect. – At least in part. Fire lingers in places like this, even more so than other places.
Leila looked at Afterglow.
– All fire is partly the remnants of the formation of the Universe, Afterglow said. – The fire was first and we are its Shadow.
It sizzled in the air, a low hum not in any way reaching them through their ears. They stopped where the terrain began descending, where the triple cities revealed themselves to them in their strangeness and glory, where they had a clear line of sight to Jupiter's Cauldron. Afterglow dried a little saliva from her jaw, as potent memories threatened to overwhelm her. The others possibly noticed, but their attention was drawn elsewhere, far at sea.
– Something is happening out there, isn't it? Lester said.
They studied it, stared at it, as bad weather spread from a fairly small point and the wind started blowing. It happened in a matter of minutes. They walked down the mountainside, caught in the sudden torrential rain. Lightning flared the eastern sky. The warm water sizzled as it hit their skin.
Leila closed her eyes as she walked, an ambiguous grin spreading on her

face.

Everybody watched as the rain hit Afterglow, glimpsing the occasional ghostly bluish taint as the droplets jumped from her skin.

– I feel better, now, honest, Leila said, her voice still shaking, – but I am still nauseous.

– You will feel like that at every new stage of your growth, Afterglow said.

She waved her hands in the air and both the air and rain sparkled and burned like would dry wood and they looked at it and her, still awestruck beyond words.

– That is the tiny price of Magick.

The triple cities rose to greet them, as they moved down the final hillside.

– I was wrong earlier, Leila said. – I said that these streets are similar to those on Earth. They aren't, aren't similar at all. These are places where people live, not merely existing. Whatever is fucked up with the people in this realm, it isn't that.

Some of the old excitement had returned to her voice and demeanor. The others caught themselves appreciating, savoring that.

– Were we… brought here? Joshua caught up with Afterglow and confronted her. – Is this our fate?

She teased him with a shrug and a devil-may-care smile.

– Humanity's greatest philosophers have debated this issue for millennia, have they not? I know for a fact that three powerful and determined human beings singled me out in my youth, but I remain unconvinced. Are we the victim of providence, the whims of the gods or are we the master of our own destiny?

People began filling the streets around them. The hum of city life sounded louder in their ears, juxtaposing on their lingering experience of the wilderness. There were cars not far away, following the modest, but evident main road out of the city.

A man stood on the sidewalk, on the corner between a dark alley and a brighter street. A car stopped right in front of him. Afterglow froze and the others, following her cue did, too.

The hood opened, opened by itself, like a jaw. The man's eyes turned distant. He seemed to leave his body. There was nothing left in there. He fell, it could even be claimed that he jumped into the jaws. The man caught in the metal jaws was devoured as they watched. Several of them screamed, even as they were unable to truly give voice to their terror.

– That's gross, Martha said disgusted, strangely unaffected.

The car burped with a pleased grin.

It approached them. It was clearly headed for them, even though there were several turns it could choose in the upcoming junction. Kathryn could easily visualize its path from there to here.

– Stand back, Afterglow cautioned them in the same calm voice she had used several nights ago.

This car had completely transparent windows. They could all see the driver, could see that he was the only one in the car. He was smiling. The smile did send shivers down Kathryn's spine, and of a kind she was unable to hold back.

The car stopped, stopped right in front of them, just as they had seen it do in their fever visions seconds earlier. The tires screeched and the metal whined.

– You have grown powerful, Blue Flame, he said. – And you have gathered powerful allies in your court, even though you have still a bit left to go before that potential is realized.

Kathryn did not respond in any way. It tickled in her hands. She wanted to fire a focused burst of power at the monstrosity in front of her, wanted it badly, no matter the risks and consequences.

– We are coming for you, Afterglow. When you least of all expect us, we will be there.

He drove off, left them as a nightmare lingering in the bright morning.

– That was one of my enemies' most recent and powerful tools, weapons magnified, Afterglow said. – I trust this lesson is not lost on you. They killed that man, a total unknown, in a deliberately horrible way, just to deliver a message.

It was not. She easily saw that, sensed that. Cold sweat covered everybody's skin.

– There is something about that man, that *creature* giving me the willies, Cindy stated.

Everybody nodded, both to the others and to themselves.

– It seems like I have outstayed my welcome in the triple cities, and so, by extension have you, Kathryn said.

She was unable to keep her surging unease from them.

– It's a good thing that we have already decided to depart then, Lester remarked casually. – As I understand it we need time.

– Time is all we need, Afterglow stated solemnly.

They saw how she got busy, how she turned even more driven. They followed her as she rushed through the Howell streets. The last stretch of their journey still made them breathless. Even though it was not physically exhausting the sense of jeopardy felt tangible and real.

On the base of the eastern mountainside between the city and the sea,

there was a property clearly distinguishing itself from its surroundings. The gate was closed and locked and everything, the entire estate seemed to be abandoned.
– We demand payment, Afterglow shouted. – We demand payment, NOW!
They heard a click and the gate opened. Everybody rushed inside. Sentries appeared, seemingly out of nowhere.
– And what has Afterglow chosen as payment? One of them queried.
– Sanctuary, she replied.
The door to the main building opened. The sentries made an honor guard for the guests. The travelers entered into a long hall brightened and darkened by torches and lamps.
It still looked pretty much like a modern place, and that was indeed how the travelers would have seen it only a few days ago, but now they knew different and viewed the world differently.
The door at the end of the hall opened, only slightly ajar. They were unable to see much inside.
– Cautious much? Stuart mumbled.
They stepped into what was a carefully selected stage. Two growling black panthers sat at each side of the carpet leading to the table at the other side of the room. Three people sat on the far side of the dark oak furniture, representatives of a faction opposing the influence of the Rosen and Maximus clans.
Afterglow sensed, without trying that her companions reacted to the presence of the panthers, the unleashed black panthers, even as she practically ignored that, too, and focused on the two men and one woman by the dark oak table.
– Congratulations, Afterglow, the woman greeted her. – Your reputation truly precedes you. You fixed our problem, one that everybody else, everybody else still alive told us could not be solved.
– Most people suffer from limited self-esteem, Afterglow shrugged.
– My name is Isobel Lysande, the woman said. – My colleagues at my side are Adrian Wonk and Mortimer Woodstone. The two between us and you are Cole and Jessie Park. We are the Ironwood.
Kathryn's trigger fingers itched harder than ever.
The intelligence in the yellowish, greenish panther eyes suddenly seemed obvious. Afterglow heard Leila gasp.
They changed, their appearance flowed like wildfire. Five, six, ten seconds later two more humans stood there nude and sweaty, their smiles a growl, more than a hint of danger.
– We are honored to make the acquaintance of Kathryn Caldwell and her

travelers, Cole Park snarled.

They all saw how Afterglow took that statement exactly for what it was worth. Her grin contained every nuance of her response.

Cole and Jessie dressed. It hardly made them seem less wild.

– We offer sanctuary to you freely, not as a part of the payment, Isobel said. – The service you have rendered us can not properly be measured.

– That is kind of you, Afterglow acknowledged. – Thank you!

– It is a wise choice on our part. Adrian spoke for the first time. – The enmity between you and the Maximus and Rosen clans had already reached epic proportions before this latest development. The fact that you are still breathing speaks highly of your survival skills. It also tells us that the clans can not truly touch an experienced sorcerer, one wielding the old power, no matter how far and high their influence reaches.

– Even vast powers beyond our realm and sphere can not touch Afterglow, Isobel mused softly.

A soft burst of excitement charged through Afterglow. They knew, a fact that told her even more about them.

– You have adequate defenses here, I gather, she said casually.

– You know we have, or you would not have bothered coming.

– We offer sanctuary, Jessie said, her green eyes gleaming. – Offer hospitality, support and friendship.

– You have our thanks and gratitude, Afterglow said, – and we accept, even though we will not need it for long.

– We know. Jessie nodded. – You are leaving the realm, but we feel confident that you will return. You always do.

You always do.

Once again Kathryn felt the poignant charge down her spine. She turned towards her companions.

– I and my apprentice have business to attend to in town, Kathryn said. – I need to pick up a few things for the Journey. I trust you will all be safe here in my absence.

Alice was at her side before she had started speaking.

– We are no longer children afraid of the dark, Cindy said with her hollow voice. – And we have you to thank for that. We will be fine.

Afterglow nodded, nodded to them all.

She turned and left, and Alice followed her down the long, dark corridor. They walked outside. There was no one there, no one visible to ordinary senses, but Afterglow and Alice easily sensed the sentries hiding in the shadows.

They sensed the defenses active in this place. And they also easily detected the secondary, currently inactive wards, if possible even more impressive. It would have felt like overkill, if they had not known what they knew.

The two of them returned to the streets, where one casual, careless move could prove fatal. They were out in the open, exposed, and it was nothing new to them.

– We are running through a gauntlet, are we not, master?

That word brought forth unease to Afterglow's already troubled mind. She shook it off.

– Of a sort. At least it can, at any given time, during specific circumstances become one.

They turned south, towards the eastern harbor. A small string orchestra played not far away, on Ivy Avenue. They had no problems hearing the music. Their ears told them the two men and two women played on the Square. To all their other senses the music seemed to come from everywhere simultaneously. They turned the corner and walked down the harbor, with its many taverns and entertainment establishments and steamy air. The singer, the same singer with a guitar still performed at the place on the right.

– He has not improved, Kathryn mumbled. – There just is no fucking hope for him!

Alice stifled a giggle with a hand.

The big clock on the wall actually showed the right time. Incredibly enough it did. Afterglow pondered that stunning fact for a moment, before casually discarding it.

The harbor was crowded tonight, as it was every night. People sat outdoors, enjoying their beer. The moisture in the air remained. It had stopped raining. People kept whetting their dry throats.

Afterglow stopped. She took another look at the clock, the no longer ailing clock, and Alice did, too, and this time it gained a significance of some kind, one not so easily discarded. They studied the people, all the people present, the sense of menace evident, but still non-disclosed.

– They do not have a clue, do they? Alice said softly.

– They do not, Afterglow confirmed.

A man spoke very loud and drank a lot. Quite a few of those present listened to him with awe in their eyes. Another sat by himself at a far off table. No one seemed to be aware of his presence at all. A couple danced on a table, their precarious balancing act turning more precarious by the second. A woman danced alone, seemingly oblivious to her surroundings. From the inside, from the dark shadows created by candles and lamps more loud and low sounds reached those who would listen.

– The clock has always been late, Kathryn said incredulous, feeling a very strong need to speak out. – For as long as I have lived here, it has never shown anything even approaching the right time.

Her words brought acknowledgement from some of those enjoying their intoxicating fluids.

There was light in the pier seven building, the same light that was always there.

A burst of irritation once more focused Afterglow's attention.

– So, my apprentice, do you sense hostile thoughts or inquiring minds tailing us this fine evening?

– Alice does not, the girl frowned. – There is nothing or no one detectable no matter where Alice directs her attention.

– I thought so, Afterglow acknowledged. – A worrying sign for sure.

She walked inside the nearest tavern, into a steamy room with a few available tables. Alice was about to head for the bar, but Afterglow stopped her with a slight move of the hand. Kathryn walked to the bar and Alice followed her. She bought two pints and handed one to Alice. They walked to the nearest table and sat down there.

– Cheers, Afterglow said raising her glass.

– Cheers, master, Alice cried.

Glasses met and parted. Alice looked at the sorcerer with huge, curious eyes.

– They serve tasty ale here, she declared.

Afterglow did not respond. She seemed to be lost in thought, even as she drank her ale.

But Alice was not fooled. Afterglow knew she was not. She saw easily how Alice saw how the other's eyes kept moving swiftly in her skull.

A man screamed somewhere. It was a loud scream and sounded like a death rattle. Afterglow (and Alice) hardly seemed to notice.

They drank more ale. It tasted great on the tongue, far greater than they could recall.

– I guess life is a series of steps making up a path, Afterglow pondered. – That thought has struck my mind before, of course, but never more so than after our recent dramatic experiences, than on this very night.

Alice listened to her as if golden words flowed from her mouth. Kathryn Caldwell ignored the warm, little voice within tempting her with its promise.

A juggler performed on the small stage. He juggled torches, knives and sticks. She recognized something in him. His hands moved the air. It distracted her.

– He has… talent? Alice mused. – Potential?

– Undiscovered, unrealized, but There, Afterglow acknowledged.

Behind him, on the wall a giant painting of a juggler seemed to mirror his movements, or, like the two of them imagined in glimpses: he mirrored the painting.

– He is a mirror image, Alice stated slowly, with a distant look in her eyes. – He is here, but never truly here.

A knife slipped in his hand, cutting his skin. The next torch on its way into his mangled hand never made it and seemed to jump from it and onto the wall, the painting, and it caught fire like dry wood and in an instant it had practically consumed itself. In one, brief blink the entire wall had caught fire. People screamed, but watched the scene with evident fascination in the eyes mirroring the plasma tongues dancing in the sizzling air.

Coughing people fled the establishment and Afterglow and Alice joined them, glimpsing the moment they exited the premises how the staff rushed forward in an attempt to put out the explosive fire.

The juggler was nowhere to be seen.

Afterglow and apprentice breathed the air. It felt crisp and refreshing juxtaposed with the poisonous smoke flowing from the doomed building behind them. Snake-like flames licked the surrounding houses. Water already flowed from hoses and hit the still fairly untouched walls.

It did no good against the flames already surrounding the building with the juggler and his painting, but seemed effective in protecting the rest.

The sorcerer returned to the building housing her home, her apprentice trailing her. They imagined that prevailing flames touched their backs. The entrance looked neither different nor threatening. The stairs resembled stairs and nothing but. The elevator was just an elevator. Her palm tingled when she pushed it at the handprint on the wall, like it was supposed to. Nothing had disturbed the wards, the ether in her Place of Power.

– It feels like we have been away forever, Alice said softly.

The outside and inside twilight dominated the place. Afterglow did not turn on any lights. She turned towards the apprentice with a stern, steady look.

– You are completely open to me, now. There is nothing even resembling walls or distortions anymore.

Alice froze, realization slowly impaling her.

– I know you killed your uncle and aunt, and your cousins.

Alice's innocent expression froze. She hesitated only a moment or two before shrugging, relenting. But her sweet voice was still very much there as she spoke her cruel words.

– Yes, I did. They all offended me. Uncle insisted on keeping me at the pleasure dome, the place turning me into a pleasant puppet and my aunt and cousins were all nagging me and encouraging me to conform and to honor the family tradition, the Mortimer family tradition of submission and pleasantries. They suffered greatly and their suffering and death created great magick.

Alice's expression turned begging and incredulous.

– How did you *know?* I swear there were times even I was not aware of my true nature. I have hidden myself so well, even from myself.

– I recognized the signs. I have always had a similar gift to conceal my inner being, to split it in two and present only one to the world. I kept one side of myself hidden from you like you tried to keep one of yours hidden from me.

The girl practically changed on the spot, as her insides stood revealed. The cunning and wickedness shadowed her pretty face.

– You have opened up to me, have you not, more than with any other person since you Fell?

The shock was still written in the young face, but faded with the innocence.

– You had help, had you not? Afterglow asked casually, ignoring the tantrum, the unpleasant words.

– I had voices whisper in my mind, yes. I made a deal with them. It was not really a sacrifice at all. They wanted me to attach myself to you and I willingly obliged. It is as I told you: you have survived the Kal Chek, the Ascension *twice*. You are the sole heir to the power of the Blue Flame, the fucking *Blue Flame*. The blood of the Bone People flows through your veins. And then there is the small matter of your… your brethren, with powers perhaps even rivaling yours. How could I *not* wish to be your apprentice, your devoted slave, to glow in the presence of you all? I knew you would make mincemeat of everybody seeking your destruction, that you would prove worthy of your apprentice's devotion.

Her eyes, her very being revealed, now, were still filled with admiration, with worship.

Afterglow's voice, when she spoke hardly sounded like a voice at all.

– You are like an overgrown kitten, still suckling at your mother's nipples. You disgust me!

The apprentice shook with the onslaught of the sorcerer's contempt.

Then, in one slip, one glimpse where the sorcerer lost her focus the girl saw what Afterglow had concealed from her, the giant behind the giant and it made her gasp in even further rapture.

– I see you, see the true you. Afterglow is indeed gifted and clever, so beyond powerful.

The girl fell on her knees and cast her eyes down, stricken beyond words, shivering in ecstasy.

– Hail Queen Cathy of the nine realms. Alice is proud to be Her lowly subject and will follow Her every command with eagerness beyond worship. She will be one of many knives slicing the throat of Her enemies.

The eyes cleared, but kept shining.

– Yes, that is the name Alice keeps hearing in her mind, the name that will be shouted from the rooftops to the deepest cellar in thy empire.

Afterglow walked to the sink, turning the tap, gathering a little water in her palm. She returned to the kneeling, blissful girl and splashed the water on her forehead. It burned the skin. The girl released a happy moan.

– You are now a witch, Kathryn said, – a sorcerer in your own right. I give you your devours, your life, and wish you good luck.

The smile faded on the innocent face.

– I can feel it, Alice frowned, – feel the power and its control rise within me.

She remained on her knees.

– Thank you, My Queen. Now, I can serve you so much better.

Afterglow ignored her. She walked to the closet where she stored her things. She pulled out a rucksack, the black blade, the pair of bracelets and a few other items.

– You are l-leaving, Alice asked, incredulous again, – truly leaving?

– It is long overdue, Afterglow nodded. – I am done with this place and I am done with you. Nothing keeps me here anymore.

– But I am the one that should be leaving, Alice said.

– You may do so, but that is your decision, not mine. I am leaving. If you want to stay, consider this place my parting gift to you.

– Alice is honored, the girl said, – thank you. She knows the queen will be back, when she is ready, and Alice will prepare everything for her return.

Afterglow put the half-full sack on her back, making sure it did not close off her access to the sword. She nodded pleased and headed for the door.

– There is still so much you can teach me, Alice said. – You are so much crueler than I am.

Even as she walked with her back turned the older woman saw the girl kneel and her eyes cast to the floor in what was an undeniable subservient posture.

The elevator door closed behind Afterglow, cutting off the voice, the last bit of poison stemming from her former apprentice.

The road ahead opened wide for Afterglow.

CHAPTER SEVENTEEN

The world had changed. She had changed.

The colors looked different. The ocean scent had a different flavor.

She stepped out of the elevator. The moment she drew breath, as she walked down the stairs the air tasted so much better in her mouth. It felt like it filled her body.

Beatrice waited for her in the lobby. The sight did not really worry her or brought much anxiety to her mind, not as much as it once would have.

– You feel good about yourself, now, do you not? Even though seemingly sweet Alice, our extended arm managed to fool you through all the tests you put her through. Her devotion to you is total, you know. We could never truly sway her from that. She is exactly like you described her, a little girl suckling her mother's nipples. There is nothing she will not do for you.

Afterglow did not reply. She did stop and she did face the ethereal girl confronting her.

– You should not, though, the spirit said. – There is certainly no reason why you should, not now, and not by the past we share.

Kathryn strived to keep her voice even, even though she knew she did not fool the creature.

– I found friendship, secrets and boundless passion. You too would have if you had not been so criminally self-absorbed.

Beatrice laughed, a hard, cruel laughter that sounded very real.

– I discarded all that, like yesterday's laundry. My birthright was to transform, to transcend, to *ascend*… until you ruined everything for me.

The voice turned poisonous, snarling.

– And you will pay. You will pay in blood and spirit, with your very soul.

And that was all there was to it this time. The apparition faded away. Kathryn felt base, unavoidable relief.

She rubbed her wet lips, as she walked through the door and returned to the busy streets.

People stared at her with their dull eyes. That had not changed.

Mrs. Galbraith approached her on the sidewalk, clearly willing to give her more than the usual piece of her mind. Kathryn sighed, not really that discouraged.

– You are not in a hurry, are you, Ms. Caldwell? The woman said sweetly.

– I am not in a hurry at all, Mrs. Galbraith, Afterglow said pleasantly.

– Very good, then I would like your opinion on something, if you do not mind.

Afterglow frowned, wondering if there was more than the usual hint of irony in the woman's voice.

– Follow me, please.

She did, without thinking twice about it.

Dull eyes pierced her soul and pricked her skin.

The light in pier seven beckoned. It seemed to twinkle and burn in Afterglow's mind. They crossed the street. There was no traffic, but Caldwell still heard snarling cars everywhere. She looked around her with pained eyes. There was nothing there she could pinpoint or point to. She almost doubled over in sudden nausea. When she tried to focus on the other woman she was unable to do so. It was all just a blur, a maelstrom of nothing.

They walked through the open door. A chill embraced Kathryn. She turned to ice all over.

Mrs. Galbraith turned, a wicked, excited smile transforming her mundane mug.

– That was easy enough, she spat in triumph, – almost ridiculously simple, in fact.

Cold sweat broke all over Afterglow's body. She could move, but the air felt like mud. Moving felt like a momentous effort.

Mrs. Galbraith slapped her cheek. Kathryn gasped, a sudden weakness overwhelming her.

– Stay still, that is a good girl, stay still and be a good girl.

Everything darkened around her. She stood straight and could not move, not move a limb.

The woman's voice changed dramatically, into one very familiar, but Kathryn still could not place it, not until the plush face changed as well and Susan Howard appeared before her.

– Surprise? She grinned.

A wicked and triumphant grin.

– This is such a genius setup, Susan chuckled. – I knew this great venture would succeed, of course, since I remember well that it did, but I guess there were no guarantees, not until now, when you have stepped into my maw and my dreams have become a reality, have become real.

She practically burst with triumph, with wicked pleasure.

– My master left me with very specific instructions. I could not drain you, since he has a need for all your juice. So I contain you, and keep you from accessing your powers. So simple and so hard. I am *so* good at this!

She rolled her hand into a fist. Pain charged through Afterglow, one she was totally unable to give voice to, and therefore hurt all that more.

– He gave me permission to play with you a little, though. He loves to see me play, like a cat with a mouse.

She circled the prey a little, caressing it a bit, causing it to squirm in pain and discomfort.

– My master is such a genius. Do you know what he *did?* He sent me back in time, to prepare, to catch you at what he knew would be your most vulnerable moment.

Kathryn saw herself, saw how she was caught in a tunnel of spells from the very moment she stepped outside, how the trap grew more powerful and irresistible with each step she made, until it sprung in full the moment she stepped inside the dreaded pier seven.

The building chuckled darkly in her ears, like a car's mouth. The laughter weakened her further.

– You are *needy,* are you not, Afterglow? That kind of person is always easy to control, to wrap around your finger. You thought you were so strong, so confident, and felt so good about yourself, but you are nothing but a shivering ball of insecurities.

The happy woman danced and swayed around her prey.

– He filled all the need in me, making me very powerful. I stood in the winter garden during twilight, surrounded by windows reflecting me and everything inside, and I knew I would succeed. One day I will tell you about your friend Cochran, how satisfying it was to take him out, to make him suffer. He still is, you know, suffering, and it will never stop, and you will know that beyond doubt when you join him in eternal pain. I walked with him, to my estranged family, and they did not recognize me. They were not even close. I did not recognize me. I was such a bore, but now I am everything I have ever dreamed of being. Cochran was a sloppy, unskilled and weak prick and that cost him, cost him everything, and it was all so very satisfying.

The wicked, ecstatic smile seemed to spread to her entire body.

She snapped her fingers.

– Listen up.

And Kathryn, with her addled mind and puppet body turned very attentive.

– You are a package, nothing but a delivery, and like all good packages you will not be idle. Do you understand, puppet?

– I understand.

She hardly heard her own voice, hardly had a sense of self at all. It was all turned off.

– Walk then, sweet Kathryn, into the maws of fate. I have places to go, people to meet and when you and I meet again everything will be different.

It was like a map drew itself in Kathryn's mind. Susan faded away before her eyes. Afterglow started walking. She left pier seven and yet again returned to the busy streets of Howell. Her walk felt stiff, doll-like, but she suspected that other people hardly noticed that at all.

She choked, frightened, panic-stricken, unable to express herself in any way. The roar of a thousand maws rose in her addled mind.

Her path took her off the eastern harbor. She turned right and walked up Ivy Avenue. The scream bottled itself up in her throat, not even close at giving voice to itself. The map kept drawing itself in her head, showing her beyond fear where she was heading, where the dreaded path would take her.

She turned right again, setting the course for the western harbor. The dark streets and alleys did not really impress themselves on her. Nothing did, except the command droning on inside her head and puppet body. Fog drifted in from the south tonight. It seemed to envelop her, invade her mind. Whispers urged her on. She did not understand what the voices kept saying, but she obeyed them like a lullaby in her confused mind. A tear flowed down her cheek. She blinked, but kept moving, kept putting one foot in front of the other.

Narrow streets and alleys shrunk even more in her eyes as she approached the ferry harbor, passed the guesthouse to the left where most of the passengers of the wayward ship were holed up, frightened and distressed. The green color looked grayish and pale. Her feet stepped on the still bloody ground. She struggled, she did in an effort to free herself from the terrible hold of the spell, in vain. Every time she tried, the slightest resistance on her part brought pain and desolation and all bad things. She became hardly more than a tiny speck drifting in the wind.

The ferry awaited her, covered in mist and cold. There were no other people present, no one she could see, not on the harbor or in the warehouse or anywhere onboard. She imagined she saw cruel eyes studying her with badly concealed expectation. The mouth, the hungry mouth opened up before her, only for her. She walked inside. The maw closed. She sat down. The ferry started on its journey across the sound. The lone woman sat absolutely still during the entire journey.

She imagined things happened outside the seafaring vehicle, even inside, close to her ears and eyes and mouth, but she did not sense any of it. Oblivious to the world she neither blinked nor moved.

The mainland faded behind her. The Island grew to a mountain in her unmoving eyes. It pierced the ceiling of her sky.

She hardly noticed when the ferry hit land, attached itself to the quay. The journey ended. She rose on numb feet. The door opened. She walked outside. Susan waited for her with an ecstatic smile on her red-painted lips.

– You are here, she marveled. – Just like you are supposed to be. This is fantastic. This is absolutely fantastic.

This was a different, previous version of Susan, not the confident, cruel sorcerer Afterglow had encountered less than an hour ago, but still an insecure, unfulfilled apprentice.

– You are a package, are you not, nothing more than package?

– I am a package, Kathryn replied evenly, as she kept staring straight ahead. – I am not idle.

Susan giggled in incredulity and triumph. She was suddenly drunk with power.

– Come then, package, come with me!

The map, the droning whispers inside Kathryn agreed. She walked through the door Susan opened for her. Susan sat down in the driver's seat, and they were on their way.

– You know where you are headed, do you not? She said deviously. – You know what fate awaits you.

– I know, Kathryn replied in the beyond servile voice, the horror and terror below the surface never manifesting itself openly.

– You know because I told you.

– You told me.

Susan clapped her hands in pure excitement, briefly taking her hands off the wheel.

– The great Afterglow, she chuckled, – no more than a puppet dancing on my strings.

– Puppet, Afterglow moaned in distress.

The dread kept assaulting her in droves. Impressions of her surroundings, not the surroundings themselves ripped into her. She could not help it, as the knowledge of what was happening filled every bit of her consciousness.

The road made a turn and a familiar, oh, so dark building appeared in her vision. A sound moved through her, from toe to head. She once again made an effort to break free, in total vain. She did not make a single dent in the shackles binding her.

– This is where it all began, all those years ago. Susan's face lit up some more. – This is where a young, non-descript, weenie girl took her first steps on her path to infamy. That is so cool, so very cool.

Kathryn Caldwell remembered the learning place as foreboding, but not this foreboding, not this monster haunting her every moment.

Susan stopped the car outside the main entrance.

– Come with me, weak puppet, she snarled viciously. – It will end where it began.

Caldwell trailed what seemed like a giant into the empty building. Somewhere in the darkness that was the open mouth she glimpsed Beatrice and her eager, innocent smile.

– The sacrificial lamb will not dawdle.

Susan snarled and struck a cruel blow on her butt.

Everything hurt now, hurt bad, even the slightest meanness.

Kathryn choked and could not stop choking, realizing, somewhere in her dim-witted consciousness that the spell shackled her mind just as much as it did her body. It was so effective and insidious.

The happy smile of a young girl flashed before her eyes.

– Will you help me, sweet witch?

– I will help you, Janet replied.

The giant mouth opened up to them, to young her and Beatrice, to vicious Susan and older Kathryn. The entrance welcomed them all.

They walked down, down dusty stairs, to murky depths. There was not a single person anywhere. The learning place was empty of people, abandoned to the tender mercies of the upcoming clandestine activity of the dark and vacant spaces.

The shackled and drawn Afterglow was brought to the small hall at the end of the basement corridor. Every step felt dreadfully familiar to her, as if she had just made it.

Sounds reached her through the open door, juggernauts of fear and memory. She imagined she knew exactly what awaited her in there. It was only when she stepped across the threshold that the illusion of familiarity ended and an equally horrible reality came crashing down on her.

The room looked completely different from the way she remembered it. Stane welcomed her with a cruel smile.

– There you are, he said pleased and wicked. – Better late than never.

She wanted, wanted so much to reply to him, but realized that she could no longer speak. Her larynx was as frozen as the rest of her body.

– It worked, Master, Susan cried excitedly, and then frowning confused. – Or it will work?

– I assure you it has already worked, he said, he declared with thick triumph in his voice. – The fact that the package is here is proof good enough.

He turned and switched on the lights. A sick red glow filled the room. Caldwell saw his machines, his machinery, his laboratory, with its rising fumes and flaring fluids in a vivid and clear illumination of deep and stark red.

– Yes, he told her, – I am a man and sorcerer favoring machines, thereby streamlining and simplifying the process, making it less messy, more efficient.

He was a man of words, Kathryn knew that.

And to Susan:

– Secure the package.

Susan grabbed Caldwell and pulled her to one of the central contraptions. She pushed her back at the stretcher-like vertical table and pulled straps around Caldwell's ankles, thighs, belly, neck and wrists and arms. Kathryn knew she was trapped, unable to free herself even if she could have moved.

– Does the sword sheath on your back make you uncomfortable? Poor girl…

It did. For some reason that tiny detail made the captive feel far worse. The smallest hurdle seemed to grow tall and seemingly intolerable. She sniffed like a little girl.

The wicked smile came closer, so close that it was possible to feel the heat from the blushing skin. Hands began fondling her, brutally, invasive. Caldwell whimpered in discomfort and despair, unable to feel the slightest rage.

– You are truly helpless. I can do whatever I want with you without you being able to resist. That is so cool, so very cool, and I can not wait for the moment when I spellbind you, when I catch you and make you like this.

She stepped back, blushing in pure excitement.

– Very good, now, come here, allow me to complete the circle, fulfill your education.

The apprentice rushed forward and stopped before him, glowing like a little kid about to receive sweets.

– You know what to do? You read her like an open book?

– Yes, Master, I know exactly what my final service to you will be, what needs to be done for me to truly earn my freedom. Your instructions are engraved on my astute mind.

He bowed down, sampling a piece of dirt from the floor and pushed it at her forehead.

– Congratulations, you are an apprentice no longer, but a sorcerer in your own right, able and willing to do as you please. I welcome you as a colleague and fellow independent magick-wielder.

The young woman straightened, not changing physically, but visibly changing from the inside before both their eyes.

– One more essential task remains, Susan Howard breathed. – Thank you, Stane, thank you so much.

– Step into the pod then.

The pod waited for her with its open door and weakly greenish and powerful deep red glow. The door closed. Stane pushed a button on his control pad. The very air seemed to bubble around her. She gasped, as if having difficulty breathing, as the energies coursed through her. The buildup picked up, the bubbles surrounded her.

– I see, she mumbled. – I see so much.

The other two in the room also glimpsed images around her, as if she traveled with the coach and horses through the land between the way station and the Dark Lodge.

Countless vast reaches of reality burned their eyes.

It lasted a few more seconds, and then she faded away and was gone from their sight. The pod turned dark and empty.

Stane turned towards Caldwell.

– Yes, this is my Place of Power, existing both in my house and here, an upgrade to beat all upgrades. And it is only fair that I bring you back here, to your greatest, most defining moment. There have been others, both before and after, but this, what happened here, more than anything defined you, made you the great force you have become. Every hope you might have entertained about the greatness of mankind was crushed at this place.

She sensed his confidence, his certainty of being in the right, the arrogance filling his being. And the words he spoke sounded so right, so true.

– Surely you can now appreciate my genius? I acted to make sure that what had already happened would happen. By one decisive stroke I made fate itself side with me.

Kathryn wanted to agree with him. She wanted to scream out her fearful agreement.

He switched a few buttons on the central control pad. The fluids started bubbling some more. She felt how the entire machinery came to… came to life. The parts of her in contact with it started tingling.

– You may enter, now.

He said, to someone Kathryn could not see.

A scared and timid woman Caldwell dimly recalled entered the laboratory from the outside, from the building's backyard, through the bright-lit entrance. She looked just as out of it, just as much unable to command her faculties as Caldwell felt.

– One touch, he shouted. – One touch is all it takes.

Images of the Howell streets and the woman she had had briefly hunted flowed through Caldwell's consciousness.

– You were the one that got away, that cheated. You know that is unacceptable. Those running the Gauntlet are through, gone from this world. Those are the rules.

He spoke to Kathryn all the time and ignored the other woman. She was nothing but a prop to him, a tool to utilize and discard.

There was a dull pain. Caldwell realized that he had struck her. Blood filled her mouth and amazingly cleared her head.

– You may scream, now.

And she did, and the pain rocked her to her core.

She breathed once, twice, thrice, as her ability to reason and act in a limited way returned.

– W-why?

The restraints and the spells still kept her from accessing her powers, but no longer numbed her.

– I know what you mean, even if I am surprised you would ask such a stupid question.

He struck her again, hard. Something broke. He slapped and struck her repeatedly. She moaned in horror, overwhelmed by the suddenly vivid memories, no longer able to contain even the smallest emotion.

– It is like I said: you are the one that got away. You broke our deal. I am a barterer. I live and breathe by the deal's worth. Where would I be if I allowed such a transgression to go unpunished and unheeded?

– In a ditch, she spat, suddenly filled with rage. – Exactly where you will end up.

He pushed another button. The power of the machinery cut into her.

She gasped horribly as the ravaging pain filled every piece of skin and bone and flesh she possessed.

– I love that rage. It will make everything so much potent and valuable. The Gauntlet will end and as an added bonus I will get everything Afterglow has become and ever was. Even her very potential will be mine to play with as I please. I will steal your destiny and make it mine, add its meager feast to my infinite self.

Dark lightning sparked at the edges of the apparatus.

– They say with patronizing flair that I am only an alchemist aspiring to the honor of being a sorcerer, or equally bad: that I am a sorcerer reaching below my station, but I will be more powerful than you all. I will become a god. I will become God. I will move beyond the Kal Chek, the Ascension, beyond blood and heredity and become the dominant force in the Universe.

Afterglow chuckled, forcing herself to put even more oomph into it than what was already bubbling below her surface. He froze.

– You are nothing, she grinned wickedly. – Nothing but a little boy wet with tears because they will not give you your toy.

He picked up two wires from the floor. He pushed their end at her body. Clips attached themselves to already sore skin. Her scream shook the building, shook the ether itself.

She hung there, in her constraints less than a rag doll. Her scream turned into a wail. She started sobbing and could not stop herself from sobbing. Nightmarish images accompanied the pain of the body.

– Daddy? She whispered. – Mommy, where is DADDY?

Tears flooded her bloody face. She shook as violent shakes tore into her.

Stane grabbed her jaw, almost kindly. She stared at him through a thick wall of terror and despair.

– Playing me, she mumbled. – You are playing me like a fiddle. YOU BASTARD!

When she stared at him she saw Beatrice, Peter, Florence and everyone that had ever done her harm.

She shifted between the extremes of emotions, just as helpless to control the changes the instruments imposed on her, as she was to command her limbs.

– Please, she begged him. – Please!

Despair overwhelmed her. She shook silently, without any force behind it, just hung there in her constraints. His eyes hovered above her, huge and bad.

– And I do it because I can and because you are *ripe*. Look at you! Poor Kathryn. Hardly even alive, in the normal sense, in any sense of the word. Everything you have suffered is shaking you apart. You are just a dead thing walking around, imagining you are still breathing. I am doing you a service.

She fought herself up from the mire of her desolation, pulling herself together yet again, focusing her entire attention on him, on her Enemy.

– I know about betrayal, she gasped, mumbling, fighting to speak through her ruined mouth. – It does not impress me. I was on to you from the start. I would be stupid if I was not.

He was not impressed, but just grinned and shook his head in appreciation.

– I knew you were on to me, he grinned.

– I knew you knew I was on to you, she grinned

She got to him, she knew she did, and it gave her a tiny modicum of satisfaction.

– Enough, he snapped. – If you believe you can snare me with confident words and bravado you are sadly mistaken. I have picked you apart piece by piece and now I will take what remains.

– I know what you are doing, she said, while pain kept racking her. – You're reenacting…

– Reenacting nothing, he boasted. – Though there are indeed details in Beatrice and Malone's machinations and methods that certainly are worthy of being included in my superior design.

The noise from the machinery rose to a level louder than she could bear. Her ears turned numb as invisible probes cut into her, taking her measure.

He held up a mirror. The face she glimpsed through the thick mist looked worse than ever. He slapped her lightly and something more broke somewhere. Her head fell down and rolled back and forth on her shoulders. He caressed her cheek and it hurt, hurt worse than anything. She choked and once again turned completely limp in her restraints. He nodded pleased.

– You believe this is pain, do you? You are convinced this is the worst it can get.

She frowned and nodded, looking at him through a haze of apprehension.

He snapped his fingers, and something happened, something beyond bad she was unable to wrap her feeble mind around.

A… figure appeared in the air in front of her, a man enclosed in an energy bubble with no fixed borders. He was stretched out and his body was penetrated by giant needles.

– You wanted to know what happened to Cochran? Well, here he is.

She stared at Cochran with disbelief. He hurt, she knew he did, but no sound erupted from his wide open mouth. He was still breathing somewhat, even though he was more dead than alive. He looked at her and she could not look away. It was not just the needles. The very surroundings that held him in its cruel grip hurt him, ripped his flesh and mind to pieces, and it was an ongoing, unending process of suffering, one insidious and cruel beyond anything she had imagined she could imagine. His eternal, infinite pain borrowed into her and she imagined she felt all those needles, everything the infernal process put him through.

– No, she wailed, the senseless panic actually making her able to move, – please, NO!

– You know what this is, Stane chuckled pleased. – That is so pleasing to me, so thoroughly satisfying. His suffering will continue forever… and so will yours.

Cochran faded slowly, and as he faded his pain became hers. His body… collapsed into a heap of flesh and bones, but he was still alive.

Kathryn screamed herself hoarse. Stane's machinery gutted her and cut her wide open on every single piece of her body and mind, and long after she had no more voice her flesh and bone and mind kept screaming. She became Cochran or feared she did - became his eternal punishment.

Only a wet rag remained. Nothing held her anymore, but there was no active strength left in her tortured flesh and tormented mind.

– You are ready, now, ready to give me everything you are.

The loud whimper of the deepest possible misery was the only response she was able to give him. Even the release of that tiny sound hurt, twisted her eternity one more notch.

Cochran was inside her. She felt him, felt his unending ruined beyond recovery soul.

Stane started moving his bloodied hands through the air, started making his magick. He pushed his palms at a paper spread out on the table in front of him and started speaking his spells.

The room changed again. Kathryn felt the imposing touch of his presence. She drifted off by the power of his magick. His scalpels cut her being piece by piece. She kept fighting somewhere in her tortured self, but failed. His reality invaded her, harder than before and without mercy. She tried to fight, but could not even do that. There was no will left to access. He had cut her off from herself. It was so insidious that she almost felt pride on his behalf.

He followed every nuance of her thoughts, what little was left in the ruins of her soul. She noticed as he probed all the processes of her mind.

– It is quite something is it not? His smile covered her entire vision. – You never had a chance. Existence itself was stacked against you. From the moment you were caught by my scheme you were doomed.

He rubbed her forehead.

– I know about your second, wicked personality as well, the one you and Beatrice called Cathy and made certain that both of you would be subdued. I make it my task to properly study my business partners, even my potential business partners. I suspected you already had a way out the moment you agreed to the Gauntlet and that you would not agree to it if you did not see it as crucial. You needed the Eye for something, needed it badly. What was it?

She tried to tell him, wanted to tell him. He made her want to tell him. But there was nothing there, just a hole where the memory was. She frowned and despaired and strived and chastised herself because she was unable to obey him. Tears kept flooding her sweaty and bloody and ruined face.

– No matter, he grunted, – I will find out. Eventually I will know everything about you, and you and many others will only be tiny pieces of my being. This is delicate work, after all and I can not expect everything to work without a glitch. I am a scientist, not God, not yet.

He stepped back. She felt it, as his spells and machines started draining her, as it started pulling her apart in earnest, doing so from her deepest core to her outer shell and beyond. He consulted his screen and his face brightened even more.

The other woman with the empty eyes stepped forward from the shadows. She approached the two of them.

He pushed another button. Caldwell felt it in an instant, for the second time, the charge of the Gauntlet. Suddenly she did not feel weak anymore. She was still locked away from herself, but the rising of the power was an exhilarating experience. Despair left her in a whiff and a sick smile transformed her face.

– I am still amazed by the willpower it took for you to resist the power of the Gauntlet the first time, but this time you will have no willpower to draw on. There will only be the power and the need, the irresistible need to move it forward, and then you will not be my concern anymore.

She nodded in acknowledgement, knowing his statement to be correct. It bloated her, irresistible and she was drowning. Her very self was drowning.

And she recognized that feeling, that numbness of complete surrender.

– NO! She shouted and was amazed that she could still vocalize her concerns. – No, please! No no no

The last words were nothing but whimpers.

His cruel laughter mingled with her memories as well.

It tingled within her, the buildup, as she moved, moved through the streets, as she felt good, felt so good, as the practically infinite power rose within her. Perception changed with every step she took. The drizzle of water and ash wet and dried her face. Desperation and despair kept warring within her and both won.

She peed on herself. The event brought no terror, but was a part of the massive and pure excitement filling her. The tiny frown in her deepest thoughts hardly manifested on her face. She ran, she was certain of it. Her feet moved and touched the ground, and she chased through the night. She smelled and tasted coffee, the best coffee she had ever enjoyed. The sudden astuteness pushed at her in waves. Breathing remained ragged. It was as if minutes constituted seconds and seconds constituted minutes. Every bit of fatigue seemed to evaporate from her consciousness and from her limbs. Doubt lingered for a second, then vanished. A storm…

– A storm, she gasped. – A STORM IS BREWING.

Thunder rocked the building. Stane shook imperceptibly, even as he laughed in anticipation.

A blink lasted a thousand years. She began chuckling. It flowed from her like it would a baby. She pondered what was happening to her. It felt like low burning acid flowed through her veins. And the hum, the hum inside rose to insane levels. So many people, but she did not see them. One single figure, one single woman five steps away pointed itself out to Caldwell, glowing in her wet eyes.

The music filled her, becoming something else, something far more. She hardly saw Stane anymore at all. He was merely an insignificant shadow on the edge of her reality. Her feet moved, she knew they did. She felt the soles touch the ground beneath her feet. Images assaulted her. Sounds, smells and tastes. *Touches without touches*. And whispers and insults, and hopes and dreams.

– I am *doing* it, Stane cried out, – riding, controlling one of the primal forces of existence.

She wished he, with his whining, his insignificant voice would shut up, would leave her alone.

– The Gauntlet, she mumbled, excited beyond words. – This is my moment, oh, goddess. Goddess!

It was as if every pair of eyes surrounding her stared at her, at *her*. Voices whispered and hissed. She remembered.

– I REMEMBER!

The wild laughter shook every single particle for miles, for miles squared.

She shook free of her bonds, removed them as if they were not there. Five steps, five steps were all it took to reach the glowing woman right in front of her. She grabbed the already shaking figure. The woman was caught in her grip, claws against skin. It went on forever. Caldwell screamed. It felt like she was sucked out of herself, wrenched, turned inside out, far worse than the previous time she hardly recalled anymore. She felt flesh move and settle a thousand times in her body. The pain she had felt before, Cochran's pain that she believed to be so bad was like nothing compared to this. Skin flowed like mercury. Her features changed, transformed into something new and startling. She recognized the sensation. Terror filled her once more. She remembered.

The scream ended with endless silence. Caldwell fell to the floor and collapsed there, weak as a kitten, drained and twisted inside out a million times.

The nameless woman did not see anything except Stane. He was her entire world.

– It tingles, she moaned. – It tingles BAD.

The forces already shook her, rising much faster and much more potent compared to all the previous participants in the Gauntlet. She was the end, the final progenitor.

– Walk to the pad, he directed her casually. – That's a good girl.

She had started walking before he had started talking, her moves stiff, doll-like.

He looked down on Caldwell, at her weak, wasted form.

– Look at you, he said, shaking his head. – You have become such a sweet, pretty thing. I bet you would hardly recognize yourself. Will you thank me or curse me, I wonder, when you look at yourself in a mirror?

She looked puzzled and bewildered at him, moaning at the slightest attempt at moving.

– You will recover from your weakness, of course, but by then it will not matter. I do not need to kill you and have no desire to see you dead. I want you in my Universe.

The woman stepped into the same pod Susan had used. Its door closed behind her. The discharge, the energy buildup began almost immediately. The thick wires of transparent material slowly brightened.

Waves of nausea kept coursing through Kathryn. Very little worked. Vomit pushed up her throat. She could hardly focus on Stane or anything at all.

– The power levels are amazing, he marveled, unable to look away from the display lighting up before his eyes. – I truly underestimated them, underestimated you.

His patronizing laughter shook her.

The pod at the opposite side of the room and apparatus started glowing as well. It hummed its siren call.

– Ah, that is my cue. Rejoice, pretty girl, you are about to witness the birth of God.

Kathryn crouched on her side, moving a limb here and a limb there, but unable to make a production out of it. She could not avoid seeing everything that was happening. Hope and despair kept coursing through her. One blink was forever.

There was the hum. She did not recognize it at first, in her boundless stupor, but then, there it was, a tangible and beyond potent presence. It filled her, strengthened her beyond belief.

The sphere… appeared. There was the hum a first, as it moved through empty hallways, as it broke through a thousand roofs and walls and floors, approaching from the far end of existence. The Orb of Eternity hovered halfway between the ceiling and the floor. Stane froze just in front of the pod, the seething pod. He looked at it and her with his mouth open.

– What…

He shook his head in amazement, as a kind of understanding dawned on him.

– This is your card, your final gambit? I knew you were hiding something, knew it. You are amazing, absolutely amazing.

The orb grew and changed form, and he could not take his eyes off it and neither could Kathryn.

It changed into a human being, one very similar to the crouching figure on the floor.

– Kill Stane, Afterglow said casually. – Disintegrate his very being.

The floating form tilted its head, as if listening. Then it flowed towards the frozen, incredulous man. It stopped right in front of him, facing him. He tried to move, to evade the attack, but was unable to do so, completely at the mercy of the irresistible force grabbing and shaking and attacking him. He screamed in pain, and Afterglow, suddenly filled with power laughed giddily.

Dark, seething eldritch energies flowed from the pod and enveloped the transformed Orb of Eternity. Mere traces of it touched Stane, but not doing him any good.

Stane the Barterer *screamed.* There was hardly any consciousness in that scream, that howl, only a pain transcending all pain.

pain

Pain of an entire Universe, never-ending, reducing what he had made Cochran and Caldwell feel to a trifle.

His eyes spoke volumes to Caldwell. They opened up to everything, transferring it to her. She shrugged it off in her beyond powerful glee.

He fell to the floor, lying still, cut to pieces by a power he had been utterly unable to imagine or in any way comprehend, his open eyes nothing but cold dust.

– That shut you up…

Afterglow rose on steady feet. It was as if all fatigue she had ever felt was gone from her limbs.

– I made the Orb of Eternity, she told him. – I created it from my son's bones, even as I was devouring his flesh. Every single place it visited it was my eyes and will guiding it.

The entity turned towards her. Caldwell rose from the floor and levitated in the air, like it did. They hovered there, face to face, making it seem like the easiest act in the realm.

– You are a part of me, they choired. – We are One!

There was more pain, more of a trifle, as both figures seemed to dissolve, to become millions of pieces flowing towards each other, merging into one being. Clothes worn by one fell to the floor. The new creature screamed in joy and happiness and triumph.

A thousand angles coalesced into one.

Kathryn Caldwell stood there, transformed. The voices whispered and hissed, no longer surrounding her, but resting within her, in every cell and synapse. There was a vast, deep dark ocean she floated through. There were points, pinpricks of bright light, and then there was Shadow.

We are paintings, hanging on a wall, retouched and polished, and we do not see the large holes, the large fields and chunks missing.

She easily identified the voice, identified herself.

The machinery crumbled all over the room, as if all its juice had gone away. It did not take long and there was hardly any noise to speak of. Its final parts, a few nuts and bolts rolled across the floor before lying still. The woman emerged from the remains of the pod, shaken but still alive, still vibrant, completely free from the woes of the Gauntlet. Afterglow looked at her, looked at herself through the other's eyes.

The connection to what had been Stane's house, Stane's aerie broke with a loud crack. This was now nothing more than yet another part of the school. The huge hole of nothing had vanished, vanished completely, along with everything else making this place and the other special. She had snapped her fingers and made it so. The cold grin lit up her face.

She felt it, across the sound how that house cracked in its foundations, how it in just a few minutes deteriorated and broke and turned into something that more than resembled a derelict building. It had become a dead place, totally devoid of power.

The room turned still, absolutely silent and still. She looked down at Stane.

– I knew people would come for me, and probably make a fairly good attempt at vanquishing me, and I prepared for that, for that, too, she said softly. – Get in line.

But he was already a withering husk on the floor.

– Thank you, she said with a grateful smile to the dry husk, the withered skeleton surrounded by the nuts and bolts it had loved so much.

She kicked its skull, kicked it loose from the body and it rolled across the floor, until it stopped at the opposite wall. The bones turned to dust as she watched.

Afterglow looked at herself. Her skin and hair had become dark again. The face had returned to the smooth form of its youth. There was no deformity, no scars or wrong-set bones. She looked similar to the creature Peter Malone had made.

Another form appeared in the dusty room. Kathryn faced it boldly, not without dread.

– Thank you. Beatrice stood there, no more or no less transparent. – You have just made another part of the painting, done our work for us, bringing us closer to our ultimate goal.

Afterglow shrugged, doing so very deliberately, not bothering to voice any reply.

The specter faded, faded away into nothing, still very much present.

«Life will find you, wherever you run».

Kathryn's own patronizing words to Leila returned to haunt her.

She picked up her clothes from the floor, clothing herself. They had become somewhat baggy on her. She had trouble filling them out, now, but they still fit her. The sword sheath and its contraption, and the rucksack fit just fine.

A thin voice briefly distracted Afterglow, as she headed for the exit, the door leading outside, into the backyard.

– You saved me. How can I ever repay you?

Afterglow turned, and looked back at the distraught girl.

– You can not.

Afterglow kept walking towards the door. The girl slumped there, in her pose, freezing on the spot.

– Will I ever see you again?

– No.

Afterglow walked through the bright-lit door, into the rain, and in just a few moments, a few steps she had faded away in the pitch-black night.

Afterglow's story continues in
AFTERGLOW RAIN
And concludes in
AFTERGLOW FIRE

Author's word

This is the thirteenth novel I have completed and the tenth I have published. I began its story back in 2004, at least with the world building and first chapter and layout.

As usual I set out to write something completely different from what I had previously written and it clearly is. This is something more different from my other novels than even Alarums of Reality was.

The setting is totally unlike anything I've done before, the feel and the narrative as well. I keep doing this, keep fulfilling the promise I made to myself as a young, nebulous writer.

I wrote sixteen chapters at first, but realized that an entire chapter, a big chunk of the story was missing. I also added significant pieces of the story to all the other chapters, making it longer and better explained. This is one advantage of publishing a novel about a year after you have initially completed it. You get to study it better, get several chances at improving it.

The reader won't know what is going on at first or even after a while. He or she or it will get an idea or a glimpse of an idea, but there will never be a roll of text explaining my stories in thirty seconds. They will have to experience the story in depth for that.

Sixteen chapters became seventeen and will in time approach two-hundred or more, presenting the story of The Nine from start to finish.

This is a Sword and Sorcery, Fantasy, Science Fiction and Horror real-life story…

Sometime in 2004 – 2013-05-13 and 2013-12-25
Printed version complete 2014-05-13

AFTERGLOW RAIN

She has died a million times…
Someone or something is stalking her.

Stalking her from one world to the next, from day to night, from night to day. Wherever she walks it is there. Turn one way and it is ahead. Turn another and there it is. In branches moving in the wind. In old houses where every step on the dusty floor brings a creak from the wood.

Afterglow is haunted and hunted, no matter where she goes.

Kathryn Caldwell is traveling the nine realms, all the nine realms and even beyond, in search of meaning, of anything tangible that might make her life make sense. What she finds is more mystery, more dark corners waiting for her. One revelation opens up nine more closed boxes slapping her in the face, grinning to her like banshees in the night, in the mists and twilights of the world. The nine lands in the nine realms are different, they are the same. Afterglow brushes them like the wind, and sometimes like the storm, making a brief stop, before moving on, leaving ruins in its wake.

The Storm is coming. She knows this, beyond knowing, beyond certainty. Dark blades are cutting air, cutting flesh. An army of them is awaiting Afterglow, and she finds revelations, horrors and terrors aplenty, out there, on her way to nowhere. She does not know where she is going, only that she is going there, no matter what it takes, no matter where it may take her.

Lightning strikes deep below the ground in Afterglow's path.

Other published and upcoming novels by **Amos Keppler** from **Midnight Fire Media:**

The Defenseless

The two rivers meet and join in the city of Denver, becoming one...

The two dark brothers, growing up with their sister Linda in a mundane, average suburb, a place well entrenched in modern United States and the world, have since their moment of birth been at odds with the world... and with each other.

Mike and Ted Cousin are not who they are. There is a mystery here, one of birth and upbringing, one of fate. Violence and death, blood and fire follow them all the days of their lives. The fire is resting somewhere inside... waiting for the Spark.

Their parents know something, but are not telling it. The policeman Mark Stewart and their aunt Trudy do, too. Everybody knows something, pieces of the whole, but nobody knows the whole truth, nobody telling it.

The ancient power is returning to the world, a world massively suffering from physical and spiritual poison, on the brink of collapse and a collective tailspin suicide run without its like in human history.

Magick is returning from its long exile. Thus begins the story of the wild beasts rising from their ashes.

The Spark is struck, horrible and terrifying.

First book of ten in the Janus Clan series: Ten stories of the wild man in the modern world, forty years of wandering, before the Phoenix is rising from its ashes.

ISBN 978-82-91693-08-8

ShadowWalk

The world is changing. They know this, in their core of cores, where everything moves and shifts. Night and fire have followed them all the days of their lives.

What they carry inside has always scared them, always intrigued them...

They have always felt different, apart from the crowd. And here, now, they get the confirmation they have always wanted, always yearned for, that they are truly different, a breed apart. The metamorphosis begins. Their minds, their bodies are changing in shocking and unpredictable ways, as what's on the inside is brought to the outside. And as they themselves are changing they are also changing the world.

Danger awaits them, Life awaits them, in the small, backward New England town. Magick and Mystery may be found beneath unturned stones.

People, young and old, are descending on the small, insignificant town of Northfield, New England.

Boys and girls, students at the school of Life, Seekers, yearning for what's different, what's hidden.

They're seeking within and without, high and low.

And here, in this dusty, remote place they're finding it, turning the stone, finding the strength within themselves to be themselves, to break out of confines, to the world beyond. And in time, after the initial, tentative steps, pushing down paths new and undreamed of.

And the present day order sees them for what they are... Agents of Change, a threat to any establishment, any imposed reality. The heatwave, the worst in living memory, is nothing compared to the boiling within the human heart. The Indian Summer heralds the twilight of mankind.

ISBN 978-82-91693-12-5

Your Own Fate

From The Book of Fate:

In the Book of Fate there is everything. Every incident, all times, everything that has been, that is, that will ever be, everything that might be, everything that could have been.

But who is writing it? Who is penning it? Who is turning page by page, too many to be counted, blowing in the wind? Does it perhaps write itself, with a pen moving across the yellow sheets? Or is it a hand moving the pen, one unseen, one stretching back into the past, back to the time before everything was created, creating itself from nothing?

Timothy Joyce is an enigma, a man without a past, appearing from nowhere, to go on a rampage in an astonished world.

Jeremy Zahn is hunting Timothy Joyce. It seems like he has always been hunting him, from old London, from the island of angels, where it is said they met for the first time, to the city of angels, California, the new world.

Here, on this shaky ground, following confrontations spanning the globe, its time and space the two will fight for the last time.

And the world is watching, its people shivering in their frozen hearts.

ISBN 978-82-91693-05-7

Night on Earth

This is said to be the age of enlightenment and reason...
A culmination of thousands of years' development and illumination.

The hunters are dying off, they say. Their day is done, in favor of the new, enlightened time of neon lights, technology and civilization.

But a hunter is stalking the streets of London. A creature without form, eyes and skin. In a city on the brink of chaos, of social and economic collapse, it is stalking cops, killing them in ever more horrible ways. Sheila Watts is a hunter. She's a cop.

Sheila is lost, losing herself further by the second. She's losing herself, finding herself, as she's closing in on the creature of the night, as it is closing in on her.

Sheila Watts can taste the sweet blood in her mouth...

ISBN 978-82-91693-07-1

Dreams Belong to the Night

New, emerging urban rebel guerilla groups, freedom fighters, called terrorists by enraged authorities are overwhelming Europe.

What is, in truth terrorism? Who does it to whom?
How much can a human being take of bondage, injustice, degradation and destruction of spirit... before being fed up?

Present day society is a wound not closing.
In a modern world society destroying everything making life worth living there are those, who, through coincidence and fate, have decided not to take it anymore.
And as they are making that decision, together and as individuals, they are also starting on a journey, a journey back to humanity's roots.
Judith, Sivert, Kim, Willhelm, Anya and many more.
A handful of people against an entire world.

This is their story...

ISBN 978-82-91693-11-8

Experience the defeat of civilization, of tyranny, of anti-life in:

Thunder Road - Book One: Ice and Fire

Damon Terrill is the Storm Child. He is born into the life hostile civilization's last years, as humanity starts on its return to nature, return to Life.

It started with the need for Freedom, the passion of life, and went from there, in new and unforeseen directions, in one, final attempt to get it right.

– It's the human being's path through life, Anya told them. – What challenges, destroys and strengthens it.

The Thunder Road is making a turn. It always is. Burning Ice, Biting Flame...that is how life began. And that's how it will renew itself. No matter where humans are going. And now the blade is laid bare, ready to be tempered once more. Humanity's idiocy, their hubris has finally and fully been visited upon them. The End Time, the final hour, Ragnarok is here. The sea is rising, winds are increasing in strength. A thoroughly rotten society is collapsing under its own weight.

Humans are natural nomads. Now they become nomads anew, pulled together in small tribes once more, pulled into a fellowship of fate in a final, desperate attempt to survive, to live the life humans are born to live. Finally. Damon, Anya, Andrè, Myriam and many others have started on their way Home.

To be published June 21, 2016

Falling

She can not rid herself of it, the sense of falling. It is lurking in her dreams, every time she looks at the world from the edge of her vision. The old, cruel oracle at the fair did not tell her anything she did not know.

Janet of the Blue Flame is born a sorcerer, one with powers of the mind and the body far exceeding those of most others, one in a line reaching far back in antiquity.

In this modern age she, like many others is virtually unaware of the potential resting in the murky parts of her being. She may know, deep down, but she is not aware… not until the day Malone the Sorcerer comes for her.

Malone is dark and powerful. His skills and might are unquestionable. His power speaks to her, to her murky depths, roaring in her consciousness like a storm. Janet is only Sweet Sixteen and is overwhelmed in Malone's presence. When he offers to train her, for her to become his apprentice she consents with an eagerness of a mule chasing the carrot. He is everything she is not, everything she has ever dreamed of being. She leaves her friends and family, leaves behind everything she knows and joins the mighty and enigmatic sorcerer on his quest. His harsh teaching takes her far away, into the nine realms and beyond.

He gives her her devours, gives her everything he promised and more, wishing her good luck, leaving her to pick up the pieces of her life.

Janet of the Blue Flame is ready for the world.

To be published October 31, 2015

BLACK DRAGON

One unexplainable, beyond mysterious event changed the world. In one moment, lasting an eternity the Earth and all its creatures was cast in shadow. The sun was blocked out in the sky, and people could only glimpse each other as flickering shapes in a seemingly endless night.

They called it the Great Darkness, and spent years and countless hours attempting to explain it, speculating in vain on its origin.

The results of the event weren't instantaneous, weren't obvious, but in the years to come many people transformed, and gained new and startling abilities, powers of the mind and body never before seen on this Earth.

Lady Grace, Flight Captain, Gimmick, Oracle, The Bowman, Raven Bird and many others rose from the sea of mankind, creatures straight from people's imagination, the fantastic writings of the world, crime fighters, vigilantes and master criminals similar to those previously described only in comic books living the life of their dreams.

The world changed, irrevocably, each new big and small dramatic event removing it further from what it had been, its status quo and social relations altered forever.

Unsettling dreams began haunting them, first at night, in their sleep, and then, slowly, spilling over into their days and waken lives. A creature, a terrifying nightmare rose from the primordial consciousness of them all.

They called it the Black Dragon…

To be published April 30, 2015

Secrets

These are descriptions of what cannot be described.

These words within deal with the current world as it is, its prevalent and extensive alienation, inequality and injustice, its ongoing destruction of both spirit and flesh, of everything making life worth living.

But most of all it's about the Night, the great darkness, the dark passions ruling us all, what those in charge more than anything want to take away from us.

Words have power...

Contains 140 poems written from August 2003 to July 2013.

ISBN 978-82-91693-15-6

www.ingramcontent.com/pod-product-compliance
Lightning Source LLC
Chambersburg PA
CBHW060605310726
48982CB00008B/1244/J

9788291693163